ALSO BY JUDITH A. BARRETT

MAGGIE SLOAN THRILLER SERIES

RILEY MALLOY THRILLER SERIES

GRID DOWN SURVIVAL SERIES

DONUT LADY MYSTERY SERIES

To Peggy —
You keep reading;
I'll keep writing!

I ALWAYS WANTED TO
BE A SPY

MAGGIE SLOAN THRILLER

BOOK 1

Judith Barrett

Judith A. Barrett

I ALWAYS WANTED TO BE A SPY

MAGGIE SLOAN THRILLER, BOOK 1

Published in the United States of America by Wobbly Creek, LLC

2019 Florida

wobblycreek.com

I ALWAYS WANTED TO BE A SPY is a work of fiction. Names, characters, businesses, places, events, locales, and incidents either are the products of the author's imagination or used in a fictitious manner. Any resemblance to actual persons, living or dead, or actual events is purely coincidental.

Edited by Judith Euen Davis

Cover by Wobbly Creek, LLC

ISBN 978-1-7322989-7-2

DEDICATION

I ALWAYS WANTED TO BE A SPY is dedicated to the colors black and gray and to everyone who remembers imaginary friends.

Chapter One

My eyes snapped open. I glanced around my room. The light of breaking dawn scattered the shadows. *A sound. From the kitchen.*

I eased back my bedcovers, grabbed my weapon, and padded in my bare feet to the hallway. I froze. Someone opened a cabinet. *Searching for something?* I pressed my back against the chill of the wall and slid toward the kitchen with the skill and silence of a viper. I lifted my weapon before I whirled into the kitchen.

"Margaret Sloan—stop sneaking around." I covered my ears because Mother never spoke at less than full volume. "You give me the creeps. And what are you doing with your flashlight? It's time for you to get dressed for preschool."

My name is Maggie. No real spy is named Margaret.

I stomped to my bedroom and flopped on the floor next to my dresser. I sorted through the drawers and tossed the unacceptable clothes to the corner of my room—blue, green, pink, yellow, red—not one color a respectable spy would wear.

"Spies wear black," I grumbled.

Mother appeared in the doorway of my room and frowned. "Margaret Sloan, why are all your clothes on the floor?"

"I need a black shirt and pants."

Mother turned away. "Get dressed and come to the table. Breakfast is ready."

I followed her to the dining table in my white underpants and undershirt because Mother heard me better when I got her attention. I tapped her arm and glared. "Need black pants and a black shirt."

"Why didn't you say so? Got a play at preschool? Wear your dark-blue shorts and shirt. I'll shop for your costume today."

The rest of the week, I skulked through the school hallways in my new black shirt and pants.

"Margaret, this is the fourth day in a row you've worn that same black shirt and black pair of pants. You need to change, so I can wash them. Do you have any idea how hard it is to find little girls' clothes in black?" Mother shook her finger at me and handed me a department-store bag. "This is southern Georgia. It's too hot to wear black. The only reason I bought you more is that you worry me to parental exhaustion."

I raced to my bedroom, dumped the sack onto my bed, and gaped in awe. *I had black clothes, just like a real spy.* I changed to a black T-shirt and shorts and commando-crawled down the hallway before I rolled behind a chair in the living room.

When I popped up from behind the chair, Mother gasped. "Margaret, you are just like your father."

My father wore black?

* * *

The day after I graduated from kindergarten, I woke to the aroma and sizzle of bacon mingled with the fragrance of hot, browning batter and warming maple syrup. I dashed to the kitchen.

"I knew you'd like pancakes with dark chocolate chips, Margaret. We'll walk to the library today to get you a card. I'm tired of you taking my novels before I've finished them. You need your own books."

When the door to the library whooshed open, I froze and whispered with reverence. "Books everywhere. This must be what heaven looks like."

At the end of the summer, the librarian with curly red hair and the three-inch scar on her right jaw stopped me on my way out. "Maggie, you're reading at the sixth-grade level. Good work."

* * *

I hurried into the first-grade class. *Is this the year we learn calculus?*

When I stepped into the room, I froze and blocked the doorway. Five purple chairs circled an orange rug, and a pink bookcase filled with preschool books was against the wall next to the chairs. The whiteboard in front had the word *Welcome* splashed across it with each letter a different color. My breathing became more shallow and rapid. *I'm in color overload.*

I narrowed my eyes at the cartoony, painted animals on each of the garish, brightly colored, square tables: red, yellow, blue, green, purple, orange; elephant, tiger, lion, giraffe, whale, gorilla. *Why?* My breakfast churned in my stomach, and I gulped to keep from puking.

The teacher had pulled her brown, gray-streaked hair into a low ponytail; her wire-rimmed glasses had slipped down her nose. She was younger than Mother and the same height as Mother, but Mother was slimmer. Two boys and a girl jostled me as they entered the classroom.

The teacher's smile didn't reach her eyes. "Come get your name tag and match the animal on your name tag with the correct table."

I glanced around for an escape route. *None. It will be a long year.*

The teacher narrowed her eyes. "I said come get your tag. You need to pay attention."

I narrowed my eyes too, but it just made everything fuzzy. I almost mentioned that she'd see better if she opened her eyes, but I realized not everyone is open to helpful suggestions.

She glared and tapped her hand with a pencil. I tilted my head and stared. Last week I read a story about astronauts and learned a number two pencil can write in zero gravity. *What if I'm asked to fix a spy satellite? I need a number two pencil in my backpack.*

I realized she had been talking while she tapped.

"Excuse me," she said. "This is not the first time I have told you to pay attention to my instructions. I'll ask for a conference with your mother. Maybe she can help you understand the importance of following the rules."

The next day Mother walked home from school with me after her meeting with the teacher. As I hopped up the steps to our apartment, she shook her finger and spoke in her booming volume. "Margaret, you need to do what your teacher says. You'll never be anything if you can't follow directions."

I uncovered my ears, jumped to three steps above her, and turned because Mother paid better attention when she saw my eyes. "Mother, I don't want to be anything. I want to be a spy. Spies follow people."

"So, follow people, Margaret."

Simple, yet logical. I didn't tell Mother, though.

The next day at our tiger-table art time, I focused on Thomas, my friend with the gray eyes and protruding ears. He sat on my left, and the girl with curly black hair and French braids was across from me. I created a composite of their drawings, except mine was in pencil while they picked through color markers. I finished my pencil drawing while the rest of the students colored. I examined the shapes of kids' ears and noted whether their earlobes were attached.

My observations were interrupted by taps on the table. "Ahem."

I glanced at the middle of the tiger table and noticed a math worksheet. I grabbed the paper and solved the problems before anyone else at the table finished.

Rookie mistake. A spy would not only observe but also keep track of the subject.

When the teacher stood next to my seat, I closed my eyes and breathed in the sweet aroma of roses, which was a decidedly welcome change from the room's usual odor of kid sweat and stale pee. "Why do you draw in pencil when all the colors are available?"

A trick question. Not sure zero gravity is the answer.

My mind raced to find an answer. "It makes corrections easier."

She smiled. "Perfectionist."

I learned my first life lesson. *Make the boss happy.*

* * *

After a month of second grade, I examined my face at different angles in the bathroom mirror. *School has aged me.*

I sauntered into the living room and found Mother reading one of my books in her blue recliner.

"Mother, I need my hair dyed black. Can you do it, or do we make an appointment with your hair stylist?"

Mother slammed the book shut and glared. "No, absolutely not; I will not dye your blond curls; and certainly not black. Where do you come up with these ideas? You made me lose my place."

I frowned, crossed my arms, and stomped to my room to organize the stacks of papers with all the notes I'd collected about students and teachers. *This is too hard to manage.*

I searched for the computer sales flyer; when I found it, I showed the flyer to Mother. "Mother, I need a computer."

"Why didn't you say so, Margaret? School is so much more advanced than when I was a girl. I'll check with my friends for suggestions and have one for you by the end of the week. You can use mine whenever you like until we get yours."

I widened my eyes when Mother unboxed the computer. *Only Mother would have ordered a red laptop instead of a normal black one.*

"You're surprised, aren't you?" she asked. "The computer got here much quicker than I expected too. Do you want me to set it up? My friends said I need to monitor your internet activity, so you let me know if you do anything I need to monitor. And you might need to show me how. Here are the instructions and passwords for our Wi-Fi."

I connected my laptop to the internet and developed a database for all my data.

* * *

The next day, I paused in the hallway and examined the ceiling tiles as I checked to see whether anyone had followed me before I slipped into the school library at recess. I needed an expert opinion.

"Are there any blond spies?" I asked.

The librarian brushed her blond hair off her face before she glanced at the door and whispered, "There are, but nobody sees them. Blond spies are the best."

I wonder if she's a spy.

Chapter Two

Ten Years Later

Mother rushed into the apartment and waved the mail in my face, and I flinched. "Margaret, there's a letter here for you from the university. I already opened it because I was so excited. Here, read it."

Mother handed me the letter; as I opened it, she said, "You've been awarded an academic scholarship in library and information sciences. Full scholarship, Margaret. Let's look at your spreadsheet for college costs and expenses. I know we can do this."

I read the letter. *I could live at home and ride the city bus—more cost savings.*

"Library science is perfect for you, Margaret." Mother followed me to my room and leaned over my shoulder to peer at the computer screen while I added transportation costs and removed housing from my spreadsheet. "You have always loved to read."

Librarian is an excellent cover for a spy.

* * *

The first week of my freshman year, I dyed my hair to match my black clothes.

When Mother saw my hair the next morning, she glared. "Margaret, I'm shunning you. I can't believe you dyed your hair black. Do you know anybody at school with dyed-black hair? No, you don't. A girl at the store today had a streak of pink in her blond hair, and it was really pretty. Why couldn't you dye a streak of black? No, I wouldn't like any black. I'd still shun you."

Mother wore her silky housecoat with the bright pink and turquoise flowers. I shaded my eyes before I headed to the breakfast table. *I need sunglasses.*

After I stirred my cereal and added more milk for the cereal to soak up, I caught Mother's eye. "What color is your real hair?"

"When I was a girl, my hair was light auburn. I always loved being a redhead, but then the red darkened and gray sneaked in. My hair looked like dull, out-of-date spices. I hated it, but this color suits me." She patted her copper-red hair that was perfect with her porcelain skin and intense emerald-green eyes. She was three inches taller than I was and often complained to her friends she was overweight, but I didn't agree.

* * *

My second year of college, Mother drank her second cup of coffee while I ate breakfast. "Margaret, your grades are excellent. You must be following directions."

"I read the textbook for each class the first week of the semester. Gives me time to—"

Mother jumped up from the table. "Got to run. Almost forgot I'm responsible for refreshments for my bridge club today."

She slammed the door as she dashed out, but I smiled and continued, "—update my database that tracks the physical and social characteristics of other students, instructors, and my fellow bus riders."

* * *

The final week before graduation, I read about the Gray Man. I wore my sunglasses at the dining table because the sun streamed into the room at breakfast and anyone with a good set of binoculars could peer into the apartment at any time.

A tall, bushy plant in a pot on the patio might block the view. Maybe Mother would like an azalea.

Mother scoured the local newspaper during breakfast.

I raised my voice to catch her attention. "Did you know some men are so gray they become invisible. Isn't that amazing?"

Mother scanned the obituaries—one of her hobbies—and frowned. "They aren't literally gray. It means they blend in with everyone else."

"Then they'd be called the Blend Men."

Mother pointed to the second column of the obituaries. "Oh no. These two people are three years younger than I am." She knocked over her chair as she jumped up and reached for the phone to call one of her friends.

Time to shop. I bought gray clothes, hair dye, and a plant.

Mother screamed when I came out of the bathroom that afternoon with my gray hair. "I'm shunning you again, Margaret. Maybe to the end of the week. I need to get a cat, so I have somebody to talk to. I could say things like, 'Cat, I called the plumber. The disposal doesn't work.' Or 'Cat, I love the ficus plant She-Who-We-Shun got for the patio.'"

"I'm right here, Mother."

"Cat, I have a hair appointment. Maybe She-Who-We-Shun will wait for the plumber." Mother grabbed her purse and keys and rushed out the door. I searched the apartment, just in case. No cat.

I answered the plumber's knock and invited him in. He was tall and muscular and wore his wire-rimmed glasses on top of his head. His gray hair was thick and curly, and his mustache was red with gray streaks.

"Maggie, your mother is sure proud of you. Whenever I come to fix her cantankerous dishwasher or whatever's broken, she points at your high school picture with your green eyes and blond curls. Did you know your real name's *No-Sensatall?*"

I loved his laugh. *My favorite guffaw.*

* * *

When I graduated from the library science master's program with high honors, Mother surprised me with a four-door, gently used sedan with a record of reliability. Mother called it silver. My car was gray.

"You need reliable transportation for your interviews," Mother said. "You never want to be late. When they ask you if you can follow instructions, just say yes. You don't need to talk about spy stuff."

When the flower delivery van pulled into the apartment complex, Mother peeked out the curtains. "Margaret, come see this. Somebody is getting fancy flowers. Delivered, no less. Who do you suppose it is? Somebody lah-dee-dah, I'm sure. Nobody we know." She laughed.

Her eyes widened when the delivery man strode to our door, and she gasped and clutched her chest when he knocked. She opened the door, and he handed her a large, emerald-green vase with blue and pink asters, pink carnations, and red roses.

She put the vase on the dining table and read the card. "It says, 'Thank you, Mother, for everything.' From you? They are beautiful."

She leaned over the flowers and breathed in. Tears and mascara slipped down her cheeks, and I handed her a tissue.

Time to find a job.

Chapter Three

The recruiter invited me into her office. Her sleek black desk, the cream carpet, and the abstract prints on the wall were a perfect backdrop for her soft, brown skin, thin nose, black eyes, and short, straight black hair. Her jingly jewelry entertained me while she looked over my resume.

"I'm Louisa, Maggie. I see you have a master's in library science. Have you applied for a position at the county library? Of course, you have. Let's see what else we can find."

A week later, Louisa called me. "I've lined up job interviews for you. You okay? You know most people on their first job search after college are disheartened by the number of people who don't return calls. Just the way of our busy world, I guess."

"So far, I haven't had much luck, so I appreciate the chance to interview. I'll have the rare opportunity to observe the behavior of people in their natural environment."

"Love your attitude. I'll email you a schedule. Stay in touch."

I revised my database to collect different types of hiring managers and interviewers and their physical characteristics, dress, tics, speech patterns, interview styles, and odors. I'd found my calling—job-applicant spy—except the lack of pay was quite unattractive.

* * *

I stood next to Mother while she washed breakfast dishes. "Mother, I don't have any interviews today, so I'm available to go to the grocery store for you. Do you have a list?"

"What's that, Margaret?" She cocked her head.

I spied her list on the kitchen counter and snatched it up. "I'll shop."

"That's my grocery list." She dried her hands. "Do you have time to shop this morning or do you have an interview?"

"I'll go." I waved to her and grabbed my purse on my way out the door.

When I pushed my cart to the front of the grocery store, the cashier who wore her gray hair piled on top of her head motioned for me to join her checkout line. "Maggie, your mother says you're job-hunting. There's a job fair at the pharmaceuticals distribution center this Saturday."

On job-fair day, I stood in line with two hundred and fifty other job hunters. I needed a new category for my job-search database—applicants.

The woman in front of me reminded me of a tugboat because she had broad shoulders and was all muscle. Her dark-brown eyes twinkled, and her round chocolate-cream face dimpled when she smiled. Her gray shirt said *pi Fixes Everything*.

"Honey, I'm Ella. Are you sure you're in the right line? You know we need to pick up seventy-five pounds. I bet you don't even weigh seventy-five pounds."

Her laugh was contagious. The people close by laughed with her, including me. *Can't argue with the truth.*

"I'm Maggie. Maybe by the time I get to the front of the line, management will realize they need somebody to pick up the little boxes."

"I like your attitude, girl. You just stick with me. We'll tell 'em I got the big boxes and you got the little ones."

I loved her booming laugh.

After we completed our applications, Ella and I sat together, chatted, and waited to be called for interviews. Ella was interviewed and hired to start the next day. No surprise, I wasn't. While I waited for Ella, I observed the manager types and took notes for my database.

"Want to go to lunch?" Ella asked after she completed her new-hire paperwork. "There's a diner nearby some might call sketchy, but the food's great."

The handwritten sign inside the door on a white board advertised the day's blue plate special: fried chicken livers with gravy, mashed potatoes, and peas.

We slid into a booth and ordered. When our food arrived, I stared at our dishes.

"Ella, our plates are white. Is this what we ordered?" I whispered.

"Honey, blue plate special just means the special of the day." She chuckled. "You are the most literal person I've ever known."

We picked up our forks and dug in.

"This is good, Ella. I never knew I liked chicken livers."

"You stick with me, girl. I'll get some meat on those bones." Ella boomed her big laugh, and the nearby customers and the waitress joined in.

We topped off our meal with hot homemade apple pie and ice cream.

"This is my treat, Maggie. I got a job. When you get a job, you can treat."

* * *

Louisa called the following week. "Are you available tomorrow? I have a cartoonist position at an art studio. Are you okay with a panel interview?"

"They're my favorite. I love the coworker interactions, and the undercurrent of drama and strained relationships fascinates me."

"From what I hear about this crowd, you will leave with a vastly enriched database." Louisa laughed.

The receptionist in the lobby at the art studio was younger than me; her long, dark brown hair had deep purple streaks around her face, and her blue eyes were highlighted by heavy black eyeliner and purple eyeshadow. Her tattoo of three intertwining hearts on the left side of her neck was intricate and delicate. "Margaret Sloan?"

"Maggie."

She grinned, and dimples that were incongruent with her black lipstick appeared. "Oh good. You aren't old enough to be a Margaret."

"I wish my mother knew that." I wrinkled my nose.

She laughed. "My mother called me Priscilla Jane."

"PJ. Am I right?"

"PJ is what my dad calls me. My friends call me Jane." When she pushed away from her desk, the long sleeves on her black T-shirt with sparkly silver stars across her ample chest revealed yellow and blue bruises on her wrists when they rose a few inches. "Come with me, Maggie."

Not good. Old bruises and new bruises.

She tugged at her sleeves while we walked down the hallway until we turned a corner, and she ushered me into a conference room. The six people who sat at a long table in the middle of the room stared while I counted five rows of tables and chairs behind them.

"Good luck," she whispered and left the room.

A thin man with a pinched face and a black mustache remained seated on the left side of the room. "Welcome, Ms. Sloan. I'm the panel leader. The panel will pose questions one at a time." He didn't offer to shake hands or introduce himself or the panel. He waved to a chair that faced the panel. "If you would take a seat, we can begin."

I angled the chair so I could see him, the group, and the door. As Ella would say, *Nobody here I'd trust to watch my back.*

Sitting on the far left, a man with brown-and-gray-streaked hair and a full reddish beard stared at a paper on the table in front of him. I recognized my resume. "Do you have a fine arts degree?"

"No, my degree is in library science."

"A bachelor of arts degree?" He glanced at my resume.

"Did we change to two questions each?" asked a woman at the far right end of the table.

"No, but we'll count it as one." The panel leader drummed his fingers on the arm of his chair. "Everyone, please remember, only one question. You may answer the question, Ms. Sloan."

"My degree is master of library and information sciences."

"What's your favorite color?" A woman with green-streaked brown hair and a red rash across the bridge of her nose asked as she frowned at her notepad. *Do they have assigned questions?*

The man next to her, a man with short, orange-red curly hair and a ruddy face, snorted.

"Gray," I answered.

"What tone of gray?" The woman with the rash on her nose cocked her head and furrowed her brow.

Before I could answer, the man next to her jumped in. "Sara, you already took your turn. We're allowed only one question." He jutted his chin, and his face and thick neck turned red.

A tall, beefy man with well-coiffed brown hair had slipped into the room when Sara asked her first question. His left arm appeared stiff or injured. He stood near the back wall to my right. While the panel argued, I took mental notes of the drama and strained relationships for my database.

My peripheral vision caught the new arrival's slicing motion with his right hand. The panel leader cleared his throat. "Thank you, everyone. Our time is up. Everyone back to work."

How bizarre.

The beefy man strode out the door, and the panel members grumbled and continued their argument about what constituted a single question while they shuffled out.

"Ms. Sloan, we want you to draw something we've never seen before," the panel leader said. "It can be whatever you like, and you can use the medium of your choice. I'll return in thirty minutes." He pointed to the clock on the wall in front of me.

I surveyed the array of art media on the table against the wall near the panel leader's chair. *Something they've never seen before.* I examined the room, selected my medium, and got to work. After twenty-seven minutes, I stood back, admired my creation, and added one last touch.

The panel leader returned. His eyes widened, and he stared at the wall. I congratulated myself for spying the can of silver-gray spray paint.

My four-foot-tall, gray bunny looked striking on their bland white conference-room wall.

I waited for the opportunity for further discussion, but he handed me papers to read before he left without speaking. I was sure they knew about the electronic bugs at the electrical outlet and the air-exchange vent, but I was sorry I didn't have time to work them into my presentation.

PJ came into the room. "Did you read the papers? I'll walk out with you if you like."

Before we reached the door, she stopped and smiled. "I loved the rabbit. I'll think of you every time I'm in the conference room, at least until they repaint the wall next week."

I turned to face her, and she met my gaze. "PJ, I notice things, and I know people who can help. You can call me. Anytime."

She maintained her gaze. "Thanks."

We shook hands, and when I climbed into my car and glanced at the building, she waved from the doorway.

The next day, the human resources assistant from the art studio called. "Ms. Sloan, someone else was hired for the artist's position. Your talent was refreshing, and I'm sorry I won't be working with you."

Guess I wasn't so original after all. I thought spray-painting the small security camera on the conference wall for the bunny eye was brilliant, but it must have been a trap to see who would fall for the obvious.

Ten minutes later, Mother pushed the apartment door open with her hip and carried in three grocery sacks. My phone rang, and she rushed to set her sacks down and put her ear next to mine to listen.

"Ms. Sloan, I'm the human resources manager for the county library system. Are you available for an interview? We have a position we must fill by the end of this week, or we'll lose it. Nobody's available to interview until next week. You're my final hope. Even if you last only a week, we'll be able to keep the position."

After I hung up, Mother sat at the bar with her arms crossed. "I couldn't hear. Who was it? What did they say? Do you have a job offer from somebody?"

I stepped closer to her. "I have an interview tomorrow morning with the library system."

She clasped her hands. "Margaret, if you don't get this job, I'll make an appointment for you with my hairdresser."

I wondered what color hair the two of them had in mind and shuddered.

*　*　*

The small library branch was in an older part of Harperville. I stepped inside and listened to the quiet buzz of whispered conversations and the clicks of computer keys while I breathed in the musky aroma of old books and moaned.

The head librarian, Olivia Edwards, met me at the door. She was middle-aged, solid with broad shoulders, and tall. Her skin had a ruddy tone, and her short gray hair had a few streaks of soft brown.

We passed the main desk that was on the left near the door before she ushered me into her office. "I see you are in your Gray Phase."

"Yes, I used to be in the Black Phase."

Olivia smiled. "Ahh. I did the Black Phase long ago. I kind of miss it. Let me give you a quick tour."

Olivia interrupted our tour to introduce me and to chat with patrons. She motioned to a reading room. "We're here for the people, Maggie. Books mean nothing without people to read them."

When we lingered in the children's room, Olivia said, "What do you think? Could you work here?"

I glanced around the room. The walls were painted with bright cartoony animals in a gaudy jungle. *Mother's kind of place.* Three toddlers and their mothers sat on the carpet, surrounded by piles of old and new books.

"Yes. My kind of place."

After the county called me to offer me the position at the library, which I immediately accepted, I called Ella. "I got a job. Let's celebrate with lunch. My treat."

"You tried chicken livers. I'll try something new. You pick."

We met at my favorite sushi restaurant.

"If you're eating with chopsticks, then so am I." Ella set down her fork and picked up her chopsticks.

She glared at her crisscrossed sticks and her plate. "No wonder you're so skinny. I haven't picked up a bite yet." She stabbed at her plate with one chopstick and popped a morsel of tuna into her mouth.

The waitress giggled and handed her kid-style chopsticks—chopsticks with a rubber band and a folded paper in between the sticks to hold them together.

"I like sushi. Who knew?" Ella grinned her brighten-the-world smile.

As we stepped into the heat, I pointed to the ice cream shop next door. "How about dessert? Double-dipped ice cream?"

"Don't have to ask me twice."

We gazed at the tubs of ice cream through the fogged-up display case.

"Whatcha getting, girl?" Ella asked.

I shook my head. "Dunno. All these are my favorites."

"Our special today is cherry cheesecake," the clerk said. Her oversized hairnet slipped forward off her dark brown hair in the front to her eyebrows when she spoke. She pushed the hairnet up with her forearm before she pulled up her apron to relieve its tight pressure against her swollen belly.

"I'll take the special then. Two scoops and a waffle cone."

"Same for me," Ella said. "I'll buy dessert."

I glanced at our clerk and raised my eyebrows at Ella. "I'll get the tip."

Ella smiled when I dropped two dollars into the tip jar and handed the clerk a folded twenty-dollar bill before we left. We took our cones outside and sat at the shop's picnic table.

"How's your job?" I licked a runaway stream of ice cream off the side of my cone. The light breeze and shade from the patio umbrella over our table made the Georgia heat tolerable.

"It's perfect. I've been promoted to supervisor. Can you believe it?"

"Congratulations! I'm not surprised at all. You are the hardest worker I know."

I bit off the bottom of my cone.

Ella stared at me. "Oh what the heck. Ya only live once, right?"

She bit off the bottom of her cone, and we raced to eat our ice cream and cones before the ice cream dripped all over us.

Ella beat me. "No fair," I said. "You took bigger bites. And made me laugh, and I lost valuable bite time."

Ella laughed. "You are the funniest sore loser I know."

* * *

I moved into a one-bedroom apartment and furnished it, paycheck by paycheck, with gray furniture. My place was old but clean and well maintained. The manager called the kitchen "compact." The bedroom was large enough for my single bed and a dresser, and the bathroom's sink and tub with a shower suited me just fine.

Mother came to see my new place. "This is nice. A second-floor apartment is safer than the first floor."

I wasn't sure why because all the apartments in the complex opened to a shared outside walkway. "Glad you like it, Mother."

"Here, I brought you a housewarming present. It's from the cat." She handed me a four-foot-by-two-and-a-half-foot painting of a green jungle with yellow snakes and red parrots in the trees and a bright peacock in the foreground.

Mother stepped out on the tiny balcony. "No grass, but it looks well kept. You need flowers."

"Did you get a cat?"

"No, but I may because you have your own place. I was afraid you were allergic to cats."

"I'm not allergic to any animals."

"My grandmother was allergic to cats. I always wanted a cat, but Grandmother couldn't tolerate an animal in the house."

After Mother left, I stopped by the manager's office. His tortoiseshell glasses had the thickest lenses I'd ever seen. His toupee matched the color of his neatly trimmed brown goatee. *Well done.* When I realized I was staring, I switched my gaze to his silver metal desk. "I'd like to paint my walls a soft gray."

"I'm sorry, Ms. Sloan. No gray paint." He glanced out the window. "Your mother's gone, right?"

"She talked to you, didn't she?" I narrowed my eyes.

He hung his head. "Well, yes. No gray, okay?"

Mother preempted me on this one.

* * *

I put Mother's art under my bed for safekeeping, upside down and wrapped in a sheet to keep it clean. *She might want it back sometime.*

A knock at my door surprised me, and I hurried to open it for Mother. My eyes widened, and I squealed. "Taylor! What a surprise. Do you live in these apartments too?"

Taylor grinned as she came inside. She was still shorter and slimmer than me. She hadn't changed a bit since high school, except for one thing: her hair was still cut in her signature bob, but her bangs were gone.

She grinned. "I recognized your mother, but I wouldn't have recognized you. No more black? I've been here for almost six months."

"Have you heard of the Gray Man?"

"Ahh, you're still as literal as ever." Taylor peered into my kitchen. "What are you doing for dinner? Can you cook?"

"No, can you?"

"No. Guess we can starve together, right? I have cereal at my place."

I opened my refrigerator door and pointed. "I bought groceries today. Want to eat here?"

"Sure, then tomorrow night will be my turn. I'll be right back. I've got beer."

Taylor returned and set a six-pack on the counter.

I fretted over the bread and cheese in the smoking pan. "I call this a grilled-cheese sandwich. Want to put some chips on our plates?"

Taylor counted our chips and placed them on the gray plates. "I'm a kindergarten teacher. It's critical in my world to be obsessive about equal shares."

"I always knew you'd find a way to put your talents to good use." I lifted a corner of one sandwich to peer at the bottom before I pushed the sandwiches around the pan.

Taylor set our plates on the table and frowned. "We need a food scale. Not all these chips are the same size. Where do you work? Can you tell me? Are you a spy?"

"Remember how excited we were about my library science scholarship? I'm a librarian, and I love the calm and quiet. The only time it's rowdy is when someone tries to get out of an overdue-book fine."

She giggled and raised her beer in a salute. "You're still funny. I love the energy and noise of a class full of five-year-olds. A library would be too quiet for me. I'll pick up pizza tomorrow night on my way home. Shall we invite Mr. Morgan?"

"Who's Mr. Morgan?" I flipped our sandwiches and poked at the blackened bread.

"He's the best neighbor in the world. He can cook."

Taylor's phone dinged. She read her text. "Mr. Morgan has invited us to his place for dessert. He retired from the Air Force years ago. You'll like him. He knows everything."

I served up our sandwiches. "They're burned black on only one side."

Taylor took a swig of her beer and a bite of her sandwich. "Better than I can do."

After I rinsed our dishes and scrubbed the blackened pan, we strolled to Mr. Morgan's apartment. Mr. Morgan was of medium height and wiry, with gray hair clipped close, military style. He was in his early eighties but looked at least twenty years younger.

"Welcome to the apartment complex, Maggie. I'm happy to meet you."

"Thank you, Mr. Morgan. You too."

The three of us relaxed on Mr. Morgan's patio. We sipped wine and enjoyed warm, homemade brownies.

"How do you two know each other?" Mr. Morgan passed the plate of brownies.

"We were BFFs in high school. We did everything together—school projects and track." Taylor reached for her second brownie. "These are good."

"We ran cross-country together. We were unbeatable." I put a second brownie on my plate. "Our coach asked us if we talked while we ran to pace ourselves. Of course, we did. Coach said it was a brilliant strategy. Remember, Taylor?"

"And remember our history project? Someone not well-known from the early nineteen hundreds who had a significant impact on American life? No one else thought of a spy."

"Sidney Reilly would have been a good choice," Mr. Morgan said. "Ace of Spies. Model for James Bond. First twentieth-century superspy."

"I'm impressed, Mr. Morgan. Not everybody knows about Sidney Reilly." I sipped my wine. "How did you know?"

"I know my spies." Mr. Morgan winked, and we laughed.

"Mmm, these brownies are wonderful. Taylor said you're a great cook, Mr. Morgan. I'm not. How did you learn to cook?"

"My father taught me the basics. He was a baker. One of my earliest memories was standing on a stool to weigh flour for bread. Mother was a great cook, but he took over the kitchen on Saturdays and Sundays. He always said working in the kitchen relaxed him. He should have been a chef."

"That's awesome," Taylor said. "Why didn't you become a chef?"

Mr. Morgan laughed. "Remember I said I weighed the flour? I was fascinated by the equipment. I took everything apart and put it back together. I studied engineering in college. After I graduated, I joined the Air Force. I could tinker with motors and engines and travel the world to expand my culinary knowledge. As far as I was concerned, I had a dream job. I was stationed in Italy, France, and Germany, and I spent my days off in restaurant kitchens all over Europe. Learning, tasting, and cooking."

"Do you suppose you could teach us to cook?" I asked.

Mr. Morgan poured wine into our empty glasses. "I could, but you won't learn until you want to learn."

Taylor munched on her second brownie and lifted her glass. "So true, Mr. Morgan. If I didn't already have a best friend, you'd be my best friend. Here's to you, second bestie."

I raised my glass in a toast. "Hear! Hear! BFF1 and BFF2!"

* * *

The next day, Olivia called me into her office when she arrived. "Maggie, you've been here a month. How do you like it?"

"I never realized how magical reshelving books was. I'm the book fairy when I place each book in its proper home."

Olivia laughed. "I love the organization you've brought to us. No one has ever stacked the books on the cart by aisle. If you're the book fairy, then you wield your magic-carpet cart."

To keep my observation skills honed, I developed a library-patron database. I noted physical characteristics, behavior patterns, and reading preferences.

All the peering around corners I've done for years has paid off. I'm an expert slinker.

I checked on our regulars every day, but one library patron in particular stood out: a tall man with a slender frame, light-blue eyes, sandy-brown hair and gray temples, and a scar just below his left eye. He wore jeans and faded T-shirts with long-sleeved flannel shirts not quite long enough to cover his bony wrists. Unlike our other homeless patrons, his clothes were worn but clean, and his sturdy, brown lace-up boots didn't need any repairs like so many of the others who frequented the library. His backpack was frayed, but not stained or ripped, and his stance and demeanor hinted of a military background.

He saluted when he came into the library, and I waved back. He and all the other regulars gravitated to their same seats every day; his chair was at the farthest corner from the front door. He sat there from the time we opened until we closed and got up only to get another book or to go to the restroom. On the surface, he was a homeless guy who stayed in the library to be out of the cold or heat for the day.

The perfect homeless man. A little too perfect. The hair on the back of my neck tingled. *Something familiar…*

I noticed he maintained an awareness of his surroundings, and he didn't manifest any signs of mental illness or substance abuse. He was thin but muscular, and he wasn't malnourished. Most suspicious of all was his personal hygiene. The scent of soap followed him, and his clothes were clean. *Either a spy or a fugitive.*

Chapter Four

I suspected the "homeless" man I'd observed at the library was there to sneak a secret message to someone, but I couldn't catch him in the act. Then it dawned on me—the men's room.

After he returned to his corner, I knocked on the men's restroom door. "Housekeeping."

Mother and I stayed at a hotel once. I liked the ring of authority the word *housekeeping* carried.

I hadn't been in the men's room before, but at first glance, the room was what I had envisioned—a couple of urinals on a wall and a single toilet inside a stall. A pervasive odor reminiscent of an outdoor toilet made my eyes water, and I noticed wet spots around the urinals and on the toilet seat when I peeked inside the stall. I was careful where I walked and grabbed two paper towels so I wouldn't have to touch anything.

I checked the stall and lifted the toilet-tank cover. A man with shoulder-length dark hair and a tattoo of a snake that wound from his elbow to his wrist walked in as I put the top back on the tank.

"Aha. I fixed it." I brushed past him and out the door.

Very smooth.

* * *

A few weeks later, Olivia called me into her office. The library aroma was reminiscent of old hay and vanilla. Her office fragrance reminded me of pungent flowers. Her desk was clear except for her computer. The walls of her office, however, were stacked with boxes of papers. Each container was labeled with a black permanent marker from A to Z and continued to AA and AB.

I sat on the visitor's chair in front of her desk. "Olivia, I'm curious about your boxes."

"It's the librarian's curse, Maggie. I can't throw away anything. But it's all cataloged and filed. Here's my notebook of secrets." She pulled a two-inch binder labeled *Notebook of Secrets* out of the bottom drawer and dropped it on her desk.

I stroked the sleek cover. "Olivia, I love this."

Her face went from smiles to stern, and she cleared her throat. "Maggie, you're the best librarian we've ever had. You're efficient, knowledgeable, and helpful. Children love you, and our senior patrons love you. However, you can't stalk the homeless man. Makes me nervous. And you can't go into the men's room anymore. You're not housekeeping, and I don't want any complaints."

I dropped the frequent surveillance of the "homeless man," as she called him, but I named him "Ernie." Instead, I found a location at the farthest aisle from his chair where I could see his outstretched legs. I strolled to my spot every fifteen minutes from the time the library opened until it closed.

Ernie rose from his chair and sauntered to the aisle where I lurked during one of my fifteen-minute checks. "Hi. Nice day."

I gulped. "Yeah. It is."

The next day, he came in at his usual time.

"Good morning," I said.

He saluted on his way to a reading room. I noticed he favored his left leg. He didn't have a limp, but he walked a little slower than usual, with a slight hesitation in his gait when his weight shifted to the left.

The two reading rooms were identical except the chairs in one room had red fabric seats and the seats in the other room were blue. Ernie sat alone at a table in the middle of the red room. I squinted, but I couldn't quite see the title of his book. He lifted his head and smiled.

Nice smile. I smiled back.

I headed to the office to complete the library's monthly report then stopped. *Should I tell Ernie I would be in the office for an hour or so?*

I shrugged and rolled the book cart into the red room. The sunlight streaming through the windows warmed the room even though the air conditioner was set at the mandatory seventy-two degrees. The people who grouped in the south corner of the room were our heat-seekers, as Olivia called them. I pulled out a chair at Ernie's table, and he rose his eyebrows while I scooted into place.

"You doing okay?" I asked in my hushed library voice.

Ernie glanced over my shoulder at the table behind me, and I imagined the occupants at the other table moved in a choreographed reach to turn up the volume on their hearing-aids.

"A little arthritis, but I'm fine. This warmer room is nice. Thanks for asking."

I rose and pushed the chair in. "If you need anything, I'll be in the office; I have reports to update."

He raised his eyebrows. "Thanks."

On my way to the office, I frowned. *Why did I tell him where I'd be, and why did he thank me?*

After I finished the reports. I hurried to the main desk and tried not to stare, but Ernie sat at a table outside the office with a graphic novel. I didn't know he liked graphic novels, but I've seen him read historical fiction, biographies, detective novels, and travel books. Eclectic reading choices.

The following Tuesday, Ernie didn't show up. I was surprised that I missed him except I was bored because I no longer had a good reason to slink around corners. *I'll keep it up for the practice.*

Two hours after I unlocked the doors, Olivia rushed in.

"Early appointment. Dental. Went longer than I expected." Her face was red, and she was out of breath.

Curious. She's had five appointments in the past two weeks. Must be annual checkups.

When I slipped past the elderly woman with hearing aids, another regular, she tapped me on the arm. "Where's your friend?"

I was startled because I didn't see her at first. She blended into the background when she sat at a table in the library. Her short gray hair curled around her ears, and her high cheekbones were surrounded by soft wrinkles. Her pale skin revealed the sheen of tiny hairs around her mouth. She had penciled in her eyebrows, and her eyelashes were either devoid of color or nonexistent. The sharpness in her gray eyes hinted of an awareness and intelligence I guessed was often overlooked. She didn't wear glasses, which was unusual for her age group.

I matched her quiet voice. "I don't know. Hope he's okay."

She folded her hands on the table and nodded sagely. I like how some elder folks do *sagely* so well. Impressive. I tried to mimic her nod. I needed it in my toolbox of nods.

I rolled my cart to the back of the library to Ernie's usual chair. I glanced toward a dark corner, where a little-used table sat. Someone was there, slumped in the chair. My eyes widened. *Blood spattered on the walls.*

His head drooped to one side and onto his chest; blood dripped from the chair and pooled on the floor. I moved closer but avoided stepping in the gore. My eyes widened at the sight of a knife buried in the back of his neck; my head swirled from the intense metallic odor, and my breakfast threatened my esophagus.

The room turned black, and I lost my peripheral vision. I grabbed for something to hold me up and gulped back the bile that rose in my throat as I took in a breath and faltered back to a book stack. After I slid down to the floor, I stared. *So much blood.* I wrenched my gaze to the man's face. His skin was pale gray, his pupils fixed and dilated, and his chest did not rise or fall.

I pulled myself to my knees. *I'm not checking for a pulse.* After I eased to my feet, I didn't faint, so I grabbed my cart for support then pushed it to the front and locked the doors.

I stumbled into Olivia's office and leaned against the door, which slammed shut. "We have a DB. Call PD."

Olivia was kneeling next to one of her boxes. Her head jerked. "Excuse me? What?"

I forgot Olivia is a civilian. Even worse, I dropped into cop-speak. I must be rattled. Deep breath.

"Olivia, call nine-one-one. A man is dead in the back of the library with a knife in his neck. I've locked the front door."

Olivia leapt to her feet. I stepped away from the doorway so she wouldn't knock me down if she bolted. "A man is dead? Are you sure? We're locked in? You've locked us all in with a killer?"

Ah. Good point.

I used my best in-charge voice. "I'll make sure everyone's okay. Call nine-one-one. Now."

She grabbed the phone, and my body clicked into action. I grabbed an empty book cart for protection and searched the aisles for a murderous fiend. I checked the reading rooms and the restrooms and opened the stall doors in case the killer was standing on a toilet.

I recognize everyone here. All regulars except for the deceased. Either someone here is the killer, or the killer got away before I discovered the crime scene.

I stationed myself at the front door. *What if the killer disarmed the back-door security system?*

I left the cart at the front door and scurried to the back. The panel lights were off. I rearmed the system and hurried to the front.

I was convinced nobody noticed me, but I wasn't as gray as I hoped. The elderly woman raised her penciled eyebrows when I zipped past her.

* * *

When two police cars and a fire engine pulled into the parking lot, I rushed into Olivia's office. She was still on the phone with the police dispatcher.

"Olivia, the police and fire department are here."

After I unlocked the front door, Olivia and I greeted the police officers and a fire officer, who wore a dark blue uniform with a captain's badge. The fire captain's girth strained his white dress shirt, and his forehead was damp. He was in his mid-fifties and of medium height. His hair was dyed blue-black.

Both police officers were tall. The older one was bald and muscular. His skin was pale brown, and his nametag said *Winston*. He growled. "Where's the deceased?"

"This way." Officer Winston and the fire captain followed me. When I neared the end of the aisle, I pointed. "Over there."

As I headed to the front door, the fire captain caught up with me and took my elbow. I raised my eyebrows. *Who's supporting whom?*

When I reached the front, patrons and volunteers surrounded Olivia as they pelted her with questions. Olivia held up her hands. "Hush!" Her command voice startled the group into silence. "Sit." Olivia glared, and the group complied.

The second police officer was two or three years older than me. *Ewing* was stitched on his shirt pocket. His brown hair was clipped short, military style. He stood with his hand perched on his holster and looked over my head, scanning the room. "The commander wants all of you together in one room. What do you suggest?"

"We have seventeen or so people, including us," Olivia said. "The only meeting rooms large enough are the red room and the blue room, but their walls are glass on all sides."

Officer Ewing frowned and shook his head. "Commander won't like it. Too many cell phones and cameras out there."

"We could use the children's story room, but our patrons can't sit on the small chairs," I said.

The police officer and fire captain stepped away for a private conversation, but I listened.

"Send in the crew to move chairs," the fire captain said into his radio.

The biting odor of diesel fumes and old smoke clung to the firefighters' gear and wafted behind them. They filed into the children's story room, hauled out the miniature furniture, and moved adult-sized chairs into the cleared space. I wished I'd timed them because they were fast; I counted the chairs as they sped past me.

When a firefighter carried in two more chairs, the captain asked "How many now?"

"Nineteen," I said.

He glared.

Sorry, Captain. I didn't realize I had given away the test answer.

"Everyone line up." A police officer with his gun belt cinched under his ample belly stood in the lobby next to a cardboard box on our display table. His nametag said *Robinson.* "Place your cell phones in this box, and Officer Ewing will escort you to the children's room."

Our folks shuffled to the children's room. When loud voices erupted from the room, Officer Ewing strode to the doorway. He glowered and used his authoritative voice. "Settle down."

I peeked at the skirmish. Eight adults were piled into the three overstuffed chairs the overzealous firefighters had carried into the room.

A tall woman with dark roots and dyed red hair pulled up into a ponytail peered over my head and snorted. "I missed my hair appointment, but this makes it worthwhile."

Olivia elbowed her way past the gawkers and into the room before she growled, "Everybody up. You heard me. Every one of y'all go stand over there."

Olivia waved her hand. "Clear the doorway."

She led three of our older patrons to the chairs. One of them was my elderly woman, who winked at me when she toddled into the room. I coughed to hide my snicker.

Now I know who dethroned the musical-chair winners.

After everyone was in the room, Officer Robinson addressed the gathering. "We will set up two interview rooms, and you will be escorted to your interview."

Olivia added, "My office is one, and the storage room was emptied for the second."

I moaned. Olivia and I would have to drag all the relocated furniture and boxes back to their respective locations. Our volunteers were beyond the age where we'd want them to help. Olivia glanced at me and nodded. *Did she read my mind?*

"You may use the washrooms accompanied by a chaperone," Officer Robinson announced.

We had two chaperones. They were dressed the same, and their badges read the same, *Aux Police*. Both men were wizened and in their eighties. Even I couldn't tell them apart.

Seven people rushed to the door, but Olivia had her arms crossed as she blocked the way. "We'll draw numbers."

I found a green crayon and safety scissors. I cut out slips of paper and the woman with the ponytail wrote the numbers before she gave the impromptu tickets to Olivia.

Olivia called the numbers, and our lottery winners shouted out their claims.

Officer Robinson mumbled, "We got us a party group."

Each person returned from the restroom with an eyewitness report. A young woman with short brown hair and a cast on her right leg recorded the findings.

"There's crime tape around the front of the library," the first woman to return said. One of the original soft-chair occupants, she was in her mid-fifties and buxom. Her face was ruddy, and her short brassy hair was gray at the roots.

"She's right," her chaperone said.

Those two sneaked off to peek out the front door.

Later in the morning, a frail man with brown hair, a scruffy brown beard, red-rimmed gray eyes, and a distinctive sour odor—one of our regular homeless patrons—returned. "The parking lot is filled with police cars, fire engines, ambulances, and news trucks."

"And the reporters are interviewing each other," the chaperone added.

Those two climbed up on the sink in the men's room to see the parking lot. I lowered my head so my face wouldn't give away their secret.

Later in the afternoon, one of our regulars slumped in his chair.

"Officer Robinson, I need to go to the desk," I said. A chaperone went with me, and I returned with my lunch for our diabetic, who perked up after he ate.

"Thanks," he said. "I guess my blood sugar tanked."

Officer Ewing motioned for Olivia to step out of the room. When Olivia returned, she drew me aside. "Maggie, the police released a few of the patrons. Will you help the police return cell phones to their rightful owners?"

Officer Ewing and I dragged chairs to the front door.

"How are we going to do this?" he whispered.

"Let's have them pick out their phones. You supervise while they unlock their phones, and I'll record their names and cell numbers."

"Shall we have them sign for the phones too?"

"Good idea."

One of the patrons burst into tears when she couldn't unlock her phone. Olivia swooped in and put an arm around the flustered woman. "Come sit with me a minute, and I'll fetch you a cup of water. After you relax, you can unlock your phone."

When our patron returned with Olivia, she unlocked her phone.

All phones accounted for.

Officer Ewing and I remained at the doorway and watched while reporters rushed folks that headed to the parking lot.

"Why did the reporter select the man in the middle of that group to talk to?" Officer Ewing asked.

"He's one of our more imaginative patrons. I can't wait to hear what happened according to our in-house eyewitness experts," I said.

Officer Ewing snorted. "You're the funniest librarian I've ever met."

After the library cleared, I locked up the library. The western sky was streaked with pink and orange as gray clouds moved in from the northwest, and the chirps of the tree frogs and crickets foretold of an evening sprinkle. As I ambled to my car at the end of the long, exhausting day, my cell phone rang.

Mother yelled so loud, I couldn't understand her. "Take three breaths. Start over."

"Margaret, did you know about a murder at a library? It's on the news. I got a cat. I tried to call you all day. Was the library yours? I didn't see you on TV. Come over for dinner. Bring Taylor."

Before I left the library parking lot, I texted Taylor. "Dinner at Mother's."

Chapter Five

Taylor wore navy-blue slacks and a navy-and-white-striped shirt as she stood at the curb and waved when I entered our parking lot. When she climbed in, she said, "Traffic may be bad. It took me an extra ten minutes to get home."

She turned on the radio and tuned it to a classical station.

"Good choice, Taylor," I said. "A violin concerto has got to be the best antidote to crazy traffic."

After we stopped at the fourth red light in a row, I scowled. "You called it, Taylor. We've caught every single stoplight so far."

My phone rang, and Taylor answered it. "Hello, Mrs. Sloan."

"Are you with Margaret, Taylor?" Taylor held the phone between the two of us. Mother's volume didn't require the speakerphone.

"Yes, ma'am. We're on our way to your house."

"You'll be here for dinner, right? It's almost ready."

"We'll be there in ten minutes."

Mother hung up.

The three lanes of traffic stopped, and we were trapped in the middle lane.

"Did she hear me, Maggie?" Taylor craned her neck at the cars ahead of us.

"It's hard to say. She'll call back."

Taylor dropped her head back on the headrest. "Your turn to talk to her when she calls back."

I chuckled. "Nope. Not our rule. Driver drives. Passenger manages both our phones.Looks like traffic's moving." I accelerated to the speed limit.

A black sedan in the right turn lane zipped across the traffic lanes to the dedicated left turn lane for the intersection ahead. I slammed on the brakes when he cut me off and narrowly missed hitting the red pickup on our left. I stared in the rearview mirror while the delivery truck behind us barreled toward my car. I gasped and crossed my fingers. *Don't be a distracted driver.* The truck screeched to a stop inches from my rear bumper, and I exhaled.

"Wow. We all stopped with no crashes," I said.

"My seat belt grabbed me." Taylor tugged at the belt to loosen it. "It happened so fast, no one even had time to honk. Big dirty doody-head."

I snorted. "You kindergarten teachers talk rough."

Taylor laughed. "I'm glad you were on your toes."

My phone rang. Taylor grinned. "Hello, Mrs. Sloan. We're just a few minutes away."

"Did Margaret remember to invite you to dinner at my house? Be sure to grab an umbrella. It's supposed to rain."

"Okay, Mrs. Sloan." Taylor looked at my phone. "She hung up."

As I turned into Mother's parking lot, low, distant rumbles added to the warnings of the cicadas and tree frogs.

"Tree frogs sure raise a ruckus. She might be right about the rain," Taylor said as I opened Mother's apartment door and froze.

Taylor pushed me into the apartment and closed the door. A sailfish mounted over the fireplace and a coconut fragrance mingled with seared meat greeted us. Mother rushed in from the kitchen and beamed.

"Nothing says *ocean* like a sailfish on the wall," Taylor said. "This is definitely unique, Mrs. Sloan."

"Don't you love how the dark-blue window and door trim highlights the pale-blue ceiling?" Mother pointed to the trim.

Taylor flopped down on the sofa and rubbed her hand across the lemony-yellow cover. "This reminds me of sherbet, especially with the pillows." She picked up one of the bright-orange sofa pillows and squeezed it against her chest.

"I spray-painted this wicker table I found at a thrift shop. Isn't the green a nice accent to the blue?" Mother smoothed the front of her pink-hibiscus shirt with bright-green fronds and flicked her gauzy, long green skirt before she sat in her favorite chair. "You're overwhelmed with how beautiful it is, aren't you, Margaret?"

Stunned is a better word.

"Where did you find a live pineapple plant?" Taylor asked. I followed her gaze. In the corner of the dining room near the sliding-glass door was a plant with a not-quite-ripe pineapple in the middle of the needle-tipped leaves.

My stomach was queasy from the explosion of colors. "Would you like to borrow my peacock painting?" I tried not to sound too hopeful.

"I found this in a magazine, but I added some improvements. Do you love it?" Mother waved her arm in a big arc.

"My favorite color is pink, and I love how you've captured the Key West style." Taylor rose and stroked the pink tablecloth on the dining table. "It's amazing how you've matched the tablecloth with the ribbon ties on the napkins. The green napkins remind me of the Everglades."

I glanced at the hallway. My voice rivaled Mother's for volume. "Mother, you have a cat!"

Taylor and I sat on the floor to make friends with the cat. Taylor tapped two fingers on the floor, and the gray kitten stalked her. When I giggled, he cocked his head toward me while he twitched the tip of his tail in time to Taylor's taps. He pounced on her fingers, whirled, and dashed down the hallway to Mother's bedroom.

Mother perched on the arm of her chair. "I told you I got a cat—you should pay attention. My hairdresser told me about Franklin. He's nine weeks old and already neutered. Franklin and I watched the TV coverage about the murder all afternoon, didn't we, Franklin?"

Franklin scampered to Mother when she said his name but skidded on the floor and bumped into her feet. When she walked to the kitchen, Franklin marched behind her and waved the tip of his tail.

Mother made my favorite meal, pork chops with mashed potatoes and mushroom gravy, and Taylor's favorite salad of mixed greens, carrots, radishes, onion, tomatoes, strawberries, and cucumbers, with raspberry pecan dressing.

"Save some room," Mother said when we sat at the table. "I made brownies for dessert."

While we ate, Mother told us, at maximum volume, about the murder at one of the libraries. "Was it your library, Margaret?"

My mouth was full, but Mother continued, "The library murder broke into my favorite show. The TV station better show the entire episode tomorrow, or Franklin and I will shun them."

"This salad is wonderful," Taylor said. "I love the strawberries in it."

"They don't know who the murdered man was. Or why he was there. What do people do at the library anyway? Don't they just turn in books, get more books, and leave?"

"Mother, you put mushrooms in the gravy. Thank you. I love mushrooms."

"Who would kill somebody at a library? Isn't there some rule about noise? Librarians always told me *No talking* when I was a kid. The people on TV said the library was on lockdown. Like they do at schools until parents come pick up their kids. Were you ever on lockdown, Taylor?"

"No, but a police officer came to talk—"

"I would be afraid on lockdown. The people on TV interviewed experts. Did you know there hasn't been a murder in a library for twenty-five years? Franklin likes to stay close to me."

"You're a wonderful cook, Mrs. Sloan," Taylor said.

I peeked under the table. Franklin slept on Mother's feet.

Mother talked about Franklin, the murder, the killer, and libraries. She could keep a conversation alive for hours on her own. We listened and enjoyed our dinner.

On our way home, I told Taylor I found the body. "The sight and smell of the blood was overwhelming. Especially the smell. Did you know it's trickier to kill someone without a sound than people think?"

"You've researched this, haven't you? Will you be on a watch list now?"

"I went on the watch list when I was five years old. Did you know how much misinformation is on the internet about how to kill someone with no noise?"

She laughed. "No surprise."

"The knife was embedded in the man's neck. It must have sliced the carotid artery and the larynx to have killed him without a struggle and with little sound. What I can't explain is how the killer got out of the library unseen. He would have been covered with blood because arteries spurt. I'm glad you aren't squeamish."

Taylor snorted. "A squeamish kindergarten teacher wouldn't last a week."

I chuckled. "Franklin is adorable, and I love he's gray."

My phone dinged with a text from a number I didn't know. Taylor read it to me. "New phone. Now is good. PJ." Taylor cocked her head. "What does this mean?"

I checked my mirrors and put on my right-turn signal. "Look up the phone number for the Safe House, the domestic abuse shelter."

"Here's the Safe House number." Taylor handed me her phone when I pulled into a gas station.

I sent a text: "Can pick U up anytime/where. Safe House #." Then I added the Safe House number.

Taylor and I sat in silence.

Another text: "Thnx."

"It's somebody I met on one of my interviews. I noticed that she had bruises and told her I could help."

Taylor furrowed her brow. "Will you call her? Can we go get her?"

"No, I'd love to, but we'll head home." I checked traffic and eased onto the roadway. "She trusted me enough to ask for help, so I'll have to let her tell me if she needs anything else."

* * *

When I woke the next morning, I was on the sofa and still wore my clothes from the day before. I sat up and moaned. *Achy back and stiff neck.*

I searched the sofa for my phone then found it on the floor and sighed. *No word from P.J. Taylor will want to know.* After I sent Taylor a quick text, I plugged in my phone to charge while I rushed to shower and dress for work.

When I turned the corner to the library, I wasn't surprised to see a police car in the parking lot and crime tape still around the building. The overnight rain left puddles in the parking lot, and the still-damp grass in front of the library sparkled. I didn't cut across the green space—not that I minded wet shoes, but the garden club volunteers were particular about their lawn and flowers.

The police officer leaned out his window. His brown face was round, his eyelids hooded his gray eyes, and his dark hair was damp and parted on the right. "You can't open the library until the detectives complete their investigation and the scene is secured and decontaminated."

I shrugged. "I'll get coffee then."

His bored look transformed into one of a penniless kid pressing his face against the glass of a candy store window.

I rolled my eyes. *How pitiful.* "What about you? Would you care for some coffee?"

"I would, thanks. I rushed to get here on time, and I'm kind of stuck for a while. Just cream and two sugars for me. Here's a few bucks. Let me know if I owe more."

On my way to the coffee shop, I stopped by the church. Tony, the maintenance man and an old friend of Mother's, knelt next to the memorial garden bushes with a wheelbarrow of mulch. Tony was the same age as Mother, but his dark-brown hair showed no sign of gray. He was lean and muscular. His tanned face broke into a toothy grin.

"Hey, Maggie. What's got you out so early?"

"Mr. Tony, do you suppose I could borrow a folding table and some chairs for the library?"

He brushed the dirt off the knees of his tan work pants and frowned when he stood. "You work at the library where the guy was stabbed? Doesn't seem safe to me."

"We've got all kinds of police protection, but we can't go in the library until their investigation is done. I'll set up shop outside."

"Let's get your table and chairs, then. You were always smart, Maggie. Always thinking."

We strolled to the church's storage room. "I can check in books, and I have a few books in my car. I could make a *Take One—Leave One* sign."

We loaded up the table, chairs, and a poster board for my sign.

I expect we'll see all our regulars and a new faux library crowd. It'll be interesting.

I took the officer his coffee and handed him a white sack with a breakfast taco.

"Wow." He grinned when he looked inside the sack. "You library people are awesome." He reached for his wallet on the console.

"On the house." I waved off his money and set up my table.

Within an hour, the sidewalks were crowded, and the parking lot was full. I had my theories on why people gather at a crime scene—in case of a reenactment or to see if anyone knew more than they did. Several of the regulars brought cookies and put them on my table, and almost all the regulars brought lawn chairs.

I scanned the crowd to see if there was anyone I didn't know. *I know an arsonist always returns to the fire, but I'm not sure about a killer. Need to research.*

The block-party atmosphere was festive in a macabre sort of way. I listened to the conversations for any threads of truth woven through all those stories, which was the primary point of lesson six in *Gathering Intel,* one of my favorite online courses. I scrutinized everyone, including the police officer, for signs of excessive interest or excitement.

Because you never know.

Olivia flopped into the chair next to me, adjusted her dark-tinted sunglasses, and fanned herself with one of the park brochures someone dropped off at my table. "Warm out here, isn't it? We're spoiled by air-conditioning. Did you notice today's change in dress code? Nobody's here in sweatpants, shorts, or T-shirts, and most of our gentlemen are dressed in white shirts and ties."

I nodded. "I was shocked by all the skirts, dress slacks, and blouses, and I've never seen some of our ladies wear makeup before. I'd say some of them are out of practice, but I'm not one to speak." *More information for my library-patron database—change of habits caused by the influence of outside circumstances.*

"I heard," announced a middle-aged, orange-haired woman in a booming voice, "the man who was murdered was an important politician who planned to launch his campaign from the library."

A gray-haired man in a brown suit and bright-blue tie cleared his throat. "My friend said her neighbor told her that her husband's second cousin found the body. She said her neighbor said her husband's cousin saw the murderer and tried to catch him, but the murderer sped away in a fast car just like you see in the movies. And didn't even stop at the stop sign."

I got lost at the second her.

The conversation jumped to bad drivers, cell phones, and speeders.

"I have work to catch up on." Olivia rose. "I'll be at the main library; feel free to call me if you need me. I'll be back later." Olivia stopped to chat with patrons while she made her way to her car.

"I read on the internet this morning no one was murdered. It's just a ruse to close down the library because the government ran out of money," said a thin woman with purple streaks in her black hair. "I'm going to buy some toilet paper and bread on my way home. My cousin said the store shelves will be empty tomorrow."

I was sorry to hear the no-money theory because I liked my regular paycheck. The government talk triggered a discussion about taxes. The tax conversation evolved into politics, which remarkably didn't turn into a fistfight. Politics led back to the unknown politician who was not murdered, after all; instead, he was the murderer.

Wow. I should take notes and write a book.

Two older men got into a small white pickup truck and drove away from a prime parking spot. Two other men in the same age range used their lawn chairs as walkers and shuffled to the parking place. *Original. Well done, fellas.*

When the pickup returned, the men scooted their chairs to the sidewalk. The passenger emerged with two flat cartons of doughnuts, and the driver put a box of coffee on the tailgate. A group gathered around the improvised coffee wagon, and a shoving match broke out among four of the older women over the maple-covered doughnuts. The police officer feinted a move to get out of his car, and the rowdies settled down.

One of the doughnut men cleared his throat. "My son is a chef—a famous chef—and he said a knife couldn't kill a man without a sound. He said the man was poisoned, brought to the library, and stabbed in the chest with the knife to put the authorities off track."

"No, you've got it wrong. The murdered guy was decapitated with a sword," someone in the group said. A bitter discussion erupted about sixteenth-century sword executions and ancient symbols on swords.

My elderly woman with the hearing aids joined me at my table. "I didn't know how controversial sword symbols were. I'm glad we're outside. Some of these flowery perfumes have the potential for mass suffocation. Have you noticed?"

I laughed. "That's funny."

A skirmish over lawn-chair placement erupted, but one of the nearby women said, "Behave, or you'll have to go home." The three men hung their heads and moved away from one another.

Well done. She has the mom voice.

My elderly companion said something, but I missed it.

"Sorry, I got distracted."

She smiled. "How's business?"

I glanced down at my table. "I have more books than I started with."

She motioned toward the crowd. "Learn anything? Any good theories?"

I rolled my shoulders and stretched my back. "I learned a wealth of imagination graces our library. We've got a good crop of potential writers or maybe oral storytellers."

"Isn't that the truth. Seriously, are you doing okay?"

I cocked my head and examined her face. Her eyes sparkled, and she smiled.

"I'm fine."

"Good. You know, people watch out for you, dear. Look at the time. Silly me, the bus will be here soon."

She rose and wandered over to a small group arguing over what type of knife killed the unknown politician and the famous chef. "Double murder, but there's a coverup, and we'll never hear about it," an unseen man said.

The bus came and went, but she wasn't on it.

Curious. I wonder who watches out for me. Suppose she meant angels or something? That'd be nice.

By midmorning, a mob of reporters and their camera folks crowded the parking lot and elbowed each other for positions with the library as a backdrop.

A slender, brown-skinned woman with short, curly black hair pushed a running stroller to my table. She wore a pink ballcap with a rose and *Mom* embroidered in red on the front of her cap, and the toddler wore a matching ballcap with *Kid* embroidered on hers.

"We jog by here every morning. I heard about the stabbing on the news, but no one said there'd be a circus here. I'm Deedee. This is Rose." She sat with me and handed the baby a cracker and a cup of water. "So what's the selection process for interviews? Can you tell?"

"I'm Maggie. Watch the reporters circle the small groups. They seem to target those who do most of the talking."

"You're right." She pointed at a small group on the sidewalk near the handicapped parking. "I'm a web designer. See how their background would be the flowers and the library sign? Perfect backdrop. And the man who's talking looks, I don't know, like an expert? No one has spotted him except for that young guy. He's a TV guy, I'm sure. He's got on heavy makeup."

The young man approached the group. He slipped in close to the speaker, a man with gray hair, wire-rimmed glasses, and a serious demeanor. The TV guy lifted an eyebrow, and a young woman with a camera on her shoulder appeared.

"You have a good eye. I'm impressed." I smiled.

Rose smashed the remains of her cracker into the stroller seat and tossed her water cup to the ground.

"Time to go." Deedee snatched up the cup and took off with a wave.

Late in the afternoon, Olivia appeared at my table. Her eyes were red-rimmed. "The police investigator said we can open the library in the morning. You can leave whenever you like. I'm going home."

"You okay, Olivia?" I asked.

"Didn't really sleep well. See you in the morning."

* * *

The next day, the library was back to its pre-murder routine, except there was still no sign of Ernie. Our regulars occupied their favorite spots to read or nap, and Olivia waved at those who wandered by her office while she sorted and filed papers.

I don't know what made me do it, but the online training *Leave No Stone Unturned* may have been my inspiration. I stood at the main counter near the front door and organized books while I waited for my opportunity.

Everyone seems occupied. Now's the time.

I went to the men's restroom, flipped over the tank top, and almost dropped it. Folded in half and taped with silver duct tape to the underside of the lid was a plain white envelope. I ripped it loose and stuffed it with the tape intact in my pocket. I jiggled the tank chain and replaced the tank top.

Good. No one saw me in the men's room. Correction—nobody asked, "Why were you in the men's room?"

I sauntered into the women's restroom, retrieved the envelope from my pocket, and sat down on the closed toilet lid. I peeled away the tape and unfolded the envelope. *We have a box of five hundred of these in the bottom-right-hand drawer at the check-in counter.* "To the Gray Lady" was printed on the front with a fine-tip black permanent marker. I held it up to the light.

Forgot about that blue cross-hatch pattern inside. Can't see anything. Do I read it now?

The restroom door opened. I stuffed the envelope into my pocket, flushed the toilet, and washed my hands. When I entered Olivia's office, she sat on the floor in front of an open box, with papers and her notebook of secrets next to her.

"I need to return the table and chairs. Is now a good time?"

"Go right ahead." Olivia smiled. "I love how conscientious you are."

I put my windows down on the way to the church. I loved the chance to breathe fresh air. Tony waited for me at the side door.

"Olivia called me." He carried the table and a chair inside. I followed him with the second chair. After we stacked the chairs and slid the folded table into its proper place, Tony headed toward the main church.

The ladies' room. Best place to open the envelope.

I always carried a pocketknife and a multitool in my purse. And a flashlight, bandages, hand sanitizer, tissues, matches, no-latex exam gloves, and a soft shawl that doubles as a blanket. And a small writing pad and a pen. And, of course, my wallet and sunglasses. And trail mix. And a county map and a headscarf. And my cell phone. And a charger for my phone.

At the library, the restroom sign read "Women" in block letters and exuded disinfectant. At the church, the pale blue sign on the restroom door was "Ladies" in a Florentine style of lettering. When I opened the door to a small anteroom with cream-colored walls and sage-green trim, the soft fragrance of roses wafted through the air. A small Queen Anne chair, upholstered in pale yellow and soft pink flowers, occupied a corner. A sunshine-yellow pillow with "Faith" embroidered in dark green occupied the seat of the small chair.

This chair adds to the room's look of an old-fashioned waiting room for genteel witness protection program candidates. Not quite disguised.

I chuckled and shook my head. *Spy humor. Never gets old.*

I sat in the chair, pulled out my flashlight, and scrutinized the envelope. No special markings besides "To the Gray Lady."

I frowned. *Not spelled Grey. Indicates American. Maybe.*

I used my pocketknife to slice open the envelope. Inside was a slip of paper with five lines of print.

146.20*0630*+D8DoD

UWILNO

Burn this & Env

Vaya con Dios

BFF3

The sheet of paper was a little over five inches by four inches. I measured it with the one-inch knuckle on my thumb. The other side was blank except for the printed logo of a local hotel. I looked inside the envelope and shook it. Nothing else. The first two lines didn't make any sense to me, but the last three did. *Burn the note and the envelope. Go with God.* Be safe on this dangerous mission? BFF3. Whoever wrote it knew about Taylor and Mr. Morgan.

My spine tingled, and the small hairs on the back of my neck and arms rose. My core was icy cold, and I shivered. I wrapped the shawl from my purse around my shoulders as I carefully shredded the paper into small pieces before I flushed a few of the pieces then carried the rest with me to find other restrooms.

As I headed toward the wing that led away from the main church, I stopped at the updated kitchen that boasted a pristine, heavy-duty look with the stainless-steel sink and sideboards, restaurant-style dishwasher, and industrial refrigerator and freezer, but the aroma of stale coffee, cookies, and casseroles—the traditional three C's of church socials—still lingered.

I flushed a few more pieces down the toilet of the restroom off the kitchen labeled "Staff" as far away organ music floated into the kitchen. It was a tune played by ear—hesitant, repetitive, and hopeful.

Across from the kitchen was the preschool classroom with a nearby restroom marked "Girls." The toilet was tiny, and the seat was only a foot from the floor. I dropped my few remaining pieces of paper into the toilet and flushed twice as I stared at the swirl. *Wonder if the boys' restroom has tiny urinals?*

On my way back to my car, I stopped to listen to the haunting organ music. I tiptoed to the church sanctuary and peeked inside. The smell of old wood, snuffed beeswax candles, and aging pew cushions and carpets transported me to the timeless place where all old churches reside.

Tony sat on the organ bench, but he didn't have any sheet music in front of him. He played a mournful tune—no chords, just single notes—but the melody was compelling and somehow comforting. I eased the door closed and hurried to my car.

Ten minutes. Maybe closer to fifteen. Hope I didn't miss anything at the library.

Chapter Six

The county had repaved the library parking lot with asphalt, but the circular drive near the front door was still the old concrete. When I parked at the far end of the parking lot, the squirrels in the surrounding massive oak trees chattered and scolded me for invading their territory. A flagpole stood tall in the middle of the green space, and a light breeze clanged the pull against the pole. When I walked past the flowers maintained by the garden club, I stopped to savor the fragrance.

I braced myself for the shift in environment and walked into the air-conditioned building.

"Oh, Maggie. I expected you to take longer. You know, at the church." Olivia spoke in short bursts, and her hands fluttered. "There's an investigator. In my office. He wants to talk to all the staff. Go on in."

I cocked my head and squinted at her. Did she realize what she just said? *All the staff was the two of us.*

As I approached Olivia's door, the investigator faced me. The scowl on his face—*man with a bitch face*—shifted to a strained smile. He had straight brown hair with an uneven, choppy cut, hazel eyes, and ears close to his head. His face was red and splotchy, and his nose was bulbous.

"Come in, come in. You are . . ."

"Are you the investigator?" I asked.

I narrowed my eyes and noted he was five foot, ten inches tall and two hundred forty pounds. His khaki pants and green-and-white striped shirt still showed the store-fold creases. The cuffs on his brown jacket were frayed. I glanced down. His black shoes were scuffed at the toes, and he wore white socks.

"Yes, yes, I am. Investigator Donald Chandler." He flashed a badge, returned it to his pocket, and stuck out his hand. I noticed dirt under his fingernails.

I shook his hand. "Librarian Margaret Sloan."

Hard grip. Not used to shaking hands with women.

"Nice to meet you, Maggie."

I noted the name change and gave him my best smile.

"You too, Donald." I resisted the urge to counter with Donnie.

Donald closed the door and waved at the visitor's chair in front of Olivia's desk. "Sit, sit."

He sat in Olivia's chair at the desk.

Going for the power position, are you?

I scooted my chair closer so that my knees hit the front of the desk. While Donald pulled a folded sheet of paper out of his inside jacket pocket and smoothed out the creases, I leaned forward with my elbows on the desk.

I've always read upside down. I thought everybody else did too until a kid in the fourth grade told me only aliens could rotate their eye sockets to read upside down.

When I used my mysterious side-squint on the kid, he left me alone. I smiled at the memory. *I miss that kid.*

Donald exhaled the scent of toothpaste when he talked, but an underlying sour odor emanated from his upper body. "So. We're going back over stuff. I've talked to everybody else and have some notes."

We looked at his paper. "Did you know the dead man?" he said. Donald was a slow reader and used his finger to follow each word.

"I didn't. He wasn't a regular."

The questions on his paper were numbered. Donald wrote "No" at the end of question number one, and we went to the next question. The paper read, "2. Why did you watch the man?"

"Why did you watch the homeless man?" he asked.

Wonder why he added "homeless"? Must have heard it from Olivia.

"I watch everyone in the library. I like to be available to anyone who needs any help. Some of our patrons have health problems. I watch them more closely."

"Oh. Did the homeless guy have health problems?"

Very brave, Donnie. Freelancing. Not the next question.

"I don't know."

He wrote, "Watch everyone."

Donald followed his finger while he read. "Why did you check the men's restroom?"

I fully expected him to begin his question with the words, "Number three." I'm so glad this wasn't question "Number two."

I coughed back a snicker, popped on my poker face, and cleared my throat. "An older gentleman reported a problem with the men's toilet not long ago, and I fixed it. I checked the restroom occasionally, when it was unoccupied, of course, until I was satisfied we had no additional toilet problems."

He wrote "Fixed toilet" and looked up. "Oh. Of course."

On to the next question.

This is excruciating. Wonder if I should snatch up the sheet and fill in the answers myself?

"Number four," he said. "A. Did you ever notice the man you watched give anything to anybody? B. Or talk to anyone?"

I wanted to answer "A, no, and B, no."

"No. Why?"

Donald looked around the room. The door was still closed. I resisted the urge to look around too.

He lowered his voice. "Well, don't let this get out. The homeless guy was a suspected drug dealer. The murder was about drugs."

I gasped to disguise my snort. I checked his paper.

Off script, Donnie. Buncha bull. This guy's either a fraud or a jerk. It's a toss-up.

"Oh, my. Are we in danger here?" I bit my lip to keep my face serious.

"No."

We looked at his paper. Only one more question left, but it had two parts.

"Number five. How many times did you see the deceased in the library? When was the last time?"

"One time. After he was murdered."

Donald looked at me with his eyebrows raised and his pen poised. "Oh. You never saw him before?"

I glared. *Not on your paper.*

"No, I never saw him before."

He wrote "one" and "day killed" next to the fifth question. He tapped his pen and stared at his paper. His face telegraphed his thoughts.

He didn't write "never saw him before" on his sheet because it would get him into trouble.

He clicked his pen and slipped it behind his ear.

Interesting. Not supposed to go off script.

"Do you have a card?" I asked.

Donald fumbled in his coat's breast pocket. "I guess I've run out. I'll call Ollie tomorrow or the next day. Let her know if you have something for me."

Ollie? He is presumptuous.

"Thank you, Donald. I will. But I can't imagine what it might be."

As I walked toward the door, I whirled around. "Donnie. You work for the state?"

"Naw. Oh. Yeah. Yes. The state. State investigator. Yes."

Fraud.

I loaded up a book cart to reshelve books. Donnie and Olivia stood together near the front door. Donnie waved his arms as he spoke, and Olivia laughed and playfully tapped his forearm.

He must be a charmer.

When Donnie left, Olivia smiled as she strolled to her office.

After I shelved the last book on my cart, I noticed I was near Ernie's usual chair. I sat and surveyed the sights. *What an amazing spot!*

Not only was the chair comfortable, but it was also an observation deck for the entire library. I could tell who was in each of the reading rooms off the main library. I peeked through the video racks to the front desk. When I leaned to the right with my head propped on my hand, the front door popped into sight. When I shifted to the left, I could peer down the hallway to the restrooms. I turned and had a good view of the back door. What a perfect place to observe the entire library. I breathed in. Did I catch a lingering whiff of Ernie's soap?

I rolled my cart to the red room to pick up books the patrons had left on the tables. I straightened chairs and picked up crumpled scraps of paper on the floor. When I headed to the door, I noticed a book on a chair I had pushed closer to the table.

How did I miss it? I picked up the book and stopped before I put it on the cart. *Oh, look. I missed something.*

* * *

Taylor and I picked at the food on our dinner plates—undercooked, slimy scrambled eggs and burnt bacon. I told Taylor about the investigator, but I didn't mention the envelope.

"Sounds like a piece of work," Taylor said. "What will you do? Should we take cooking lessons? This is awful."

"Maybe I forgot to tell him something." I put down my fork. "I agree. This is awful. You want a peanut butter and jelly sandwich?"

Taylor pushed her plate away. "Sure. You'll tell Olivia, so she'll call him, won't you?"

I dumped our food and carried our dishes to the sink. Taylor pulled out clean plates while I smeared smooth peanut butter and strawberry jam to the edges of slices of whole wheat bread and cut our sandwiches into triangles. "Unless you have a better idea."

"I prefer the direct approach. Your triangles are always perfect. Too bad cooking isn't geometric. If you want to be sure the call is made, you might want to call the police department yourself."

* * *

The next morning, I called the police department, and the man who answered the phone told me they no record of a state investigator named Donald Chandler. He took my name and location. "A detective will come to the library, Ms. Sloan."

I knuckle-tapped on Olivia's open door. She was sorting papers on her desk and jumped at the sharp sound. She flipped the documents over.

"Can I bother you a minute? Investigator Chandler said if I thought of anything I should let him know. I didn't get his card, so I called the police department. They'll send a detective to talk to us. There's obviously a mistake somewhere. A miscommunication."

She froze but didn't look up. "I'm sure you're right."

* * *

In the afternoon, a tall man with sandy-brown hair strode toward Olivia's office. He wore gray slacks, a crisp white shirt, and a black tie and carried a black briefcase.

If they need me, Olivia knows where to find me.

I straightened books on the shelves in one of the nonfiction aisles that was in the middle of a stack farthest from Olivia's office. A soft blue-gray cover, one of my favorite colors for a book, caught my eye. I realized I was in Logic, Section 160.

Section 160. Where's 146?

I was startled by a tap on my shoulder. I spun around. It's a good thing I hadn't signed up for karate lessons yet. Olivia stood behind me with her eyebrows raised and her mouth in a big silent O.

Amateur move on my part. Toughen up, buttercup.

"I didn't mean to startle you, Maggie. I called you, but I guess you were lost in thought. I need you to come to my office."

"Sorry, Olivia. I didn't know I was so nervous."

"Well, we might have reason to be." Her face was grim.

After we went into her office, she closed the door.

"Maggie, this is Detective Coyle from the police department."

"Parker Coyle, ma'am." He held out his hand.

Firm handshake. Direct eye contact. Blue eyes. Sandy-brown hair. Nice haircut. Clean-shaven. Six feet tall. One hundred eighty pounds. All muscle. Early thirties. Soap mixed with man smell. Cute—what? Not part of the class and neither is man smell.

Scalding heat rose from my neck to my face, and my ears burned.

"Maggie Sloan," I squeaked, then cleared my throat. "May I see your badge? Do you have an ID?" I tried to recover from the embarrassment.

"Of course. Here you are."

He handed me his badge and his ID. I compared the two and returned them. "Thank you."

"I suggest we sit," Olivia said.

Olivia sat behind her desk. Detective Coyle and I scooted the two visitors' chairs that were alongside her desk around to make a tight circle of three.

"I understand a man was here yesterday who impersonated a law-enforcement officer," Detective Coyle said. "Can you recall what he looked like and what he asked you?"

"Yes, I can. But first, do you mind if I give the police department a call?"

Olivia frowned and slid her desk phone toward me.

"It's fine, Ms. Sloan," Detective Coyle said. "Makes perfect sense to me."

I called the non-emergency number and asked to speak to a sergeant. I was on hold for a while before a gruff voice came on the phone. "Sergeant Arrington."

"Sergeant, this is Maggie Sloan at the library. Detective Parker Coyle is here, badge number twelve-fifteen. Could you verify he's with the police department, and it's no surprise to you he's here?"

"Ma'am, Detective Coyle was assigned to investigate the recent occurrences at the library, and his schedule would have him there. You have given me his badge number. If he's tall with brown hair, I believe the man with you at the library is Detective Coyle."

"Thank you, Sergeant. You've been very helpful."

"Satisfied?" the detective asked.

"Yes, thank you."

Olivia jumped up. "Well, I'll leave you to your questions. I have work to do unless there is something else. Detective?"

"No. Thank you, Mrs. Edwards."

Olivia closed the door to her office when she left.

"What can you tell me about the man from yesterday, Ms. Sloan?"

I gave Detective Coyle the physical description of the man who identified himself as Donald Chandler. I told him all the questions the "investigator" asked and the information he gave me. I included my observations that he answered to the name "Donnie" and was something of a charmer, even with the rough edges.

"He actually read from a sheet of paper?" Detective Coyle asked.

"Excruciating to watch." I closed my eyes and put the back of my hand to my forehead. "Even the memory is painful." I peeked to see his reaction. He smiled.

"I'll bet." He snorted. "Have you ever seen him before? How did you keep from laughing?"

"I've never seen him in the library, and I bit my lip."

He scanned Olivia's office. "Is it usual for a librarian's office to be organized like this?"

"I really don't know, but Olivia has it all cataloged."

"What about the number of boxes?"

I tried to see them with the eyes of someone who had just walked in. "Seems like a lot, but I tend to be more minimalist." I remembered my databases and my purse. "At least as far as boxes of paper documents are concerned."

He tapped his notebook with his pen. "The way you described Donald Chandler—it sounds like his clothes weren't his usual daily wear."

"I wouldn't be surprised if he stopped by a thrift store and bought the jacket before he came here. It had the thrift-store smell. Kind of musty. My mother used to drag me from one thrift store to another. Gave me an expert nose."

When he laughed, I wanted to hear his laugh again. "My grandmother loved garage sales. Speaking of an expert nose, my mother said Granny could sniff out a bargain a mile away. Anything you wanted or needed, she'd have it in her spare bedroom closet or in her garage. Come to think of it, her garage shelves were organized like an old hardware store"—he waved toward the boxes—"or a librarian's office."

We chuckled.

"Another question—you were pretty specific about his height and weight. How can you be so certain?"

"Well, as far as his height, look here." I walked over to the door. "Somebody who occupied this office must have once worked in a convenience store. This mark," I said, pointing, "is five feet, and this one up here is six feet. The smaller marks are in one-inch increments."

The detective shook his head. "Wow. I'm not sure I would have noticed them if you hadn't pointed them out."

"I know. It's a little bizarre, don't you think?" I returned to my chair next to him.

"What? That they're there or that you noticed?"

We laughed again. *He's teasing me.*

He cleared his throat, frowned, clicked his pen, and tapped it on his notepad.

"So, Ms. Maggie Sloan, how long have you had your charming laugh?"

Oh lord. Hot flash!

"I'm sorry," he said. "My sister says I have no social skills. I didn't mean to embarrass you."

"I'm fine. I'm not embarrassed. My sympathetic nervous system has developed this totally annoying, random dilation response to improve the oxygen flow to my face."

He laughed. "Best description of blushing I've ever heard. Charming and smart. How did you know his weight? Where's the scale?" He glanced around.

"Educated guess. After I knew his height, calculating the average weight was easy. Then from there, I estimated his weight by how overweight he appeared."

The two of us talked for over an hour. Detective Coyle took copious notes.

He looked up in the middle of writing. "How did you remember my badge number?"

I was puzzled by the question. "Is this a trick question?" I asked.

He smiled. "No, not a trick."

"Your badge number is only four digits and ten days before Christmas."

"Your memory is amazing. I just want you to know. If Donnie had been in the library before, you'd have remembered him."

I touched my face, and my skin was as hot to my hand as it felt inside.

Stop it. Wonder if I could pass it off as a premenopausal hot flash?

"I'm sorry. I apologize for not being sympathetic to your sympathetic nervous system," he said, and we laughed together.

Love that laugh. I'll blush all day long if it makes him laugh.

"Well," he cleared his throat. "Thank you for your time. You've been extremely helpful, and you can call me anytime you think of something else. Although I can't imagine what you left out. Sergeant Arrington always knows where I am if there's anything else or if there's anything I can do for you. Or better yet, here's my card, and I'll write my cell number on it."

While he wrote on his card, I gazed at his face.

Was I practicing my observation skills or was I soaking him in? My face was on fire.

He gave me his card. I could still feel the lingering warmth of his handshake after he left. Was I getting a taste of charm in action?

I need to shake this off.

I texted Taylor and Mr. Morgan. "Pizza. My treat." Taylor wouldn't see it until she got off work, but she'd appreciate a plan for supper. I needed to check 146.210. I took my cart to Section 100—Philosophy and Psychology. Section 140 is Philosophical Schools of Thought. Section 146 is Naturalism. Section 146.210 is Ritual and Belief.

We didn't have any books in the 140 range. Our books jumped from 130, Parapsychology and Occultism, to 150, Psychology. *What kinda joint is this, anyway? Weren't we supposed to be full service?*

I pulled out books from Section 180, Ancient, Medieval, and Eastern Philosophy, in case the Naturalism or Ritual and Belief books were misshelved. I sat with the books on the floor and returned each one to the shelf after reading a few pages. After an hour of reading, I dusted off the seat of my pants and stretched. Seemed only fitting to do a few yoga stretches in Section 180. *Well, that's an hour I'll never get back.* Although, I am prepared to help anyone interested in medieval philosophy.

Wonder what Detective Cutie likes to read. Should I call him?

Chapter Seven

Taylor breezed into my apartment with a bottle of white wine in her hand and a red under her arm. "Perfect night for pizza, beer, and good friends. The temperature's dropped. TV weather says we've got a front moving in. I heard thunder boomers off in the distance, so I brought extra wine in case we're stranded in a storm."

Mr. Morgan came in behind her with a salad, his homemade Italian salad dressing, and something in a foil-covered cake pan. He nudged the door closed with his foot.

"Mr. Morgan," I said. "You know it isn't necessary to bring food when we invite you to eat with us."

Taylor poked me. "Hush, Maggie. Mr. Morgan, you can bring salad and dessert anytime."

I lifted an edge of the foil covering Mr. Morgan's cake pan. "I take it back. Bring whatever you like."

"It's homemade strawberry cheesecake and needs to go into the fridge until we're ready for dessert," Mr. Morgan said.

"If Taylor and I were here alone, we'd plop on the sofa and eat pizza straight out of the carton with paper towels to clean sauce off our faces and fingers." After I put our dessert on the top shelf of the refrigerator, I pulled out the beer before Taylor grabbed the pizza out of the freezer and popped it into the oven.

Taylor set the table with the gray Fiesta ware plates and pale-gray cloth napkins Mother found in a thrift shop. "We wouldn't have homemade strawberry cheesecake, but if we did, we'd have spoons with the pan between us."

Mr. Morgan poured our beer into the cut-glass crystal goblets that Taylor gave me as an apartment-warming gift. "Anytime you need a cheesecake for your spoons, just let me know, and I'll whip one up."

After lightning cracked nearby, and the rumble of thunder rattled the windows, I lit my gray candle in a jar in case the lights went out.

"Smells like spicy woods," Taylor said. "Nice."

Taylor and I caught Mr. Morgan up on Investigator Donnie.

"Very strange," Mr. Morgan said.

"I called the police department, and a detective came to the library. Detective Coyle." My face went hot. "I've developed a sudden onset of early menopausal hot flashes. At least that's my preliminary diagnosis."

"You need to work on your blushing thing," Taylor said. "It gives away too much."

"I know." I groaned. "I've never had this problem before."

"Call it out. You know, *Look, I'm blushing*," Mr. Morgan said. "It'll stop."

"I'll give it a try. So. I need help with a puzzle. What does 146.210 mean to you?"

"I don't know. Let me check my phone." Taylor pulled up an internet search. "Hmm. Emergency evacuation plan. Or part of an IP address."

"Section 146 at the library is Naturalism; 146.210 is Ritual and Belief," I said.

"Also, Section 14-6.2-10 defines a delinquent juvenile in Rhode Island." Taylor read her phone. "How about a rimless wall-hung shower toilet? What does that even mean? Never mind. Page not found. I wanted to see a picture. Daniel Boone National Forest Section 146.210 of the Kentucky Wild Rivers Act has definitions . . ."

We chuckled at Taylor's internet obsession and the results of her searches.

"Let me see if I can find a picture—rimless wall-hung shower toilet," Taylor mumbled. "Here." She handed me her phone.

"Sure enough. Look at all the different styles." I handed the phone to Mr. Morgan.

"Bizarre." He shook his head. "I have another idea; 146.210 could be a radio frequency. Most two-meter frequencies use it for their repeaters."

I didn't understand one word he said, and Taylor's silence and puzzled face indicated she didn't either.

"I'll start over. Amateur radio—ham radio," he said. "I've been licensed for years. I still like to listen on my handheld."

"What could you do with a 146.210?" I asked. I knew I was asking an ignorant question, but I hoped Mr. Morgan could interpret. I studied his face while he grappled with an answer we might understand.

Heavy rain pounded the windows, and the sound of the wind intensified to a roar. Taylor peeked out the curtain. "The wind's knocked down some limbs. It's really blowing out there."

She sat next to me. "Not a fan of storms. We're ready for our radio class, Mr. Morgan."

Mr. Morgan explained radio frequencies and repeaters. Taylor and I were tech-savvy when it came to apps and smartphones, but this was a whole different world for us.

"My head is about to explode," I said.

Mr. Morgan rose from his chair. "How about if we call it a night? I'm starting to—pun alert—*repeat* myself."

We were so tired, we barely chuckled. Taylor grabbed a grocery-store plastic bag for rain protection to run to her apartment. Mr. Morgan brought an umbrella; he was always prepared for our unpredictable weather.

I expected my mind to race when I went to bed, but when my head touched the pillow, I tumbled into a deep sleep.

* * *

When I woke up the next morning, I jumped up, made coffee, and called Taylor. She sounded grumpy for a weekend.

I can fix grumpy. "Coffee's ready. We can go for a run."

My front door opened. Taylor was barefooted and in her pajamas. She held her running shoes and clothes. Her hair was in an early-morning ponytail.

"Here's coffee." I poured two cups. We tossed down our hot coffee and headed out to race and jump puddles.

When we returned to my apartment for our second cup of coffee, Taylor looked down. "Ugh. I'm mud-spattered. So are you. After we finish our coffee, bring your clothes to my apartment. It's my turn to do laundry," Taylor said.

"I'll shower first. I bought milk yesterday. Shall I bring it for cereal?" I asked.

Taylor was almost out the door. "Yes, and cereal too. I'm out."

"You have plans for tonight?" I asked while we ate breakfast. I caught a light whiff of peaches. Mother changed colors; Taylor rotated candles.

"My usual—lesson plans. You?"

I picked up my bowl to drink the milk. "Last week I took an online test: *Listening to Three Conversations at Once*. I missed one question, but they were wrong. I sent them an email with my correction. If I don't hear back from them by this evening, I'll find a different series."

* * *

On Sunday afternoon, Taylor and I had our typical where-shall-we-go discussion.

"We should go to the art show Mr. Morgan recommended," Taylor said.

"I'd rather go to an art show when he could go along to explain everything. Besides, would we have to dress up? Wear, like, work clothes?"

Taylor shuddered. "Movie. Let's go to a movie."

I pulled up the local movie theater site on the computer. Taylor pointed at a movie. "Here. I've waited for this. It's supposed to be gorier and scarier than the original."

I shook my head. "I can't stand scary movies. I don't like creepy music, screaming, or clowns jumping out with big knives. And have you noticed the people don't have any sense? I keep telling them—don't go into the basement, but they don't listen. Why don't they listen? I like action—if a helicopter blows up, the movie is a success as far as I'm concerned."

"I hate the violence," Taylor said.

"How can you watch a movie where people's hearts are ripped out of their chests and claim you don't like violence?"

"You know," Taylor said, "we need to find a second favorite movie for both of us."

I grinned. "Another option would be a movie we both hated. That would be different."

Taylor laughed. "You are the funniest person I know."

I stretched. "Well, if you're going to be like that, we'll go to your movie. I get to pick the ice cream place."

Taylor groaned. "Totally fair. And *ugh* to your ice cream in advance."

After the movie, we went to the ice cream shop then sat on a park bench with our cones. I bit off the bottom tip of my cone. "You know, the movie wasn't half-bad except they went into the basement. It almost had a plot."

"And this ice cream isn't terrible. It's almost not grainy."

I grinned. "A totally adequate day."

Taylor spewed her ice cream. I jumped up and danced, and ice cream dripped down my arm. "I win."

Taylor stuck her tongue out at me.

On our way home, I broke our Sunday-night rule—no talking about work. "I have this feeling. Something's going on with Olivia. She's so tense."

Taylor frowned at me. "You made the rule."

She was right.

* * *

I'm always the first one at work, but when I arrived at the library on Monday morning, Olivia waved at me from her car in the parking lot. Her typically coiffed hair was a fright of tangles. Her makeup always had the professional touch, but this morning her red lipstick was smeared across her upper lip, with nothing on the lower. She didn't look like herself without any powder, blush, or mascara.

Her window was down, and she tapped on her steering wheel. "I forgot my keys to the building. What took you so long?"

"Olivia, I'm thirty minutes early. Are you okay?"

"I got a call from Donnie last night, and he was furious I called the police. He said he's undercover with the state."

Does she really believe that?

I scratched my head. "Why did he call?"

She got out of her car, locked the door, and realized she'd left her window down. "Why did I do that?"

She raised her window, closed her car door, and frowned at her keys. "He said we must know something if we called the police, and he needed to know what we said. You did say you remembered something."

I stared at her. "Wow, I'm baffled. If Donnie's undercover with the state and knows you called the police, then why doesn't he know what we told the police? Have you had your morning coffee?"

She chewed on her thumbnail. "No."

"Well, let's grab some coffee. Your treat."

I tried for a joke, but Olivia didn't get it. Taylor would have replied with something in retaliation. "Sure, and you buy dinner."

Sometimes I forget I'm funny only to Taylor and Ella. And maybe Detective Coyle. While Olivia retrieved her purse from her car, I got a text from Taylor. "Man is the only animal that blushes or needs to. Twain." I coughed to hide my giggles when Olivia got close to my car.

Olivia rubbed her forehead. "Are you okay, Maggie? Are you coming down with something?"

"I'm fine. What about you? Have you eaten?"

She climbed into my car, and I noticed her blouse buttons were in the wrong holes. "No, but I usually only have coffee anyway."

"Your shirt looks strange. Are the buttons in the right holes? How did Donnie know you called the police?" I asked.

She looked down. "Oh, you're right. Now, how do I fix it? Well, I might have told him when he called and asked if we'd thought of anything. It just came out."

"Maybe if you get the two bottom ones right, the rest will straighten out when you go up?"

We went to a drive-through for coffee. I paid for our coffee to apologize for my weak attempt at a joke. Olivia didn't notice, and I shrugged. *So much for making amends.*

"What do we tell Donnie?" she asked.

I turned to look at her. Her face was tight, and she was close to hyperventilation. *Panic attack?*

"Olivia, take a few slow breaths for me."

She tried—I'll give her that. I sipped my coffee and choked. *Cream and sugar. Ugh. I got Olivia's coffee.*

I set down the cup in the holder. *Olivia must be agitated. She's drinking my black coffee.* I lusted for my black coffee with every sip she took. "Maybe we should get out of the middle and introduce Donnie to Detective Coyle."

Olivia threw her hand up to her face. "Oh, no."

What on earth with the Oh, no?

"Well, then, how about if we call Detective Coyle and ask him what to tell Donnie?"

According to the look on Olivia's face, I didn't have one intelligent cell in my brain.

While I waited for Olivia to come up with a response, I put on my Cinderella hat, figuratively speaking. Sometimes it's good to look at things from a different perspective. Lesson four from How to Deal with Tricky Situations. Cinderella's perspective was different for me.

Let's see. Wicked stepmother. Pumpkin. Mice. Fairy godmother. Ball. Cleaning. Glass slipper. Fancy dress. Nice hair. Blond. Blond jokes. That's it. No-Sensatall. Plumber.

"We need to call Detective Coyle and talk to him about the plumber. Remember I checked the men's room? Because the elderly gentlemen complained about the toilet? We talked about a plumber. But I fixed the toilet. Remember? Did you call a plumber after you said I shouldn't fix the men's toilet anymore?"

I bit my lip. How badly does Olivia need a straw to grasp?

Olivia frowned. "What about Donnie?"

"If Donnie calls back, we tell him we called Detective Coyle."

"What if he doesn't like it?"

I raised one eyebrow and gave her the hairy-eyeball look.

Thank you, Mother.

"Right. Right."

My logic to call Detective Coyle made no sense. If Olivia hadn't been so distracted by what Donnie might think, she'd have poo-pooed everything I said. I was so full of it.

Oh man. I'm glad Mr. Morgan and Taylor didn't hear that. I swallowed hard.

She tilted her head. "Are you okay? Are you coming down with something?"

I was a little choked up from trying not to laugh. "Allergies. Something must be in bloom."

"Everyone has allergy problems. Much worse this year." During the rest of the drive back to the library, Olivia talked about her allergies and how bad they were.

I had permission to call Detective Cutie, and my face went hot.

I mean Coyle. What's wrong with me?

After my morning checks, I interrupted Olivia, who was in the middle of a story she was telling my hard-of-hearing friend about her allergies. My friend furrowed her brow and shook her head, but her eyes twinkled when she winked at me.

I cleared my throat. "Okay if I use your office to make a phone call?"

Olivia waved her hand toward her office and didn't miss a beat of her story.

I called Detective Coyle, but he wasn't in. I left a voice message with my cell and the library phone numbers. Before I left Olivia's office, my cell rang.

"Miss Sloan?" Sergeant Arrington said. "Detective Coyle told me to call you myself if you called while he was out. Are you in any danger? Any trouble?"

"No. I'm okay."

I was surprised because nobody had ever asked if I was in any trouble. Even as a child, I never got into trouble—except for not following directions. That still stung.

"I need to talk to Detective Coyle. The guy who came to the library and claimed to be an investigator called our head librarian last night. She said he was angry she called the police."

"Did he threaten her?" Sergeant Arrington growled. I wouldn't want to be the imposter.

"I don't think so, but she was upset when I suggested we call Detective Coyle."

"But you called anyway."

I crossed my fingers and hoped I wasn't in trouble with the sergeant. "Yes."

"Coyle said you were smart."

He did? Really?

"I'll get in touch with him right away." Sergeant Arrington hung up.

I got a text from Mr. Morgan: "Nada on repeater this am."

I logged on to the county library catalog system to see if another branch had books in 146. I found 140, Philosophical Schools of Thought, and 153, Intelligence, but no books on humanism, naturalism, or any other of the isms.

I grabbed my cart, wheeled from aisle to aisle, and reshelved books. I halted when I realized I was at the scene of the murder.

Strange. The chair was away from the table, and on its seat was a red-corduroy pad. *We don't have seat pads for our chairs.* I picked up the cushion and threw it back on the chair. *A book.* The cover was a dull brick red. *Like blood.*

I grunted and pulled out the book. "Cut the melodrama."

A man in the next aisle looked around, shrugged, and strode to the front of the library with a book in his hand.

I bent over, peered under the chair, and flipped it over to check the bottom of the seat. I didn't want to come back later to find another book or note. I headed to the women's restroom, but when I realized Olivia was in my path, engaged in a deep conversation about her allergies, I diverted to her office and closed the door.

The book was *Camping in the Yukon* by Walter Chandler.

Oh great. "Sorry. No disrespect intended."

I held the book upside down by the covers, but nothing fell out. I flipped through the book but didn't find anything marked or handwritten. I looked the book up on the library system, and it didn't show as checked out. I turned to page 146. "How to Build a Snow Cave." When I flipped to page 210, I found the alphabetized index from "Nature calls" to "Sheets." Some of the topics sounded interesting. "Ojibway snowshoes," for example; I turned to page fifty-one and read about the only snowshoes made of wood and tied at toe and tail. I was ready to sit and read more when Olivia walked in.

"Sorry, didn't mean to interrupt your reading," she said.

"Just a little research to help out a twelve-year-old." I cocked my head. *But this is your office, Olivia.*

"That's nice. Oh, I came to tell you Detective Coyle is here." She left after the detective walked in. This was becoming my office.

"Well?" he said.

I cleared my throat. "The imposter investigator called Olivia last night, and I'm not sure why, but she's worried he was angry with her. You might want to talk to her."

"Sounds good, and then we'll go to lunch." Like we went to lunch all the time.

My heart pounded, and I gulped. "Sure."

I found Olivia in the red room. "Detective Coyle would like to talk to you in your office." I didn't join them because I couldn't control my eye rolls.

They talked for almost an hour. After I checked out *Camping in the Yukon,* I dropped it into the drawer with my purse. I reshelved books, took the trash to the dumpster, rearranged all the tables and chairs in the blue room, and cleaned the women's room.

I walked past the hearing-aid woman. She pointed to an elderly man with his glasses on the top of his head; his head bobbed as he dozed at a table with an open book in front of him. "You are a whirlwind today. I'll give you a nickel if you close his book."

I gave her the "Mother" look. She laughed, and the elderly man snorted awake at the sound and frowned. "Shhhhh."

She said in a quiet voice, "Well played, Library Girl."

When Detective Coyle came out of Olivia's office, I stopped at her doorway. "Be back in a bit."

Olivia looked up. Her eyes were red, and mascara streaked down her cheeks. I hoped she hadn't confessed to the murder because I was hungry.

Chapter Eight

Detective Coyle smiled. "Ready for lunch?"

When I didn't see a police car in the parking lot, I realized a detective would have an unmarked car. *Will I ride in the back seat with wire mesh between us?*

The detective impressed me when he accompanied me to the passenger's side and opened the door. *Didn't expect that.*

I peered at the interior: a police radio and microphone were attached to the dash. *No surprise there.* I had anticipated papers, pens, and a clipboard on the seat and empty cups and food wrappers on the floor, but his vehicle was neat and organized, and the small crate on the back seat served as a portable file cabinet.

When we left the library, I asked, "Are we going to lunch so no one can eavesdrop? Is Olivia's office bugged?"

He glanced at me. "Did you know your mother called the police station?"

"Nooo."

"Yep. She called to ask if you were safe at the library. More accurately, she bellowed."

"That's my mother. I may cut her out of my will." I glanced at him.

He chuckled. *He laughed at my joke.*

"Sergeant Arrington took her call. I understand they bellowed at each other." When traffic was clear, he turned right. I stared while his arm muscles flexed, but I pretended I was checking for oncoming traffic.

I smiled. "I can hear it. I love it."

"She said you are an important spy."

"What?" I closed my eyes. *Can a person die from embarrassment?*

"Her words."

I stared at his muscles and his chin. I broke my gaze and glanced out my window. "Well, I'm not, but I always wanted to be a spy. I've sometimes wondered if she knew."

"Then why are you a librarian?" he asked. We stopped at a traffic light, and he looked at me. I willed myself not to blush, but my face caught on fire. He turned his head toward the road ahead. I caught a sliver of a smile.

"The library is heaven on earth," I said.

"Because it's quiet?"

"You got it." We laughed. *He did. He totally got it.*

This was the point where I could have told him about Ernie, how I found the envelope, what the paper said, the ham radio, the book, naturalism, and even the rimless toilet hanging on the wall in the shower. But I didn't. It all sounded too bizarre.

"We know who the deceased was," Detective Coyle said. "We aren't sure, but I have a theory about why he was at the library."

He braked hard when a car whipped out in front of us from a side street. My seat belt grabbed me. He turned to me. "You okay?"

"I'm fine. Who was he? What was he doing? Why he was murdered?"

"Guy's lucky I'm not in a patrol car. The deceased man—it appears he was either spying on someone or waiting to talk to someone. My theory is he was watching you."

"What? I was monitoring the homeless man while the deceased guy spied on me?"

"You did make it kind of easy for him."

"Oh. But why?"

This sounded even more bizarre than the toilet on the shower wall.

"I hoped you'd tell me." He turned left into a diner parking lot. "How's this?"

"Fine. You know I have no idea why anyone would keep an eye on me."

I frowned and remembered my elderly friend saying that people watched out for me.

"There's an answer. We just don't know what it is yet." He narrowed his eyes and peered at me. "You okay?"

"Yep. Ready for lunch."

When we walked into the diner, the chalkboard at the entrance announced the special was a blue cheese burger. The diner aroma was heady—seared meat on the grill and fresh-cut potatoes, not frozen, sizzled in the fryer. I may not know how to cook, but my nose is a foodie.

The waitress came to our booth. "What would y'all like?"

"Special and fries. And iced tea," I said.

"Same for me," Detective Coyle said.

"I wanted to be a chef when I was a kid," he said in between bites. "Dad was a police officer. It took him a while to understood why his son wanted to cook."

I sipped my tea. "I never learned to cook. I didn't spend much time in the kitchen. Ours was too noisy."

He laughed. "I baked my first cake when I was five. Mom gave me free rein in the kitchen."

"That's awesome."

He reached for the catsup, squirted a pool on his plate, and dipped a fry. "I think so too. When I was seven, I learned to toss pizza dough. Dad bought me a pizza stone for my eighth birthday. He told me he was proud to have a kid who could cook. He'd sit with me in the kitchen while I chopped and sautéed. We talked about school, cooking, football, his job, girls. Everything."

"Sounds like he's a great man. Very wise."

He grinned. "Yeah, he is. He's retired now and volunteers with kids."

"I always wanted to be a spy. When I was four, I convinced Mother to buy me black clothing. I wore black until college when I learned about the Gray Man. Maybe sometimes I'm too literal. Mother tried to tell me a Gray Man isn't actually gray, but how could she know anything about spies?"

"Makes sense to me. After all, she was talking to the expert, right?"

"So true." I laughed. "I took every free online spy course I could find. I read every book written about spies—fiction and nonfiction. So, yes, in one sense, I'm an expert. But I have no experience. You know what you call someone who is an expert with no experience?"

"I have no idea."

"A rookie."

Parker chuckled. "Maggie, you might be literal, but you are brilliant. You described our rookies at the police department to a T."

Somewhere around mustard on my chin and needing more napkins we had reached the point of "Parker" and "Maggie."

Our server asked, "Dessert?"

I groaned.

Parker said, "We'll have to come just for dessert sometime."

"Sounds good to me." I beamed. *Oh boy, oh boy.*

"How could your spy expertise cause you to be a threat to anyone?" Parker asked on our way back to the library. "There has to be something else. I'm stumped for now. I need to do some more digging. Okay if I get back to you in a day or so?"

"Sure."

It would be more than okay. It would be positively magnificent.

"Meanwhile, don't do any spying, and if you think of anything, tell your mother." We laughed. "Although that may not be a bad idea. She'd call Sergeant Arrington. Seriously, call me or text me."

After we reached the library parking lot, he turned to me with a stern look. "Seriously, stop."

Seriously? Not happening.

In my most sincere tone, I said, "Of course."

He gave me a look of disbelief and shook his head.

I reached for the door handle. I expected him to say, "Liar, liar, pants on fire."

When I got out, he said, "I'll call you later."

What is later? Ten minutes? Two weeks? Never, like the job interviews? Or let's do lunch? Except we already did.

"Certainly," I trilled and closed the door. He groaned. Maybe my cheerful demeanor was a little overboard.

I strolled into the library as Olivia poked her head out of her office, backed up, and eased the door shut behind her. Everyone within view stared at me.

What's wrong with these people? I just went to lunch in a cop car, for cryin' out loud.

I locked my purse in my drawer near the checkout station, loaded up a cart with books, and placed them in aisle order. My automatic routine gave me a chance to think, except my mind was a blank. *Do I have thinker's block?*

"Dearie, a question." My empty train of thought was interrupted when the elderly woman with hearing aids slipped up behind me. People all around us lifted their heads at the sound.

I didn't realize how tall she was. She looked small and frail when she sat. She must unfold when she stood. She was at least six inches taller than me, and her posture was stately. She was within the average weight range for her height, which was unusual in comparison with the other patrons at the library her age, or even twenty years younger. Her gray hair was cut in the latest style. Her face was soft with wrinkles; otherwise, I'd accuse her of masquerading as elderly for the senior discounts.

Still smiling, she whispered, "I have an important message for you."

I spoke loud enough for our audience to hear. "Of course."

She showed me a small slip of paper with scribbling on it and whispered, "Day eight." The words were so soft I thought she'd spoken in my head. I took the paper from her.

I maintained a volume for all to hear. "Next aisle over."

Another piece of paper for the fire. Wonder if I should invest in a propane torch?

She smiled, patted my hand, and spoke in a normal tone. "Thank you. You've been a big help. I can find it from here."

"You're welcome."

I returned her smile. *Is she BFF3?* I read the paper. *Day eight. D8. DOD. Date of Death.*

Olivia came out of her office. "What did Ms. Lillian need? She never asks for help. What did she want? What's on the paper?"

Olivia knew the people, but I knew the library contents better than she did. It shouldn't have been a surprise Ms. Lillian would ask me for information.

"She wanted a graphic novel, and I told her where they are. You can help her if you like."

"No, no. I don't know anything about graphic novels. Aren't those for kids?"

"I suspect she wants to understand what her grandkids read."

"Right, right."

Olivia sounds just like Donnie. Stop. No jumping to conclusions.

I got a text from Mr. Morgan: "Dinner at six."

I wasn't sure I could eat again today, but I couldn't pass up dinner at Mr. Morgan's.

I got a call from Parker at four thirty. We went through the lunch-was-great conversation, and then he said, "I need to talk to you, but I'm working late tonight on a case. Do you eat breakfast?"

Oh, Lord. I'll put on ten pounds this week.

"I love breakfast." I glanced down, and my pants became tighter. *Cut it out, smarty-pants.* I chuckled but managed to turn it into a fake sneeze.

"Bless you," he said. "Shall I pick you up in the morning about six? Or would it be better if we meet at the library parking lot?"

"Library parking lot."

Of course, then everyone would assume I was out all night with him. But if he picked me up at the apartment, I wouldn't have any way to get home. *My reputation could use a little pizzazz.*

* * *

When Mr. Morgan opened his apartment door, Taylor and I were pulled in by the aroma wafting from the kitchen.

"Mmm. Smells heavenly," I said.

He waved at the cheese, crackers, and two wine glasses on the kitchen bar.

Taylor inspected a cracker and nibbled on a corner. "Are these homemade?"

"Yes. You two deserve a treat. How are they?"

"Amazing," Taylor said.

We stuffed cheese and crackers into our mouths while Mr. Morgan poured red wine.

"Red meat, right? Beef?" I asked while I munched crackers.

He placed our salads on the table, lit the candles, and refilled our wine glasses.

"Salad looks great. What's in it?" Taylor asked.

"Wild greens with raspberries and pecans. The raspberry vinaigrette is homemade."

After we finished our salads, I cleared our plates while Mr. Morgan brought prime rib to the table, and Taylor followed him with tiny red potatoes with the skins on and a vegetable.

"Roasted potatoes?" I asked.

"Right. Olive oil and rosemary. And the brussels sprouts are roasted too. The roasting's what makes the char."

So the vegetables aren't burnt? I speared one of the brussels sprouts and bit into an edge. Taylor cringed. She must not have liked brussels sprouts either.

"Wow, these are good," I said.

"Of course, I knew they would be," Taylor said. Her smug tone matched her smug expression. I raised my eyebrows, and she grinned.

At the end of our meal, we all cleared the table, Mr. Morgan put the dishes in the dishwasher, and Taylor and I washed the pots and pans. We were a team.

"Shall we talk over dessert?" Mr. Morgan said.

Dessert was brownies with chocolate frosting and our favorite homemade gelato with ragged drizzles of chocolate.

"Donnie called Olivia." My words were muffled because I was holding a mouthful of gelato in my mouth to absorb the flavors. I gave up and swallowed the melted deliciousness. "I'm pretty sure she told Donnie I called Parker."

Taylor raised her eyebrows. "Parker?"

"You can't just casually mention *Parker* without details," Mr. Morgan said. "It's the BFF rule."

"After Detective Coyle talked to Olivia, we went to lunch. We ate and talked about when we were kids, and he laughed at my jokes. He's got brown hair, blue eyes, and he's tall . . ." I remembered Parker's warm touch and blushed.

"Were you going to add dreamy?" Mr. Morgan winked and chuckled.

"Harry's tall too," Taylor said. "He's a third-grade teacher at my school, but he's been there for three years. I met him my first day of school. His name's Harold, but he told me to call him Harry. Our classes have a ten-minute overlap at lunchtime."

"Taylor, everybody's tall to us," I said.

Taylor sipped her wine. "Yep. Either tall or really tall, right? So it takes some fast footwork to drop into the teachers' lounge before Harry leaves."

"And, of course, you have to be nonchalant." Mr. Morgan chuckled.

"Right. Not always easy. Last week, one of my kids threw up right before lunch, and I had to clean the floor. I was running late, so I sprinted down the hallway to get to the teachers' lounge. The principal turned a corner in front of me. I skipped down the hall and announced, 'It's Don't Skip School Day.' At first, she looked at me like I was loony then she skipped the other way."

Mr. Morgan and I laughed with Taylor.

"I've listened to the radio every morning," he said. "So far, nothing to hear except radio checks and the ham coffee group who discuss their plans for the day while they drive to the diner where they're having coffee. What's interesting is there are two or so new hams. I can tell by their call signs. It isn't unusual for new hams to start with radio checks, but they are on the air every morning, almost like a training session. Might be reading too much into it."

I carried our bowls to the kitchen and returned. "I have a snippet of information. Something's scheduled for tomorrow or Wednesday, but I don't know anything else like who, what, or where. Day eight from the date of death of the guy murdered in the library is all I know."

"Seriously?" Mr. Morgan said. "How did you hear that?"

My head snapped in his direction. "A confidential source."

"Confidential from us?" Taylor narrowed her eyes.

"For everyone's safety." I had spent all day thinking about how to explain "day eight." I envisioned what Smokey Bear would say and hit a blank wall, but then I remembered McGruff the Crime Dog.

Security. Keep the doors locked.

Taylor brushed the crumbs on the tablecloth into a napkin and shook the napkin contents into the trash. "Makes sense. I'll keep it as confidential as all the things my kindergartners tell me about what happened at home the day before. And let me tell you—no, wait. I can't."

She waited for the appreciative chuckles. We obliged.

"Mr. Morgan, do you have a lady friend?" Taylor said.

He wiggled his eyebrows. "I have many lady friends."

"No, I mean a special lady friend. It would be nice if we had a dinner party and invited Parker, Harry, and your lady friend. We can have it at my apartment, but you have to cook."

"We have more room here. You two can bring flowers and wine. We'll do it up right. Give me a little time to decide who I would invite."

"Look at the time." Taylor yawned. "Ten o'clock. Late. It's past bedtime for this kindergarten teacher."

"And the retired gentleman." Mr. Morgan yawned.

"Librarian." I mumbled and tried to stifle my yawn. *And I have a date in the morning. Meeting. I have a morning meeting.*

Chapter Nine

My alarm went off at five fifteen. I had planned to set my alarm for four thirty so I'd have enough time to make coffee, shower, blow-dry my hair, put on my makeup, and pick out my outfit. I must have been tired because I forgot I don't wear makeup, it takes only a second to select clothes for the day with a closet full of gray, and I don't blow-dry my hair because the dryer is too noisy.

Parker's car was in the lot when I pulled into the library at five forty-five. I parked at the far end in the staff section. Parker strode over and opened my door.

"You should keep your door locked until you have everything in your hand and you are ready to walk inside."

What does he think I am? An amateur? I wrinkled my nose. *Probably. Because I am.*

On our way to his car, he kicked at a small rock, and it skittered across the asphalt. "Sorry, I'm a little on edge. Okay if we try another diner? It's my favorite breakfast place and a little farther out, but they buy their eggs from a local farmer when egg production is high."

He opened the passenger door, and I climbed in. "I've never eaten an actual farm egg—sounds great."

We rode to breakfast in a comfortable silence. We parked in front of an old train passenger car. A faded wooden sign over the door proclaimed RE GIE'S DINER. *Love the missing G. Adds character.*

Parker led the way to the farthest booth on the left. I scooted in with my back to the door, and he sat across from me.

A tall, slender waitress with brown hair pulled into a high ponytail bounced out of the kitchen with two cups and a pot of coffee. She looked like a dancer. "Hi, Parker. And?"

"Kate, this is my friend Maggie," Parker said. "Maggie, this is my sister, Kate."

Kate set down the cups and held out her hand. "Pleased to meet you."

Strong handshake. I liked her. "You too."

Kate grabbed silverware and napkins and placed them on the table. "Maggie, how do you like your eggs? And would you rather have bacon or sausage?"

"Over medium. And bacon, please."

"And one of our homemade cinnamon rolls. What about you, Parker? Your usual?"

"You got it."

"Maggie, I'm the server, busboy, and cook. If you need more coffee, Parker will take care of it for you. And if I get too busy before you leave, don't be surprised if Parker jumps up to take over in the kitchen. This diner has been a family-run business for four generations. Can you wait tables?"

"Kate, let Maggie drink her coffee. And breakfast?"

"On it." Kate hurried to the kitchen.

"So what's up?" I asked.

"Enjoy your coffee. Kate will be here soon with breakfast. We have to eat it while it's hot, or she'll take it away and fix new plates."

A large brown dog with a gray face and gray whiskers lumbered out of the kitchen. She made herself comfortable on the floor under our booth.

Parker reached down to scratch her neck and ears. "Hello, girl. Maggie, this is Lucy."

I held my hand down close to Lucy, and she sniffed my fingers. I passed the sniff test, and she let me rub her face. She flopped over onto my feet; I was accepted.

"Lucy might be losing her sight, but she loves to run with someone," Parker said.

Kate carried out plates of food. "Here ya go."

She set down my bacon and eggs, a plate with a six-inch diameter cinnamon roll, and bowls of grits and sausage gravy. I glanced around to see if someone else had come in. "All that food for us?"

The dark-orange yolks sat high on the whites and looked like suns on top of fluffy clouds. The eggs were creamy, and their fresh taste was like nothing I had imagined. They immediately ruined my appetite for watery, tasteless, store-bought eggs.

I said, "Wow."

Parker grinned. "Exactly."

I spooned the gravy on top of the grits and took a bite. "I love grits, but this is heavenly. I love the creamy, spicy-hot sausage gravy mixed with the salty and sweet taste of corn."

I cut my cinnamon roll into quarters while Parker jumped up and refreshed our coffee. I bit into my cinnamon roll. The thin frosting oozed onto my lower lip and fingers. I scraped my lower lip with my teeth and popped my sticky fingers into my mouth. Then I wiped my face and fingers with a napkin.

Taylor and Mr. Morgan would love it here.

Kate glided in and smiled her approval. "Well done. More coffee?"

She refilled our cups without waiting for an answer. After we ate what we could, Kate took our dishes. "I set a sack on the counter with a box of cinnamon rolls for you. I'll be busy with dishes in the kitchen. Holler if someone comes in."

Parker leaned back. "Did you apply for a job at a bank?"

"I did. My recruiter arranged an interview for me at the large bank in town, and I interviewed there not long after I met with a panel at the art studio. Short interview, but he did ask good questions. I didn't hear anything back from them, but no surprise. I learned few businesses bother to respond to applicants."

"Could you describe him?"

"Sure. I've got my interview notes. I can refer to them. When do you want it?"

Parker grabbed the pot of coffee and refreshed our cups. "Where are your notes? At your apartment?"

I sipped my coffee. I would be wired all day. "Yep. I can scan them or write something up this evening and email it to you."

Parker stood up and grabbed the sack on the counter. "Why don't we run by your place this morning? We've got plenty of time before you need to be at work."

"Okay. We can do that too."

I didn't see what difference a few hours made, but I didn't mind. "So what about my interview would make somebody want to watch me?"

"Do I turn here?"

Deflection, thy middle name is Parker.

We parked at the apartment complex, and Parker accompanied me up the steps. After I unlocked my door, he put his hand on my shoulder and entered the apartment before I did.

While I pulled my notes out of my file cabinet, he checked the windows and doors. "Your door needs a deadbolt. Do you have a locksmith?"

"No, but Mr. Morgan can install one for me."

"Tell Mr. Morgan to call me if he has any questions about placement."

I handed him my notes, and he read through them.

"These are very thorough. Do you have anything to add? You might want to review what's there."

"The bank was one of my favorite interviews. I was impressed with the efficiency of the interviewer because he had more than one position to fill."

Parker frowned. "You said the doors were locked when you got there, and the interview guy let you in, then locked the door behind you?"

"Yes. The interview guy—he didn't give me a name—didn't let me in until I said I was there for an interview, and he asked which position. We sat at the first desk, and he said they were undergoing a lock-in audit. After the interview, he thanked me, escorted me to the door, and locked it behind me. The questions and answers are in my notes."

I pointed to the page. "The physical description is as complete as I can be."

Parker picked up my box of interview notes. "You must have interviewed with every business in Harperville. Can I take all your notes? I'll get them back to you."

"Sure. I have everything in my database, and I could re-create my notes if I needed to."

"Don't tell anyone that." Parker spoke in a stern voice. "And don't tell anyone about your database or your interview notes."

I shrugged. "Sure. Oh, look at the time. I need to be at the library in thirty minutes."

"Lock up. You know, we could go lights-and-sirens to get you there on time if we need to."

He guffawed at the look of horror on my face, so I punched his arm.

"Ow. Sorry." He rubbed his arm and laughed some more.

On our way to the library, I got a text from Mr. Morgan. "Might be something today. Need to talk to Parker."

I texted him back. "I'll give him your number."

I turned to Parker. "The text was from Mr. Morgan. He needs to talk to you."

I wrote down Mr. Morgan's number and handed it to Parker when I got out of the car. He did get me to work early enough to suit me. Without lights and sirens.

I was reluctant to go inside; I wanted to bask in my pleasant morning. "Thanks for breakfast. I enjoyed meeting Kate and Lucy."

I gushed. Embarrassing. Fire rushed up my neck and face.

"Don't forget your cinnamon rolls."

* * *

All I expected was my three-quarters of a cinnamon roll, but my sack was heavy. When I reached the desk, I opened it and discovered a dozen cinnamon rolls. I cut them into quarters and put them on the literature table near the front desk. I printed out a note: *For our faithful readers— Enjoy. Courtesy of RE GIE'S DINER. Support our local businesses.*

When Olivia waved at me from her office, I was relieved to see she was back to her usual, fastidious appearance. After I loaded my book cart and pushed it toward the first aisle, she came up behind me and tapped me on my shoulder.

Olivia, you have got to stop sneaking up on me. You aren't me.

I turned and smiled.

"Are you busy?" she asked.

"The usual." I pointed at my cart.

"Can you stop a minute and come in my office? I need to talk to you."

I'll bet this is more about Donnie.

We went into her office, and she closed the door. "Your car was here when I came in to get an early start. I thought you were already here, but no lights were on."

Ah. We're here for a fishing expedition.

"But here I am." I used my cheeriest voice and changed my tone to one of concern. "So what's up? Is there a problem?"

I strained to hear her quiet voice. "I got another call from Donnie."

We were in her office. Why did she whisper?

"Anything you need for me to do?" My normal voice sounded booming in comparison to hers.

She rubbed her neck, went to the window, peeked out of the blinds, and returned to her chair. "Donnie said I was in trouble because I brought in what he called *the locals*."

I glanced at the window and frowned. "What kind of trouble? Why didn't he say anything when he was here the first time? Librarians understand confidentiality."

She half stood, dropped back into her seat, and put her head in her hands. "Big trouble. I don't know what kind of trouble."

"Have you talked to a lawyer?" I rose and rolled my shoulders to dispel the edginess Olivia's agitated state gave me.

Her head snapped up. "What? Why would I need a lawyer?"

"It seems to me if you are in big trouble with a state investigator, you might need legal counsel in case there's some law about calling in the locals."

Olivia rubbed her forehead. "My ex-husband's cousin is a lawyer, but he only does wills."

"That's perfect. You've got someone you can call for a referral." I turned to leave.

"I'll call him. Wait. I have something I want you to keep for me. And keep it confidential."

She handed me a manila envelope, wrapped several times over with silver duct tape. I loved the gray tape.

She mouthed her words. "Don't let anyone know you have it. I'll get it back from you later. Okay?"

I whispered to let her know I understood. "Right."

She brushed back her hair and spoke in a normal tone. "Oh, I have an appointment. I should be back in an hour or so. I'll text you if it's longer."

After I left her office, I picked up my purse on the way to the women's room. The envelope didn't fit, so I put it up the front of my shirt and down my pants. My packet was secure but stiff, and I couldn't bend over. *Small price to pay for confidentiality.* I took my phone out of my purse so Olivia could contact me if something came up, but I'd worn the only pair of slacks I owned with no pockets. I put my phone in my bra and flushed the toilet. After I washed my hands, I headed back to my purse drawer. *I feel like I'm walking like a robot. Or a zombie.* I snickered. *If Taylor were here, we'd dare each other to walk like a zombie.*

After I locked my purse in the drawer, I set my keys next to the books on the cart and picked up where I'd left off. When I got to the Philosophy section, someone was on the other side of the stack. His head jerked from one side to the other, and he flinched at every sound. *Looks familiar; remarkable resemblance to the interview guy from the bank.* I pulled out two books from the shelf but didn't have any better view of him. *Runaway imagination alert.* I snickered.

After I put away all the books on my cart, I went to the reading rooms to collect more books. As usual, several regulars stopped me. We all knew the questions were an excuse to break the suffocating, silent loneliness wrapped around their lives, but I was happy to oblige. Someday I might need a young person to look me in the eye and speak to me with respect.

As I picked up books in the red room, the fire alarm went off.

A gray-haired woman sitting at a table grabbed her cane. "Again? The fire alarm here goes off just about every week. Can't we just call the fire department and tell them we're not on fire?"

A volunteer strode over to help her. "Here, Madge. Lean on me."

"You know, if this library were a commercial business, there would be outrageously expensive fines for these nuisance calls to the fire department."

"You're right, Madge." The volunteer offered his arm, and the two of them shuffled to the front door.

"We've gotten pretty good at getting out fast, though," one of our homeless patrons said, following Madge and the volunteer.

My assignment was to search all the public areas to be sure no one remained in the hypothetically burning building. Olivia's job was to do a sweep of the staff offices. I was always the last one out. I joined the patrons and volunteers at the designated gathering spot at the far end of the parking lot and waited for the fire-department engine company to arrive. I scanned the area and didn't see Olivia, but her car was in her usual parking spot. She must have returned earlier than she expected. *Not good.*

Everyone was forbidden to go back into the building until the fire department declared an all-clear. An excellent rule. Smart. Even with a defective fire alarm. Safety first.

My phone rang. Parker. I fished him out of my bosom and blushed only a little.

He said, "Something big . . . What's that? A fire alarm?"

"Yes. Everyone's outside. But Olivia's missing. Her car's here. Gotta go."

"No, wait. Don't do anything—"

I didn't hear the rest because I hung up—and put the cell back into my bra.

I pointed at one of the volunteers. "You. You're in charge until I get back. I need to see why Olivia didn't come out with us. Tell the fire department."

I picked the perfect person. When I glanced back, he had corralled everyone into a tight circle.

He needs to be in charge all the time. I can never get them to stay in the same zip code.

When I reached the walkway to the library door, the sound of a thunderous explosion rushed toward me, but I couldn't get away. I was blown backward across the roadway and into the gardening circle. I was on my face in the grass, and a loud *whoosh* roared over my head. I tried to move because I was smashing the flowers. I choked on a rush of acrid fumes that reminded me of burning plastic and rejoiced in the sweet floral aroma around my face. No sounds.

This is nice. It's quiet. I'll rest here and move later.

* * *

Lights. Too bright. Can't see. Eerie. No sound. Tired.

I woke. *Still bright lights.* I squinted. *Dang it. Hospital. I need out of here. Need to find Olivia.* I tried to move, and someone bent close to me. She wore gray. *Maybe I'm in heaven.*

She smiled and moved her mouth. I frowned. *Is she talking or playing a joke?* I looked around to see if Taylor was there.

Nope. Bummer. But then there's no reason for Taylor to be in heaven. Not that Taylor couldn't make it into heaven . . . Exhausted, I slept.

The next time I woke, I remembered to squint because of the lights. Someone sat in a chair next to me. Wonder if they came to help me find Olivia?

I tried. "Find Olivia."

But I didn't hear anything. No noise came out of my mouth. The someone jumped up. I was a little startled. Heaven was way different than I thought. I worked to focus my eyes.

Wow. Looks like Parker. I like heaven.

He was very close to my face. He smiled. I tried to smile. His mouth moved. I gazed at his lips. I tried to lift my hand to his face, but my arm didn't cooperate. A tear escaped, and he brushed my cheek with his fingertips. *I really like heaven.*

Tired again. I slept.

I opened one eye. *Still with the lights.* Did I want to deal with the glare? I felt a touch on my cheek and opened my eyes. Taylor.

"Pretty girl," I said.

I didn't hear anything, so I must have only thought it. Taylor's face was in front of me. She stuck out her tongue at me. *Taylor, don't do that in heaven. There might be rules.*

And then, just because, heaven forgive me, I stuck my tongue out at her. She laughed and cried. And disappeared. *Where did she go?* She returned with a small dry-erase board she must have stolen.

I'm pretty sure there's a rule about stealing from the angels.

She wrote: "You were hurt. Maybe can't hear. Can you blink?"

I did a blink, blink, blink for her.

She wrote: "Woo-hoo!"

She erased the board. "One blink is yes. Two blinks no. Okay?"

I blinked once.

She wrote: "Your boyfriend's name is Fred."

I blinked twice. And stuck out my tongue. Taylor laughed again. *This is fun.*

She wrote: "You said pretty girl. Weak voice." She erased the board then wrote more.

"Can you hear any noise? Sound?" I blinked no. She wrote, and I blinked.

"Find Olivia," I said. She blinked no at me.

"Duct tape," I said. Taylor frowned.

I was tired. When I woke up, something was different.

Chapter Ten

Before I opened my eyes, I listened. *Did I hear something muffled? Maybe like underwater, but not really.* I opened my eyes, and another hospital gray angel smiled at me. I think I smiled at her. She moved her mouth like she was talking. I closed my eyes and felt a touch on my arm. I looked at the angel. She smiled, showed me Taylor's stolen whiteboard, and wiggled her eyebrows. Kinda cool.

She wrote: "Blinks? 1 Yes, 2 No?"

I blinked once.

She erased. She wrote: "Want to see Fred?"

I blinked twice.

The angel smiled. *I have to think of a way to get even with Taylor.*

Other hands reached for the board. They wrote "Your Nurse" and held it in front of the angel. They erased that and wrote "Your Doctor," and the woman with the board held it in front of herself.

"Your patient," I said.

They laughed without sound. *Okay, they could be my nurse and my doctor.*

"Taylor's boyfriend is Elmo." Did they understand me?

My nurse's face crinkled, and her shoulders shook. She wrote: "Good one."

My doctor looked in my eyes and ears. She opened her mouth wide and pointed at me. I copied her, and she looked down my throat. She poked and prodded, and my nurse wrote on a clipboard and asked me questions on the angel board. I blinked. It was easier than trying to talk.

My doctor and my nurse huddled over the clipboard, and I closed my eyes. My nurse tapped me on the arm and showed me the angel board. "Hearing loss from explosion. We hope temporary. Head fine. Broken pelvis healing. Broken arms healing. Broken legs healing. Pretty much a mess." When I laughed, she added, "Nice laugh."

I was tired, and closed my eyes. I think people visited me, but it might all have been dreams. I dreamed Mother came to see me. She talked to me until my nurse came in and walked her out. I wasn't sure if Mother understood I didn't hear her. Mother came to see me again and again. She was stubborn that way, even in my dreams.

Mr. Morgan came to see me. He smiled and performed a mimed finger-puppet show for me. The kindness of his effort to cheer me warmed my heart.

Taylor came to see me every day. She wrote on the board: "Your mom got a call from someone—praying 4 U & U owe her lunch. Friend?"

"Yes. Sweet Ella."

Taylor sat with me, combed my hair, braided it, and put fingernail polish on my accessible fingers and toes. I had no idea what color. I frowned because I couldn't see my toes, and she was having too much fun.

"Take a picture so I can see my toes."

She blinked no.

"You are so not funny, Taylor." I tried to scowl.

She blinked yes. Couldn't help it. I smiled.

"Where's Olivia?"

Taylor's shoulders slumped, and her eyes filled with tears.

She picked up the whiteboard and wrote: "Olivia in library. Sorry."

Tears ran down my face, and Taylor held my hand and wiped away tears. A nurse appeared at my door. She glanced at us and eased the door closed.

Taylor brought makeup for my face. My nurse shook her head. I loved my nurse. Definitely an angel. Taylor growled at anyone who tried to kick her out. I couldn't hear her, but even her eyes telegraphed *growly*. I loved her fierce face.

Parker came to see me as much as Taylor did, if not more. When he left, he'd always kiss my forehead. I loved my forehead.

I woke up and tried to listen for any noises. I inhaled; maybe it would help me hear better. I focused on hearing. "Beep, beep, beep." The sound quit when I exhaled. *Oh great. I can only hear if I don't breathe.* I inhaled and listened to the beeps.

"Beep, beep, beep, beep."

I held my breath as long as I could and listened to the beeps. When I exhaled, my nurse appeared in the doorway. She looked winded and scared.

I said, "Hi."

"What on earth happened?"

"Held my breath." I closed my eyes and slept.

"Good morning." A much-too-cheerful voice woke me.

I made a mistake. My life was simpler when I couldn't hear.

"We're taking a bath this morning."

Oh, joy.

"You first." I closed my eyes.

The voice laughed. "You are so funny."

Maybe I can tolerate her after all.

I opened my eyes. She had a pleasant face and a nice laugh.

Nice is good.

We took our bath.

* * *

Recovery from blast trauma was a real pain. None of my spy training prepared me for physical therapy, but I was determined to walk.

"Maggie, ease up," my doctor said. "You've chased off four therapists."

I snorted. "They need to toughen up."

After I took my first step holding on to the walker, I let go for my second step.

"Don't do that," the therapist on my left growled, catching me before my face hit the floor. "You'll get us all fired if you break your nose."

"Maggie, you can't let go until you can stand without falling," my doctor said.

Doctor's orders—stand. I stood with my nemesis, the walker, in front of me. It taunted me to stand on my own. After I imagined the Buckingham Palace guards, I let go of the walker and stood tall alongside them. If I wobbled, I'd glance at the guards, and we'd push back our hips and lift our chins for balance. I loved the Buckingham Palace guards. We stood and took one step. They didn't fall, and I didn't either. I left therapy drenched with sweat.

My nurse smiled. "Maggie, you're a beast. Keep it up; break those therapists."

When I was wheeled into the therapy room the next day, three therapists met me at the door and grinned. Their T-shirts needed to say *Therapists Scoff at Pain. Yours.*

"We're upping the ante." My left-side therapist pushed my wheelchair to a raised deck with three steps and wooden railings on both sides of the stairs.

I need reinforcements. Somebody tougher than therapists. *Spike.*

Spike was a retired police detective and a legend when I was a kid. The big kids said Spike was so tough, bad guys would turn themselves in. Spike was five eight and almost as broad as he was tall, but his mass was all muscle. He had a thick neck and biceps bigger than most kids' heads. He had thick brown hair, a broken nose, bushy eyebrows, and a leathery face from years of playing ball in the sandlots with kids. His smile was like a shark's or a panda's, depending on his intent. Kids worked hard for his panda smile.

I glanced to my right. Spike was with me. He smiled, punched my arm, and swept his hand toward the steps. *Ladies first.*

I raised my foot, and when Spike stepped with me, I didn't scream. I brought my other foot up, lifted my head, and exhaled. Spike raised his arms in victory, and I raised my arms in victory just like Spike.

"No!" the therapists screamed in unison, and the one on my left caught me before I hit the back of my head. *We did it, Spike.* His face crinkled into a panda smile. When the nurse's aide wheeled me out of the therapy room at the end of my session, I noticed the therapists were in a huddle.

When the aide rolled me into therapy the next day, Joanna, the therapist supervisor, was the only one in the room. She was slender and taller than any of the others. She reminded me of a volleyball player and wore a look of determination. *She doesn't lose.*

Joanna pulled her gray hair into a ponytail. "Maggie, you and I will do this. Just you and me, girl."

Finally. Somebody who could keep up with me and wasn't squeamish.

She rolled me back to the door, locked the wheels, and handed me two one-pound weights. "Carry those to the stairs and walk up the stairs."

It took me a week to lug the weights all the way from the door to the stairs, and two more weeks to carry those suckers up the stairs. Joanna dashed any hopes I had for a break when she met me at the door with *two-pound* weights. *Devilish.*

By the end of the week, I'd conquered the two-pound-weight challenge.

The following week, she didn't meet me at the door with any weights.

"Have I mastered all your hurdles?"

Joanna chuckled. "See the chair?" She waved at a straight-back cane-seat chair in the middle of the room.

What if I say no? Spike shook his head at me.

"Fold your arms across your chest, sit back in the chair, and stand up. Oh, and keep your back straight when you rise."

Easy. Spike raised his eyebrows.

"I can do this," I said to Spike.

"So do it then," Joanna said.

I was talking to you, Spike. I glared as he motioned toward the chair.

I walked to the chair and folded my arms before I sat then leaned back.

"No," said Joanna. "Don't lean. Scoot your butt to the back of the chair."

I tried. "It's hard to scoot on this cane seat."

Joanna chortled. "I'll just sit over here and watch. Want me to time you?"

"No," I grunted. After I scooted back, I realized my feet didn't reach the floor. I'd have to scooch forward without using my hands.

"I'll have great butt muscles after this is done," I grumbled. "And these sweatpants don't help with the scoot."

Joanna cackled.

"I hate that you love your job," I said. She laughed even harder. After I mastered sitting and standing, Joanna handed me a medium-sized cardboard box.

"It has books in it, Library Girl. Only two books right now, but we'll add more," she said. "Sit and stand with your box."

The following week, my doctor came to observe my progress while Joanna and I played our version of Follow the Leader. Joanna glanced up when the doctor walked in and hesitated.

I chided her. "Joanna, don't ease up because my doctor's here. My doctor can take it, and if she can't, she can leave. Right, Doc?"

Joanna's intricate routine included jumping jacks, ten push-ups, and a floor hip-rotation exercise. I folded after the fourth push-up. She hopped on one foot across the room and did a cartwheel. My hop-on-one-foot was a failure; I didn't even attempt the cartwheel. At the end of our session, both of us were drenched and laughing. Before the doctor left, she raised her fist in the air. "Keep it up."

PT wore me out. I slept for two hours after my session.

A cheery, almost musical, voice woke me. "Ms. Sloan?"

"Maggie," I replied automatically. I opened my eyes, and a miniature Ella was next to my bed—same build, same great smile, but six inches shorter.

"I'm Brenda, your occupational therapist." She waved a yellow stretchy band.

"I just got back from therapy," I grumbled as I sat up.

"Oh honey, that was physical therapy. They're brutes but don't tell them I said that. They're all about strength and endurance. I'll help you with the finer things in life. We'll get your coordination and fine motor skills back."

"Will you help me dance again?" I practiced my panda smile.

"I'll make you a better dancer than you ever were before," she cackled. "You'll be able to tell your right foot from your left. How's that?"

I snickered. "Fair enough." *Well played, Brenda.*

* * *

"I'll miss you, Maggie," my doctor said. "I've signed your discharge from the hospital; your next stop is a rehab facility that is one of the best in the state."

"I couldn't have done it without my team." Palace guards, Spike, Brenda, and Joanna. And my nurse. Nobody had ever called me a beast before, and my doctor, who didn't fire Joanna.

Mother and Franklin, in his carrier, waited for me in the hall. "Are you all packed, Maggie? I guess you would be. You didn't bring much with you. Franklin and I will go with you to wait for the transport van." Taylor told me Franklin went everywhere with Mother.

My doctor joined us at the elevator. "Mrs. Sloan, Maggie has made wonderful progress here. I am a little concerned because no rehab facility can push her as much as she's used to. Maggie, you call me if it doesn't work out."

Franklin mewed. I shared his concern.

"What can I do to help?" Mother asked.

"Probably just call, don't visit," my doctor said. "I've observed Maggie in physical therapy, and she drives herself. She'll get to full recovery much quicker if we let her work at her own grueling pace."

"She's always been like that," Mother said. *Was that pride in her voice?*

Mother patted my arm when the transport van arrived then she and Franklin hurried to her car. *She didn't want me to see the tears.* Joanna appeared next to me before the driver loaded me and my wheelchair.

"Their record minimum stay is two days," she whispered. "Beat it. Walk away."

I did, but I suspect I won't be welcomed back.. The administrator even paid for the cab to take me home out of his own pocket. "I've called the property manager, and he'll be waiting for you. Lord help him." He shook his head.

* * *

I was home earlier than everyone expected—except for my hospital team and me. The property manager met the cab and took my elbow to help me out. "Good thing I got the call to let me know you were on your way. I wouldn't have known you. I've got the master key; I'll let you into your apartment."

After he unlocked the door and left, I leaned against the door and gazed with relief at my beautiful gray apartment. I rubbed my hand across the rough corduroy sofa, the sleek dining table, the smooth kitchen counters, and the cold porcelain bathtub. I caressed my soft towels and hugged my feather pillows. I was home. I kicked off my shoes and flopped onto my nonhospital bed.

After I woke, I went to Mr. Morgan's and knocked on his door.

When he opened the door, I said, "I didn't call because I don't have a cell phone. Or a purse, wallet, or ID. But it's me."

He grinned. "Come on in."

I was short-winded. "My day wore me out more than I expected."

He helped me to his blue sofa as I examined his apartment. "I'm glad you didn't change anything."

Mr. Morgan handed me a napkin and a cold glass that dripped with condensation. "Have some iced tea."

I sipped my tea. "Nobody brews tea like you. I love the lime wedge."

"Here you go." He handed me a plate with two brownies.

"Magical healing medicine." I toasted him with a brownie before I took a big bite.

"I should have known you'd bust out of rehab," he said. "Ready to make some plans?"

I raised my hand to hide my mouthful of brownie. "Yep."

He grabbed a pad of paper and a pen from his desk and sat next to me. "Let's list what you need to replace."

While we talked, Mr. Morgan sent a text to Taylor and Parker. "Just let them know where you are. Do you feel like a ride?"

"I'd love it."

"Let's get a cell phone first. You can go in if you like, or you can wait in the car."

"I've got energy to burn. I'm ready."

Mr. Morgan laughed and helped me down the stairs to his car.

"This is what we know about the blast," Mr. Morgan said on our way to the store. "From the fire marshal's findings, the fire alarm was set off manually in Olivia's office. Nothing else definitive. The official theory is somebody showed up, threatened to set off the explosion in the library, and Olivia set off the alarm. Maybe the two of them fought, but the explosives went off."

"So Olivia saved everyone in the library." Tears trickled down my cheeks. *I always thought Olivia was a lightweight, but she was a hero.*

"Yes. She received a posthumous citation for bravery from both the fire department and the police department. The library set up a scholarship fund in her name."

When we got to the store, Mr. Morgan parked in the shade.

"Why don't you stay here and rest? I'll leave the engine running to keep the car cool."

I was too tired to argue. After he got out of the car, I locked the doors and leaned my seat back to rest my eyes. I woke when Mr. Morgan tapped on the driver's window.

"Here's your new phone. It'll need to charge first."

"Do you have any idea what happened to the envelope?"

Mr. Morgan's eyes widened. "I'm surprised you remembered. The rescue team was focused on whisking you off to the hospital. One of the library volunteers picked the envelope up off the ground and brought it to your apartment."

I leaned on the armrest and rubbed my forehead. "That's sweet. Sun's bright."

"Let's stop and pick you up some sunglasses. Taylor and I were at your apartment removing perishables from the refrigerator because it'd be a while before you'd be home. We weren't allowed to visit you in the hospital yet and were desperate for something to do. The volunteer gave me your envelope when I answered the door."

"You didn't open it?"

"Should I have? I didn't see any reason to."

He pulled into a drugstore parking lot. "Let's get you some sunglasses."

Mr. Morgan selected the type of sunglasses based on UV protection and scratch resistance. "Here, try these." He handed me three different styles.

I selected the pair with gray lenses and a pale-gray frame and put them on. "Feels fine."

"My idea. My treat," Mr. Morgan said, and we were back on the road again.

I gazed at the passing landscape. "Can we put the windows down just a bit? I missed fresh air. Olivia gave me the envelope for safekeeping, but I don't know what's in it."

Mr. Morgan put his window a third of the way down. "Don't want to give you a chill. Let me know if I should put it back up. Should we give Parker a call?"

"I don't know. There's a bunch of stuff I haven't told him. He'll be mad."

"Maggie, you suffered a full body blast from an explosion and survived. You terrorized an entire department of physical therapists. You got kicked out of a highly respected rehabilitation facility. You have a huge fan club that consists of the police department, fire department, hospital staff, librarians everywhere, and library patrons. You can do this."

"Maybe. Anything more about Donnie or the homeless man? What about the guy who was killed?"

"As far as I know, there's nothing."

"What about the library?"

Mr. Morgan glanced at me. "There's no library left."

I put my head back. "I need a nap."

"I'll give you my key to your apartment. We'll get you situated and plug in your phone to charge. Call or text me when you wake up. I'll make dinner tonight and invite Taylor and Parker. We'll eat at your place so you can rest whenever you like. Sound good?"

"Yes. Good plan."

Mr. Morgan offered me his arm, and we walked to my apartment. When we were inside, I lay down on the couch.

"I can plug in your phone and put it on the table where you can reach it," he said.

I waved my hand. My attempt at a *thank you*.

Mr. Morgan stepped to the hallway and peered at the thermostat. "Are you comfortable? I can adjust the temperature."

"It's good."

When he came back to the living room, he glared. "Are you sure you're comfortable there?"

"I'm fine," I mumbled.

"I'm leaving then. I'll take your key and have another copy made."

"Thanks for everything."

The door clicked, and I closed my eyes.

A knock at my door woke me. When the door opened, I smiled at Taylor.

"I didn't want you to get up if you didn't feel like it. Where's your medicine? Want to take a shower? I'll change your sheets. You're home. Your apartment smells like it's been closed up. Okay if I open some windows?"

Yay, Taylor's here. I sat up, but I was wobbly. "Shower sounds great and so does fresh air."

Taylor brought me a glass of water. "Take your time." She opened all the apartment windows. I inhaled the smell of flowers and dumpsters and listened to the roar of the landscaping company's mowers.

"I'm sorting through your medicine," Taylor called from the kitchen.

"Here." She stood next to me with three pill bottles and a glass of water.

I took the pills, drained the glass, and headed to the shower. While I lingered under the spray of warm water, I gazed at my shampoo, my conditioner, and my bath gel.

"Ahh. My shower."

When I dried off, I looked in the mirror and got a shock.

I shouted, "Taylor!"

She came running. "What, Maggie, what?"

I stood naked in front of the mirror, except I had disappeared; instead a stranger stared back at me. "What happened to my hair? Why am I all bony?"

"They wouldn't let me color your hair in the hospital, and you've been on a hospital diet. Didn't you see yourself at the hospital? Mr. Morgan will take care of the diet thing. And by the way, I love your warm, light-brown hair. We should take you for a haircut tomorrow."

"Brown?" I pulled a handful of wet hair to the front of my face. *My hair was blond when I first dyed it black almost seven years ago.*

"The real Gray Man would have brown hair," Taylor said.

"Might be a nice change." I wrapped the towel around me. "I was too busy sparring with Joanna to pay attention to how I looked." *It'd be a good disguise. Twenty-two-year-old with brown hair would blend in. Except for the skeleton body.*

I dressed in my soft, gray clothes and found Taylor in my bedroom.

Taylor made my bed with fresh sheets. I inhaled the aroma from the doorway. She fluffed the pillows and tossed them onto the bed. "Dude, your shirt is three sizes too big for your scrawny self, and are you okay with holding up your pants with one hand? It looks a little awkward. I'll tell you what—let me grab you something."

Taylor rushed out of my apartment and returned with a minty-green shirt and creamy brown sweatpants.

"I'm sorry about the colors, but these will fit you until we can get a few outfits in your new size."

I put the Taylor clothes on. *At least they aren't pink.*

Taylor was right. I didn't have to hold the pants up, and I didn't feel like a tent hung from my shoulders.

"Thanks, Taylor. These are nice. Was I really that fat?" *I knew I was twenty or thirty pounds heavier than Taylor, but I always chalked it up to bone structure.*

"No, Maggie. You're just skin and bones now."

Taylor fixed me some hot tea, then braided my hair into a single braid. She texted Parker and Mr. Morgan to let them know I was awake. I listened while Taylor talked about Harry. *I need to build up my stamina for a party, so I can meet Harry.*

I called the hospital and asked for Physical Therapy then Joanna, and her voicemail answered.

"Joanna, this is Maggie Sloan. Rehab kicked me out in one day. Not even an overnight. Do you have some tips for me to get some strength back? Thanks." And I left her my cell phone number and email address.

My imagination took over for a minute. When Spike and a palace guard nodded their approval, I cocked my head and squinted. *What are you two doing here?*

I relaxed on the gray sofa, sipped my tea, and enjoyed the excitement in Taylor's voice. I breathed in the flowery odor of my bath soap and shampoo. *No hospital smell.*

The door opened, and Parker burst in and strode to the kitchen. "Taylor, where's Maggie?"

Taylor looked past him. "Uh."

Parker cocked his head.

I cleared my throat. "I dunno. On the sofa? Is this a trick question?"

Parker wheeled around. "Maggie?"

I was swept up off the sofa, with my feet dangling, and wrapped in a huge hug.

"Oof."

Parker almost dropped me. "I'm so sorry. Did I hug you too tight? Are you okay?"

I wrapped my arms around the neck of the man who had kissed my forehead every day for the past four months. "I'm fine except I need another hug."

I melted into his hug. I'd looked forward to being smashed into Parker since forever. He buried his face in my hair. "Umm. You smell good. What did you do to your hair? I like it."

I smothered myself in Parker's chest and inhaled the essence of Parker—soap, deodorant, and sweat. *He likes my hair.*

"Can we sit?" My legs were ready to give out.

Parker helped me to the sofa. "I'm so sorry."

"Please don't say you're sorry. I'll get stronger. You'll see."

Taylor got a text. "Be right back; Mr. Morgan needs help with the groceries."

While Mr. Morgan cooked, I napped, and when I woke, we ate.

After cleanup, Mr. Morgan said, "I brought the envelope with me."

I pursed my lips. I'd planned to wait a week or two. Like when I was strong enough to run away.

Parker frowned. "What envelope?"

I steeled myself. "Olivia gave me an envelope the morning of the explosion and asked me to keep it for her. She said she'd let me know when she needed it. I stuck it into my pants and shirt for safekeeping."

Parker frowned. "What? Why?"

"It seemed like the best way to keep it safe, and I didn't have any pockets." It sounded strange when I said it aloud.

"I meant, why did she give it to you? And now I want to know why you didn't put it in your purse or in a drawer?"

"No room in my purse. And I don't know. It made sense then."

"In hindsight, your choice was brilliant," Taylor said. "It may have saved you. I'll bet the envelope provided some protection for your chest and abdomen. Did you know you had no internal injuries? The nurses talked about how amazing that was. Your chest protector must have been why. And witnesses said the blast threw you into the grass face down before the ball of fire flew over you. Your doctor said that saved you from burn injuries."

As Mr. Morgan handed me the envelope, Taylor said, "See? The envelope protected you when you landed on the ground."

I inspected the envelope before I gave it to Parker. The duct tape was ragged and dirty on one side, but the other side was in perfect shape.

Chapter Eleven

Taylor sat next to me on the sofa. I flashed on Olivia handing me the envelope and the sensation of being tossed by the explosion, and I shuddered as I was swamped with anxiety. When I cringed and put my hands over my ears, Taylor scooted closer, eased a hand away from my head, and sandwiched my hand with hers. I relaxed. *I need to relearn my poker face.*

Parker used his pocketknife to slit open the envelope. He slid out a newspaper clipping, two old photos, a marriage license, two birth certificates, and a heavy cardboard insert. He handed me the newspaper excerpt.

"This is Donnie." I showed Taylor the clipping of Donnie in front of a courthouse with his head down and his eyes shielded by his hand.

"He looks like a crook," Taylor said.

I snickered. "Good eye."

Parker shook the envelope. "The caption and article aren't here. This marriage license was for John Edwards and Olivia Chandler. The date is twenty-seven years ago."

Taylor and I looked at the pictures. One was a wedding photo.

"This is Olivia. She looks so young," I said. "The groom looks familiar, but I can't quite place him."

"What is this second picture? *Notebook of Secrets*? What's that?" Taylor asked.

I stared at the picture. "Olivia said it was the catalog for all the boxes in her office. Why would she take a picture of it, though?"

"We'll never know what was in her boxes. Why was her binder so important she took a picture of it? Seems like this is a big loss for us," Parker said.

Mr. Morgan examined the birth certificates. "These are for Donald Chandler and Olivia Chandler with the same mother and father listed— Mary Alice and Walter Chandler. Donnie is Olivia's younger brother."

I jerked my head up. "Olivia's brother? That explains why she was worried about him being angry at her. And I just remembered something. He called her *Ollie*."

"Yes, but it opens up more questions," Taylor said. "Like, why did she go along with his investigator or whatever charade?" She passed the pictures to Mr. Morgan, and he handed her the birth certificates.

"I don't know whether the feds have the DNA for Olivia and the male killed in the explosion," Parker said. "It would be pretty remote. They were at the source of the explosion, and the result was a fireball. If they do, it's an easy test to see if the male was Olivia's brother."

"This envelope explains a few things, but I can't help wonder what Olivia planned to do with it and why she gave it to Maggie," Mr. Morgan said.

It also explains the Camping in the Yukon *book by Walter Chandler. But not who left it and why.*

"Maggie, you're wilting," Taylor said. "I'll close the windows before Mr. Morgan and I leave. You can rest. Parker's got this. Right, Parker?"

Parker's eyes narrowed. "Right." His tone suggested I wasn't saying something. I put on a pitiful-me look. I'm not sure he bought it.

"Maggie, we'll work on our list tomorrow." Mr. Morgan rose from the chair.

"Thank you."

"What list?" Parker asked.

"Maggie's purse and contents burned in the fire," Mr. Morgan said. "We have a list of what needs to be replaced. Which reminds me— Maggie, your spare car keys were here, so Taylor and I picked up your car from the library parking lot after the explosion and started it every other day. Also, we picked up your mail. We took mail we thought were bills to your mother. She paid them and said to tell you happy birthday. Your mail is on the table."

Taylor dashed to the door. "Maggie, don't lock up quite yet. I'll be right back."

Taylor returned with several casual cotton shirts and pants. "Here you go. This will get you through the week. Then if you're up to it, we can shop this weekend. If you don't feel like it, we'll do laundry."

"You're cute in that green, Maggie," Parker said. "Brings out your eyes."

Detective Fashion Guy. Wait, brings out my eyes?

Parker put his arm around me. "I'm glad you're home. See you tomorrow." He hugged me and kissed my forehead and mouth. *Mmm.*

After everyone left, I put on my old flannel nightgown and fell into nice crisp sheets that didn't smell like a hospital. Rumbles of thunder shook the windows, and rain slammed against the glass. The rhythmic sound of the rain relaxed me.

* * *

At six thirty the next morning, I woke to the ding of a text.

Parker.

"U ok 4 bfast?"

No, I'm not.

I answered his text. "Ok. What time?"

I threw the bed linens into a semblance of neatness and slow-dashed to the shower.

By the time I turned on the water, my phone dinged.

"7."

Are you serious? "Ok."

When I got out of my shower, I realized Taylor had organized the shirts and pants into sets. *You are one smart cookie, T. I have no idea of what colors to wear together. Oh. Mr. Morgan.*

"Going 2 bfast w/ Parker."

"Me 2. T can't."

I was ready a few minutes before seven, but I didn't have enough time to make coffee. When I stepped outside, Mr. Morgan stood at my door with two cups of coffee in his hand. *Fresh morning air and coffee. Ahhhhh.*

The damp air was chilly. I rubbed the goosebumps on my arms, went back inside, and grabbed my gray sweatshirt. It swallowed me and looked a little dull next to my new Taylor clothes, but in a familiar, comforting way. *T's colors are pretty, but gray is an old friend.*

Mr. Morgan offered me his arm when Parker turned into the parking lot. While we walked to the car, a loud wolf whistle from the second-floor breezeway broke the early-morning silence. I looked up—Taylor.

She waved and shouted while she ran to her car. "You look hot, girlfriend."

She'll get us evicted from the apartments just like she got us tossed out of heaven. I stuck my tongue out at her, and she laughed then reciprocated.

"She's right, you know," Mr. Morgan said.

"Thank you." My face warmed, and Mr. Morgan chuckled.

Parker jumped out of his car and opened the passenger door of the squad car. Mr. Morgan walked over to his old coupe.

"Maggie, something's come up, and I'll have to leave for a meeting after we eat," Parker said. "Okay if you ride back with Mr. Morgan?"

"Sure." I glanced at the back of the car, and my jaw dropped. Spike and Palace Guard had jumped into the back of the police car and held their wrists like they were handcuffed. I snicker-sneezed. While Parker walked around the car, I looked forward and hissed. "What are you two doing here?"

When I glanced at the back seat, the two of them grinned. I rolled my eyes just as Parker climbed into the driver's seat.

"You okay?" he asked.

"Sure." I put on my poker face, and Parker frowned.

Parker sees past my poker face. Dang.

Mr. Morgan followed us to the diner. When Parker opened the diner door for me, I inhaled the fragrant aromas of bacon and cinnamon rolls.

I turned to Parker. "Thank you so much. I needed Kate's diner therapy."

Parker grinned.

I didn't know if Parker prewarned Kate, or if she was that sharp, but she shouted when I entered the diner. "Maggie!"

My money's on sharp.

When Lucy waggled to me and offered me her face, I rubbed her head and neck. "Missed you, Lucy."

"Kate, remember Mr. Morgan?" Parker asked.

"Sure do. Nice to see you again."

"It's been a long time—too long." Mr. Morgan smiled.

Kate waved us toward the end booth. *Must be Parker's regular booth.* "Mr. Morgan, how do you like your eggs? And do you want bacon or sausage?"

"Over easy and sausage."

Kate poured coffee while we took our seats. Parker and I were on one side of the booth, Mr. Morgan on the other. Spike and Palace Guard crowded in with Mr. Morgan as Kate twirled away toward the kitchen. Our entrance, seating, and Kate's exit were like an intricate, choreographed ballet.

"I am so happy to be here." I smiled as I surveyed the old diner.

Parker frowned. "I hope it doesn't wear you out."

"I might not be as delicate as you think, Parker."

When Kate snort-laughed from the kitchen, Parker rolled his eyes.

Mr. Morgan cleared his throat. "Our priority today is to replace Maggie's driver's license. Maggie's mother helped me with most of the paperwork, so it won't be too hard. I think all the other things we have on our list we can do online."

She did? That's kind of amazing.

"More coffee?" Kate reappeared and refilled our cups without waiting.

"Want to know what I heard on the radio on day eight?" Mr. Morgan asked while he stirred his coffee.

"Oh yes," I said.

"Time to hit the books." He raised his eyebrows.

The hair on the back of my neck stood up, and my arms became cold despite my sweatshirt. "Whoa. Really?"

"I'd been listening for about an hour when I heard the book comment a little before seven. Before that, the only talk was just typical ham chatter: radio checks. After three of the regulars coordinated a meeting, the new ones talked about meeting later in the day. One of them said 'time to hit the books' and cleared. I texted you and called Parker. After I left him a message, Sergeant Arrington called me back."

"I walked in while Sarge was on the phone," Parker said. "Mr. Morgan also told the sergeant the call signs of the two new guys; when Sarge checked, both of the call signs belonged to new hams out of state who were unaware someone had used their radio IDs."

Kate brought our food, and our talk stopped; instead, we ate. Correction—we feasted. My plate wasn't clean, but I did my best.

Kate inspected my plate when she cleared it. "Good job, girlfriend."

"Thanks, Kate. Ready to go, Mr. Morgan?"

"I am so sorry, Maggie. We should have left earlier," Mr. Morgan said.

Parker frowned. "Knew this would wear you out."

I leaned over and kissed Parker near his ear. "I'm not worn out. I'm in stamina training."

Kate laughed. "You're doing great, Maggie. Isn't she, Parker?"

I didn't hear what he mumbled, but Kate winked, and I snickered. Parker walked me to Mr. Morgan's car and whispered after he kissed my forehead. "See you later, honey."

* * *

I must have dozed off on the ride to the apartment because I startled awake when we pulled into the apartment parking lot. After Mr. Morgan walked me to my door, I went inside and kicked off my shoes then fell into bed face down. I loved my bed—no hospital smell.

When I woke, I was proud of myself because I'd been asleep for only an hour. I brewed a cup of hot tea and attacked my mail. I flipped the stack over to start with oldest first, just like Ella taught me—first in, first out.

I found a letter from the county dated four months ago. I was on permanent disability with full pay, and I had thirty days to appeal. *What did they do? Send me this letter the afternoon of the explosion?*

I found another letter from the county. And another, and another. I opened one, and enclosed was a check for two weeks' pay. I checked for an expiration date. I pulled out all the letters from the county and put them in a stack.

Mr. Morgan sent me a text. "Call."

"Want to get your replacement driver's license?" he asked.

"Give me fifteen minutes."

I changed out of my sleep-crumpled clothes. The next outfit was a light-turquoise shirt and dark-turquoise pants. *Nice two-tone.*

My hair braid fell apart during my morning nap, and I couldn't rebraid it right or, more accurately, at all, so I pulled it into a low curly ponytail. I knew a driver's license meant a new photo, so I added the lipstick and blush Taylor left. After I examined my face, I washed my cheeks and mouth. *Ugh. Clown.*

Mr. Morgan came by my apartment then walked me to the parking lot, and we were on our way.

I stared at the passing scenery and sighed. "I don't understand why I'm so exhausted. I did an hour of physical therapy every day in the hospital. I shouldn't be so worn out."

"Your body went through a lot with the explosion. Your therapies helped your strength and balance. Now we work on your resilience."

"I'm sure you're right." I closed my eyes to build up my stamina.

Mr. Morgan parked in a spot close to the door and hustled around to the passenger's side to help me out. "The Department of Motor Vehicles isn't known for their customer service, but your mother gave me all the paperwork we'd need. If the process is too arduous, we can come back another day. Just let me know."

We were out in less than fifteen minutes. I eased into the passenger' seat. "That was a pleasant surprise. I was braced to spend the entire morning there."

"Guess they got tired of being easy pickins for has-been comedians," Mr. Morgan said. "You can get your replacement credit and debit cards online. You have your driver's license; we can get you a new voter's registration card next if you like. It's just a block away."

The voter's registration card took only another five minutes.

"Lunch now?" Mr. Morgan asked.

"Yes."

"Do you want to go to a restaurant or would you rather grab groceries and have lunch at your apartment? What do you feel like?"

"Groceries. I'm not sure I could sit that long in a restaurant and don't think I could stomach anything that even remotely resembled hospital food."

He smiled. "Fair enough. No hospitals."

After shopping, I marked the expiration dates on the fronts of boxes and cans and rearranged the shelf items with the oldest ones in front for inventory management, just like Ella taught me. Mr. Morgan made ham and swiss cheese sandwiches on rye bread—my favorite. After we ate, he left. I requested new credit and debit cards online before I collapsed on my gray sofa. When I woke, I discovered an email from Joanna.

"Knew you'd do it. Volunteer at the animal shelter but not the office. Walk dogs and clean kennels."

I realized Spike and Palace Guard were behind me; after they read the email over my shoulder, they patted my back.

Glad you two approve.

When I called the shelter, the volunteer coordinator told me the link to the online volunteer information page and application.

"Let's start my car to make sure it'll run when I'm ready to go to the shelter."

When Palace Guard, Spike, and I got to my car, I looked at the keys in my hand. I'd picked up the wrong set. I held the spare keys for my apartment and Mother's, Taylor's, and Mr. Morgan's apartments. When I turned to go back to call Mr. Morgan, I noticed a note under the windshield wiper on the driver's side.

What's with the notes?

I removed the paper and unfolded it as Palace Guard and Spike crowded me to read over my shoulder: "BOOM." Palace Guard narrowed his eyes as he scanned the parking lot, and Spike moved so he had my back.

While Spike covered the rear, Palace Guard led the way as I hurried to my apartment. After I was inside, I sat on the floor and shook. Spike sat next to me and helped me to focus and slow down my breathing rate. "I might need some real people on guard too."

Spike crossed his arms.

"You pouting?"

I called Parker. His phone rolled to voice mail—not unexpected. I tried to be calm, but if calm is one and hysterical is ten, then my message was a solid eight.

My phone rang almost as soon as I hung up, and I smiled because I'd know that growl anywhere. "Maggie, this is Sergeant Arrington. Parker and the bomb squad are on the way. Parker said for you to call Mr. Morgan to stay with you."

I texted Mr. Morgan. I didn't want to scare him with the Hysterical Maggie.

"Can U come over? Need a little help."

He knocked seconds later. I opened the door, and Mr. Morgan helped me to the sofa. He got the hysterical version, ten plus.

"Maggie, we need to talk as soon as you slow down." He left for a few moments and returned with brownies and ice cream. "You needed serious comfort food therapy."

Mr. Morgan brewed two cups of tea, but before he dished up pecan crunch to go with our brownies, cars screeched into the parking lot. He hurried to the window and peeked out. "The police cordoned off most of the lot and blocked the entrance to the apartment complex with patrol cars."

Parker and a tall, slender police officer with curly brown hair rushed into the apartment.

"Maggie. Details," Parker said in a voice almost as growly as Sergeant Arrington's. The police officer peered out the back window, strolled through the apartment, and stationed himself at the front door.

I gave Parker the note. It was handprinted in large block letters with a permanent marker, and it was damp from being against the wet windshield. The other side had stains of water drops from the trees but was otherwise dry.

Mr. Morgan handed me a spoon and a bowl with a brownie and a generous helping of ice cream. *Fortitude food.* I scooped up a healthy spoonful of ice cream and let it melt in my mouth.

"My guess is the note was left sometime after the rain stopped late last night." I scooped up another bite of brownie and ice cream.

"The last time I started the car was two days ago." Mr. Morgan placed my cup of tea on the coffee table in front of me.

"Okay, thanks. Let's go, Kevin. Maggie, stay inside." Parker and the officer left.

Mr. Morgan turned on the TV and found his favorite cooking show. I stretched out on the sofa and dozed.

After a few hours, Parker came back to the apartment alone, and his face was grim. "I thought at first the note was a threat. Now I wonder if it was a warning. The bomb squad defused and removed an explosive and will be gone soon. There's a forensic team documenting the scene, and they'll be here a while. The federal guys will lead the investigation."

Mr. Morgan rinsed and set our bowls in the top rack of the dishwasher. "I don't believe Maggie is safe here."

"I agree," Parker said.

"I have a sister in South Carolina. Maggie can stay with her," Mr. Morgan said.

"I don't want her too far away. She needs to be close and with someone who can keep her safe."

"She's sitting right here," I said, only slightly annoyed.

"Sorry, Maggie," Parker said. "We're just worried. Let's look at the possibilities—moving in with Taylor would be great except she's in the same apartment complex. Moving in with her mother wouldn't work because that's another known address associated with Maggie."

"I could hire a bodyguard," Mr. Morgan said.

"I don't want to be somewhere alone with somebody I don't know. I'd be afraid to sleep. And where would the bodyguard and I stay?" I said.

Parker held up a hand with his palm out. "Okay, I've got it, and it's somewhere you'll feel safe and can sleep, Maggie. Mr. Morgan, it would be better if you and Taylor don't know where she is, at least until we have a better idea of what's going on."

"If she keeps her cell phone but has her location turned off, would she be safe?"

"It isn't possible to turn off emergency services, but no one else can track her with the location turned off."

"Then I'm okay," Mr. Morgan said. "We can get in touch with each other and won't put her in danger."

I looked from one man to the other while they talked. I was an invisible observer at a ping-pong match. Then I realized I was also the ping-pong ball and lay back on the sofa. *Gotta work on endurance.*

"I sent Taylor a text and asked her to shop for Maggie before she comes home from work," Parker said.

I didn't have the energy to argue with protective men, but I was too restless to sit. I left them to work out my future while I wandered into the kitchen for a glass of iced tea and worked on a packing list. After I turned off the location services for both my phone and my laptop, I uninstalled apps I didn't need and cleared my browser history. I sorted through the mail, opened all the letters with checks, and deposited the funds online. I signed on to the county system and set up direct deposit. Mother and I shared our bank accounts; she had kept my account balance above the minimum and paid the three bills that weren't automatically paid online.

"Who can track my credit or debit purchases?" I asked.

Parker looked up. "Only you and your bank unless your account is hacked."

"I've got new credit cards on the way. If Mr. Morgan picks up my mail, can he get them to me somehow?"

"Yes, we can manage that," Parker said.

Mr. Morgan looked up at the clock. "Taylor just got off work. Time for me to cook. You'll stay, right, Parker?"

"Damn straight."

I was worn out. "Time for me to lie down."

"I'll be right here," Parker said.

I woke up just before Taylor appeared with four bags of clothes. "Here you go, Maggie, try all the outfits on. I want to see how they fit."

As I rose to go to the bedroom to change, my phone dinged with a text from Mr. Morgan. "Dinner."

After Taylor dumped all the new clothes onto my bed, I spotted underthings and breathed a sigh of relief. *No more droopy drawers.* We removed all the tags and tossed the clothes into the washer.

"We're washing out sizing—the chemicals on fabric to keep it crisp-looking in the store." I reminded Taylor, keeping our long-standing argument alive.

"No, we're washing away store cooties."

"You spend your day with five-year-olds." I snickered.

On our way to Mr. Morgan's, a thought occurred to me. "Taylor, do the tops and bottoms have matching tags, so I know what to wear?"

"I'll make a chart for you."

I saw Spike smile out of the corner of my eye.

Hey, Spike. You still with me?

He pointed at Palace Guard and smiled again.

I don't care if you two are the aftereffects from all the surgery drugs or from landing on my face. I like having you around. I smiled.

"Glad you're smiling." Taylor smiled, and so did Spike and Palace Guard.

Parker was not smiling when we got to Mr. Morgan's. "You girls ready to eat? I'm starving."

"Nice to know you get grumpy when you're hungry, Mr. Detective," I said, and Taylor snickered.

Parker held my chair for me, and then he held Taylor's chair for her. While the four of us ate, talked, and laughed, a sudden wave of melancholy swept over me.

This is the end of a wonderful chapter of my life.

I shook it off. Taylor frowned. "Do you feel okay? Do you have a fever?"

"No. I'm fine." I should have known better. I can't fool Taylor. *I need to work on my spy skills. I'm evidently an open book to these people.*

"Sure you are," she said. "So what is it, really?"

"I don't want to leave you and Mr. Morgan. I don't like what's happened at all."

"I hate it too," Taylor said.

"I hate it as much as I hated running laps in basic training," Mr. Morgan said.

Taylor giggled. "I hate it as much as I hated being the shortest girl on the basketball team."

Parker rubbed his neck. "I hate it as much as I hated being creamed by a two-hundred-pound eighth grader in junior varsity football."

My turn. "I hate it as much as I hated not knowing what color Taylor painted my toenails in the hospital, except not really."

Even Taylor laughed.

Mr. Morgan wiped his eyes. "Oh, if you had only seen—"

"You would have loved them," interrupted Taylor. She jumped up. "I'll move your clothes from the washer to the dryer."

Parker scowled. "I'll go with you."

When they returned, Taylor said, "Clothes are in the dryer. Maggie, Parker and my dad want me to move back home with my parents and brothers for a while. Keep my apartment but stay with the folks, but I'll be close."

"I may go visit my sister," Mr. Morgan said. "But I can be back here in a heartbeat."

I fought the tears, but I wasn't successful. "Thank you. It means a lot for you two to be safe."

Parker cleared his throat. "I'll be on top of a dragon, clearing the countryside of bad guys."

We all laughed about the dragon, but clearing the countryside? *True. Very Parker.*

Taylor packed all my clothes into my gray carry-on travel bag she found in my closet and put my goes-with chart on the top of the clothes before she zipped up the case.

"I put in a little makeup with your clothes," she said. "Maybe whoever you stay with can critique your makeup if you try it. Should be easy for you, and it would be another big change away from the Gray Lady. Leave your hair long and wear it in a ponytail."

I was afraid I'd never see Taylor again. We hugged and cried while Parker carried my things to his car.

"Oh, I almost forgot your new purse." Taylor handed me a soft, pale-gold faux-leather purse. I looked inside and found a wallet and sunglasses. I put my driver's license and voter registration in the wallet and found a ten-dollar bill.

"An old tradition," she said. "Never give anyone an empty wallet. Money follows money."

"Thank you," We hugged again, and tears slipped down our cheeks.

Mr. Morgan handed me a gift sack. "This has some of my crackers, some cheese, and brownies. It also has the wine you like and a glass because it would be horrible to be off somewhere strange without your wine and a wine glass." We hugged.

"You are a sage man," I said.

"I know." His eyes twinkled.

Parker came inside. "Maggie? Ready?"

No. I'm staying with Taylor and Mr. Morgan. We'll build a bunker.

Spike shook his head. Palace Guard glowered.

"Yes. Let's do this."

We meandered through a shopping-mall lot and cruised a lumberyard.

Parker eased the car next to an open-market stand on the side of the road.

"Let's see what they've got."

I checked the fruit while Parker gazed at the sky and glanced at cars on the road. A young girl with double braids stood near the cash register. "Let me know if I can help."

"Apples?" I asked.

"Sounds good, honey." Parker smiled.

I picked out two apples, and Parker paid the clerk.

"Need a sack?" the young girl asked.

"No, thanks. We'll be eating them for a snack," Parker said.

"There's a water spigot right over there if you want to wash them off." She ripped two paper towels off a roll, offered them to me, and grinned.

"You are my kind of girl. Thank you." I smiled and rinsed and dried the apples.

We circled through a neighborhood, ate our apples, and stopped at a drug store for cough drops.

"I don't think anyone followed us," Parker said. He headed out to the country and turned at a dirt road with no houses in sight.

Parker slowed the car and pulled over on the grassy shoulder. "We'll wait. Kate will pick you up in less than five minutes. You'll be safe with her. She was with the FBI until she took leave to help with Uncle Reggie's diner four years ago. He died last year, and she stayed on for the customers. It's been a much-needed break for her, but she's getting restless. It'll be good for her to have some company. You okay?"

Kate was FBI, and I was . . . I wasn't sure what I was, but yes, I was okay.

Chapter Twelve

Parker eased the car into the brush before we climbed out of his car. We stood near the road, but not too close. Parker stood between me and the road, Palace Guard assumed his sentry stance, and Spike had our backs.

I know you are only here in my imagination, but thank you, guys.

The night was clear. I gazed at more stars in the sky than I'd ever seen in town. Beautiful until the gnats and the mosquitos buzzed me. I waved and slapped. *I need to add bug-repellent spray to my supplies.*

Lights headed toward us, and we stepped behind a tree. The vehicle slammed to a stop then Kate jumped out. "Let's go, Maggie."

I grabbed my things. Kate took the larger bag and threw it into the trunk of her old Dodge Dart. Lucy was in the back seat, and she grinned and wagged her tail. Spike and Palace Guard jumped in next to Lucy. I raised my eyebrows when she looked at them.

"Hi, girl."

I got a thump, thump, thump in return. When Kate did a fast U-turn, she threw all of us off-balance. Lucy shared the small back seat with two large, imaginary men who had squashed her into the corner behind me when Kate turned.

Kate looked in her rearview mirror. "What's wrong with you, girl? Can't get comfortable? We'll be home soon."

Lucy glared at me. "Your fault."

"Sorry, Lucy."

She scrambled over Spike, flopped down in the middle, and put her head on Palace Guard's leg. He rubbed her ear. *Good, she's more comfortable.* Palace Guard looked more comfortable too, but Spike was crowded into the corner behind me.

We went straight to the diner. And by straight, I mean like when a honeybee flies back to the hive by way of all the clover patches within twenty miles.

The cabin was hidden in the trees behind the diner's dumpster. We went inside, and it glowed with a welcoming feeling of home.

"This little cabin is deceptive," Kate said. "The original cabin was built in the 1920s and was one bedroom, a bathroom, a kitchen with a breakfast area, and a sitting room with a fireplace. Uncle Reggie remodeled it for his family in 1970, and again in 1990. It has two bedrooms and two bathrooms, a larger kitchen than the original, and a great room with a fireplace. You'll have your own bedroom and bathroom. Lucy can't see very well, but she is a killer of a guard dog and will protect us with her life. Parker said he told you I'm FBI—I'm used to working with a team, so if I give you an instruction, do it. We can always have any discussion later. Make sense?"

"Perfectly."

"I get up at four thirty, make coffee, take a shower, and then go to the diner around five. You may want to keep the same schedule."

"My physical therapist said I should volunteer at an animal shelter. Walk dogs and clean kennels to get stronger. I can walk Lucy and clean the cabin and diner."

"Okay, but remember you just got out of the hospital, so you'll need to take frequent breaks, and Lucy does too."

"Thanks for everything, Kate."

"Get yourself situated and set your alarm for four thirty. Let me know if you need anything. Oh, and leave your door open at least enough for Lucy. If she can't get into your room, she'll sit outside your door and whine all night." Kate chuckled. "Your choice."

My bedroom was larger than I expected. The queen-sized bed was covered by a prairie-star patchwork quilt. I inhaled and caught a whiff of pine. I spied a small basket of pinecones on the natural-pine dresser and found hangers in the closet. I opened my suitcase and unpacked.

It didn't take me long to put my clothes away, my suitcase in the closet, and Taylor's chart on the dresser. I unpacked the toiletries and electronics out of my backpack and plugged in my phone to charge next to the bed. I almost collapsed on the bed when I realized I was bone-tired.

I turned off the lights and snuggled down into the comfortable bed as the sounds of "click, click, click" came toward my room. Lucy rested her head on my bed and sniffed my exposed arm.

"Good night, Lucy."

After she click, click, clicked away, I listened to the rhythmic clicks during the night and relaxed. When my cell phone alarm beeped, I showered and checked the Taylor Guide before I dressed in jeans and a blue chambray shirt. I brushed my sandy-brown hair into a ponytail and hurried to the kitchen. Kate was already there in jeans, a purple-and-gray plaid shirt, and brown work boots. She grabbed the blue enamel coffeepot off the stove and poured two cups.

"Do you cook?" Kate asked.

"Not really. I've warmed up pizza. Oh, and heated a can of soup." I crossed my fingers and hoped a lack of cooking skills didn't get me kicked out of the cabin.

"That's excellent." Kate joined me at the table.

My jaw dropped. "Really?"

She laughed. "If you don't cook, you don't have any bad habits. Tell me how you learned your library job. Was your degree in library science?"

"Yes, but a library science degree is all theory. My first day at the library I studied the library layout. My major routine responsibility was to return books to their proper shelf. I put the books on my cart in the same order as the library aisles. At first, I got a few wrong, but I knew the library backward and forward in less than a week."

"Good, because cooking in a diner is exactly like your process for reshelving books. Our menu is simple, and everything we cook is fast, with no deviation in quality ever. The grits and gravy, for example, would taste the same if you made them or if I made them. The ingredients are always put together in the same order and cooked the same way, exactly like you rolled down the aisle and inserted each book in its rightful place. Today we'll make cinnamon rolls, but all you need to do is watch."

At the diner, Kate showed me how she made coffee then I perched on a stool while Kate made cinnamon rolls.

Easy for her. I'll never make cinnamon rolls.

When headlights appeared in the parking lot, Kate grabbed her apron and her Bulldogs baseball cap. "Your assignment for the morning is to take Lucy for a short walk then check out the cupboards, refrigerators, and freezers to get an idea of where staples and supplies are stored before you take Lucy to the cabin to relax. I'll come get you before lunch."

She pointed at Lucy's leash and hurried to wait on customers. I examined the contents in the refrigerators, freezers, and cupboards and smiled. *I see the pattern of organization.*

After Lucy and I strolled down a path, it turned toward the woods; Lucy stopped to sniff the trail before we turned to go back.

"Sorry, girl. We have Kate's orders to pace ourselves."

After we returned to the cabin, I wrapped myself up in the blue afghan from the wooden rocking chair before I lay down on my bed, and Lucy flopped down across the bedroom doorway. I closed my eyes and relaxed as Lucy snored, and maybe I did too.

* * *

On the third day, Kate trusted me to make coffee; on the fourth day, I made the cinnamon rolls with help.

"Well done. Proud of you," Kate said as Spike and Palace Guard applauded; when I bowed, Kate rolled her eyes.

The next day was my solo cinnamon-rolls assignment. They were a hit with our diner customers, which means nobody noticed any difference. Coffee and cinnamon rolls became my permanent assignments, and I loved it.

"Maggie, what are you most afraid of cooking?" Kate asked on our break.

I wished I'd had the good sense to lie and say toast. "Eggs. No way could I ever cook eggs."

Kate pulled out four muffin tins and set them on the counter together to make a square. "Look at the square like it is made up of rows and columns. Each row is a style to cook eggs. Let's call the first row *scrambled* and the second row *fried*. The columns are times. For now, we'll call them minutes eight through one—longest to shortest."

"So if I want to make a soft scrambled egg, I'd put it in the scrambled row and column two minutes. A fried egg over medium goes into the fried row, column five minutes?"

"You got it." Kate beamed.

I cooked and plated up the eggs for a table of six, and Kate delivered hot food to the table. I kept my egg pans ready and followed my muffin-tin rows and columns. After Kate served our last customer, Spike and I raised our arms up in victory and danced.

"You're a cook, Maggie, not a dancer."

Kate is too serious. I rolled my eyes then caught her cover a smile with her hand.

After eggs, the next lesson was grits and gravy, and last was bacon and sausage. Kate showed me how she ground and mixed her own sausage. "We tell any new customers all we have is hot sausage. Every time I made mild, I got complaints the sausage was too hot. So I make sausage the way I want to and call it hot."

I followed the instructions in Kate's recipe notebook. After another week, I had mastered the breakfast menu. Kate and I sat at the counter and drank coffee at the end of the morning rush.

"You're a genuine short-order cook. Congratulations." Kate lifted her cup in a salute.

"I love the kitchen. I never knew how heady the blended aroma of cinnamon and bacon with the underlying tones of dishwasher detergent was."

"You're goofy. Break is over."

I got an email from Mother: "Margaret, I have hearing aids. Your doctor in the hospital sent me to a doctor who tested my hearing. My new doctor said I lost my hearing from a disease like mumps after I learned to talk."

I knew Mother had visited a variety of doctors when she was young, but I never understood why, and it never occurred to me she couldn't hear. *I wonder if she talked all the time so no one would know.*

I replied: "Great news, Mother."

I settled into my new career of short-order cook and loved the daily routine of a simple lifestyle. *Silly me.*

"Now we need to train you," Kate said. "You need the strength and skills to defend yourself."

My training was intense. When Spike and Palace Guard cringed, I grumbled. *You imaginary guys aren't much help, you know. Why don't you tell me how great I'm doing?*

Spike shook his head, and Palace Guard looked down. *Challenge accepted.*

I worked even harder. I learned to roll, dodge, kick, block, and use Kate's weight and height against her. My weight and height were not an advantage.

During our second week of training, Kate picked up her water bottle and took a swig at the end of a workout. "Your biggest advantage is that your looks are deceiving. You're slender and short. Your surprising strength and skill give you a tremendous edge. If you attack first, you win. If they attack first and you fight back, you win. You ever been around guns?"

I shook my head.

"We'll start with the basics," Kate said. "I'll teach you to clean guns—take them apart and put them back together. I have a deal with the local range, and they'll be happy for us to clean their rental guns."

I disassembled, cleaned, and reassembled every type of rental pistol imaginable. It took me six days to pass Kate's inspection, but when I got it down, I was fast.

"Ever thought about being a gunsmith?" Kate asked.

"No. Never. Is that what I'm doing?"

She laughed. "No. You're just cleaning guns, but you're good at it."

What do gunsmiths do and when will my gunsmith training start?

Kate looked at my face and laughed even harder. Even Spike and Palace Guard laughed.

Not funny. I glowered.

After dark, we watched a meteor shower while we sat on the porch. "Have you done any camping?" Kate asked.

Uh-oh. She'll take me twenty miles out into the wilderness and give me one day to get back. Let's see. What do I pack? Bug spray, for sure.

"Not yet."

"Let's add camping skills to your toolkit. I've got a tent and a sleeping bag for you. Pitch the tent behind the cabin tomorrow."

Kate sat on the back porch and read a book while I spent three hours trying to put up the tent. After the tent quit collapsing, I unrolled the sleeping bag and placed it on the ground.

After supper, Kate, Lucy, and I relaxed on the porch, and I sprayed myself with bug repellent. *If any mosquitos land on me, they will drown.*

"Bedtime." Kate headed to the cabin door, and I stepped off the porch with my flashlight. Lucy eased down the steps and followed me.

"Lucy, you have to come inside," Kate said. "I'm afraid you might wander off."

Lucy switched her gaze from me to Kate before she trotted to Kate.

The variety of menacing sounds— hoots, chirps, crackles, snaps, rustles, and scratches— kept me awake. I sat with my back against the tent and hugged my knees. I stared at the tent flap and waited for a bear to charge through and rip me to pieces. When my head drooped from exhaustion, Spike showed me hopping-bunny-ear fingers, and I heard only rabbits scampering through the forest. Snapping, scratching, scrambling? *Just bunnies.*

* * *

I woke up the next morning feeling like I'd slept on a bed of nails.

"How'd you sleep?" Kate asked over our morning coffee.

"Fine." *No sense in giving her any ideas.*

"After breakfast is over, we'll go to the gun range," Kate said. "The diner has always closed for the annual three-day shoot because Uncle Reggie was one of the top competitors. We'll clean the rental guns. It's a good way for you to be around the sound of gunshots. You'll be jumpy at first, but II have good hearing protection for both of us. If you hate it, you don't have to go back."

Hats off to Kate. She's pushing me every way imaginable.

Kate was right—a shooting match was an excellent place to hear gunshots, and I jumped with every crack and pop. When the competitors took a break from shooting, I disassembled, cleaned, and reassembled the rentals.

At the end of the day, I pushed away from the range table. "My neck and back are stiff."

"No wonder. You were tense the entire day. We'll loosen up your muscles when we get to the cabin."

When I climbed out of the car, Kate ambushed me and tossed me to the ground. Before I sat up, she flipped me again.

"You win. My muscles aren't tense." Kate laughed, and I took her down. She was on her back still laughing while I ran to the back of the cabin.

"Truce," she called when she came in the front door. "Let's get our supper going."

"Good job today," she said over our meal of steak and salad.

"Thanks. Felt good."

"This week we'll chop wood, split kindling, lay a fire, cook on the fire, and collect water. Forecast is for thunderstorms later this week. That's an excellent opportunity to start a fire in the rain." Kate slipped her plate into the sudsy water while I washed dishes.

"We?" I snorted.

While Kate put away dishes, I cleared an area of leaves, pinecones, rocks, and sticks and pitched my tent in the torture-free zone. I found a yoga mat in my closet and placed it under my sleeping bag.

The next day, I was surprised I didn't jump much at all during the shooting match. We ran when we got back to the diner because Kate liked to mix it up. I pushed hard to keep up with her and looked forward to the third day at the range.

* * *

We sat out of sight in the back room of the gun-range store and cleaned guns. We listened to the bragging, whining, and trash talk of the competitors—mostly men, but a few women. Kate and I snickered at the comments. I froze at the sound of a voice.

Kate spoke in a quiet voice. "What is it?"

"Donnie. The phony investigator. He's here," I whispered.

"What does he look like?" Kate asked.

"Five foot ten, two hundred forty pounds. Hazel eyes and straight brown hair. Red, blotchy face and bulbous nose."

Kate stepped out of our back room. A shiver at the base of my spine ran up my back, and my breathing was rapid and shallow. I thought the library and explosion were behind me, but hearing Donnie brought it all back like a time-warp nightmare.

What's taking Kate so long? I knew I looked different, but I didn't know if I'd be recognizable. I sat in silence and cleaned guns. *All these guns, and I don't know how to use one of them. Need bullets, anyway.*

Spike was at my elbow, and Palace Guard stood at the door. Palace Guard breathed out with pursed lips and gave me a hand signal to slow down. I held my breath and mimicked Palace Guard's slow exhale.

I frowned as Kate talked to a man and laughed while they talked about guns and the shoot, but I didn't recognize the man's voice. *I will kick her ass tonight.*

Spike laughed.

I narrowed my eyes. *Yours too.*

He grinned.

Kate sauntered into the room. "A guy out there matched your description. A friend took a picture of me with your guy in the background, and he'll send me the pic for you to verify it's Donnie. The only reasons people come to a meet is to watch a friend or relative or to compete. He didn't have any gear or seem to be here with anyone, and he didn't stay for the next competition round."

"I might need more than just Spike and Palace Guard," I mumbled. Spike looked shocked, and Palace Guard's face was stormy.

"What?" Kate asked.

"Nothing. Sorry, guys," I replied to Kate and apologized to Spike and Palace Guard.

Spike crossed his arms, and Palace Guard narrowed his eyes. *Okay, okay.*

"Well, actually, my imaginary men, Spike and Palace Guard, wanted you to know about them. They have been with me since my physical therapy sessions in the hospital and were the reason I got through physical therapy and healed so quickly. I know they are imaginary, but they've helped me, and we've been through a lot together."

"They're imaginary, and they've been with you since the hospital? I might need a little time to process." Kate examined my face. "You aren't kidding. So, Palace Guard, like Buckingham Palace? Who's Spike?"

"Yes, like Buckingham Palace. Spike's a legend from my childhood. He pulled kids off the street and taught them to read and play ball. Nobody's tougher than Spike."

Kate raised her eyebrows. "I guess if you have imaginary men, might as well have the best."

When Spike's and Palace Guard's chests puffed up, I smiled.

While we cleaned guns, I planned my ambush. After Kate received the photo her friend took with Donnie in the background, she showed it to me.

Donnie faced to the side toward the front door. "His hair's a little longer and cut in a different style, but it's Donnie."

Kate forwarded the pic to Parker.

On our way back to the diner I rolled down my window for fresh air. "I want to buy a gun tomorrow. And I want to learn to shoot."

"Okay. We'll get you a concealed-carry permit class."

Kate's phone rang.

"Trouble," she said. "It's Parker."

Kate's always right—we were in trouble. I rolled up my window, and Kate handed me the phone to hold between us.

"What were you thinking? Why go to the gun competition?"

Kate said, "No one knew—"

Parker interrupted. "I don't care if you think no one knew you were there, but you're wrong because somebody must have, and I can't believe you went into the store. Are you trying to give me a heart attack?"

Kate made a yakety-yak motion with her fingers, and I put my hand over my mouth to silence my giggle.

"You still there?" Parker didn't wait for an answer. "What was Donald Chandler doing at the gun range? How did he know where Maggie was? And taking a picture? What if he'd seen you? I should have been there. I'm coming to the cabin. Don't go anywhere else."

Kate asked, "You done?"

I thought he was going to rant some more, but he must have been finished because he hung up.

"I know he'll want you to leave," she said, "but you should stay."

"Yep." I glanced back. Spike and Palace Guard nodded in agreement.

"Spike and Palace Guard agree, don't they?"

"Actually, they do." I looked at her in amazement.

"I knew it."

We returned in silence with two large, smug, imaginary men in the back seat.

"Bathrooms and bedrooms or kitchen and living room?" Kate pulled in at the cabin.

"I'll take bathrooms and bedrooms." I found some old-fashioned powder cleanser under the kitchen sink. I shook the cleaner on my shower floor and scrubbed.

"Hey, Kate. Did you know this powder cleanser has to be rinsed?" I ran the shower a few minutes and swished the water around then ran more water before I returned the powder to the kitchen.

"Here, use this." Kate handed me the kitchen cleanser.

I scrubbed the sinks, toilets, and Kate's shower in the amount of time it took me to clean and rinse my shower. I stood back to admire my handiwork and realized the bathroom floors were dingy. I swept and mopped the floors and wiped down the walls and baseboards. I eyed the ceiling. *No ladder. It'll have to do.*

I dusted, swept, and mopped the bedrooms and returned the broom, mop, and bucket to the pantry. "Kitchen and living room look great. Cabin's spotless. What do we do now?"

"Not enough time for a run." Kate frowned.

When we flopped on the sofa, Lucy padded over and squeezed in between us before she stretched, and I lost my space. I rose then paced.

"Taylor bought makeup for me. Nothing's safer than applying makeup, right?" I retrieved the sack from Taylor and handed it to Kate.

Kate looked through the bottles, jars, and tubes. "Taylor has a good sense of style. These are good colors for you. You'll look totally natural. Let's give it a try."

We stood in front of the mirror in my bathroom.

"Wet your sponge with warm water and dab on the foundation. Fast. Like you'd dab paint on a canvas." Kate peered at me in the mirror. "Dust your eyelids with the eyeshadow like you brush crumbs off your shirt. Do a fake smile and dust your cheeks where they're prominent with the blush. Brush away crumbs again."

"You're going too fast. Slow down."

"Pick up the pace. You're thinking too much. Open your mouth so you won't blink. Brush on the mascara. Light touch. Two passes. Watch me put on my lipstick. Now you."

I examined my face in the mirror. "I look like a clown."

"No, you don't. It's subtle. Nice. You'll have to have a picture taken for your concealed permit. You should take it with your makeup."

I opened my mouth to argue, but Lucy barked, and a car parked behind the diner.

"Stay in the bathroom." Kate turned lights off behind her.

A knock at the door sounded like a code to me.

I heard Kate open the door and Parker's voice. "Where is she?"

"Come on out, Maggie," Kate said.

Parker looked at me with what might have been suspicion, and even I thought I was an imposter.

"You hate it, right?" I was ready to run to the bathroom and wash my face.

He smiled. "Trick question?"

He took two steps, and his hug had my feet dangling.

"Be careful, Parker," Kate said. "She knows how to get out of a hug."

He laughed as he set my feet on the floor. "Show me."

Chapter Thirteen

I grabbed his arm and leaned down as I flipped him over my back to the floor.

He looked up at me. "This isn't fair. I can't take you on."

"Yes, you can," I said.

He picked me up and tossed me like a bowling ball. I slid across the floor and spun on my back like a break-dancer before I bounded to my feet.

"Game on." I rushed him.

When we were winded and flat on our backs on the floor, we rolled toward each other and laughed. Parker had a bloody nose and a bruise on his cheek, and I had bruises on my arms and an abrasion on my shoulder. Parker offered me his hand and pulled me to my feet. I hugged him.

"Beer or wine? This deserves a victory celebration," Kate said.

"Beer for me," Parker said.

"Wine," I mumbled into Parker's chest. Kate poured wine and grabbed a bottle of beer. I released my bruised man and put cheese and crackers on a plate.

Parker lit the tinder in the fireplace, and the fire heated the little cabin a few degrees past toasty.

"Nice woodsy atmosphere, but now it's too hot." Kate opened the back door.

Our world was perfect—the crackle of the fire, the smell of oak wood smoke, and the fresh night air. Parker settled down on the faded blue-and-red-plaid sofa and put his sock feet up on the scarred-pine coffee table. I sat cross-legged next to Parker, and Kate curled up in her old cracked-leather recliner.

"Very well done. Both of you—student and trainer," Parker said.

We saluted each other with our drinks.

When Parker put his arm around me, I scooted closer. He traced my jawline with his finger. "At first, I was afraid I'd hurt you, and then I was afraid you'd hurt me if I didn't take you down. You're amazing."

"I planned to kick Kate's ass tonight. You did her a favor," I said.

Kate snorted. "Ha."

"I came out here with this big speech in mind about how you needed to go somewhere else, Maggie, but now I'm not so sure," Parker said.

"I'd like to know what's going on," I said.

"Fair enough. The fire marshal found, sorry if this is gruesome, enough of two bodies just outside the library at the back door to run dental records. The medical examiner's office positively identified Olivia but hasn't identified the other yet. They are pretty sure the second was male. We thought Donnie died in the explosion, but I guess we were wrong."

Parker rose and set another log on the hot coals. I crossed my arms until he returned and resumed his spot next to me. I leaned on his shoulder and inhaled his soap and sweat. The log's bark caught a spark and flared up.

"The paper from the note on your windshield had no fingerprints and was generic and cheap. The apartment security camera showed someone with an umbrella who walked close to the car not long after the rain stopped, but we can't tell whether the person was close enough to put a note on the car. A handicap transport van parked in its usual spot early in the morning the three days before the explosion, and it blocked the security camera's view of your car for about twenty minutes each day. A long time."

The log dropped with a clunk, and a few coals escaped the firebox. Parker rose and pushed them back with the poker. When he sank on the sofa, I snuggled into him.

"There haven't been any threats since you left. Mr. Morgan stayed, and Taylor is with her parents. Your mother has her new hearing aids, and she and Sergeant Arrington met for coffee."

I sat up. "My mother and Sergeant Arrington got together? Like on a date? Good for them. Do they bellow at each other?"

He chuckled. "Your mother has softened our crusty Sarge. A little scary to hear the sergeant whisper on the phone."

"Sounds sweet. I see no reason for me to leave."

Parker turned to his sister. "Kate, what about you?"

"I agree with Maggie. I'd like to know why Donnie was at the competition, though. Not a coincidence." Kate wrinkled her nose.

"I'll follow up on Chandler." Parker removed his arm from around me and extricated himself from our entwined legs. "Sorry, Maggie. I have to get back."

"Not half as sorry as I am."

I accompanied him to his car and brushed mosquitos away from my ears and arms. He leaned down, took my face into his hands, and kissed my mouth with sweet tenderness. I melted into his kiss, and he pulled me closer. He nibbled my lower lip and teased my mouth open. I returned his deep kiss and smacked my arms and neck.

Parker hugged me and laughed. "Go inside, Maggie. I'll see you later."

When I turned to go inside, he gave me a light swat on the bottom before he climbed into his car. I swung my hips in an exaggerated version of a sexy walk before I turned with my hand on one hip and fluttered my eyelashes as I grinned and waved.

"Dang it, Maggie," he called while he backed down the driveway. "I miss you already."

* * *

The next day, Kate helped me pick out a handgun. While we waited at the counter for the paperwork to be completed, a man walked into the shop. His hair was gray; he was slender to the point of wiry, and his hands were scarred and leathery. He wore scuffed cowboy boots and faded blue jeans. STAFF was printed in large yellow letters on the chest pocket of his black T-shirt.

"Maggie bought a pistol, Buck. Do you have time to teach her the basics?" Kate asked.

He slapped me on the back. If I hadn't been braced against the counter, he'd have sent me across the room. "With your skill in cleaning guns, it'd be a pleasure to teach you to shoot."

* * *

We spent the first day on safety. The next day, we took my gun to the range.

"We'll work on stance and aiming without your gun. Position yourself to shoot and hold up your hands like you're holding your gun."

I faced the target with my right leg forward, pointed my right hand, and used my left hand to support my right.

"Good start. Stay square to the target. Put your feet a shoulder's width apart and move your right foot back a little. You want your right toe to be in line with your left instep."

I was as awkward as I was when I learned a new dance step.

"How does it feel? Natural? Uncomfortable?"

"Not uncomfortable, but not natural. I had to look at my feet to find my instep."

"It'll take a little practice. Flex your knees a little. Lean forward slightly. Remember to keep your head level. It'll help you to maintain your balance. Now?"

"Good. Feels good."

"Walk to the store. When you get back, take your stance."

Spike and Palace Guard high-fived.

I walked, returned, and took my stance.

"Good," Buck said.

Spike signed "Again," and so did Buck. Spike and Buck crossed their arms.

"You've got it. Let's shoot your target," Buck said after my fifth repetition.

I shot a round, and the four of us reviewed my target.

"Good cluster. Four more rounds." Buck patted my back. I had widened my stance and didn't fall. After I shot the remaining rounds, we walked into the store, and I cleaned my pistol.

Buck laughed. "I've never seen a new shooter clean a gun. You've had a good first day. Reggie always said it was important to be proficient with two different kinds of pistols; we'll add maybe a revolver and a rifle. Won't take long for you."

* * *

A week later, Kate's phone rang while we cleaned the diner after breakfast. She glanced at her phone. "It's Parker. Gotta go outside."

Cell reception was sketchy inside the diner, but I frowned. *Parker never calls in the morning, because that's when we're busy. Something's wrong.*

After I cleaned the oven, I shifted to the grill, and Kate returned with a scowl. "Parker said an unknown assailant attacked and robbed an elderly woman three days ago and left her for dead. She's still in critical condition in ICU but will recover. Yesterday she woke up and said, 'Tell the Gray Lady John Updike.' All the nurses at the hospital knew who the Gray Lady was. She was so insistent and agitated that one of the nurses called Parker. What does it mean?"

I froze. "John Updike wrote *Rabbit, Run*. Do they know who she is?"

Kate leaned against the counter. "Her name is Lillian Brewer. Parker thought you might understand the message."

A chill ran down my back, and the hairs on my arm stood up. "Lillian is from the library. She told me 'day eight.' Tell Parker we need to leave. He might want to alert Mr. Morgan, Taylor, and Mother."

Kate rushed outside to call Parker. I finished the grill, refilled the napkin containers, and wiped down the countertop.

Kate returned, and her face was grim. "I'd like to leave after dark. I'll put up my *Gone Fishing* sign before we leave. The locals won't think anything of it."

Kate picked up the plates I'd pulled from the dishwasher and put them in the cupboard as she continued, "I need to check my car for a GPS tracker. Would you take the perishables out of the refrigerator and carry them to the cabin? There shouldn't be much. The stuff in the freezer will be okay, but why don't you pull out some bacon, a few steaks, maybe a roast or two, and a few packs of chicken."

I loaded butter, eggs, milk, bacon, sausage, and the frozen meat into a basket and carried the heavy load to the cabin refrigerator.

When I stepped outside, Kate was sitting on the porch with her face in her hands. "I found a GPS tracker on my car and moved it to a tree. I'm kicking myself for not checking earlier. I sent a quick text to Parker to let him know. Because now I'm paranoid, I checked the diner. No electronic bugs there. I'll check the cabin."

I waited in the doorway.

"All clear. I have a packing list for clothes and personal items; you can use it as a guide." Kate handed me the list and one of her backpacks. "We have a few basic supplies at our destination, but I'll fill a large cooler with perishables. Grab a box or two and fill them with food and staples from the cupboards."

After I packed, I stood with my hands on my hips and surveyed the boxes we'd staged at the front door. "Now what?"

"We're going to travel most of the night. We need a power nap. I'll set an alarm."

"Not sure I can sleep," I mumbled on my way to my room. Lucy followed me.

* * *

"I slept. Did you?" Kate leaned against my bedroom door and yawned.

I opened my eyes and stretched. "Must have. You woke me up from a great dream."

Kate grilled steaks, and I tossed a salad. After supper, we relaxed on the back porch with hot tea while the sky changed colors from blue to pink to orange.

"Let's load the car before we need any inside lights." Kate rose. "I'll set timers for the lights."

After I rolled the ice chest out, Kate and I team-lifted it into the trunk before I carried out the boxes and backpacks to the car in three trips. "Everything fits into the trunk except one large box."

Kate examined the trunk and stuffed our jackets, pillows, sheets, and our sleeping bags into the voids. "The box can go behind the passenger's seat. It's pulled forward the farthest."

"It fits with room to spare." I channeled my nervous energy and swept the dirt around the front of the cabin to the car. We went to the back porch to sit, but we paced instead.

"I can't wait until dark," Kate said. "Let's leave now."

After I took Lucy for a short walk, she jumped into the back seat and claimed the middle. Kate locked the cabin and put the sign in the diner window.

Kate turned her head toward the back seat. "Are Spike and Palace Guard with us?"

I checked. Spike was behind me, and Palace Guard was behind Kate. Lucy settled in with her head on Palace Guard. Spike was shifted toward the middle with his feet in front of Lucy. Spike gave me the thumbs-up. Palace Guard rubbed Lucy's face and ears and looked straight ahead while Lucy breathed what sounded like a soft purr.

"Yes. They are."

"I feel a lot better with your imaginary guys along. Is that nuts?"

"I do too. And yes. Totally nuts."

Kate turned onto the highway. "We'll be on the road for about four hours. We won't use rest areas, but we'll stop for breaks. We're going to a hunting cabin. It's basic. I already warned you, right? The kitchen has a small stove with an oven and a small refrigerator. Not exactly what we're used to at the diner, but the appliances work and are reliable. The kitchen is a corner of the living area. The living area has an old sofa and two chairs."

"I'm a diner cook. You'll have to teach me how to be a hunting cabin cook." I wiggled my eyebrows.

Kate swatted my arm. "You're goofy. We have running water and a bathroom with a shower and a toilet. The bedroom has two twin beds, not bunkbeds, thank goodness. The mattresses are thin. We'll use our sleeping bags over them. The washing machine is on the back porch. No dryer. We'll wash the cabin's towels, sheets, and blankets in the morning and hang them out to dry. Our priority for tomorrow will be to clean the cabin, especially the kitchen, and take inventory. There are supposed to be cleaning supplies, but if there aren't, we'll have to go to a store. I'm not crazy about the idea."

"I'm just grateful we aren't camping. Running water and an inside toilet—we're set. Right, gentlemen?"

Spike wiggled two thumbs up.

Kate pulled into a small roadside park with no amenities for our first break. "This will be a quick stop."

Lucy refused to get out of the car even though I tried to coax her with a treat. "Come on, girl. Lucy, I peed. It's your turn. You pee outside all the time."

She glared at me as if to say, "I never."

Kate and Spike pushed and scooted Lucy to the edge of the seat; after she lumbered out of the car, Kate slammed the door. "Go pee, girl."

Lucy sat near the car and faced us. The four of us turned our backs so she'd have privacy. I listened to Lucy sneak to the grass while Kate peeked over her shoulder. "Success."

We were finally on the road again—two kick-ass women, two imaginary men, and a prima donna dog.

An odor wafted from the back seat.

"Lucy," Kate scolded.

When I looked back, Lucy stared at Spike, and he laughed.

"Spike, did you let the poor dog take the blame?"

Lucy wagged her tail. With every thump, she whapped Spike in the face and grinned. Palace Guard smiled and rolled his eyes. I laughed.

"What's going on back there?" Kate asked. "I'm the driver and need to focus. Tell me."

"Lucy's tail wags smacked Spike in the face, and she was proud of herself and her girl revenge."

"It isn't fair I'm the only one who can't see the imaginary men."

"Maybe you're too grown up," I said.

Kate growled, "Take it back, or I'm kicking you out of the car."

"Okay, I apologize." I giggled. "You are totally not grown up."

"Apology accepted." Kate turned to stick her tongue out at me. "Hey, I just saw something out of the corner of my eye. Is Spike wearing a blue shirt?"

"Yep."

"For real?"

"Yep."

"Ha. I'm officially as immature and nuts as you are."

I snorted, and Spike laughed.

Kate turned onto another highway. "I'm glad the imaginary men are here."

"Me too." The landscape rolled by. We rode in silence for an hour.

"You will know," I said.

"Did you say something?" Kate asked.

"I got a note right after the library murder. U-W-I-L-N-O in all capital letters was on the note. I thought I needed to break a code, but now I understand. I do know where to start—the bank and my job hunting."

I talked through my job applications and interviews. Kate was quiet, and the imaginary men leaned over the seat to listen.

I frowned. "I don't know, though, how it all fits together."

"If we need any supplies, I'll pick up some sticky notes," Kate said. "I need to see it before I can find a thread. The answer's there somewhere. I just can't see it."

We turned west, and the blue sky changed to orange and pink, and then gray.

"Does Parker know all of this?" Kate asked.

I shook my head. "No, I never realized it was all related. It seemed like a scatter of isolated incidents."

"Call him and fill him in," Kate said.

"That sucks."

"I know," she said, "but we won't have much of a cell signal later, and I don't want us to blow up without Parker knowing as much as we do."

"Well, since you put it so delicately, I will."

Kate chuckled, and I called Parker. He answered right away and sounded alert. *Dang.* I told him the whole story. He asked questions and asked me to go back a few times.

"Thanks, Maggie," he said when I finished. "You're sure there's nothing else?"

"No. That's it."

"Okay. Thanks, and I'm not happy." He hung up.

Kate asked, "What did he say?"

"He said he's not happy."

"Might be a good sign—he didn't say he was angry."

Palace Guard patted my shoulder. Spike and Lucy slept.

Kate turned left onto a dirt road with narrow shoulders. After a mile, Kate pulled off into the brush and stopped. We stepped outside to listen for traffic behind us. My hearing tested fine before I left the hospital, but if Kate heard something that I didn't, I needed to know. We took another bio break, except this time we didn't wake Lucy.

We stood in the brush until Kate motioned toward her car.

"I don't think anybody followed us," Kate said.

After a few more miles, she turned right onto a dirt road with no shoulders. The poorly maintained road was rutted, and the ride jarred and threw us around.

"We're bouncing like a rubber dinghy on a choppy open sea." My words bounced along with the car.

We pulled into an overgrown path Kate claimed was a driveway. We were at a rustic cabin, but it looked like a shed in the shadows cast by the half moon. Kate walked around the cabin, unlocked the door, and checked inside while I waited in the car.

When she was satisfied we were safe, she turned on the lights inside the cabin, and we unloaded the car assisted by the glow of the faint trunk light. We dropped Lucy's favorite dog bed on the floor for her. She fussed with her bed until she was satisfied and fell asleep. I understood. I wanted to fluff my sleeping bag.

Kate opened the small white refrigerator. "It's empty, clean, and cold enough for our food."

"Good news." I scooted the cooler closer. While I filled the refrigerator and freezer, Kate turned the kitchen faucet on full until the water ran clear.

I checked the bathroom. "Toilet flushes."

"Cleaning will be our priority tomorrow. When I shined the flashlight into the dark corners, no critters scurried away, and there's no evidence of any in the kitchen. We have no roaches and no mice," Kate said.

"Best news I've had all day, except it's kind of pitiful when you think about it."

"Yep. Don't think," Kate said. "I'll show you how to check for bedbugs."

More good news—bug-free.

"We can throw our sleeping bags on the beds. You ready to call it a night?"

* * *

The smell of coffee woke me. When I stumbled barefooted into the combination living room and kitchen, Kate poured me a cup. She was dressed in jeans and an olive-green T-shirt.

"If you wash dishes and set the table, I'll make biscuits and fry bacon and eggs while you get dressed," she said.

"Sounds great."

"Wash only what we need for breakfast. We'll do the rest later."

Kate found homemade strawberry jam in the cupboard and showed me how to check a jar for a good seal.

"Listen," she said while she tapped the lid with a spoon. "Bing, bing is good. Thunk, thunk, the jar's not sealed."

"You'll teach me how to make biscuits, right?" I asked after we ate. "Who canned the strawberry jam?"

"Mom did. Biscuits are easy. I'll show you."

I finished my coffee. "I'll get the laundry going." I gathered linens and carried them to the washer on the back porch. When I returned to the kitchen, Kate had washed our dishes and pulled out a notebook for a shopping list.

"We need more laundry detergent and bleach," I said.

Kate added them to her list. "Let's pull everything out of the cupboards, check expiration dates, and wipe out the cabinets."

After we emptied the cupboards, Kate said, "I'll scrub. Will you check the wash?"

I threw towels over the old line and hoped they wouldn't fall. I wasn't sure how many more loads the frayed line had left in its life. When I went into the kitchen, I added clothespins and a clothesline to the list.

Didn't take me long to scrub the tiny bathroom, but I used up all the cleanser. More for the list. I found the woodshed with stacked wood but no ax or a saw. Again, the list.

"I found flashlights and replaced the batteries," Kate said. "But the weather radio doesn't work, even with fresh batteries."

"Did you expect a list this long?" I asked.

"Not at all. I found a jar of peanut butter, and we have our strawberry jam. I'll make sandwiches for lunch," Kate said.

"My favorite sandwich," I said between bites. "Let's limit our exposure with one trip and get everything."

Kate took her last bite. "I should go alone. If anybody's trying to find us, they'll search for two women."

"True, but if we both go, we'll finish in half the time. We can split up the list and shop then check out independently. Is there a store where we can get everything we want? If we need items from a second store, you can drop me off at the first one and go to the second store solo. We can coordinate with texts. What about Lucy? Will she be okay if we leave her?"

"Lucy will be fine." Kate pursed her lips. "I hate to admit it, but that's a solid plan. Let's organize the list into two lists. You want to take the first cut, and I'll take Lucy for a long walk?"

I created the two lists and checked the laundry on my clothesline. The towels were still damp. I folded and put the sheets away before Kate and Lucy returned.

"Lucy enjoyed stretching her legs," Kate said. "We even ran a little. I'm sure she'll be happy to relax this afternoon."

Kate compared the lists. "I'll take the list with the ax. If our superstore doesn't have it, I can dash to the hardware store."

"Guys with us?" Kate asked when she turned onto the highway.

"No, they stayed to keep Lucy company."

Kate dropped me off in the parking lot near one entrance and parked near a door on the other side of the building. I headed to the checkout and texted Kate. "Done."

She replied, "5 min."

I scooted to the pharmacy section and picked up more bug repellent and antibiotic ointment. By the time I got to the checkout counter, Kate texted, "Cking out."

On our way back to the cabin, Kate said, "Much smoother than I expected. Better call Parker. We can let him know we made it okay. Maybe he'll go up a notch from not happy to kind of happy."

I called Parker. He fired off questions the second he answered the phone. I had trouble keeping up.

"Yes, we're okay. We got to the cabin around two. Right. No cell coverage there. We went shopping. We're on our way back. Yes, we were careful. Nobody saw us. No, we weren't in the store together. What's up?"

"Can you go to speakerphone? I need both of you to hear this," he said.

I pressed the button. "You're on speakerphone, Parker. Both of us can hear you."

"An explosion at the diner occurred around four this morning."

Chapter Fourteen

Kate and I looked at each other. She shook her head. I was stunned.

"The fire from the explosion was intense," Parker said. "The diner is gone, and even the cabin burned to the ground. The fire department arrived within ten minutes, but the structures were engulfed in flames. Right now, the assumption is Kate was in the cabin; no one has mentioned Maggie, but I'm sure she was the target. Thanks for the call last night because I'd be a wreck if I didn't know you were nowhere close to the cabin."

"I don't know how the initial connection was made between Maggie and me for the GPS tracker to be put on my car," Kate said.

"Maggie went to the diner twice," Parker said. "The second time, she rode home with Mr. Morgan. I'll check his car. Someone's tracking her somehow."

"Parker, how do we get in contact with you?" Kate asked. "Do you know of a place within walking distance of the cabin where we can catch a signal?"

"Go toward the old Smith farm. You may get some bars on the hill."

"How about if I call you tomorrow morning at nine? If I can't get a signal, I'll drive toward town. I'll stop when I can get through."

After I hung up the phone, it hit me. *The diner and the cabin are gone.*

"I'm so sorry about the diner and the beautiful cabin."

Kate's face was tight, and her lips were pressed together. "I know. Me too. But what's important is we're okay."

I rubbed my forehead. "What could I possibly know to cause someone to chase me with explosives?"

When we got to the cabin, Kate unlocked the door. Spike and Palace Guard sat on the sofa with Lucy between them. Lucy yawned, eased her front legs to the floor one at a time, slid her back legs off together in slow motion, and lumbered over.

"Thanks for taking care of Lucy." I bit my lip. "We talked to Parker, and there was an explosion at the diner early this morning. The cabin's gone too. It's good we left last night."

Spike glowered, and Palace Guard narrowed his eyes.

Kate and I unloaded the car in silence. While Kate put our items away, I tossed the last of the dirty clothes and linens into the washer and strung up my new clothesline.

"Hey, Kate," I yelled from the yard. "I just strung up a diamond necklace. This is beautiful."

She stuck her head out the back door. "You are not only immature and nuts, but you're also weird."

"You're just jealous. I got a diamond necklace. All you got was an ax."

I hung up the next batch from the washer and carried the dry load inside. While I folded, I inhaled the fresh smell and rubbed my hands across the stiffness of the towels dried by the light breeze.

"I've put everything away. I'm ready for a shower," Kate said. "After I get cleaned up, I'll start supper. You can take a shower before or after supper. Whatever works for you."

"Before supper. Otherwise, there's no way I'd lift my arms to eat without ruining my own appetite."

Kate laughed. "That's how I feel about me."

As we ate, Kate said, "While you were in the shower, I checked everywhere for any transmitting electronic gadgets. We're clear."

"I'll do the dishes if you want to take Lucy for a long walk. Then maybe we can work on our sticky notes."

"We'll walk to the hill to see if I have a cell signal and stroll around the perimeter. Lucy's eyesight is shot, but her nose and hearing can keep up with the best of them. I'll feel more comfortable if Lucy's comfortable."

When Kate returned, we wrote on our notes. We stepped back, and I counted. "There's twenty-seven on the wall."

"I don't know if this is good or bad." Kate peered at the wall of notes. "I don't even know if we've covered everything. Do you see that most of them are questions? We don't know many facts."

"I'm beat. I have to go to bed."

"I'll be there before you turn off the light. I'll take one more walk around the cabin. Want to go, Lucy?"

Kate turned off the light when she came into the bedroom. Lucy slept in the living room on her dog bed. My mind raced—no sleep for me tonight. I almost got up to make some hot tea, but I didn't want to disturb the lightly snoring Kate. I thought about the diner and the cabin, Parker, and all our notes, and I listened to the night noises and the patter of light rain.

I was still awake at dawn when pale-gray fog blanketed the window. I grabbed my clothes and a sweatshirt, sneaked out of the bedroom to let Kate sleep in, and stepped outside to a chilly, damp morning. The low fog smothered the grass like gray fuzz. The tree branches dripped, and the porch was wet. When Lucy came to check on me, I coaxed her outside for a walk.

Kate joined us on the porch after we returned and handed me a cup of coffee. "I didn't hear the rain, did you?"

"It was a light rain."

"I don't know whether those sticky notes are helpful or not. I'm stunned by how much we don't know. I've got cinnamon rolls in the oven. Ready to go inside?"

While I washed dishes, Kate rearranged notes and drummed her fingers on the table. "I'm nervous about leaving the cabin unguarded."

Spike was near Lucy, and Palace Guard was stationed at the back door. I snickered when they puffed up their chests and frowned.

"What's funny?" Kate asked.

"Spike and Palace Guard were insulted when you said the cabin would be unguarded. I laughed because their reaction was instantaneous."

"Oh, for crying out loud," Kate huffed. "What do we do?"

"Let's leave Lucy. She'll be safe with them. The walk might be a little much for her after yesterday." I looked at Spike. "And we should lock the doors. They'll get her out if they need to. I don't know how, but they will."

Kate shook her head. "I have a hard time understanding how imaginary Spike and imaginary Palace Guard could take care of Lucy."

Spike shrugged, and Palace Guard gave a slight nod.

"Well, if it makes you feel any better, they agree with you. Should we take some water with us? Are you ready to go?"

Kate grabbed two bottles of water from the cabinet. She locked the door behind us, and we left. I needed to stretch my legs, but Kate's fast pace was a challenge. When we reached the hill, I was ready for a break.

Kate called Parker, and he asked her to turn on the speakerphone. "There's been a break in the case. The investigation team arrested Mr. Morgan early this morning. They questioned him about the murder and the explosion at the library. I haven't heard what the charges are yet."

My face grew hot. "That is absolutely nuts."

"I'm sorry, Maggie, but solid evidence ties him to the murder of the man in the library and maybe the library explosion."

I stamped my foot. "Somebody made a huge mistake."

"Sorry, Maggie," Parker said. "I liked Mr. Morgan too."

I wanted to shake some sense into the investigation team. "They're wrong."

"Well, it's all I have. The chief says you two are safe now."

I growled. "Easy for him to say."

"What evidence is there?" Kate asked.

"It hasn't been made public yet," Parker said. "There's a press conference this afternoon. Want to call me around five? I want to check Mr. Morgan's car."

"Will do," Kate said.

I scowled. Kate hung up the phone.

"They are wrong." I fumed.

"I know he's your friend. I hope you are right."

"The chief is wrong too," I said. "We need to stay on alert."

"I agree. Let's get back to Lucy and her guards."

"One more thing. Send Parker a text and ask about Lillian's condition."

We waited for Parker to text back. "Better," Kate said. "Out of ICU."

"Good. I've been anxious about her. When we talk to Parker later, we can ask if she identified her attacker."

"I'd send another text, but I want to get back to Lucy. Okay with you?"

"Absolutely."

"Let's run." Kate took off. I tried, but I couldn't keep up.

When I stopped, Kate looked back. "We'll walk and run. I don't want to leave you by yourself."

I pushed myself hard. Joanna would have been proud. I was relieved to see the cabin intact.

Kate ran to the cabin and unlocked the door. When Kate insisted, a sleepy Lucy sauntered out the door and down the steps for a short walk. Spike and Palace Guard patted each other on the back.

"Are they there?" Kate asked.

"Yes. They are proud of taking good care of Lucy."

"Tell them thank you."

"They heard you. You're welcome."

I was restless. I wanted to rescue Mr. Morgan and find the bad guys. I scrubbed floors and baseboards instead. All my activity disturbed Lucy's routine, so she went out to the porch to relax in the warm sun.

"I need to split firewood," Kate said.

After the floors dried, I made ham sandwiches then Kate and I ate lunch on the porch with Lucy.

"If the chief were right, we'd go to the range this afternoon," I said.

"Have you changed your mind?" Kate said. I think she intended to say, "Have you lost your mind?"

"No. I'm just grumbling."

"Let's do a walk around the cabin to see where we'd like to set up traps."

"What kind of traps?" I envisioned deep pits with spears to impale intruders. I'd whittle the spears. Kate could dig the holes.

"Tripwire traps. Early-warning-system traps."

I didn't tell Kate about my pit idea, although it sounded like a much more exciting way to spend the afternoon.

We hiked out to the road and picked our way through the woods and brush around the cabin. We didn't see or hear anything except for our woodland birds.

"When I was a kid, I strung cans with rocks in them across paths. My version of warning traps." Kate chuckled. "One of my traps tripped Dad on his way to his equipment shed. Got in trouble for that one."

"Sounds like you trained for the FBI before you walked."

She laughed. "Can you imagine if the two of us had gone to the same school?"

"We'll have to ask Taylor if she has any future FBI or spy kids in her kindergarten class."

The cabin warmed up while we were on our walk. I opened the front and back doors to catch a breeze, and Kate opened windows. I poured two glasses of cold tea, and we sat on the porch until it was time to leave to call Parker.

Finally.

We jogged and arrived at the hill that overlooked the Smiths' farm a few minutes before call time. I wanted a farm with rolling hills and pastures where the cows headed toward their barn. I'd always lived in town, but I belonged in the country.

The west wind picked up before it shifted to a northwest wind. I shielded my eyes from the sun with my arm. "Clouds are gathering. Look at the loft. We may have a storm later."

Kate called Parker with the speaker on.

"This is public knowledge and from the press conference. Do you remember Everett Duncan, the First National Bank president who disappeared about five or six months ago?"

Kate did, but I didn't.

"The department investigated Everett Duncan's disappearance, but reports surfaced he left town with his girlfriend. The man stabbed at the library was a bank examiner, an auditor for First National Bank. His name was Bob Zephfer. Mr. Morgan and Everett Duncan are related by marriage. Everett Duncan's ex-wife was Mr. Morgan's late wife's cousin. Mr. Morgan confronted Bob Zephfer in a coffee shop three days before Zephfer was killed. After the manager threatened to call the police, Mr. Morgan left in a huff. Zephfer tried to laugh it off as a misunderstanding, but the manager said the argument was more heated than a simple argument."

"That's all they've got?" I asked. "Seems pretty flimsy to me. And what does an argument have to do with the explosion?"

"When a reporter asked the department spokesperson about the library explosion, she said the incident was still under investigation. She did say Mr. Morgan hadn't answered any questions, per his lawyer's instructions."

Kate put her index finger up to her lips.

"Sounds like that's that, then. Good to know it's solved," she said. "I'm ready for a break. When can we go to the lake?"

I raised my eyebrows. *A lake?*

"I don't know. It may be a few weeks. I'm pretty much swamped right now. I've still got two hours' worth of work to do tonight."

"We can plan later, then."

And we hung up.

"Lake?" I asked, but my tone said, "Are you nuts?"

Kate headed to the cabin, and I fell into step beside her. "Either someone was with him, or someone was eavesdropping. He'll be here in two days."

"How do you know? What did I miss?"

"You missed growing up with a sibling." Kate laughed. "When he talked about the public-knowledge stuff, he let us know someone was listening. Thanks for asking a question, so it didn't sound like he and I were talking some secret code. Which we were. The lake was a way to ask when he would be here. What was important about the two hours' work was the two. He couldn't be here in two hours. He wouldn't wait two weeks, so he'll be here in two days."

"Wow. You got all that. So that's why you told me to hush, and why you sounded so casual."

When I stopped, Kate turned to look at me. "Yep. And now we have more questions. Like, why was Bob Zephfer in the library? And what did Mr. Morgan and Zephfer argue about? Oh, and where is Everett Duncan? Who was his girlfriend and where is she?"

I shuffled to catch up to Kate because of the vines on the forest floor. "I've got more. The bank where I interviewed was the First National Bank. Now we need to know who interviewed me. Was it Mr. Duncan? Our *solved* case just opened up another pack of sticky notes."

Kate laughed. "You're right. Want to race back?" And she took off.

"Wait—I wasn't ready."

Kate beat me back to the cabin. No surprise there. She sprang into her victory dance when she saw me on the path to the cabin.

"You know I would have won if I'd left while you were still on the phone with Parker."

"Yes, but then I wouldn't have told you what he said."

"True enough." We snickered because we were downright hilarious.

While Kate pummeled and tossed pizza dough, I scribbled the new notes. The sky darkened, and a storm rolled in. Thunder boomed, lightning cracked, rain pounded on the roof and windows and roared down the gutters, and the wind howled through the trees and rattled the windows. Lucy stayed close to me.

When Kate pulled the pizza out of the oven, our electricity went off. Kate lit two oil lanterns and opened two beers to go with our pizza. While we ate, the sticky notes dropped off the wall from the humidity.

"We'll arrange them again in the morning, on the table this time. I'm too tired to think," Kate said.

"They might make more sense where they are." I stared at the scattered paper.

While I picked up the notes and put them into a basket, Kate lit a fire in the fireplace. It helped to chase the chill and dampness out of the small cabin while the storm raged on. We munched on brownies and drank a beer for dessert.

I didn't want to think about explosions, killings, assaults, banks, basements, or any other scary things. I stared at the fire. "Do you have a boyfriend?"

"Where did that come from?"

"I'm burned out. I need to talk about what normal people talk about. So do you?"

Kate gazed at the fire. "My husband Ryan was killed four years ago. He was a marine and my best friend. I know it's what everybody says, but he really was. When he died, I took a leave of absence. Uncle Reggie asked me to take over the diner for a while so he could enjoy retirement then told me I was welcome to stay at the diner as long as I liked. When Uncle Reggie died a year ago, I wasn't ready to leave the customers quite yet. Some of them have been coming to the diner almost every day for forty years. I can't tell you how many times I've sneaked cinnamon rolls into an ICU. You might say I have about thirty boyfriends."

"I'm sorry about Ryan."

Kate rose, poked at the fire, and added another log. "I know. Me too. You would have liked him. He always made me laugh, and he would have loved your sense of humor. Now, what about you?"

I shifted on the sofa and sat cross-legged. "My best friend in middle school was a boy who wanted to be a spy. We talked spy stuff and made up scenarios before school and at lunch. I loved my spy boy. But then he met a girl who wanted to be a dog trainer or maybe a bird watcher. He changed his mind from spy and wanted to be a veterinarian. Broke my heart. I felt abandoned and turned to my spy studies for solace. My goal was introvertness."

"Introvertness?" Kate raised her eyebrows.

"Of course. Introvert to the extreme. It was easy because the ratio of girls to boys in the library science classes was five to one. The boys were full of themselves—insufferable."

Kate snorted. "I can see it."

"Mother decided I needed to expand my social life so I joined the literary society. It was perfect—a whole club of introverts that discussed books online."

Kate laughed. "What about after college?"

"You know your diner customers? They all came to the library. I may have as many boyfriends as you do."

Sharing a laugh with Kate was refreshing., and even Lucy grinned; Spike smiled, and Palace Guard gave me a thumbs-up.

* * *

The next morning, I took Lucy for a slow run while Kate cooked. After breakfast, we took coffee outside before we tackled our household chores then hovered around the kitchen table with our notes.

"Let's go with the best guess." Kate rolled her shoulders.

"Sometimes your first instinct is right. Are cliches ever true?" I asked.

After a half hour of staring at our notes and moving each one from one spot to another, I stretched and touched my toes. "When the tiger yawns, run."

"Where did that come from?" Kate looked up from the table.

"I just made it up. Do you like it?"

"I can't argue the originality. Let's take Lucy outside and go for a walk."

"Good idea. I only see what we don't know."

Kate coaxed Lucy outside. Clouds hid the sun, but the humidity stuck to my skin like a spiderweb I couldn't brush away. When we were ten feet from the back door, Lucy turned to go back to the cabin.

"What's wrong, girl? You afraid we'll make you run again?" I stood with my hands on my hips. When Spike and Palace Guard copied me, I snickered.

Kate opened the back door and called Lucy inside. "Let's run, but you set the pace. Remember an overcast sky with high humidity can be deceptive. We need to build you up."

Kate turned us around on our run before I was ready. When we got back to the cabin, I made it inside and flopped onto the sofa, but I didn't collapse in exhaustion. *Joanna would approved.*

"Lunch?" I asked. "I'll make sandwiches."

We ate on the porch while the cicadas buzzed and the hawks cruised overhead.

"Kate, do you know if any libraries are outside?"

"What? Are you asking for a friend?"

I chuckled, and Kate snorted.

I rose and stretched my back. "I have a different plan of attack."

"Oh, Lord." Kate rolled her eyes.

"No, really. Instead of dissecting each note, which is what I keep doing, we talk about theories then see what fits."

Kate frowned. "Don't get it."

"So we have all these explosions. Somebody has explosives. Maybe a highway contractor. What if our highway contractor took out a big loan at the bank? And the bank president approved it. But highway man had no intentions of paying it back, so he killed the bank president, but he didn't know the bank president had embezzled funds. The disappearance of the bank president triggered an audit. What if it was highway man interviewed me? And he needs me out of the way because I saw him at the bank."

"And highway man killed the bank examiner. But why was the bank examiner at the library?"

I paced. "The bank examiner was there to see if I knew anything about the bank president."

"Let's walk. What's the tie there? I don't get it unless the bank examiner thought you were the bank president's girlfriend."

We strolled down the path through the woods and turned back.

"Hmm. What if Olivia was the bank president's girlfriend?" I stopped when we reached the cabin.

"Hang on. I'll be right back." Kate returned with two glasses of iced tea and two brownies. "Brain food." She grinned. "The bank examiner was killed because he watched Olivia, or Olivia and highway man worked together."

I munched on my brownie. "Maybe Ernie was just a homeless guy. Donnie showed up to see if I knew anything about the bank examiner or why he was killed, except Donnie asked about Ernie, which doesn't fit. Maybe I wasn't supposed to realize he was there about the bank examiner. I wanted Donnie to be the killer, but he would have stood out in the library like a stink bomb at a debutante ball."

"Stink bomb?" Kate laughed. "Whoever left the note in the men's bathroom knew about the plan for an explosion after the bank examiner was murdered."

"My turn to go inside. More tea?" I asked; Kate shook her head.

I brought out a pad and a pen. "The note writer would need to be part of the inner circle to know about the planned explosion. What if highway man was under investigation for explosives shortages and the undercover investigator wrote the note? Maybe Olivia? She knew I checked the toilet."

Kate finished off her glass of tea. "I see how difficult this would be to solve. Do you see how many agencies would be involved in the investigation?"

"We need Scotland Yard," I said.

"No kidding. Let's give it a rest. I'll put all our notes back into the basket. We need to do something else."

"One more thing. Some of our notes may be unrelated to anything."

"We have questions, a timeline, strays, holes, red herrings, and theories that don't fit. Lovely." Kate rolled her eyes.

Chapter Fifteen

I explained my pit idea.

"Me dig? And you whittle? I've got a better idea. How about if we pick wild blackberries? We'll bake a blackberry cobbler."

"I've never picked blackberries and never made a cobbler. Sounds good to me."

"Put on jeans and a long-sleeved shirt," Kate said.

I understood why after we were out in the brambles.

"It's a rule to blow on blackberries before you eat them. Then you'll blow away any spiders."

Sounded logical. I picked a blackberry, blew on it, blew a second time for good measure, and popped it into my mouth. *Wow, sweet.*

We hiked, searched, and picked. My right hand and lips were purple, and so were Kate's. I couldn't remember when I had so much fun and so many scratches. When we returned to the cabin with our blackberries, Kate insisted we take showers.

"Best way to check for ticks and wash our scratches."

I found a tick in my armpit and squealed. Kate picked it off with tweezers. I flushed the tick and waited while the water in the toilet bowl swirled and emptied.

Kate called from the kitchen. "What are you doing?"

"Waiting for the tick to emerge from the depths of the sewer."

"We don't have a sewer," Kate said. "We have a septic tank."

I wandered into the kitchen. "Can I have a flashlight to keep in the bathroom so I can check for the tick? Just in case. I discovered I have a tick phobia."

"You'll get over it, but I have a spare flashlight. Want to make fresh coffee while I shower?" Kate waved at the stove. "I'll put on a pot of chicken. Add some veggies, and we can have chicken soup with cobbler for dessert."

I set the coffeepot on the burner to perk and grabbed the peeler for the carrots and potatoes. I wished Taylor were here. She'd like to learn how to cook too. And Mr. Morgan could explain. And Mother, so I could hear her talk. *Whoa. I really am homesick.*

I cut up carrots, celery, and potatoes and tossed them into the soup pot. I found a small can of chopped green chilies and dumped them in. I added a few spices: rosemary, thyme, and a bay leaf. The coffeepot gurgled and perked. Coffee in the evening used to keep me awake, but it put me to sleep at the tiny cabin. The incredible aroma of homemade chicken soup and fresh coffee filled the air.

When Kate came to the kitchen, she mixed the ingredients for cornbread and popped the cast iron skillet into the oven. Next, Kate taught me how to make simple blackberry cobbler.

"This is easy. Why did I not know this?"

"We'll put the cobbler into the oven when the cornbread comes out."

We took our coffee out to the porch to wait for the cornbread. We convinced Lucy to come with us, and Spike and Palace Guard followed Lucy.

"Spike, you and Palace Guard hover over Lucy. Is she okay?" I asked.

Spike pointed at Kate and me at the same time. Then he drew a circle in the air with his finger and pointed to himself, Palace Guard, and Lucy.

"Kate and I can look after each other and you two will look after Lucy?"

Palace Guard signed thumbs-up.

"I followed what you said. Good to know Lucy is okay," Kate said.

* * *

We slurped our chicken soup and ate our cornbread slathered with butter.

"We have over fifty notes," Kate said. "I counted. Your yawning tiger made me think. Elephants."

"You just outdid me on the off-the-wall comments. What about elephants?"

"We've ignored the elephant in the room: Mr. Morgan. We don't have one note with his name, and he's been arrested. I'm sure he guessed you would be at the diner. Didn't you say Parker mentioned you'd be somewhere safe with someone you knew, and Mr. Morgan was right there?"

"Yes, and there's the Indian elephant story," I said. "Three blind men touched the elephant in different places. The man who touched the leg said it was a tree. The man who touched the tail said it was a rope. The man who touched the side said it was a wall. And all three argued they were right and the other two were wrong."

"One more elephant thing. How do you eat an elephant? One bite at a time. We tried to fit our entire elephant onto a tiny spoon."

"So where does that leave us?" I asked.

"In a circus, the best I can see." Kate laughed, and we laughed with her.

While I cleared the table, Kate rummaged in the freezer. "Aha! A quart of vanilla ice cream got shoved into the back. I don't know how we missed it. There's enough left for a dollop on top of our warm cobbler."

I love pie, but I'd never had a cobbler, and I'd never eaten wild blackberries.

"Warm blackberry cobbler with melting ice cream is now my favorite dessert." The hot cobbler and ice cream burned my tongue and froze the roof of my mouth.

"Me too, unless we have brownies."

* * *

"When will Parker be here?" I asked at breakfast. "Did you catch a hint?"

"He'll either be here for supper or show up hungry. Let's make my tamale casserole—it's simple and easy to warm up. We can forage for wild greens for a salad."

"A day without theories and notes sounds great."

We jumped into our morning chores. It didn't look like rain anytime soon, so we did laundry. After lunch, Kate took Lucy for a short run while I folded clothes.

"What about ticks?" I asked. "Do we have any tick-deterrent spray?" I had added ticks to my list of bugs to stress about.

"Tuck your pants into your socks and your shirt into your pants. Oh, and wear your floppy hat. It'll cover your head and the back of your neck. Go for the no-direct-path-to-your-skin look."

I felt a little goofy with my pants tucked into my socks, but being less stylish was a small price to pay to block ticks. *No Maggie skin here, ticks.*

I got an in-depth nature lesson on weeds. Kate pointed out edible and inedible plants. She sang out in delight when she spied wild asparagus. It didn't look like the fat sticks of asparagus in the grocery store. We snapped the slender, delicate stems.

"I didn't know dandelions were edible." I examine my handful of leaves.

Kate picked wild raspberries.

"Maggie, look. Poison ivy," she said. "You know leaves of three, right? Leave it be."

I was amazed at how much she knew. "Pinch these leaves." She pointed at a spindly plant.

I sniffed. "Peppermint. Mmm."

Our stroll through the woods to investigate plants was relaxing, and the number of tiny flowers surprised me.

"You have to look to see them," Kate said.

"I didn't know you were a philosopher."

Kate flipped her hair with one hand. "Oh, yes. I'm very complex."

"And don't forget immature."

I ran because Kate was after me. When we got back to the cabin, I jumped into the shower.

"No ticks!" I yelled.

While Kate showered, I took Lucy for a walk. When Lucy and I returned, Kate had browned the ground meat with garlic and onion and added all the other ingredients. I followed the recipe for the cornmeal topping, and we popped the casserole in the oven. Another easy recipe with a fabulous aroma.

"I brewed tea and steeped it with wild peppermint. Let's take our iced tea to the back porch," Kate said. Lucy flopped down in the dirt to soak up the sunshine. A mockingbird serenaded us as it ran through its repertoire of songs.

Kate rocked with her eyes closed. "Nice lazy aft—"

Lucy gave a low growl and snuffled a quiet "woof."

Kate hissed. "Take Lucy inside."

Lucy and I went into the cabin. Spike and Palace Guard slipped out the door just before I eased it shut. Lucy positioned herself near the front door. I stayed close to the back door. We listened. Lucy gave a quiet, short whine and ran to the back door.

I heard Kate step onto the back porch, and she opened the door.

"If it's Parker, he'll stop the car about halfway to the house and walk the rest of the way. He'll holler at us to let us know he's close."

We soon heard the shout. "Halloo, the cabin."

Kate was right—Parker.

Kate shouted. "We hear ya. Turning the hounds loose."

Kate opened the back door. Lucy ran around to the front and tore down the driveway.

"That girl knows her Parker," Kate said.

Parker and an excited Lucy trotted up the path. "What's for supper?"

Kate dug her elbow into my side. "Salad. Thought it would be nice to eat light and healthy."

Parker hung his head. "Oh man. I coulda stopped for an overcooked-shoe-leather burger on a dried-out bun."

We laughed.

"How about tamale casserole to go with the salad? Will it beat your burger?" Kate asked.

"You know it does. Can I have a beer?"

Parker strode to the porch. He hugged me and whispered. "Don't hurt me." He kissed me full on the mouth when I laughed. He let me go and hugged his sister. My mouth still tingled as the three of us went inside. Parker grabbed three beers. "I got beer. Want to sit on the back porch? I need fresh air."

We sipped, gazed at the clouds and birds overhead, and listened to the sounds around the cabin.

"Kate, go for a walk with me out to my car," Parker said. When they walked away, he said "Family stuff" over his shoulder.

I didn't know if I was hurt or curious. *Kate and I are family. I'm pretty sure.*

I sat on the porch floor with Lucy's head on my lap.

"You're family too, Lucy. Maybe he meant brother–sister."

I finished my beer then Lucy and I went inside. After I set the table, I washed the greens and put them on a paper towel to dry. I turned down the oven then paced until I decided I could scrub down the bathroom, but before I started, they returned with full grocery sacks.

"I stopped and got some staples. Beer, cheese, crackers, chips, and apples." Parker placed the sacks he carried on the table.

"Maggie," Kate said, "I'll pull the salad together if you put the groceries away. We'll talk after we eat."

Parker pulled out the casserole and grabbed the salad dressing. The aroma of the hot casserole's meat and spices hit my nose, and my tummy rumbled. Kate poured three glasses of iced tea.

"How do you like the tamale casserole?" Kate blew on another forkful.

"I've never eaten anything like it because Mother always said spices hurt her stomach. It does have a nice kick, but it's not too spicy for me."

"Are these wild greens? Really fresh salad," Parker said.

"We picked them today," Kate said.

I sipped my tea. "Tamale casserole and wild salad. My new favorite meal."

After we ate, Parker cleared the table, and I slipped the dishes into the hot, soapy water to soak. Kate scraped the leftover casserole into a small container.

Kate refilled our glasses with tea, and we moved to the back porch. "Kate's boss called me, Maggie." Parker sat on the top step. "He tried to get in touch with her, so I'm the messenger. He wants her to return to work to lead a team."

"Maggie, they want me to investigate the disappearance of the First National Bank president," Kate said.

"Scotland Yard." I raised my eyebrows.

"Exactly." She laughed at Parker's puzzled face. "It's a long story. And only interesting if you were there."

"You'll accept the offer, right?" I asked.

"My only hesitation is leaving you here alone. I wonder if you'd be better off in town."

Spike and Palace Guard looked quite huffy when Kate said I'd be alone. I gave Kate a look—raised eyebrows and a pointed gaze toward Lucy.

She glanced at Parker. "Well, yes, I'd leave Lucy."

I narrowed my eyes at her. She was not off the hook.

"Okay, I know you won't be here by yourself."

Spike and Palace Guard high-fived, and Lucy grinned.

Parker said, "Do I have a say?"

"No," Kate and I said in unison.

"Anyway. I agree it's a good idea to stay. In fact, what if Taylor came here too? The school put her on leave after Mr. Morgan's arrest because they said she was a risk to the students. Her folks considered sending her to stay with a relative. They discussed it with their friends and neighbors and practically broadcast the latitude and longitude coordinates. We'd divert her here if she's interested."

"No offense, but I'm not sure Maggie is ready to manage an untrained civilian." Kate frowned.

Wow—I'm trained? And not a civilian?

"What if we send Taylor to two weeks of training? She wouldn't be close to the level of Maggie, but she'd at least be more prepared to defend herself."

Wouldn't be close to my level? I'm a standard?

When I glanced at Spike, he grinned, so I stuck my tongue out at him, and Kate coughed. I knew she hid a laugh.

"Where for training?" she asked.

"Tia. The training is intense, but she's good."

"I agree on one condition—I test Taylor to see how she can handle herself."

Should I object? Kate's tough.

"Two weeks is an awfully short time." *Somebody had to say it.*

Kate raised her eyebrows. "You've forgotten how far along you were after two weeks. You threw me down before the end of the first week."

"But Taylor's little."

"So are you, honey." Parker laughed. "Kate, he'll want you there quicker than two weeks, you know."

This Parker guy's a keeper.

"Maybe we can compromise with a week or ten days if I can't get two. After one week, I can check Taylor's progress. I'll walk out to our cell-signal site and give the boss a call. Who's going with me?"

"I want to go," I said. "But one important question: do we have dessert now or after the call?"

"Let's make it after the call. Okay if we leave Lucy here?" Kate squinted at Lucy. Spike and Palace Guard moved closer to Lucy.

"Yep."

"What, have you two developed a code and left me out?" Parker asked.

"Pretty much," Kate said.

Parker pouted, and I laughed. The three of us walked to the hill. I wore a long-sleeved shirt, not so much for the ticks as the mosquitos because this was the time of night their Maggie radar was on high alert.

"Parker, I love to sit beside Maggie because the mosquitos leave me alone. She's a mosquito magnet."

"Cause she's sweet," he said.

Kate pointed her finger at her mouth and made a gagging sound.

Even though Kate set a brisk pace, I kept up with her.

"Just to let you know, I'll need to leave after dessert," Parker said. "I'm officially not here. Sergeant Arrington is covering for me until I'm back at the office. If the weather and the traffic hold, I'll be home by one tonight. I can go to work an hour or so late in the morning."

I had plans. I'd let Kate stay in my tent with my mosquitos, but then my visions of steamy bedtime scenes evaporated. "Bummer."

"I totally agree, sweetie."

While Kate was on the phone, Parker took my hand. We walked a few yards away. With a smile, he tilted my head up with his thumb and gave me a sweet, tender kiss. I met his gaze, and he leaned in. His mouth caressed my lower lip. He nibbled it, and my heart raced in anticipation. He kissed me hard, and I wrapped my arms around his neck. He pulled me closer and lifted me off the ground.

An airlifted kiss. Lip-locked in the stratosphere.

My hands explored the back of his head, ears, and neck. I memorized every bump on his head, the curve of his ears, and the feel of his hair. I wrapped my arms around him tighter. I wanted to melt into his face. His hands explored my shoulders, my back—

"Hey, ready to go?"

Kate was what's known as a buzzkill. I had been floating in a glorious dream until her voice dumped me onto a floor of ice. Thud.

Parker eased me away from him. He gazed into my eyes and gently put my feet on the ground. "What did he say?" He scrutinized my face and caressed my lips with his fingertips.

"One week. One week from today. How fast can we move Taylor?"

"I'll take care of it tomorrow." He turned toward her. "I'll call Tia and Taylor on my way home. After I talk to Taylor and explain what we have in mind, I'll call her parents. Taylor and I will discuss how much to tell them."

Kate headed toward the cabin. "Maggie, I'm not crazy about leaving you alone for a week, but we'll take advantage of the time we have left and train."

Parker took my hand, and we followed her. "More training sounds great. Parker, can we set up regular calls?"

"Might not want to do regular calls," Kate said. "You don't want a predictable schedule."

"Good point. Why not schedule the next call at the end of each call? We'll need to work around my schedule anyway."

"What about a cell phone signal booster?" I said. "I wouldn't have to leave the cabin and go to the hill to receive calls or texts."

"Honey, you're brilliant. I'll have Sergeant Arrington research it."

Honey is brilliant.

"How do you know all this stuff, Maggie?" Kate asked.

"Kate, you are so funny. I think that about you all the time."

"Hey, what about me?" Parker worked on a fake scowl.

"You're cute," I said. I tried for an innocent smile, but it came out closer to wicked.

Lucy's tail wagged at full speed when she spotted us. While Kate warmed up the cobbler, Lucy and I walked a short path. When we returned, Lucy sat, and Parker gave her the treat she earned.

"I'll bring ice cream with me next visit if you make another cobbler," Parker said.

"Deal. And pick up a cookbook for Maggie." Kate handed him a grocery list.

"Maggie, you can cook or bake whatever you want. You just need a cookbook for the measurements and ideas. So, this is our plan: Parker will pick me up, and I'll check on Taylor before I report to work. I'll leave my car here for you for transportation in case of an emergency."

Parker hugged Kate. He gave me a hug and a long, sweet kiss, but it was much too short. Then he was gone.

"You know I'm scared, right, Kate?"

"I know. I am too. We won't be by the end of the week. Let's start with a walk around the cabin and talk about vulnerabilities and maybe some strategies. You know you're strong and smart. You can take care of yourself. We've got a week to make you a leader so you can take care of yourself and keep Taylor safe. I have every confidence in you."

"Let's do this." I spoke with more conviction than I felt.

Chapter Sixteen

Kate woke me while it was still dark. "Let's run before breakfast." We ran the driveway, the washboard dirt road, and the smooth-scraped dirt road almost to the highway, and then we ran back. While Kate cooked breakfast, I tossed our dirty clothes into the washer.

After breakfast, I hung the laundry; When I leaned over to pick up the basket, Kate slammed me to the ground and put her foot on the back of my neck.

We went for another run after lunch. When Kate was a few yards ahead of me, I barreled into her and knocked her down then veered into the woods and slipped back to the cabin.

When she returned to the cabin, we sat on the back porch with cold tea. Kate saluted me with her glass. "This training is doing as much for me as it is for you. I didn't realize how soft I'd gotten."

"You, soft? Isn't that like calling my yawning tiger cuddly?"

Kate spewed her tea. It's a rare day when I can catch Kate off guard twice.

"I miss the range. I haven't practiced in ages." I drained my glass.

"Shooting is like any other skill. Proficiency levels drop off with no practice. We have enough room here. We can set up a temporary range for ourselves. I'd worry someone might hear, but it's close to hunting season. It wouldn't be unusual to hear gunshots off in the distance around here, and no one is close."

Kate set up our targets. I was rusty at first, but I was back to my old level by the second day.

"Does Taylor's training include shooting?" I asked on our break.

"It does, but did you know her dad taught her to shoot? Her dad is a hunter and all his children hunt. Taylor got her first turkey at fifteen."

I brushed my hair away from my sweaty forehead. "Impressive. Taylor never said she hunted."

"Maybe she was worried about your reaction."

"Maybe so. I remember a girl at school saying farm eggs were gross; she said she ate real eggs her mom bought at the grocery store, and I agreed. Did we believe eggs popped out of machines into egg cartons on conveyor belts in a factory, and meat came on a tray and was wrapped in plastic?" I rolled my eyes.

"Ryan grew up on a farm. He always said we'd have chickens someday. We'd look at coop designs together and talk about how to protect the chickens from predators." Kate smiled. "I'd almost forgotten about that. He'd approve of us living in the cabin and foraging for our salads."

Kate stood up and blindsided me. I was on my belly, and she sat on my back.

Dang, she's good.

I flipped her to the ground, jumped up, and ran away.

Kate lay in the dirt and laughed.

"Good one," she called.

I was good at running away until Kate threw in a twist on the third day after I ambushed her and ran away.

"Bang!" she shouted. "I just shot you in the back. You're dead. Your next lesson is to make sure your attacker is incapacitated or at least stunned before you run. Lunch first."

"You have to make lunch. I'm dead." I zombie-walked to the cabin.

* * *

"Since I don't want you to leave me dead or incapacitated, we'll walk through some scenarios." Kate bit into her sandwich.

We devoted the afternoon to attackers—attacker with a knife, a gun, a stick, or a bat; attacker with unknown weapons or multiple weapons; multiple attackers; crazed attackers, either psychotic or on drugs.

"I don't want to train you to pull back a punch because we tend to perform under stress the way we trained. Instead, I want to train your brain and muscles to react to the conditions. Make sense?"

We trained the rest of the day with me and an imaginary attacker. I was in the middle of a scenario when Spike stepped in. At first, I was startled, but I followed through with a punch to his throat, and when he went down, I ran.

"Good work, Maggie." Kate toasted with her iced tea from the porch. "It looked realistic, just like you knocked an attacker down, then ran. You threw a throat punch, right?"

Spike sat on the ground and grinned, and I did too.

"Oh Lord, don't tell me. You punched Spike."

I applauded, and Spike jumped up and bowed.

"You and I don't need to practice this anymore. If Spike wants to continue your training, that's up to you. Or the two of you. Or three. Whatever."

She stomped into the cabin. I wasn't sure if she was angry, confused, or proud. I didn't go in right away to find out.

Kate replaced my attacker training with splitting wood and carrying it to the woodshed.

"Splitting wood is hard." I wiped my face on my shirtsleeve.

"People pay an outrageous amount of money at gyms to do what you're doing. This is the fastest way to build up your strength."

I leaned on the ax handle. "I hope so because this is tough."

Not sure if we're training or she's getting even. I didn't ask. I grabbed another log to split.

* * *

At dusk on the last evening before Parker was scheduled to pick up Kate, we relaxed on the back porch. The sky darkened, and shadows moved in. The tree frogs ratcheted up into quite a racket.

"Think it might rain tonight? The tree frogs sound like it will," I said.

"Possibility. They are carrying on, aren't they?"

"I like this light breeze. No mosquitos."

Kate pointed at a barred owl swooping down into a clearing and then back into the trees. We listened to its signature hoo-hoot call.

"It's been an intense week." I placed my arms behind me for support and leaned back. "I ache all over and feel stronger and more confident, all at the same time."

"Good," Kate said. "If you didn't ache, then we slacked off."

I glared. "We?"

Kate cackled.

We sipped our wine and munched brownies in silence. Lucy picked up her head and sniffed. I looked in the direction of her twitching nose and nudged Kate. Lucy had spotted a beautiful doe only a few yards away. The doe stood still as she watched us until she flicked her ears, flipped her tail, and leapt into the woods.

We relaxed until the breeze died down and the buzzes and bites broke my mood to soak in nature. "We have to go in now. Mosquitos are feasting."

"Best send-off party ever," Kate said. "I love the woods."

I swatted while I ran inside. "Absolutely amazing."

I woke up in the middle of the night to the rhythm of soft rain. I smiled. *Thank you, tree frogs.*

* * *

The next morning, we were up before dawn for our run, as usual. After I cleared our breakfast dishes, Lucy clicked to the front door and whined.

"Halloo, the cabin."

"Parker's smart. Here in time for breakfast," Kate said.

I almost knocked him down when I ran out and jumped up to hug him.

"Got the cell signal booster for you, sweetie, and there are groceries in my car."

I walked with him to help carry groceries into the cabin. He brought in a flat of mixed perennial flowers. "Thought you might like these to plant for the butterflies."

"They're beautiful. Thank you." I kissed his cheek. "I'll set up the signal booster, and we can test it after you have breakfast."

While Parker ate his eggs, bacon, and cinnamon roll, Kate packed. I slumped on my bed in a cloud of gloom.

"I've been alone since . . ." Kate cleared her throat. "A long time. It was hard at first, but then being alone was like an old friend. My hardest adjustment was the sounds—noises I didn't recognize or sounded scary. I realized if Lucy wasn't spooked, then I shouldn't be either. Check with Lucy before you're too spooked and keep your pistol on your hip."

"Thanks for everything." My heart said *Don't go*.

Parker called Sergeant Arrington to test the signal booster. After he talked to him for a few minutes, he said, "Good connection."

"Tell Sergeant Arrington well done," I said.

Parker grinned. "Sarge says thanks and call your mother."

Kate announced, "Time to leave."

When I cried, Kate hugged me, and Parker gave me a sweet kiss followed by another kiss that made my toes curl. Palace Guard, Spike, Lucy, and I stood on the front porch and waved while the two of them walked down the path to Parker's car.

I remained on the front porch until I couldn't hear the car anymore. When I went inside, the cabin was eerie without Kate. I washed dishes, stripped beds, started laundry, and planted the flowers.

"You know I keep thinking Kate will ambush me at any minute," I said.

Spike danced around me and jabbed the air.

While the laundry dried, I ran and left Lucy and her companions in charge of the cabin. When I got back, it still wasn't time for lunch.

Gonna be a long week.

At bedtime, I worried I'd have trouble sleeping. I wasn't sure if my sense of peace was from the fresh air or Lucy's comforting snores or both, but I slept through the night.

The next morning, Lucy and I went for a walk and a short run before breakfast. After breakfast, I split wood. When I came inside, Spike waved his hand in front of his face and held his nose. *Subtle.* I showered.

After lunch, I took Sergeant Arrington's advice and called Mother. She must have been coached not to ask me where I was. Our call seemed a little strange until I realized she wasn't yelling. I listened to her in awe because I had never heard her speak in a normal tone before. Mother's voice was a pleasant lilt with a soft drawl.

Who knew?

Most of her conversation was "my Duane this" and "my Duane that." I figured out Sergeant Arrington was her "Duane." I loved the joy in her voice. I almost told her I missed her, but I didn't want to scare her.

Lucy supervised me while I cleaned the cabin. "Let's go for a walk, girl. We can look for dandelion leaves for a salad."

When we returned, I flipped through my new cookbook and found an intriguing recipe, chicken pasta with lemon and artichokes. Kate and I had laughed when we found the jar of artichokes in the almost empty cupboard. I meant to adjust the recipe to a single serving, but when I plated my food, I realized I had plenty of food for another meal. I found my niche. *Chef of leftovers.* Spike and Palace Guard laughed with me.

I was almost ready for bed when I got a text from Kate. "Saw T. Doing great." I didn't reply. We agreed to keep calls and texts to a minimum. I was surprised at how much I wanted to text back. At least "thnx," or maybe "come back," but I resisted.

* * *

I set a single place for breakfast, but I didn't eat alone because Spike and Palace Guard sat with me. I washed my few dishes and placed them in the drying rack. "Spike, could we train on incapacitating like Kate suggested?"

He nodded. Palace Guard pointed to himself.

"Thanks, Palace Guard."

We developed a system of sorts to keep score. When I hit the mark, they went down and stayed down while I ran away. They taught Lucy to bark when they pointed at her. Lucy's bark was my signal I'd been shot. The rule was I continued to run when she barked because maybe they missed, but I lost points for being shot. Spike kept score.

"Spike, you cheated. I quit!" I fumed and stomped off. Palace Guard waited for me at the porch and grinned.

"You're right. I should have known he'd cheat. He's taught me to fight dirty. You keep score. And referee."

Spike stood next to me, and he hung his head.

"Okay, you're sorry. But you still need to teach me to be tough." We high-fived.

My imaginary Palace Guard had to break up only one fight between me and Spike, my cheating imaginary trainer. It didn't take me long to learn to fight like a street thug to keep from losing points. Palace Guard called for a midmorning break before I overheated from exertion.

I sat on the back porch and drank cool, delicious water. I held my hair up off my neck and let the light breeze from the northwest cool and dry my hot, sweaty skin. The unexpected crackle of car tires grinding into the rutted dirt road startled us, and Lucy growled. Quiet and low.

We slipped into the cabin. I put my cell phone on vibrate and left the three of them inside. I crept out the back door and settled down in the blind Kate and I had built. I listened to the growl of a car's engine as a vehicle crawled past the driveway. After it was gone, the grasshoppers chirped. When the vehicle returned, the grasshoppers hushed and the light breeze stilled. The crunch of tires broke the silence. My ears strained to hear engine noise after the car sped away. I sat in the blind for two more hours before I retreated to the cabin. I took Lucy out and stayed with her while she took her doggie break.

Later in the afternoon, Lucy and I went for a quiet perimeter walk. Kate's nature and plant lessons also taught me to be aware of anything unusual. The only disturbances I found were signs of deer.

The cabin needs to look like no one's here.

I put away tools, closed the woodshed door, and rolled up the water hose. I left the empty clothesline up but took down the small basket of clothespins I'd hung on a tree branch. I folded up the porch chairs and put them in the storage bin.

My companions and I inspected the cabin perimeter.

"What do you think? Looks unoccupied? I'll figure out how to manage after dark."

I spotted a yellow piece of paper under the sofa and pulled out a sticky note marked BFF3.

Can't be Taylor or Mr. Morgan. They are BFF1 and BFF2. Lillian? Ernie? Olivia? A library volunteer? Whoever wrote the note was my BFF3.

"BFF3 knew about BFF1 and BFF2; otherwise, she or he would be just plain BFF, right?" I slammed my hand on the table. "I can do these circles all day. Olivia, right?" Palace Guard raised his eyebrows. *Maybe Olivia.*

I tossed BFF3 into the basket with the rest.

"I need to clear my head. Watch Lucy while I go for a run?"

Palace Guard frowned. Spike shook his head.

"Okay, fine. Then one of you run with me."

By the time I laced my shoes and looked up, Palace Guard was poised next to me. He wore running shoes, shorts, and a blue shirt. His shirt said "CHELSEA F.C." *I'd heard about Chelsea soccer* . . . "Oh—you Brits. Football Club."

Palace Guard grinned. He was off duty or on duty incognito.

We took off. He was fast, and I pushed to keep up with him. We ran to the cell phone hill.

"Break," I called as I leaned against a tree.

Palace Guard grinned, and I hated him. After I wheeled around and ran back to the cabin, he passed me. Yep, I definitely hated him.

When I got back to the cabin, Palace Guard waited for me on the back porch in his guard uniform.

"No fair!" I yelled. His hair even looked wet, like he had just taken a shower. Palace Guard and Spike laughed.

"It's easy when you're imaginary." I huffed, stormed into the cabin, and slammed the door.

That evening, I sat at the table with my plate of warmed-up leftovers and cold tea. My arm didn't have the strength to pick up a fork, but when my stomach took over, I dug in.

A sour odor threatened to ruin my appetite while I ate. I realized the reek was the most overwhelming when I lifted my arm to put my fork in my mouth.

Embarrassing to be offended by my own armpits.

"I stink," I said while I ate. In the first place, I didn't realize I'd said it out loud, and second, I don't know why the two men thought it was so hilarious. "You know, I'm supposed to learn how to be alone. How to go all zen or something. You two are . . . are . . ."

What are they? Imaginary men? My best friends after Taylor and Mr. Morgan?

"Infuriating. And my very best imaginary friends."

Shower, then bed.

* * *

The next four days were the same: fight to the death with Spike, do my chores, relax during the heat of the day, get my butt run off by Palace Guard, eat, shower, collapse. Every day I died fewer times and took fewer breaks than the day before.

The fifth day, I smiled while I ate breakfast. *Only two more days until Taylor Day.*

"What else do I need to work on?"

Spike pointed his finger like a gun and pulled the trigger. Palace Guard slashed with his hand.

"I'm afraid to shoot because of the noise, but I need tactical training. And I haven't done any knife work at all. Can we work on both?"

The morning knife training went slow. Palace Guard would make some offensive moves, and I'd copy him. Spike critiqued and motioned. "Again."

After lunch, the training shifted to defense. Palace Guard was offense; Spike, defense. I tried to copy Spike. I was lousy at first, but when I gained confidence, I improved much faster than I expected.

I took a break in the shade with a big glass of water. "I didn't realize how afraid I was of the knife. This training booted knife fear out of my life."

I leaned against the tree until Palace Guard appeared with his CHELSEA F.C. shirt and bounced on his toes. I hurried inside and changed my shoes before I ran out the front door and down the path to the hill.

I swear my Brit said, *"Cor."*

I ran as hard as I could—I ran like a cheetah chased me. I ran like a Palace Guard was after me and reached the hill first. When I turned around, Palace Guard barreled down the path with the obvious intent to knock me off my feet. I used my new evasive skills and took off for the cabin. He trampled grass and leaves behind me, but I knew if I looked, I'd slow down. I just ran. *Lucy's bang bark.* I ran the zigzag pattern Spike taught me. I ran into the woods but maintained my forward progress. I jumped over logs and crashed through bushes. This wasn't a quiet run. This was a *save my life* run.

I slowed down when I got near the cabin and put myself into stealth mode. I stopped before I ran into the clearing to see if I was safe to continue. Spike stood on the path with his back to me while Palace Guard ran toward the cabin. I ran faster than I ever had before and slammed into Spike's back. I rolled over to my feet, and my jaw dropped: Spike had gone down. Palace Guard congratulated me with a salute.

"You two are awesome trainers."

They beamed. I bent over and put my hands on my knees. My other option was to collapse.

"Let's take a celebratory jog down the driveway path and back." Palace Guard and I headed out. On the way to the road, I spotted some wild raspberries and a good patch of what looked like purslane. *I'll have to come back and check it out.*

On our way back, Palace Guard stopped. I listened to the crunch of tires. A car on the road headed toward us. *Again?* We took off for the cabin.

When we got to the cabin, I eased the door shut behind me. I sat down on the floor beside Lucy and hugged my knees. After my heart rate slowed, I stepped outside to listen. Palace Guard went with me, and Spike stayed with Lucy.

I slipped to my blind and crouched down. Palace Guard walked around the side of the cabin toward the front. *He's going to walk to the road.*

The sound of the car engine became louder, but it didn't have a signature sputter or cough.

Gasoline engine. Not diesel. Or at least, not a typical noisy diesel. Oh fine. Then, not a motorcycle. Whatever. I'm a lousy spy.

I sat in my blind, listened, and pouted.

I listened to the car engine until I couldn't hear it anymore. I listened to the silence. I realized no birds were singing.

It's going to rain.

Rain would be good. After a while, the car returned, and it headed toward the road to the highway. It sounded like the vehicle traveled at a dangerous rate of speed for the condition of the dirt road.

Do you suppose Palace Guard scared them?

The vision of the tall, stately guard in his Chelsea Football Club gear made me smile. I waited for Palace Guard to return. When he appeared, I pulled myself up then the two of us walked to the cabin.

I ate a sandwich before it got dark. No lights after dark except in the bathroom with the door closed. While I ate, I debated whether I should text Parker.

And if I did, what would I text? "Car x2, signed Scaredy Cat."

Nope, not going there.

Shower, then bed. I stayed awake and listened. Rain. It turned to a hard, driving rain with thunder and lightning.

Bad guys are too delicate to be out in this storm. I fell asleep wrapped in the comfort of the crashing thunder, howling wind, and pelting sheets of rain.

* * *

I jumped out of bed the next morning. *It's Taylor Day.*

While the coffee pot sang its perking song, Lucy and I went outside to look around. We found tree limbs down but no damage to the cabin or any of the sheds. A large branch, more massive than I could drag, lay across the driveway path about twenty yards from the cabin's clearing.

"Should I grab the saw and ax? Maybe it's better to leave it there. It sure makes the driveway look like a dead end. Don't you agree, Lucy?" Lucy grinned, and I scratched her ears.

We explored the woods, and I found a way to get out Kate's car. I'd have to take down two small trees, but it would be easy.

When Lucy and I returned to the cabin, I had a text from Kate.

"T not coming. U b ok?" I sat down in shock.

"No, I will not be okay!" I screamed at the phone.

Spike, Palace Guard, and Lucy crowded around me. Spike and Palace Guard looked at my phone. Spike scowled, and Palace Guard patted my shoulder. I was somehow comforted. "I wanted to see Taylor. You're right. I'll be okay."

"Yes," I texted back. Right after breakfast, I got another text.

Yay. From Parker.

"C u 9 pm meet at road & driveway need supplies?"

"Usual + oatmeal apples blueberries buttermilk."

Spike and Palace Guard read over my shoulder.

"I want to make buttermilk pancakes from scratch, and blueberry pancakes are my favorite."

Parker will be here tonight!

I did a fast cabin cleanup, and then the four of us went outside for more training. Spike and I worked on my knife skills until he pointed at Lucy to do the gunshot bark, and she did.

"Dammit, Spike. That's cheating." I was ready to call it quits.

Spike grinned and winked. I fell to the ground. *Dead is dead. Obviously my motto.* When I opened one eye and looked up, Spike and Palace Guard laughed.

"Okay, so the scenario is I go to a gunfight with a knife. So what do I do?"

Spike and Palace Guard walked through several scenarios.

"The idea is, then, I always assume the other guy has a gun."

They walked through a few more scenarios. I realized tall, muscular Palace Guard played the role of me. I wanted to ask him if I was as prissy as he was, but I was afraid he'd be offended.

"It seems my best defense is to go on offense, but it would have to be quick. Element of surprise, right?"

Spike leaned down, picked up the knife, and threw it at a tree five yards away.

"Can you teach me?" We spent most of the morning searching for my knife. Time after time, I threw it everywhere except into a tree.

I picked up my knife and scolded it. "Tree. Any tree."

Then it clicked. My arm and wrist got the message to slow down and take control of the knife and to develop the feel for when to turn it loose. It was like when I learned to ride a bicycle.

The knife and I are one, and the world is mine. I did a dance I called *Knife Dance.*

I was in the middle of my lunch when my phone rang. The sudden sound startled me. *Kate.*

"This has to be quick. I'm picking you up this afternoon. Empty the fridge. Pack all your things. I'll be there as soon as I can. I'll text you when I'm about twenty minutes away. Ignore all texts or calls until then. Remember, ignore. Clear?"

"Clear."

After she hung up, Spike and Palace Guard frowned.

"I don't know what this is all about either, but she's our team leader."

I went into the woods and dug a hole and buried the few perishables. I saved the carton of ice cream Parker brought for my afternoon snack. I showered and then started a small load of laundry.

When I threw the towel into the washing machine, Spike laughed. He raised his hands in the air and did his victory dance.

"Ha ha. I threw in the towel, but it's a washing machine. It doesn't mean you win."

He continued to dance and wave his arms.

"Okay. You win." I glowered.

Palace Guard shook his head.

By early afternoon, I had packed for the trip. I grabbed a spoon and the carton of chocolate ice cream for my break, relaxed on the back porch, and listened to the birds. *I'm going to miss the cabin.*

After I washed my spoon and put it away, I swept the cabin and cleaned the bathroom and kitchen sinks. I gathered trash and stuck the sack into my backpack to carry away with me.

When my phone rang, I shook my head. "Kate said ignore."

Parker.

"I hate this." I walked away from the phone, holding my hands over my ears. I checked later. No message.

Chapter Seventeen

When I got the "20 min out" text from Kate, I slung my backpack over my shoulder and carried my bags down the driveway. The few clouds that drifted in from the west and a light breeze brought relief from the usual heat and humidity. The song of the cardinals, "Pretty, pretty, pretty," promised no rain. Lucy and I reached the fallen tree limb as Kate drove up in a black SUV. Her face was grim. When she rolled down her window and frowned at the log, I said, "Storm."

She pressed a button, and the back hatch opened. I tossed my bags into the back, and we all climbed into the vehicle; she was still silent. I raised my eyebrows when she reached the end of the driveway and glanced to the right, but she ignored me as she turned her head to the left. Kate pulled onto the road and accelerated. Her eyes were narrowed, her mouth was set, and she had a tight grip on the steering wheel. When I glanced at the backseat occupants, Spike and Palace Guard looked as concerned as I felt. After a half hour of silence, Kate pulled into a roadside park.

"Maggie, I have terrible news. I need to get out of the car. Let's sit at the picnic table."

I didn't know what Kate was about to say, but I knew I didn't want to hear it. She grabbed two bottles of water and strode to a splintered picnic table in the shade. Kate faced the road as she sat on the table. She had tears in her eyes and anguish on her face. She handed me a bottle and sipped on hers. "I don't know how to say this."

Then don't say it. Don't. I closed my eyes and sat on the bench across from Kate.

She cleared her throat. "There's no way to soften this. Parker is dead."

I examined her face and waited for her to correct herself. I shook my head.

You're wrong, Kate.

She looked away then stared at her hands. "He was ambushed at his apartment parking lot early this morning. A group of kids at a school bus stop were close to him when the shooting started. Two of the kids were hit, but they'll be okay. He killed the three men who ambushed him, but he was shot multiple times and died from his wounds on the scene. One kid reported a fourth man, but all the other witnesses who took cover or ran to help the kids described only three. The kid said he was close to Parker when this fourth man—an old man with a hurt arm is how the kid described him—walked up to where Parker lay wounded, shot him in the head, took his wallet and phone, and walked away. Parker's phone and wallet are missing."

My world shifted to slow motion. Sounds were muffled. A weight grew in my chest and crushed my heart and my soul. I was overwhelmed by waves of nausea and slumped on the bench seat.

I didn't get to say goodbye. If only I'd texted him last night. He should have been at the cabin. How can Kate be so calm? He's her brother.

I looked at Kate through a wall of tears. She had turned her back to me. Her shoulders shook as she sobbed. We sat at the picnic table for a long time, drowning in grief. We mourned the loss of a warrior with all the fierceness of ages past before language existed. After a time, the tears dried up, and there was nothing left except emptiness. *No Parker.*

I handed her my cell phone. "I got a text this morning. Then a phone call after you said you'd pick me up. I didn't answer the call."

Kate looked at the text from Parker's phone. "Damn," she said under her breath. "Let's get out of here."

After we were back on the road, Kate glanced at me. "I'll catch you up. First, the investigators dropped the charges against Mr. Morgan. Second, the coroner identified the guy with Olivia. He worked in construction and was very deep in debt. They found his car with a timer and a primer in the trunk not far from the library. He took out a huge insurance policy on himself a few days before the explosion. Of course, the insurance company claims suicide. Parker and I are—were—convinced you were the target. This is too hard." She tried to clear her throat.

"It's pretty clear Olivia pulled the fire alarm to evacuate the building. We suspect she fought with him, and he set off the explosion. He had ties with different construction companies. All the companies we checked reported small amounts of explosives missing after they completed a physical inventory."

"Do they know his name? Who was the beneficiary of his insurance policy?" I asked.

Kate looked at me with an expression I didn't understand. "I should have thought about that. I'll get the information for us."

"It's back to the elephant. I don't want to miss anything."

I looked out my side window. *Parker should be here.*

"Investigators found the bank president's decomposed body on his boat. His wallet contained quite a bit of cash, so we know the motive wasn't robbery. It looked like somebody tried to make his boat sink, but either they didn't know how or didn't have enough time. The interesting part is his girlfriend was Olivia."

"What?" I rubbed my forehead. *Too much to process.*

"Your mother kept your apartment rent up-to-date, but you're welcome to stay with me," Kate continued. "Taylor moved home with her parents, but Mr. Morgan is still there."

"I've been spoiled; I couldn't live in an apartment. I need a place with a little land around it."

"I understand." Kate's smile was weak, but it was the first one I'd seen all day.

I tried to smile too. "I know this is a lot to ask, but I'd like for Lucy to stay with me. She's used to her outside time and a little space, and we'd be good company for each other. Of course, she'd still be your dog."

Kate's voice was thick. "Lucy has never been an apartment dog. I hadn't thought about it before, but she'd hate apartment life. It makes sense for her to be where she has a little freedom, and she can guard you."

I looked away. "How about if we all go to your apartment for today, and I'll start house hunting tomorrow. What about my car? Is it still at my apartment?"

"Your car was impounded for evidence. I'm not sure when you can get it back. You may have to lease for a while."

"I need a car, and Mother can help me find a place to live. She has contacts."

I called Mother.

"My Duane told me about Parker," she said. "He's devastated with grief. He said the whole department is. He told me you and Parker were good friends."

She talked for thirty minutes about Taylor, Mr. Morgan, her Duane, and a dozen people I didn't know before I interrupted her.

"Mother, I need a small house outside of town with a little land around it. Not too expensive, but not too rundown. Oh, and dogs allowed."

She hung up. She was on it.

"Could we go car shopping after we get to town? I should have asked her to find me a car too. I'll bet she'd have one in the parking lot when we got to your apartment."

Our forced smiles were betrayed by escaping tears. When I glanced at the back, Spike and Palace Guard nodded in sympathy.

"I have a strange question." Kate brushed at the dampness on her face. "If Lucy stayed with me, and you had your own place, where would Spike and Palace Guard stay?"

I looked in the back seat. Spike's face was red with anger. Palace Guard had the darkest scowl I'd ever seen.

"Whoa. Tough call."

"Thought so. Another question, what can I do for you?"

I opened my mouth to say "nothing," then glanced at Spike. He held up his hand and made shooting motions.

"I need range practice. If you have any time on your days off, would you go with me?"

"Spike's recommendation, right?" The tightness in her face eased.

As we pulled into Kate's apartment parking lot, my phone rang.

"Margaret, my friend Harriet has three places lined up for you to see in the morning," Mother said. "Franklin and I can pick you up and take you to Harriet's office. We'll have to follow Harriet because she's allergic to cats. Franklin is insulted—"

"Mother, Kate and I are car shopping this afternoon, so I'll have a car."

"You need to go where they'll treat you right. I'll text you several places to buy a good used car." She hung up.

Two minutes later I got a text with the names, addresses, phone numbers, and best contact name for three car dealers. I showed my phone to Kate.

"Let's go here first." She pointed to the second dealer.

Kate took Lucy for a walk while I took my bags into her apartment. Kate and I grabbed sandwiches on our way to buy a car.

"An SUV would be a little more expensive, but there would be enough room for Lucy and the two imaginary men. Right?" I said.

Kate shook her head. "Who knew imaginary men were a factor in buying a car?"

I was relieved Kate agreed Lucy should stay with me. I couldn't bear to part with Lucy, but it hurt to be around Kate. *I need time to deal with my grief.*

I realized Kate needed private time to mourn her brother. A tear slipped down my face. It had escaped and overflowed on its own. I brushed it away. *Toughen up, Buttercup. There'll be plenty of time for tears later.*

Mother called again. "I've looked up safety and repair ratings for cars and have a short list for you to consider. Kate with you? I'll text you the list."

She hung up, and a few seconds later I had the list. We parked and approached the dealership showroom.

A heavy-set, sweating salesman in a bright-blue sports jacket opened the door for us.

"This is what I want." I showed him my list.

"What you girls want is over there." He waved in the direction of a row of cars on their side lot.

I cringed at his choice of words.

"Okay, sonny." Kate dismissed him with a growl.

He disappeared into the dealership, and a short, middle-aged woman waddled to join us at the row of SUVs.

"I'm Roxie, the sales manager." We shook hands. "Your mother said you'd come here. Can I see your list?"

She led us to the middle of the row. "We've got two like you want. Your choice. They're alike except for the color. Silver or traditional blue."

"Traditional blue."

Kate raised her eyebrows, and I snickered. "You thought gray, didn't you? PG would like the blue."

"Let's get you inside and get the paperwork going," Roxie said.

After I read and signed all the forms, Kate and I sat in the customer waiting area. She scrolled through her phone, and I flipped through magazines. After a half hour, I realized she didn't need to stay.

"Kate, if you want to go home and let Lucy out, I'm okay. There's no reason for you to wait for paperwork."

Kate put her phone down. "Sure?"

"I'm sure Lucy is more than ready to go for a long walk."

I was more relaxed after Kate left. *I'm glad I realized how much Kate needed her space too.*

After an hour, Roxie came into the waiting room. "Paperwork's done. I apologize for your long wait. I'd tell you our system was down, but the truth is, our system is antiquated. Here are your keys. Your car has been washed and is right out there. Let me know if there's anything I can do for you." She pointed to the side door and handed me a packet of papers with her business card stapled to the front and my keys.

I adjusted the seat, mirrors, and radio and fiddled with the lights and the windshield wipers. I loved the new-car smell. *I wonder where they get the spray for their used cars.*

I sent Kate a text to let her know I was good to go and drove to Kate's apartment in my new-smelling traditional-blue SUV.

Kate poured two glasses of wine and set cheese and crackers on the table for us. We munched and drank in silence. My glass of wine must have had sandman sprinkles in it because I was tired almost to the point of complete exhaustion. Kate had made up her sofa bed.

"I'm shorter than you are," I said. "It's fine for me, and it makes no sense for you not to sleep in your own bed."

Discussion closed. Both of us were too beat to argue.

* * *

I woke up early. *I miss Parker.* I shook off the melancholy and started a pot of coffee before I took Lucy for a walk. When we returned to the apartment, Kate was in the shower. I folded the sheets and closed up the sofa bed. I had high hopes that it was only an overnight stay. While I showered, Kate cooked breakfast.

"I have a few things to wrap up, and I have to meet with my dad. Here's my spare key." Kate hugged Lucy and left.

I called Ella. "It's Maggie. My boyfriend died."

We talked for a long time.

* * *

Lucy and the imaginary men climbed into my new-smell car to go to the realtor's office.

"If Lucy doesn't like a place, we walk away, right?"

My smile was weak as Palace Guard and Spike shook hands.

When we pulled into the realtor's office, Harriet jumped into the front seat and gave me her business card. Her black pencil skirt rose up to midthigh when she sat. I worried her stiletto heels might cut into my floormat, but she kicked off her shoes after she got in, and her brown eyes twinkled as she smiled.

Harriet was in her mid-forties and had brown highlighted hair and flawless makeup and nails. The neckline of her sleeveless white blouse plunged like it belonged on an evening gown or bathing suit. She had a bright red, patent leather purse slung over her shoulder and carried a clipboard and a file folder with a printed SLOAN label.

She tugged at her skirt and pulled up the bodice of her shirt. "This is a sweetheart neckline. It's supposed to be the latest fashion, but I'm not convinced it has the professional-realtor look. I have it on my *donate* list."

I like Harriet.

"What do you think?" Harriet asked when I pulled into the driveway of the first house.

I rolled down my window. "I like the look of the white cottage with the roses across the front, but I'd worry about Lucy with no fence, and the house is too close to the road. I don't need to look inside."

"We'll just put this on our *Maybe* list," Harriet said.

Harriet directed me down a dirt road to the second house, a small pale-blue cottage with gray trim. We pulled through an open gate.

"The chain-link fence goes all the way around the house. The overall property includes the field surrounded with the three-rail fence." Harriet got out of the car and left her folder on her seat. "This little gem was a guest house and was built in the 1930s, but the plumbing and wiring were updated five years ago. Let's go in for a tour."

"Wood-burning fireplace. I like it. This is more of a great room, isn't it?"

"Open-living concept." Harriet laughed. "Before its time. Two bedrooms down the hall. The one on the right is a guest bedroom. The larger bedroom straight ahead has a small bathroom with a shower. The larger bathroom is on your left."

I peeked in the larger bathroom. "Stacked washer and dryer in here. Does it stay?"

"Sure does. No garage, of course, but the driveway has plenty of room for parking close to the house." Harriet opened the back door.

"A back porch. I love it." I walked out onto the porch and soaked up the country air and aromas. The grasses undulated with the light breeze out of the north. I caught the aroma of hay and fresh manure, and the horses on the farm to the north whinnied. Lucy stepped off the porch and lifted her head to sniff the air.

"Well? *Strong* list? I think Lucy likes it," Harriet said.

"I think you're right."

"I have one more for us to see. The third house is closer to town if that's a consideration."

I pulled into the driveway of the third house and parked in front of a single-car garage. The redbrick ranch-style home was close to the county road but not as close as the first one.

"Now this one has a living room with a wood-burning fireplace, a small eat-in kitchen, three bedrooms, and one bathroom. There's also a full-sized washer and dryer in the garage. Let's check this one out."

We toured the house. No back porch.

"A garage is nice. We'll put it on the *Contender* list," Harriet said.

I got the impression if we looked at six houses, we'd have six lists. I considered asking to see more to check out my theory.

"Let's talk monthly rent," Harriet said on our way to her office. "We looked at them in the order of cost, with the first one being the lowest and the last one the highest. All of them are available for immediate occupancy."

I glanced back at Spike and Palace Guard, who waved two fingers. My choice too, and Lucy liked the smells. No contest. *Strong* wins.

"The blue cottage," I said.

"Won't take long for the paperwork. I can get you the key by lunchtime."

Harriet called Mother, and I took Lucy for a walk. When we returned, Harriet caught me up on their conversation. "Your mom arranged for movers to pick up your furniture at your apartment this afternoon. She'll meet them there to supervise. She sounded excited to have a chance to help you. She said her good friend suggested a home security system. I agree."

I chuckled at the pent-up mother hen energy. "Mother is a force."

After Harriet and I finished the paperwork, I wrote the check for the first and last month's rent and the security deposit.

"I didn't want to sway your opinion, but I'm excited you chose the blue cottage because I own it, and I'd love to have you as my tenant. Here are your keys—I changed locks after the last tenant moved out. Your mother and her gentleman friend will pick out your home security system, and I'll have it installed. I'll call you."

I sent Kate a text with the address and invited her to come by after work. Lucy, the imaginary men, and I packed a few boxes at my apartment, picked up my clothes from Kate's apartment, and shopped for groceries, cleaning supplies, paper products, tools, wine, and two rocking chairs for the porch.

After the movers left the house, I made my bed, assembled the rocking chairs, sent Mother a thank-you text, and chopped vegetables for a salad.

Lucy yipped when Kate drove up. After Kate climbed out of her car and trod to the porch, her shoulders slumped. She had dark circles under her eyes.

"You look exhausted," she said.

I raised my eyebrows. *Takes one to know one.*

"Come in for a tour then we can eat."

After we ate, we carried our wine to the porch.

"Maggie, my dad asked if you'd sit with us." Kate choked on the words and cleared her throat. "Sit with the family at Parker's service."

The tears got away from me. *Parker's family is so gracious. They were supposed to be . . . I don't know what.*

Kate had tears in her eyes too.

I took in a big breath and blew it out slowly. "Thanks."

Kate set down her wine glass. "I need to try to get some rest."

After Kate left, I texted my new address to Mr. Morgan and to Taylor. My imaginary men and I sat on the porch while the clouds raced by. After Lucy wandered around the yard and checked the smells, she padded up the steps and flopped at my feet. I listened to the tree frogs and cicadas sing their evening rain song.

After the sky changed from blue to pink to the orange-red of dusk, the sun dipped into the horizon. When the onslaught of mosquitos chased us inside, I put away clothes and unpacked the kitchen boxes.

The rest of the week was a blur. Mother helped me shop for clothes to wear to Parker's service, and we found a dress in Parker's favorite color, a soft sage green.

Taylor called. "Maggie, I can't come to Parker's service. I'm in Pennsylvania, and my parents don't want me to return to town quite yet." She burst into tears, and we sobbed together on the phone.

Mother made an appointment for a haircut and color and met me at the hair salon. I was grateful she and her hairdresser held their own conversation because the normalness of social chatter was beyond what I could manage.

"I am thrilled with your hair." Mother beamed when the hairdresser spun me around to look. I shuddered when I looked in the mirror.

"I didn't take much off the length, and you'll get used to the color. The shades of brown and dark blond give your hair depth." The hairdresser patted my shoulder, and when I rose, she hugged me. "I am so sorry for you loss, Maggie." Tears slipped down her cheek, and I hurried outside to wait for Mother; otherwise, I would have broken down.

When I got home, the home-security system with alarms on the windows and doors had been installed. I was surprised the system included cameras around the house and at the gate. *Kind of slick.*

Parker's funeral service didn't give me closure, but it was a milestone.

After Parker's funeral.

After Parker's funeral, my imaginary men and I double-downed on my training. Sometimes I'd run with tears streaming down my face and my nose dripping. After Parker's funeral, I resolved to find out who was behind the explosions and the murders. And to kill Parker's murderer.

Chapter Eighteen

Two weeks and three days after Parker's funeral, I sat on the back porch with my morning coffee. "Lucy's vision may not be as bad as we thought. Have you noticed she never misses Spike's bang-bark command? Look at her. She loves to watch the butterflies."

Lucy padded over to me and nuzzled my knee.

"Okay, girl. I did say your name." I laughed and rubbed her face. "So what's next on our training, guys? No bang?"

Palace Guard jumped off the porch, ran to the middle of the yard, and dove into a prone shooting position. Spike bowed at the waist and swept his arm toward the yard. I took it as a *your turn* invitation.

Palace Guard returned to the porch. We ran together, and when he dropped to a prone position, I copied him. By noon, my drop was simultaneous with his, but I was itchy from flopping on the grass.

After my shower, I smeared peanut butter on two slices of multigrain bread, arranged my banana slices to cover but not overlap, and cut my sandwich into four perfect triangles.

"You know, I haven't seen or heard from Kate since the funeral." Palace Guard raised his eyebrows. "Oh. She hasn't heard from me either."

I sent her a text between bites. "Go to range?"

I was surprised to get an immediate response: "Saturday? 10 am?"

"Great."

Before we went outside for more training, I sent Kate another text. "Olivia next of kin? Anyone collect her clothes for donation?"

I received a reply an hour or so later. "No one. You want to file as emergency contact?"

"Yes."

"Check with the county. See if you can get a copy of her emergency contact info. Call me."

I called the county, and my call was forwarded to the right person.

"Olivia Edwards named you her emergency contact," she said.

"Really? I'm surprised. I didn't know who she had listed. She died suddenly, and her apartment needs to be cleaned before it's rented. She doesn't have any close relatives. I wanted to sort through her belongings for donations because I don't want a stranger to do it, and the apartment manager needs a copy of the emergency contact before she will let me into the apartment." I realized I'd said everything in one breath.

"Of course, honey. I'm so sorry for your loss. I'll make a copy, and you can come down and pick it up, or I'll mail it to you."

I chose the pick-it-up option and called Kate.

"I'm listed as the contact. I'll pick up the form this afternoon."

"Meet me at Olivia's apartment in the morning with the copy of Olivia's emergency contact form." She hung up.

I left Lucy with the guys and found the woman I'd talked to when I called the county office building. The nameplate on her desk said MRS R. YODER. Her chin-length brown hair framed her round face, and the lenses on her glasses magnified her blue eyes. We chatted about the weather, and she gave me copies of Olivia's paperwork.

"Do you know anything about my disability? I'd like to know when I can return to work at the library."

Mrs. Yoder turned to her computer and scrolled through my records. Her eyes were moist when she switched her gaze to me. "Honey, you're on permanent disability. You were hurt very badly. It was in the papers and on the TV. Do you have a handicap tag for your car? I'll make sure they send you the paperwork."

"But I'm much better."

"That's nice, dear. You take care of yourself."

She hugged me gently before I left. Her kindness almost overwhelmed me. *If I ever feel lonely, I'll go to the county office building and ask some random nice person a question.*

* * *

I opened the front door, and Lucy eased off the sofa like a lazy snake.

"Let's go for a run." She scrambled to the back door.

Lucy led the way, and Palace Guard ran alongside her. Spike and I raced each other but were careful not to pressure Lucy. *Silly competitive Spike.* Definitely a challenge to stay one footfall ahead of him.

* * *

When I arrived at Olivia's apartment complex the next morning, I pulled over and double-checked the address before I pulled in because the landscaping looked like a magazine cover. I drove around a traffic circle with three bubbling fountains in the middle. On my way to the parking area, I gawked at a lake with separate biking and walking paths and covered picnic areas. When I spotted Kate's car, I parked next to it.

"Ooh la la," she said when she locked her car. "You library people must rake in the big bucks."

I was so stunned by the opulence I didn't have a snappy response. "Holy moly" was all I came up with.

When a young man in a crisp gray shirt and black slacks appeared in front of us, I admired his attire.

Good job double-blending.

"May I help you?" His condescending tone dripped with the implication: *You are trespassing, obviously poor peasants.*

I was impressed by the depth of disdain he conveyed in those four polite words.

Kate glared at him, whipped out her badge, and growled. "We're here to see the manager." Her warrior tone carried the implication: *Get outta my face, knave.*

He didn't break into an actual run, but he led us to the manager's office at such a fast pace that I had trouble keeping up.

"This is why I like to work with you," I said in a quiet voice.

Kate, the lioness, grinned. *I need Kate to teach me the warrior tone.*

We scooted past the L-shaped Olympic-sized pool with a section of swim lanes and an area to relax, splash, and float. Next to the pool was an oversized hot tub, a sauna, and a cabana with a bar. The back wall was decorated with fishnets and starfish. Maybe the apartment complex called it a spa. When we reached the artfully laid brick walkway near the apartment office, I lingered behind the knave to see if he removed his shoes.

The carpet in the lobby was white, the furnishings had a sleek look I'd seen in a designer magazine at the dentist's, and the fragrance of vanilla and peaches filled the room. The knave walked us to the manager's office, and she whirled around in her chair.

"Police," the knave squeaked.

I showed her the paperwork from the county.

"May I make a copy for our records?" Her gray shirt had *Manager* in fancy script embroidered on the chest pocket.

"No," Kate said. "Ms. Sloan will sign any release forms you may have, but these records are confidential forms from the county."

Not sure if that's true. Kate must be tired of all the pretentiousness.

"Yes. Well, Ms. Sloan, may I see your identification? And sign this for the keys." Ms. Manager reached inside her left-hand drawer and pulled out a form.

It was blank. Kate crossed her arms. After Ms. Manager filled in the form, Kate read it and gave it to me. I signed, and Ms. Manager handed me the keys.

"The lease is paid through the end of the year. No refund. You are welcome to extend the lease for another year."

No mention of cost for the year's lease. *If you have to ask, you can't afford it.* Kate stepped toward the door.

"The lease includes a weekly cleaning, all utilities, and, of course, all the amenities. We took the apartment off the cleaning schedule."

I raised my eyebrows, and Kate stopped. "We'll put it back on the schedule for next week. We didn't expect . . . well . . . I'll just change the records to show you as the tenant, Ms. Sloan. And here's the paperwork to extend the lease."

"What's your pet policy?" I asked.

Kate wheeled around, took three strides, and stood next to me. I sensed the fury of her scowl without even looking. *Better get this answer right, Ms. Manager.*

Ms. Manager smiled. "Cats and dogs are welcomed—no size restrictions. No exotics, though. You don't have an exotic, do you? We have a nice Bark Park, Doggie and KittyCat Salon, and SweetiePie Pet Day Care."

Kate snorted. I agreed. *Lucy in SweetiePie Pet Day Care? Oh my.*

Ms. Manager led us to Olivia's apartment, made sure all three copies of my door keys worked, and left.

"Decorated by a designer." Kate scanned the living room. "Wonder if the furniture is included in the lease or if Olivia owned it. We should check."

I took off my shoes. "I like the fireplace, even if it is gas. White carpet and a white sofa wouldn't be my choice." I sat on the sofa and felt like I'd dropped onto a rock. "Oof. What's the point of an uncomfortable sofa?"

I rose, moved to the dining area, and rubbed my hand over the sleek, golden brown teakwood table. "I like this."

I pulled out a chair and sat. "Sturdy and comfortable. Maybe Olivia hosted dinner parties."

Kate opened the refrigerator. "Cheese, wine, and beer. No food."

She flipped open cupboard doors. "Wine, whiskey, rum, vodka, and snack crackers." She pulled out a cracker and bit into it. "Stale."

I sat at the kitchen bar and rested my elbows on the cold brown-and-gray granite. The padded brown-leather seats were a nice contrast to the stark white. "Barstools are comfortable."

I moved to the kitchen to watch Kate go through the small amount of trash. "Nothing of interest here. The stovetop looks like it's never been used."

I opened the brushed silver oven door. "You're right. The racks still have cardboard taped to the corners. No dinner parties."

While Kate opened kitchen drawers, I wandered to the bedrooms. When I returned, Kate had removed and stacked the drawers on the countertop and examined the bottoms. "Haven't found anything in the kitchen."

"The door I thought was a closet in the hall is a half bath," I said. "There are two master bedrooms with walk-in closets and master bathrooms. Both bedrooms have king-sized beds. One bedroom closet has clothes organized by color. Definitely Olivia's. The other bedroom closet is bare. White towels, white bedspreads."

"They're coverlets—that's what you call expensive bedspreads." Kate pulled out the oversized stainless-steel refrigerator and checked behind it. "Let's attack one room at a time. We can start with Olivia's bedroom. I've got boxes in my car. Be right back."

I stripped the king-sized bed and flipped the mattresses. I folded the sheets and put them into one of the larger boxes Kate brought up.

"I stashed some bottled water in the fridge. We may be a while," Kate said. "I had some coffee in my car and stuck it in the cupboard as a contingency."

I shook out the bed linens from the closet, refolded them, and added them to the box. When I opened the bedside-table drawer, I found stacks of small notepads with different hotel names on them. I gasped. "Kate, here's a pad with the same hotel name and address as the UWILNO note. Maybe Olivia was BFF3."

Kate examined the notepad. "There's no imprint, but some sheets have been torn off. It isn't hard evidence, but you're probably right."

I removed the drawer, flipped it over, and found a manila envelope duct-taped to the bottom of the drawer. I opened it and found a small notebook labeled *Notebook of Secrets 2*. I flipped through the journal, which was a catalog of sorts—just as I expected.

"I'm positive Olivia was BFF3. This envelope was taped to the bottom of the drawer with her signature silver duct tape. If we find a bunch of documents, I'll bet this is the catalog for them. It's in code, but I'll bet it's decipherable."

Kate removed artwork from the walls and checked behind the frames. "Look at this. I found a wall safe behind a print. Numeric pad for a lock."

Kate frowned at the lock. "I'll try the apartment number."

"Bingo." She pulled out several small boxes and a stack of fat manila envelopes.

"Put the safe contents and your notebook of secrets in the box I marked *Knickknacks to Be Donated*. Put a few of those bedsheets into a smaller box and mark it *Important Papers*."

I stepped into the master closet, and my eyes widened. It was bigger than my entire house. I opened the drawers of the built-in dresser. "Jewelry in the closet," I called out. "I recognize silver, gold, turquoise, and diamonds, but I can't identify the rest."

"We need to find you a good lawyer." Kate looked over my shoulder. "Some might be costume jewelry, but I'm no expert. We'll put the boxes we labeled *To Be Donated* in your car. Everything else will go into my car."

We scoured the apartment. We examined each item and put it back or into a *Donate* or *Important* box.

"Let's take a break," Kate said.

We sat at the kitchen bar with our bottles of water.

"Before we leave for the day, I want to take all the electrical plates and the air vents off. Which do you want?" Kate asked.

"Electrical plates. I can reach them."

I found a pair of diamond earrings. Kate found more papers.

"Paper covers rock. I win," Kate said.

"Immature," I grumbled.

We carried the boxes labeled *Donate* to my car and the rest of the boxes to Kate's car. I stuffed Olivia's mail from the locked mailboxes into a recycle bag Kate found under Olivia's kitchen sink.

"We'll meet at your house. I'll bring lunch." Kate rolled up her window and left.

While I showered, Spike and Palace Guard stayed outside with Lucy and guarded the house. The only immediate danger I feared was running zigzag for the woods covered only with foamy shower wash if Lucy gave her bang bark.

* * *

Lucy yipped as Kate and her dad, Glenn, stepped out of a white truck. Glenn was a tall man, just like Parker, or maybe Parker was just like his dad. Glenn's hair was curly and gray, but he didn't have the typical, middle-aged man spread. His face crinkled when he smiled even though his blue eyes were sad—like they'd seen too much tragedy over the years. Lucy wriggled her entire back end and whined a high-pitched doggie giggle.

"Hello, girl. I missed you too." Glenn stooped, and Lucy flopped on her back for a belly rub.

Glenn helped me carry boxes from my car into the house. Kate brought in a large sack of tacos and a twelve-pack of cold beer for our lunch and my refrigerator.

After we ate, Glenn, Lucy, and the imaginary men went to the back porch. Glenn grabbed a beer and a book.

Kate and I pulled all the papers out of the donation boxes and read and sorted. I recognized patterns in the marks on the documents. *Notebook of Secrets 2* had similar marks, but I needed time to crack the code.

After two hours, Kate said, "Let's run."

We shot out the front door and raced up the road. The neighbors to the north of me had a horse farm; the neighbors to the south, a goat farm. When we ran north, the horses galloped along the fence with us. When we wheeled around, the horses whinnied and snorted. We increased our pace and dashed past my house and to the south. The goats at the farm south of the house jumped and leaped while we raced. We turned around at the far end of the goat farm. When we got closer to my house, Lucy barked with excitement and Glenn cheered us on. We ran harder. Kate won. Of course.

We sprawled in our chairs on the back porch and gulped water.

"You didn't really win, Kate. Your legs are twice as long as mine, and my legs have to run two miles for every one of yours, so technically, I won."

Glenn laughed.

"Sore loser," Kate said.

I glared at the laughing Spike and Palace Guard.

"Spike and Palace Guard still here?" Kate asked.

I raised my eyebrows. "You know they are."

"Woo-hoo. Team is together." She waved her arms and swayed in her chair.

"Oh please, Kate, don't encourage them."

Spike and Palace Guard did a victory dance.

"Cut it out. You guys didn't win." I tried to sound grumpy, but I laughed.

"I'll get an explanation eventually, right?" Glenn said.

I had forgotten he was there. I didn't remember my dad, but I had a sudden "Uh-oh, Dad is here" feeling in my stomach. From the look on Kate's face, she had the same thought; even warriors answer to Dad.

"How about now, Dad?" Kate leaned back in her chair. "It all started after the explosion at the library." The two of us explained how my imaginary men helped me.

"And Lucy sees them?" he asked.

Kate, Spike, Palace Guard, and I nodded.

"I trust Lucy's judgment. I can't explain it, but I'm sure your imaginary men will keep you and Lucy safe."

"Really?" I tried not to sound too surprised.

"Yep. If it were just the two of you, I'd wonder what you were up to. And I've thought for a while Lucy saw somebody or something I couldn't see."

Spike and Palace Guard blushed, and I smiled because I understood—Glenn was the Original Force.

"What? What did Spike and Palace Guard say?" Kate asked.

"They said, 'Thank you.'"

Spike and Palace Guard did the wave, and I rubbed my forehead to keep from rolling my eyes.

"Break's over," Kate announced, and we went back to our work of reading and sorting.

Kate looked over a document in her hand. "This is interesting. I found a will."

She flipped to the last page. "This will is dated the same month as the explosion. It looks like Olivia left her brother and her ex-husband each a dollar. She set up an annuity for a domestic-abuse shelter, and everything else appears to go to you."

"What?" I pushed my chair back and hurried to look over Kate's shoulder.

Kate read through the will. "It looks like Olivia inherited most of her money as the oldest child. From what I can tell, Donnie must have received at least a stipend, and I haven't found mention of any other family."

I dropped into my chair and shook my head. *No family to worry about her.*

Glenn came in from the porch. "Eavesdropped. Can I help?"

He sat at the table with us, stacked financial-looking papers and statements into a pile, and flipped through them.

"Maggie," he said, "you need a lawyer and a financial advisor. I've got a good financial advisor I can recommend. I don't know about lawyers."

"My mother knows everybody. I'll ask her."

And I need to invite Mother and her Duane to my new house.

We read and sorted into three stacks—*Keep*, *File*, and *Toss*. Harriet would have been proud of us.

"Here's some real estate documents and several lease agreements." I pointed to my stack. "I don't recognize any names except for Everett Duncan. Wonder why Olivia has these?"

I stretched and called Mother. "Mother, I need a good lawyer. You have any suggestions? And would you like to have dinner at my house one day next week?"

"Margaret, what a wonderful invitation. I'll check Duane's schedule with him and get back to you."

"I'm open, Mother. Just let me know."

She hung up before I said goodbye. I wasn't sure if she didn't like long goodbyes or if phone conversations were still hard for her.

Kate and Glenn left late in the afternoon. I was exhausted but restless.

"Would you like to go for a ride, Lucy?" Her tail swung into high gear.

The four of us piled into the SUV. I took my companions to visit the posh apartment. I was a little surprised or maybe disappointed the knave didn't meet us. I grabbed Lucy's leash for show when we climbed out of the SUV.

Lucy investigated and snuffled every inch along the walkway. After she completed her thorough search for lizards and frogs in the apartment, we went to the Bark Park.

Bark Park was unoccupied. When Lucy discovered a basket of dog toys near the entrance, she picked up a hard ball with a bell inside it and dropped it at my feet. I threw it, and Lucy charged after it.

I clapped my hands. "Bring the ball here, Lucy. Here you go, girl. Bring me the ball."

She snatched up the ball, ran in a circle, and grinned. I caught on and chased her. She let me catch her, and I threw the ball again. While I wore myself out, Spike and Palace Guard relaxed on a bench. After a half hour, Lucy picked up the ball, trotted to the gate, and dropped it into the basket. Time to go.

"Thank you, Lucy. Good exercise." I leaned on the fence until I caught my breath.

After we returned to my house, I fed Lucy and ate leftover tacos then picked up the historical fiction book Glenn left. I wouldn't have chosen it, but the story pulled me in. I wanted to read one more chapter, but after I closed my eyes then my head jerked, I stumbled to bed.

The next morning, I woke to Lucy snores and bird songs. *Best sounds in the world.* After I let Lucy outside, I turned on the burner under a pot of coffee. The fenced yard gave Lucy the freedom to be outside as long as she liked.

I should ask Glenn about a doggie door for Lucy.

Kate and I were alone on the pistol range until eleven when a group showed up.

"The range manager is an old friend. Want to clean guns?" Kate asked.

"You know I do."

We sat in the back office, cleaned rental guns, and talked about Parker. Sometimes it's cathartic to laugh and cry with a good friend.

After I got home from the range, Mother called. "Your appointment with the lawyer is on Monday at ten. Best in the county. Duane and I can come for dinner on Wednesday. Six, right? Gotta run. Nail appointment in thirty minutes." She hung up.

In the afternoon, Lucy and I went to the hardware store to look at lawn mowers and grills. I found a young store employee in the bug-zapper aisle. She was short and slender, and her dark skin matched her dark eyes. "I need a grill, but I don't know what my options are."

"Do you know if you want charcoal or propane?"

I shook my head.

"Here's a brochure. Let's go over the features of both. That might help you."

We sat together on a lawn swing, and I listened to the pros and cons. "I'm leaning toward propane."

"I use my propane grill all the time. In fact, Mama got a huge propane grill for her house, so I'd do the grillin' when she hosted the family barbeques. You'll love hanging out at the grill." She lowered her voice and leaned toward me. "Grillin' means I don't have to talk to Aunt Ethel. She can't stand to be around the smoke."

We giggled.

"Thanks for everything. Including the grill master hint."

Lucy and I wandered to the garden center and picked out a green flower pot, a bag of soil, and perennial flowers for our butterflies.

"Okay if I give your dog a treat?" the store clerk asked when we checked out. She and Lucy looked at me with identical sweet grins on their faces and hope in their eyes.

"She'd love it."

After we got home, Lucy and I dumped the soil into the new pot before we planted and watered the flowers. I brushed off my hands, and Lucy and I strolled up the road to visit the horses. The horses pranced to the fence when Lucy appeared, and they visited nose to nose.

On our way back, Lucy gave the bang bark. I ran for the house, and Lucy chased after me. We zigged to the back when we got to the driveway. I was ready to crack some imaginary heads, but Spike and Palace Guard weren't laughing. Spike pointed toward a car headed up the road from the south. The car crept by. I strained to see, but I didn't have a good view of the license plate because of the distance to the road.

I miss Parker.

I sent Kate a text: "Need to chat. Call?"

Kate called.

"Lucy and I were walking back from the horse farm when she gave her bang bark. When we got home, a car drove by real slow."

"You want a patrol car to cruise by?"

"No. It didn't stop. I'll check the security camera to see if I caught a tag. One more thing, I need your dad to advise me at the hardware store. I want a grill—maybe propane. Need to talk about this big yard and how to mow it. I need his advice and his truck."

"I'll call ya back."

We looked at the security video. Maybe just one occupant. Mud over the license plate. Kate called me back in less than ten minutes.

"Did you catch anything on your security camera?"

"Nope. Mud on the license plate."

"No surprise. On your lawn and grill, Dad said he would love to advise you. How about if he meets you at one o'clock at the hardware store tomorrow? And I'm supposed to ask if we could invite ourselves to your house for dinner tomorrow. Dad said he'd provide the steaks so you two can test drive your new grill. Mom wants to come too. She wants to bring her famous potato salad and cherry pie."

"Sounds great."

Kate's tone turned serious. "Maggie, if you ever don't feel safe, you are more than welcome to stay with me or with Mom and Dad; they offered too."

Tears slid down my face.

"You are amazing." I sniffled. "You know that, right?"

"Yep."

I love that family.

I opened a beer and took it outside to the back porch. The four of us relaxed, and I gazed at the clouds and the sky until twilight crept up on us.

"Mother was always up before dawn to witness the sunrise every morning. I didn't understand until now. She greeted the rising sun, and we trail the setting sun."

When the mosquitos chased us inside, I fed Lucy and made myself a salad. I had a feeling the calories I'd be consuming would carry me into next week.

Three of us hovered around the security cameras while Lucy napped. When I tired of moths flying around the lights, I read Glenn's book until I realized I'd fallen asleep in my chair.

* * *

First thing after breakfast, I wiped out the refrigerator because I didn't want to be embarrassed in case Kate's mom opened it. Spike swiped his finger on the fireplace mantel like he was a dust inspector. I knew he was making fun of me, but I still laughed.

Lucy and I met Glenn and Kate at the hardware store, and Spike and Palace Guard tagged along. Kate and Lucy wandered off accompanied by the imaginary men to find grilling utensils, while Glenn and I discussed grills.

"What do you need in a grill?" Glenn asked.

"One flexible enough to barbeque for just me or a group up to twelve or so people. I don't need fancy dials or a smoker, but the propane tank has to be easy to get to."

"You'll like a thermometer too. Let's look at those."

At the checkout counter, Kate announced the grill was a housewarming gift from her. When she insisted, I said, "Thank you. Very much."

I whispered, "You pulled a pretty good ambush, there, Fed Girl. Well done. I'll get even."

Spike and Palace Guard elbowed each other. Maybe they had some ideas.

Glenn looked at us with a frown. I think he tried to hear what I whispered.

"I have every confidence in your skills," Kate announced in a loud voice. She followed up with a wicked grin.

* * *

While Glenn and I put the grill together, we talked about the yard.

Glenn said, "You might want to check with your landlady. Two acres seems like a lot for you to mow. You wouldn't want to do it with a regular push lawn mower. You might want to get a regular mower and take care of the yard around the house yourself. But you do want the rest mowed. Otherwise, you'll have problems with ticks when you run."

When he said "ticks" I was ready to call Harriet right away, but I decided to wait until Monday. We talked about electric mowers and gas mowers. I leaned toward a gas mower.

"We'll have to make sure you can pull the cord to start the engine, but I expect you'll be fine," Glenn said. "You're a lot stronger than you look. I can teach you about engine maintenance and repair too, if you're interested."

"Absolutely. I never had the opportunity for any hands-on learning. I'd love it."

"You are an amazing person, Maggie," Kate called from the porch. She and Lucy were on a break after playing with the new ball.

"Doesn't make us even," I retorted.

"You know," Glenn said, "I'm getting a sense of what it would be like to have two daughters."

I laughed along with Glenn and Kate, but I almost cried. *Sometimes I'm sappy.*

"I have a question, Glenn. What do you think about a dog door for Lucy?" I asked.

"I'd worry about someone else using it when you aren't here, but if you take Lucy with you, you could close it up. If you leave Lucy here, she wouldn't be by herself, right? But would she be safe? Kate?"

"What do the imaginary men think, Maggie?"

I was embarrassed I hadn't thought to ask them. Both of them shook their heads.

"They said no to the dog door, but I don't know why."

Spike pointed to his eyes.

"Spike says she's safer in the house with her failing sight."

Palace Guard held up his fists.

"Palace Guard says they can protect her inside."

Glenn cleared his throat. "Settled, then. And I can't believe I'm saying this. Your imaginary men are smart."

I helped Glenn put away his tools and created a list for my next trip to the hardware store. We planned to get a mower later in the week or next weekend, but I'd check the sales flyers. Glenn left to pick up Kate's mom, Jennifer; Kate stayed.

We pulled out our sticky notes and added the car going past the house.

"I can informally look into Donnie a little more. Do you think he was in the car?" Kate asked.

"I don't know."

"I wonder if they followed you with a paper trail. They still may not know what you look like now. I wonder if there's a way we can use your new appearance to our advantage?"

"If the Gray Lady lured them to a secluded spot, you could grab them."

Kate laughed. "I did ask for that, didn't I? I can't say why, but it might be smart to have a gray sweatshirt for you to throw on."

"My gray clothes don't fit anymore."

"Can I use your car?"

Kate was back in less than thirty minutes. "I got you gray sweatpants, three shirts, and a sweatshirt. Maybe the sweatshirt will bulk you up."

"I'll throw these into the washer."

Kate flopped down on the sofa. "When laundry is the highlight of our day, we need a hobby or something—besides escaping explosions and finding bad guys."

"I experimented with flavors of iced tea. Want to try some raspberry tea?"

We put away the sticky notes, drank raspberry tea, and did another pass through the *Toss* papers. We ended up putting 90 percent of them into a new category we called *Shred Maybe*.

"I'm not sure if Olivia was a packrat or if we are missing something." Kate rubbed her forehead.

"I'll put all these expired coupons in an envelope. Did she just collect coupons, or do they have any significance? Look, they are all marked. I haven't cross-referenced them yet with the notebook." My head hurt.

"Let's pack up and get away from the table."

Chapter Nineteen

Kate, Lucy, and I went for a quick run around the two acres. If I ran fast, the ticks couldn't latch on to me. After we got back to the house, I jumped into the shower. *No ticks.*

"Your squeamishness is contagious. I'm taking a quick shower too," Kate grumbled.

When Glenn and Mrs. Coyle pulled into the driveway, Lucy pranced and wagged.

"She loves Mom and Dad," Kate said. "Look at her tail go. If it went any faster, her rear legs would lift off the ground."

I had trouble calling Mrs. Coyle "Jennifer," but she had corrected me more than once, and I wanted to respect her wishes. *Maybe it didn't have to be about me.* I could step out of my personal comfort zone to make her feel welcome and comfortable in my home. I inhaled and breathed out. "Jennifer. Jennifer. Jennifer." The practice helped.

The entire Coyle family was tall except for Jennifer. She was short— maybe not quite as short as I am, but short by Coyle standards. She was slender, and her short blond hair had a halo of silver around her face. She wore white linen capris and a pale, sage-green shirt with butterflies. I swooned in my heart over the butterflies. "I'm so happy to see you, Jennifer. Thanks for coming."

When I hugged her, Jennifer beamed; Glenn beamed. When Kate punched my arm, I stuck my tongue out at her behind her mother's back. Glenn shook his head and chuckled. "Girls."

Glenn explained the steps to prepare the steaks for the grill, and we went out to fire it up with our requisite beers. Glenn said we'd do all the steaks medium rare.

He pushed on each steak with two fingers. "Feel the give, Maggie? Rare. When they are medium rare, we'll pull them off the grill to rest. We could use a meat thermometer, but there's no substitute for touch."

I inhaled the aroma of the meat and caught the primal allure of standing around a fire with meat cooking.

"Feel this, Maggie. Medium rare."

I pulled the steaks off the grill and carried them inside on a platter. When Spike and Palace Guard applauded, I bowed. *Grill drama.*

Glenn followed me and continued the grill lesson. "Medium steaks feel like shoe leather. If someone wants a well-done steak, then let your steak rest, eat it, finish your beer, then pull the steak off the grill."

When I giggled, Jennifer cleared her throat.

"Sorry," Glenn said. "Didn't mean to trash steak preferences. Maybe take your steak off the grill, hand them the tongs, and tell them you're a beginner. It's what I do."

"You do not," Jennifer said. "I'll get Maggie a meat thermometer."

I ate half my steak. I promised Glenn I would eat my leftovers cold, sliced thin. The potato salad was scrumptious, but I declined seconds. I wanted to save room for cherry pie and ice cream. I asked Jennifer if she'd teach me how to make the pie.

She patted my arm and smiled. "You are so sweet."

My face warmed. I wasn't sweet—I had a sweet tooth.

After we were at the one-belt-notch-past-stuffed stage, Kate took Lucy for a walk while Glenn went outside and scrubbed the grill. Jennifer packaged up the leftovers, and I washed and dried dishes.

I glanced over at the lumberjack-sized portion of potato salad Jennifer spooned into a container for me and the three-quarters of a pie she slid into my refrigerator. "You've given me more than I can eat. Maybe just a little less potato salad and two slices of cherry pie?"

She frowned. "You might have company. If you don't, you're set for the rest of the week."

Glenn washed his hands at the sink and grinned. "I never win either."

"I did invite Mother and Sergeant Arrington to dinner on Wednesday night," I said. "What about cheeseburgers? Too casual?"

Jennifer shook her head. "Not at all. Cheeseburgers are perfect with potato salad and cherry pie."

After they left, I put my feet up. It had been a glorious day, and it hit me.

Parker should have been here too.

Tears rolled down my face. I wiped the tears away, but I couldn't wipe away thoughts of Parker. I took Lucy outside and gazed at the stars.

Parker would like it here. Lucy and I shuffled to bed.

* * *

The next morning, I called Mr. Morgan. "Come have dinner at my new place. This evening. I'll cook."

"What do I bring?"

"Nothing. I'm a fabulous cook. Really. And I have leftovers from Jennifer Coyle."

"You cook? Are you sure? What do you want me to bring?"

I tried to put a growl in my voice, but it came out as a giggle. "Kate taught me to cook. Bring your appetite. I promise you won't go home hungry."

"How would you feel if I brought a guest? It's okay to say no. I don't want to put any pressure on you, especially since—maybe it's a bad idea; next time might be better."

"No, it would be great. I would love it. Bring a guest. One of your lady friends?"

He laughed. "An old friend."

You old stinker. You're leaving me in suspense on purpose.

I didn't find any wild blackberries around the house, so I bought blackberries at the grocery store. I was shocked the grocery store didn't carry dandelion greens. I planned on ham steak, potato salad, and tossed salad with the dessert choice of blackberry cobbler or cherry pie for dessert. I wanted to invite Kate but worried she'd feel obligated.

I stopped at the hardware store and picked up another rocking chair and another big pot of perennial flowers. I missed the butterflies, and the flowers reminded me of Parker.

After I put the groceries away, Palace Guard and I went for a hard run around the property. When we got close to the house, Lucy gave her bang bark, and I turned and zigzagged into the woods. Palace Guard gave me the all-clear, and we trotted to the house. Spike gave me a double thumbs-up. I might be in mourning, but Spike and Palace Guard helped me stay sharp and not distracted.

I searched the spare bedroom closet, where I'd stashed unopened boxes, and found last year's Christmas present from Mother. She told me it was table linens. I unwrapped the package and discovered a red tablecloth, red and orange placemats, and orange napkins. At first, they looked garish, but when I stepped back and squinted at them with my sunglasses on, they didn't look too bad on my dining table.

I showered and put on jeans and a blue short-sleeved shirt, except Mother called it a blouse—maybe because it had buttons. It didn't have a sweetheart neckline.

I was jittery because this was my first-ever, actual dinner party. I looked at Spike, and he breathed in and blew it out. I copied him.

"Thanks. It helped."

Lucy woofed. Mr. Morgan's car pulled in. I went outside to greet him and his guest. Mr. Morgan opened the passenger-side door. His guest's cane looked hand-carved. She turned and grinned at me. *Lillian!*

I squealed. "What a wonderful surprise. I'm so happy to see both of you."

Mr. Morgan brought wine, homemade crackers, and cheese. No surprise there. I grabbed three wine glasses and put the cheese and crackers on a plate while Mr. Morgan helped Lillian get settled in the living room. Mr. Morgan opened the wine.

"Is this your new disguise, dear?" Lillian asked. "Are you camouflaged as normal?"

I laughed. "I like that. Yes, I am."

"You've done a great job. You look nothing like the Gray Lady. I wouldn't have recognized you or even noticed you in a store."

"We're so sorry about Parker," Mr. Morgan said. "You know he cleared me. We can talk after dinner if you like."

"I'd like that."

"My physical therapist is Joanna," Lillian said. "She's challenged me to beat your recovery time."

I laughed. "Joanna is amazing and tough. You're in good hands. I'm glad you're doing so well."

"May I have a tour of your new home?" Lillian asked.

After the quick house tour, we stepped out onto the back porch, and Lucy padded out with us.

"This is very nice," Lillian said. "A little secluded, but with a good view of all your immediate surroundings. Good defensive position."

Good defensive position? Exactly who is Lillian?

During dinner, Mr. Morgan and Lillian complimented me on my cooking. When I blushed, Mr. Morgan winked at me.

"I love to sit on the back porch, but I've learned dusk is prime time for bugs out in the country, especially mosquitos." I cleared our dishes from the table while Mr. Morgan helped Lillian rise from her chair.

After we moved to the living room for dessert, Lillian and I sat together on the sofa while Mr. Morgan made himself comfortable in the overstuffed chair.

"I like the quilt you put on the gray sofa. The colors perk up the room," Lillian said.

"Thank you. I'm still not sure about the color thing. You know you were a complete surprise this evening."

"Lillian and I have known each other for years," Mr. Morgan said.

"We worked together in the Criminal Division of the Department of Justice before we retired," Lillian added.

Why did I not know this before?

"What about your arrest, Mr. Morgan? I thought it was awful—can you talk about it?"

"You may have heard I argued with Bob Zephfer, the bank examiner who was stabbed at the library. It's true—we did argue. His audit found Duncan's bank embezzlement, and he came across Olivia in conjunction with Duncan. He dug deeper at the bank and made some erroneous assumptions about Olivia and other evidence. We argued because I tried to warn him he'd stumbled into the middle of something big. He was angry because I wouldn't give him any details. I told him to talk to his supervisor, and he said he didn't run to his supervisor with every unsubstantiated claim. I told him he had made a big mistake. Our discussion might be called heated by the casual observer, and we did get loud. He said I was an old fool. I may have called him a reckless blowhard. Make that allegedly."

"I'll remember," I said. "Allegedly reckless blowhard."

Lillian snickered. "Zephfer went to the library to talk to Olivia, but the bad guys thought he planned to talk to you, not Olivia. He was murdered because they were certain he was ready to expose them. We also think the murderer is the same man who planted the explosives at the library, and Olivia knew him."

"So I'm supposed to be a confidential informant, which is like a spy, right?"

"Might be why you're a target," Mr. Morgan said.

"What am I informing about?"

"We don't know." Lillian frowned. "What do you think it might be?"

"What about Parker? Was he killed because of me?"

Mr. Morgan answered. "That's the official conclusion, but I don't agree. It's too easy." He glanced at Lillian.

"Sometimes, though, the simple answer is the only answer," Lillian said.

"This is all so complex; so many pieces." I rubbed my forehead and rose to put my wine glass in the sink. "Lillian, why were you attacked? Do you care for more iced tea?"

"Yes, please. The investigation deemed it a random attack on an old lady, which was incorrect," she said. "I was on the bank's board of directors for a few years. My attacker was Donald Chandler. He told me he knew I was on the board and retired from the Department of Justice. He wanted to know what the DOJ had on Everett Duncan, the bank president, and I told him I didn't know because I was retired."

I set Lillian's glass on the table next to her.

"Thank you, dear. Chandler said he would beat it out of me. The police said they checked the hospitals for a man with a broken collarbone, broken arm, and broken nose and jaw two weeks later when I was able to tell them what I did. They said Donnie probably went to a large city for his injuries and claimed unknown assailants."

"You're awesome, Lillian."

Lillian waved her hand. "I should have taken him out, but I was a little slow, and he got the upper hand for a while. I was Army before the DOJ. I've tried to keep in shape."

"Don't be modest, Lillian," Mr. Morgan said. "Maggie, she was a crack shot. She's a legend."

Lillian shook her head. "It was ages ago. One good thing did come out of my entanglement with Donnie, though. My hearing aids got lost in the fray, and I got new, more advanced ones. No more replacing batteries. They self-charge."

Lillian looked so pleased that I had to smile with her. *I always want to look at the bright side of everything too.*

"As far as Everett Duncan, he was under investigation by the Department of the Treasury, not the DOJ," she continued. "Donnie didn't ask me about IRS or Treasury. He made it easy to deny knowing anything."

"Lillian and I think the bad guys are looking for the confidential informant," Mr. Morgan said, "But we aren't positive."

"Scotland Yard," I said.

"What do you mean, dear?" Lillian asked.

I brought out the basket of sticky notes.

"Kate and I used notes to try to put the pieces together, but it would take Scotland Yard to solve the puzzle."

I put the notes on the trunk I used as a coffee table and knelt on the floor across from Lillian. The three of us moved slips of paper around, but most of them didn't fit with anything else.

"Dear, most of these are questions," Lillian said. "Did you draw any conclusions from these?"

"No conclusions. Just more questions." We chuckled.

"I've got something you can add," Mr. Morgan said. "The 'boom' note isn't on any of your stickies." Mr. Morgan cleared his throat. "I wrote the note after I saw Donnie mess with your car then I switched the door keys with your car keys. An anonymous note was all I could come up with on such short notice. Might not have been the best choice, and I'm really sorry I scared you. Parker guessed and asked me later."

"You did what? Parker said he thought the message was a warning. Why didn't you tell me?"

"I thought I'd catch you before you saw it. I put it there just in case you—not my best decision. I wanted to tell you earlier—" He shook his head. "What about having someone here with you? Someone you can trust?"

I looked at Lucy, Spike, and Palace Guard. "I've got it covered."

"You're right. Lucy is an excellent watchdog."

Lillian raised her head and frowned. "I have something to add too, dear. I apologize for not telling you sooner. Olivia trusted me because she knew me from the bank. She told me something big would happen eight days after the murder. She said she had a plan to tell you. That's how I knew about 'day eight.'"

My mouth opened but nothing came out. I dropped into the chair across from Lillian. "Wow."

* * *

I had a restless night—troubling dreams I didn't remember. At three, I woke up with a start. Spike and Palace Guard were next to my bed. When Palace Guard pointed to the front of the house, I peeked out the front window then stepped back. *A car is idling at the gate.*

We slipped through the dark to the computer and checked the security camera. *Donnie was at the gate.*

I texted Kate: "Donnie at gate."

She texted back: "Deputy on the way."

Donnie was alone and didn't notice the camera. When I heard another car on the road, Donnie jumped into his car and sped off to the north. Before he cleared the horse property, a sheriff's deputy car zoomed from the south past my house as sirens approached from the north.

My phone rang. *Kate.*

"You okay? How did you know he was out there?"

"Spike and Palace Guard woke me up. We're fine."

"Donnie is under arrest."

I was restless. I coaxed Lucy out back while the coffee perked then I ran to the gate and back while Lucy wandered in the grass. After Lucy was ready to go inside, I stood in front of the computer while I sipped on my coffee and scrolled through the night's security video. It showed Donnie drive up and the deputy's car fly by.

After breakfast and a shower, I called Harriet.

"Would it be possible for you to have the property outside the fence area of the house mowed regularly?"

"Of course. I should have thought of it. I'll have my landscapers trim and mow it once a week. I'll have them mow inside the fenced area too, if you like."

"I can take care of the grass inside the fence. I'd worry someone might forget to close the gate, and Lucy might wander off."

"They'll start next week."

Goodbye, ticks.

When I met Glenn outside the lawyer's office, he handed me a cardboard box. "The financial paperwork and the will's here. Text me after your appointment, and I'll meet you at the hardware store."

I shook my head. "Can't. Lucy would be heartbroken if I went to her favorite store without her. She'd smell hardware on me. How about after lunch sometime?"

He laughed. "Two o'clock, and you're right about the hardware smell—you'd be in big trouble. Which reminds me, I'm supposed to invite you to our house for dinner tonight. Can you make it? Bring Lucy and the guys, if they'd like to come."

"I would never miss a Jennifer meal. Thank you."

The lawyer's office was in a small house four blocks from the courthouse. The old parquet floors and rich woodwork showed the scars of years of use. The assistant's computer on an old wooden desk was the only modern furnishing in the room. The assistant was on the phone when I walked in. Her skin was dark, her eyes were black, and her short, tight curls hugged her scalp. She had a ring piercing below her lower lip on the right side and a small scar in the middle of her chin. The color of her long fingernails matched the turquoise of her necklace. She waved at the single visitor's chair, an overstuffed armchair next to a square mission-style table.

After she ended her phone call, she smiled. "Hi. You're Ms. Sloan? Sorry to keep you waiting. I'm Shantelle. This way, please." She led me down a short hallway and tapped on a door.

The lawyer, Amy Rodriquez, looked like she was Mother's age. Her coal-black hair was pulled into a tight bun and had a streak of silver near the right side of her temple. She was tall, but not quite as tall as Kate. She wore black pumps, a slim black skirt, and a brilliant orange blouse. Her ample bosom strained at the fabric, and her skirt revealed the faint outline of an old-fashioned girdle. We shook hands.

"Sit." She pointed to the straight-back chairs at the conference table.

I set the box of papers on the table and sat. As she scanned each sheet and sorted them into stacks, she didn't speak. Shantelle slipped into the conference room and glided out with the papers.

Ms. Rodriquez glanced through the will and jotted a few illegible notes on a pad of yellow paper. She tapped her pen on her page. "Ms. Sloan, we'll need some time to go through the papers. Do you want me to serve as your lawyer after I provide the analysis of the documents? Based on this preliminary review, I urge you to hire a lawyer to represent your interests."

Shantelle placed my original documents next to Ms. Rodriquez and slipped out the door.

I didn't realize Palace Guard was with me until he leaned over the lawyer's shoulder and read what she wrote on the yellow pad. He nodded.

"I would like for you to represent my interests," I said.

"Good. I'll need a retainer."

I wrote a check, and after she gave me a receipt, we shook hands. She was all business. When Palace Guard patted her on the back, she jerked to look over her shoulder. While Palace Guard laughed, I gave him a hard stare and bit my lip.

I chided him on the way home. "I can't believe you patted her back. You know when you laughed, I almost laughed too. How did she feel you pat her on the back, anyway?"

I glanced in the rearview mirror. He looked contrite.

"Sorry. I guess I went on a rant. I'm glad you were there. Thanks for letting me know I should go with her as my lawyer."

He gave me a nod.

Good. My apology was accepted. I rolled my eyes. *By an imaginary Palace Guard.* I snickered as I glanced at Palace Guard, and he grinned.

Palace Guard and I were home early enough in the day to take Lucy for a comfortable run, Lucy style. Lucy alternately sniffed the air and the ground to discover new odors and enjoy the memory of scents from the past. After the outing, I swept the floors and showered before lunch. I was too stinky to shop for a lawn mower in a hardware store.

The four of us piled into the car to meet Glenn, who waited for us at the store entrance. Lucy's tail went into overdrive.

He greeted his girl with a face rub. "Got your guys with you?"

"They stay pretty close to Lucy, so yes."

"You know we're both nuts, talking like this, right?"

"Oh yes."

Lucy and her entourage stopped. "Sorry. No offense intended," I said.

Glenn stared at Lucy. "I'm sorry I can't see them."

"Me too. You know if it weren't for Lucy, I'd think I was whacko."

Spike did a silly dance around me—his version of a whacko dance.

I laughed. "Cut it out."

"I don't want to know." Glenn rolled his eyes. "Let's go buy a lawnmower."

When we reached the lawnmowers, Glenn pointed. "Here's a no-pull-cord electric starter. The one-touch height adjustment would be good for you, and you need safety controls to stop the blade but not the engine."

We looked at power, engines, and decks, and I picked out a mower with Glenn's guidance. A young store clerk rushed to help Glenn load the mower onto the flat.

"You'll need a gas can and a spare." Glenn set two on top of the mower.

I found work gloves in the next aisle over. "I can't find leather work gloves small enough for my hands," I grumbled. "Oh wait. Here's a size small behind the extra-large."

"We'll have them load your mower into the back of my truck, and I'll put it together for you. I'll stop and fill the gas cans on the way to your house."

When Glenn arrived at the house, Lucy did her *Glenn's Here* dance even though we were with him only twenty minutes earlier. After he assembled the mower, Glenn gave me a quick maintenance lesson and guided me through starting the machine. After he left, I mowed my yard.

When I finished, I was sticky and exhausted as I flopped belly down in the fragrant grass.

When my phone rang,. I dragged my achy body over to the porch to answer. It was Jennifer.

"Glenn said he invited you to our house for dinner, but he couldn't remember if he told you what time. Can you come at six? We've invited some other people too."

"Thank you. We'll be there."

After I hung up, I turned to the imaginary men. "We've been invited to the Coyles' for our first dinner party. Everybody has to behave, got it?" I used my stern Mother voice. When they saluted me, I giggled.

I wore jeans and an orange T-shirt that Spike selected. I stressed over whether my clothes were acceptable, until Palace Guard gave me the thumbs up. If my jeans and shirt were good enough for Buckingham Palace, they'd be fine for an American dinner party.

When we arrived, the driveway and the curb in front of their house were crowded with cars. I panicked. *I'm not ready to be around a bunch of strangers.*

I rubbed my neck and glanced at the back seat. Spike wore a black mock turtleneck, and Palace Guard sported a collared royal-blue knit shirt.

"You two look very nice. Parties make me nervous. At least, I think they do. I've never been to one."

I sniffed. "I like the cologne. Yours, Spike?"

Spike blushed.

"I win, right? You blushed, right?" Palace Guard and I laughed.

Spike poked my shoulder.

"Okay, we'll go in."

I shuffled toward the house like a death-row inmate taking the last few steps to the electric chair. I stopped on the front porch and debated leaving. After Lucy nudged my knee, and Palace Guard pushed me, I banged into the door; it must have been good enough for a knock because Kate threw the door open and practically dragged me inside. She wore jeans and a pink T-shirt.

After Spike jumped behind her and made a karate move, he winked.

What a wonderful idea.

I grabbed Kate and flipped her to the floor then I ran toward the back of the house. When I crashed into Glenn in the kitchen, Kate was hot on my heels.

"Hello, Maggie. Do I want to know what's going on here?" Glenn cocked his head.

Kate tried to stop, but she slid into me. By then, she and I were laughing and so were the imaginary men; Lucy joined in as she barked and danced.

Jennifer walked into the room. "Glenn, did you start this?"

We howled. All five of us—Kate, the imaginary men, me, and even Lucy, who got the joke and joined in with a she-wolf howl.

Glenn raised his arms in surrender. "Oh, Lord."

"Still getting into trouble, Maggie?" *Taylor!* She was in jeans and a lavender blouse.

When I ran to hug her, she slammed me to the floor. *Tiny Taylor nailed me.*

I stayed on the floor, laughing. "Big mistake sending you to Tia. You're a kindergarten teacher ninja."

Taylor giggled and karate-chopped the air.

Glenn shook his head. "I am so glad I had only one daughter."

Jennifer helped me up. She was the only one I trusted.

Mr. Morgan stuck his head inside the back door. "You folks just going to lie around, or would you like to come out on the patio and have a beer?"

I stayed close to Jennifer. I noticed Kate was arm in arm with her mother on the other side, and Taylor glommed on to Glenn. I snickered.

Aren't we the suspicious lot?

When I stepped outside, I spotted Lillian, Mother, and Sergeant Arrington at a patio table. Sergeant Arrington rose and grabbed me into a big Sarge hug.

"Maggie," he roared. "I'm so happy to see you."

"Me too," I mumbled into his massive chest.

When Sarge released me, Lillian hugged me. Mother smiled and patted me on the shoulder; we were never huggers at our house.

Mr. Morgan handed me a beer, and I joined Glenn at the grill. As far as I was concerned, Glenn was the grill master, and I was there to learn. I sneaked a peek at Mother and Sergeant Arrington. Mother wore her red hibiscus shirt, a red skirt, and red high heels. Sarge wore khaki pants and a white short-sleeved shirt. They smiled at each other and leaned to touch shoulders. When I raised my beer in salute, Sergeant Arrington smiled and blushed. My eyes widened, and I choked on my beer.

Glenn and I grilled steaks and portabella mushrooms. Jennifer served roasted rosemary potato wedges, asparagus from her garden, and tossed salad with tangerines and toasted pecans. Mr. Morgan brought his famous deviled eggs, and Lillian brought homemade rolls. Kate made my raspberry-infused iced tea. We feasted on warm brownies with vanilla-bean ice cream for dessert.

"Harry and I spend most evenings and weekends together," Taylor said. "He'd have joined us, but he coaches a tee-ball team twice a week.

Harry applied for a position at an inner-city public school. He says he wants to make a difference for the kids, and the school has been losing teachers. I might apply there too. Things between us could get . . . We'll have to see."

I'm not ready to listen to her talk about how wonderful Harry is. It isn't fair. I miss Parker.

"Speaking of men—my physical therapist's assistant has a crush on me." Lillian had a twinkle in her eye.

"I'm not surprised. Your recovery has been amazing, and your spirit is inspirational." Jennifer passed the roasted potatoes to Mr. Morgan.

After dessert, Sergeant, Mother, and Taylor made their farewells, and Mr. Morgan took Lillian home. After everyone left, Kate and I went for a run.

When we returned, Mr. Morgan and Glenn were waiting for us.

"Kate, your mother was looking for you," Glenn said. "She has some questions."

After she left the room, Glenn handed me a bottle of water. "Maggie, we need to talk. Let's go out back."

After the three of us sat at the patio table, Glenn said, "We didn't want to talk in front of Kate, because she's active duty. Ray and I are retired, and you aren't on a payroll. Let's sit."

Ray? Mr. Morgan has a first name?

"We have official information, off the record." Mr. Morgan nibbled on a cookie he'd grabbed off a plate in the kitchen. "For example, Donnie was released on bail. His slick lawyer managed to convince the judge Donnie wasn't a flight risk, and an elderly and traumatized woman could be mistaken in her memory of the attacker."

"That's the dumbest thing I've ever heard. Who would ever believe such nonsense about Lillian?"

"I agree," Glenn said. "Another point of interest is the judge put the bail at the highest possible amount."

Mr. Morgan tapped the table. "We learned his bail was paid for him, but we don't know by whom."

"We have a theory," Glenn said. "I suspect Olivia's ex was mixed up in it somehow too. I'd like to review Olivia's papers tomorrow if you aren't busy."

"Was there anyone else at the bank when you interviewed? Did you hear any voices?" Mr. Morgan asked.

I turned to Mr. Morgan. "A janitor was mopping a small hallway close to the front door. The voices of a man and a woman came from the main hall, but their voices weren't clear enough for me to understand what they said."

"The woman was Lillian," Mr. Morgan said. "The man was Bob Zephfer, the auditor. The man who interviewed you was John Edwards, Olivia's ex-husband. Bob Zephfer was there to talk to the two board members, Lillian and Edwards. Lillian said she didn't know Edwards left their meeting for an interview with you, and Lillian never mentioned a janitor. She must not have noticed him."

I frowned. *That's odd. Lillian notices everything.*

Glenn moved to his grill and scrubbed the grates with his wire brush. "We focused on John Edwards as the brains of the operation. He's the owner of a construction company. His company is a major contractor for roads and tunnels. Was the janitor Donnie?"

"No, not Donnie. I caught a glimpse of his face. He was tall—tall as you, Glenn, but heavier than you are. His build reminded me of an old football player who quit working out. Caucasian, bald or shaved head. Had a graying mustache."

"Oh Lord," groaned Glenn while he wiped down his grill. "Your observation talents and recall are phenomenal. I have to ask about scars."

I frowned. "No, I didn't notice any scars, but his left arm appeared dysfunctional. Maybe from a mild stroke or permanent injury."

"How did you see so much? Did you stare at him? Did he come talk to you?" Mr. Morgan asked.

"Mother says I observed people while I was still in the hospital after I was born. She exaggerates. I do know I've observed people as long as I can remember because I always wanted to be a spy."

"Lillian and I have this little business. Maybe we can talk sometime when all this settles down," Mr. Morgan said.

"You must have seen someone where they didn't expect to be recognized," Glenn said. "And somehow, what you knew, Parker knew. How could that be?"

"There must be something we're missing." Mr. Morgan rubbed the back of his neck.

"My job-applicant database." My skin turned clammy, and when I shivered, Glenn pulled a chair next to me and put his arm around my shoulder.

"Parker had copies of all my notes. I need to go back over them and look at them like Parker would."

"Need help?" Glenn asked.

"Yes, I'd like for you to review them after I see what's there first."

"I want to focus on Donnie," Mr. Morgan said. "I'll dig into how his bail was paid and backtrack from there."

"I know your lawyer has Olivia's documents, but I'd like to focus on them from a retired detective's viewpoint," Glenn said.

"Could we get back together in three or four days? Maybe lunch?" Mr. Morgan swatted his arm.

The setting sun and dusky sky was an open invitation for mosquitos. I waved two away and smacked a third.

Glenn rose. "Let's go in. We can meet here for lunch. I'll grill or pick up something if Jen's busy. Find Kate, Maggie. I'll bet she's ready to leave, and you look tired."

"A little."

After I said goodbye, the four of us piled into my car. I glanced at my rearview mirror. "You guys have some theories, don't you?"

Spike shrugged, and Palace Guard turned his head away. *I'll bet they do.*

Chapter Twenty

When we got home, I stood next to the car and listened to the cicadas while Palace Guard did a perimeter check. I unlocked the front door, and the last remnants of the sun disappeared while Spike cleared the house, and Lucy investigated the yard. After the house was declared safe, we all went inside.

I turned on the computer and searched my database. I searched for *male* and *bald* or *toupee*. Quickest disguise for a bald man would be a hat or a toupee, and I'm good at spotting hairpieces. I filtered my search with *older*, *overweight*, and *tall*—all of the janitor's fundamental characteristics.

I leaned back in my chair. Seven men—the janitor, a man at the cartoon place, a manager type at the warehouse, two applicants in line at the warehouse, a manager at my grocery store, and Sergeant Arrington. I threw out Sergeant Arrington because he was much taller than the janitor and his hair was a little thin, but not at the point of bald. I corrected my database.

Mother would kill me if I said Sergeant Arrington was a killer.

I popped open a beer and spread Olivia's documents, folders, and envelopes across the dining-room table. *Need a picture of Everett Duncan.*

After two hours, I sat with a warm beer and a dull ache in my lower back. *I'm out of ideas.* I poured my warm beer into the sink. Palace Guard pouted.

"Sorry. I forgot you Brits drink warm beer."

I stretched my back. "Lucy, let's go for a run." Lucy opened her eyes and lifted her head.

Palace Guard and Spike scowled.

"In the backyard. You happy?"

Palace Guard and Spike smiled.

"You two have turned into helicopter parents."

The two of them did a helicopter jig—like a fancy foot-jig except with the addition of arms whirling and waving overhead and gyrations of bobbing and weaving.

Why do I have immature imaginary men?

Lucy ran at the Lucy pace. Run. Stop. Sniff. Pee. Run. Walk. Stop. Sniff. After she turn toward the house, she repeated her routine.

"I need to do a few perimeters." I ran along the fence line in the dark until my heart pounded and my legs ached. When my phone rang, the screen showed "Ella."

"Hey. The boss man, Evan Dunnelly, was asking around about a skinny, short white girl who wore all gray and applied for a job here a while back. Don't know nobody like that, and nobody else did either. Just wanted you to know. He's trouble and bad things are going on. You need me, you call me."

She hung up.

What is this? Everybody hangs up on me.

I sniffed my armpit. Spike and Palace Guard made gagging faces.

"Ha ha."

When I returned to Olivia's documents, folders, and envelopes, I came across a manila envelope marked "E.D." with pictures in it that looked like travel pictures. When I shook it over the table, a tiny flash drive fell out. The number on the drive, twelve, cross-referenced in the notebook to 610, which is Medical Sciences and Medicine. I noticed more and more twelves on documents. I looked through the pictures—ocean, beaches, and hotel towels with the hotel names embroidered on them. *Fancy.* I inserted the flash drive into the slot on my laptop. My eyes widened at photos of Olivia with a man at beaches and hotels. Olivia and the man had big smiles and their arms were around each other.

If the man with Olivia was Everett Duncan then he moonlighted as a janitor. He wore a peppered-gray toupee. I knew it was a hairpiece because the hairline was perfect. A man in his late fifties to early sixties would have at least a slightly receding hairline. Everything else—his height, weight, eyebrows, eyes, cheekbones, hands, stance, even his left stiff arm—was the janitor. *Gotcha.* His death was a sham.

I grabbed a cold beer and drank it while I stood at the computer desk and looked at Everett Duncan, bank president and janitor. Rhett Dunn, art studio manager. Evan Dunnelly, warehouse manager. Undead man. Killer.

Just need to weave all these threads together into a delicate tapestry.

I backed up my database and the pictures. Mother and I shared a cloud provider, but I'm not sure she knew how to access it. I sent Sergeant Arrington an email and told him about Mother's storage space. I didn't mention what I'd added. He was my backup to my backup.

I went through the documents, folders, and envelopes again, armed with the awareness of the relationships of the bank, warehouse, and art studio.

Now I knew what to look for, and I found the art studio's address on purchase orders for pharmaceuticals—antibiotics, cancer meds, pain meds—placed with companies in China, India, and Hong Kong. The warehouse was the Ship To address. The costs for the drugs were fractions of a penny per pill. I found a mention of a "Director" three times, but no details. I had several folders with unreadable, smudged letters—the first letter was E, L, or F, and the second letter was B or D. I organized documents and scanned them into folders in my cloud for two hours.

I stretched, picked up all the papers, dropped them into a clothes basket, and carried the basket to my room.

"Let's go outside before bed, Lucy. My eyeballs are burning from the computer screen."

We went out back. The night air was cold and damp. The sky was clear, but the moon was only a pale sliver. When Lucy wandered off into the dark, I walked toward the back fence and realized the back gate was open.

As I hurried to the gate to close it before Lucy wandered out, someone grabbed me from behind. I bent in half like I had collapsed and grabbed the knife strapped to my leg then whirled and sliced. I was rewarded with a roar. The sound of a single *click* grabbed my attention. I rushed toward the sound, threw myself into a low dive, feet first, and connected with bone. The dive was met with a satisfying crunch, and the bullet zinged high above me.

The backyard lights flooded the yard. I counted three men in my yard, and all three of them wore night-vision goggles. One was on the ground with a blood-soaked shirt. The second was on the ground with a leg askew and a bone sticking out.

The third man ripped off his goggles and headed toward the gun, which had flown out of the second man's hand and lay on the ground. Spike and Lucy ran to the house. Palace Guard raced from the house toward the gun and sent it sailing across the yard with a kick. I pulled out my pistol and squeezed. The third man dropped to the ground. I jumped up, and Palace Guard and I ran to the house.

I slammed and locked the door. *Hyperventilate later.* I grabbed my phone, texted Kate "Help," and called 911.

"I was attacked by three men in my backyard." I slid to the floor. Spike sat on one side of me, with Palace Guard on the other. Lucy climbed onto Spike's lap. I managed to repeat my name and address slowly and coherently.

"Stay on the phone," the dispatcher said. "Are they still there?"

Sirens. My favorite sound. "I need to unlock the front door, or they'll bust it down when they try to get in."

"Don't unlock any doors." The dispatcher's voice changed from a monotone to one with a higher pitch, and I understood the hint of panic. It was his version of "Don't go into the basement."

I rolled my eyes and hung up the phone. Palace Guard pointed; I still held the pistol in my right hand. After he offered me a hand up, I set the gun on the dining table and unlocked the front door. Palace Guard helped me to the sofa, and the four of us sat and waited for the deputies. Or Kate, Glenn, or Sergeant Arrington. *Wonder who will get here first?*

Spike had a fierce look.

"Is that your Kate face? Are you betting Kate will be first? I agree."

Kate burst into the house, followed by Glenn. The deputies swarmed the yard, and shouts came from the backyard.

"Now what?" Kate asked as Spike stood next to her with his hands on his hips.

"Oh lord, Spike." I snorted. "Sorry, Kate. Somebody opened the back gate. I was afraid Lucy might get lost. We bet you'd be here first. Unanimous."

"You hurt?" She pointed at my right arm. My right hand and arm were bloody, and it looked like I'd smeared blood on my shirt.

"It's not mine."

"Thought so. Go wash up and put on a clean shirt."

Sergeant Arrington appeared at the front door while I changed.

"Maggie?" he roared.

"Sarge, Maggie's fine. She's a little shaken and needs to clean up," Kate said. "Bad guys out back."

After two hours of questions, Kate called a halt and ordered me to go to bed. "I'll be here when you wake up."

* * *

The smell of coffee woke me up. I stumbled to the kitchen. Kate poured a cup and handed it to me. "About time you got up," Kate said. "Thank goodness you keep a well-stocked kitchen—somebody trained you well. I'm ready to throw the cinnamon rolls in the oven; you want your usual?"

"Sure do." I collapsed in a chair at the dining table. I wasn't sure what my usual was, but Kate was the cook. Whatever she put in front of me would be delicious and more than I could eat.

Kate grabbed bacon and eggs out of the refrigerator. "I haven't figured out how the yard lights went on. Do you have them on a timer?"

I looked at Palace Guard, and he looked away.

"You might say so," I said.

Kate gave the grits a quick stir, browned the roux for gravy, and dropped the bacon in a cast-iron skillet. Watching her at the stove was like watching a symphony orchestra's maestro.

"We need music." I turned the radio on. "So, do we know who those guys are?"

"Hired thugs who claimed they didn't know who hired them. Where did you aim your shot?"

"Left kneecap. I got it, right? He went down right away."

"Yep. Pretty much shattered. Another guy has an open tib-fib fracture. Your knife work on the last guy sliced across the tendons in both arms, and the abdominal slice nicked his liver. Your backyard looked like a war zone. I soaked your shirt in cold water."

"Thanks. It felt like a war for a minute there. I followed the rules—incapacitate, run, call for the cavalry, and fall apart."

Kate laughed. "Your training never included 'fall apart.' Did it, guys?"

Spike and Palace Guard shook their heads.

"I'm an advanced student. I added the last part myself." I flipped my hair.

Kate swatted me with a kitchen towel, but she must have felt sorry for me because any other time she'd have slammed me to the floor.

When Spike raised his eyebrows, I shook my head. *No ambush. Breakfast is ready.*

We ate in silence then after I ate my fill, I pushed my plate back.

Kate grinned. "You're such a lightweight." I was too stuffed to take her on, so I stuck out my tongue. Lucy yipped.

"Glenn?" I asked. Palace Guard went to the window and nodded.

I cleared our dishes, and Kate opened the door. Glenn strode in and headed to the coffeepot.

"You have breakfast, Dad?"

"Your mother doesn't let me out of the house without breakfast, but I wouldn't mind a cinnamon roll for dessert," he said. "Maggie, we need to talk."

I started another pot of coffee while Kate plated up a cinnamon roll for Glenn and cut a second one in half for the two of us to share.

"When I go home I need to have a good reason why you aren't with me," he said.

"Uh-oh. Mom's on the warpath," Kate said.

Glenn and Kate looked at me like it was my turn to talk. I grabbed forks, set them on the table, and sat down with my chin propped on my hand. "It's not a good idea. We'd just put Jennifer in danger. I don't have any facts to back it up, but I'm convinced we've got a leak somewhere. Somebody close to us is a source of information for Everett Duncan or whoever. You two are the only ones I trust right now. And, of course, my imaginary men."

Kate narrowed her eyes. "What about your mother, the sergeant, Taylor, Mr. Morgan, Lillian?"

Spike and Palace Guard stepped next to me. Palace Guard shook his head. I broke off a piece of cinnamon roll and popped it into my mouth. *Can't talk with food in my mouth.*

"If I can say something here," Glenn said. "If there is a leak, and it wouldn't take much to convince me there is, then our person who provides the information might be perfectly innocent and not realize the wrong people are listening to them."

I licked my fingers and grabbed a napkin. "Olivia documented and cataloged everything. I haven't gone through all the papers; however, I see some patterns. I just don't have anything for Scotland Yard yet."

"Who?" Glenn asked.

"She means me," Kate said. "The official me. So what do you think, Maggie? The unofficial me is asking."

"The overall boss stepped in because Everett Duncan is not dead, and there is an internal power struggle."

Glenn walked to the coffeepot with his cup and refilled it. "Anyone else?"

Kate and I held our cups up, and Glenn poured.

"So what do I tell Jennifer?" Glenn asked.

"Whatever you like. You Coyles are good at stuff like that." I grinned.

"What do your imaginary men say?" he asked.

Spike and Palace Guard stepped closer to me. "I'm better off here."

"Can you show me some of the documents?" Glenn asked.

"I'm going to work. Keep me informed, Maggie," Kate said.

Glenn read, reviewed, and organized more of Olivia's documents. I scanned and uploaded to the cloud.

After Glenn left, I sat down with a pad of paper and called Mother. "What do you know about Everett Duncan, the bank president, and his wife?"

"Everett's hair was gray, but it was so thin and fine, he kept it clipped short, and it made him look bald. He wore a toupee, but if he was going to spend the money for an expensive toupee, why a gray one? I didn't understand unless he wanted to present the distinguished banker look."

Mother talked for over an hour, and I scribbled as fast as I could. My hand cramped up before she wound down, but I kept writing.

"That's about it, Margaret. I can ask around some if you like."

My heart rate tripled, but I went for nonchalance. "No, it's okay. Like you said, my boss was his girlfriend. I was just curious."

"Duane and I might take a little weekend excursion, maybe fishing. You don't mind, do you?"

Why would I mind? Oh.

"Sounds nice."

"Thank you, Margaret. I was afraid, well, you know." Mother giggled and hung up, and I shook my head.

"Mother's going away for the weekend with her boyfriend. She said fishing, but I didn't know she liked to fish."

Spike and Palace Guard looked worried.

"Naw, it's okay. I like Sergeant Arrington."

Palace Guard patted my back.

I needed to clear my head before I tackled my pages of notes. "Let's go outside."

Before my shoes were on and tied, Palace Guard was ready to go. Lucy and Spike stayed on the porch. We stretched and ran our usual route north past the horses, turned around to go south past the goats, and back to the house. We ran hard, and I was drenched. After we got back, Palace Guard crossed his arms until I stretched again.

I poured a glass of raspberry tea and took my notes to the porch to read. After a half hour, I returned to Olivia's papers. I found letters from Everett to Olivia. Some of them were personal to the point of icky. I read on and discovered a disturbing revelation. Everett was interested in investing in the medical-marijuana market and mentioned "high profitability."

I sent Kate a text. "Go shoot?"

"Ten am tomorrow at the range."

* * *

Next morning was a discussion, of sorts, of who would stay with Lucy and who would go with me to the range. I wasn't involved, so I pulled my range gear together. I boxed up all the documentation, threw stinky clothes on top, and shoved the box into my closet. When I walked out to the car, Spike was with me.

Kate's car wasn't in the range parking lot, so I signed in, and Spike accompanied me to the pistol range. After I shot two rounds, Spike pointed at my phone. He wore hearing protection.

"Proud of yourself?" He grinned as I read the text from Kate. "Work no play."

"Bummer."

After I finished my morning shoot, I spread out my cleaning supplies on the table in the store's back room. After I cleaned my gun, a familiar voice in the store caught my attention.

I peeked through the door and turned back to Spike. My face must have shown my shock because Spike stepped toward me.

I mouthed. "Ernie. The homeless guy."

Spike's eyes narrowed. Even though he wasn't around pre-explosion, he knew about the homeless guy. Spike stepped out of the back room, and I followed him. I didn't know how, but he was positioned to protect me.

Lillian stood next to a counter behind Ernie. She glanced at the range clerk then at me. "Hi, I heard you were here. Got time for a cup of coffee?"

Spike frowned and shook his head.

A million thoughts raced through my head. *This is beyond bizarre.*

"Sure."

Spike swung into the passenger's seat. I'm sure he wanted me to have the full benefit of his displeasure. His arms were crossed, and his mouth was tight as he glared at me. We followed Lillian and Ernie to a café.

"I know you aren't happy about this, but I can't pass it up."

He shook his head.

"I understand. And I'm arguing with an imaginary man."

Spike tightened his mouth even more.

"You holding back a panda smile or a shark smile?"

Spike turned his head away.

When we got to the café, Spike slid into the booth, and I sat next to him; I was prepared to bolt.

Lillian slipped in across from Spike, and Ernie sat across from me. His gaunt face was clean shaven, and his sandy brown hair was short and styled.

I glared. "What's going on?"

"You need to try the muffins," Lillian said. "They're wonderful."

We ordered coffee and muffins. I asked for my blueberry muffin to be split and grilled.

While we waited, I glared at Lillian and frowned at Ernie.

He cleared his throat. "My name is Gary."

"Dear, this will be a bit of a surprise for you." Lillian reached across the table to pat my hand.

"Gary Sloan."

Spike and I looked at each other. *What the hell?* Not sure which one of us thought it.

"Gary Sloan," I said. "Really?"

Ernie closed his eyes, rubbed his forehead, and peered at me with sadness and pain in his face.

Or else he's a good actor. I looked at Spike because I wasn't sure who said that either. Spike shrugged.

I tapped my fingers on my coffee cup. My voice was hard. "My father's name was Gary. Mother said my father was *gone*. My whole life, I thought gone meant dead."

"I went undercover. I was young and overzealous. I left when you were three," Gary said. "I expected to be gone for four or five months— six months, max. I was more successful than anyone expected, which was good from an undercover standpoint, but bad for my family. I couldn't leave my position—too many people's lives depended on me. And my family was potential leverage. I got word—"

He looked away. When he turned back, his eyes glistened as he examined my face and gazed into my eyes. I glared back at him.

"You have your mother's eyes."

I snorted and gave him my best "Seriously?" look. It must have been close enough because he shifted his gaze to look at the floor.

He cleared his throat. "I got word to your mother to divorce me. I set up an annuity for her and you, but I abandoned my family."

I pursed my lips. "Certainly did."

"This was a bad idea. I'll go." Gary placed his hands on the seat to scoot out.

Lillian reached out and touched his arm. "Wait. Tell her the rest."

"No, Lillian. Let him go," I said.

He sat back with a slight smile. "You have your mother's fire."

"Take it back."

"What?"

"You heard me. Take it back, or I'll kick your ass," I hissed.

His smile erupted into a belly laugh. "Okay, I take it back. You have your own brand of fire. Well done."

"Good. Because she would do it," Lillian said.

Spike gave Lillian two thumbs up.

I put my head down to hide my smile. Gary looked straight at Spike then frowned as he rubbed his face.

"I guarded you at the library," Gary said. "You made Everett Duncan nervous with the rabbit incident. Did you know you spray-painted his security camera?"

"Yep, but I didn't get a chance to ask about the two electronic bugs in the room."

"It's good for me you didn't. They were mine, and Duncan didn't know about them. I pulled away from the library because Duncan thought I worked for his competitors who triggered the audit, and he was worried I planned to contact Olivia. Again, the bugs. Duncan was nervous about the auditor, so he had the auditor killed; I think his competitors killed Duncan."

I wasn't ready to trust Gary, even if he did see Spike. Spike raised his eyebrows, and I glared at him then blinked twice. Spike knew about the blinks. Twice is no.

Gary looked in Spike's direction, narrowed his eyes, and rubbed them. "I must be tired. Keep seeing shadows or something."

"Tell her," Lillian said.

"Donald Chandler planted the explosives at the diner and your car. I have information I'll get to Kate through Lillian. I need to disappear for a few weeks, not twenty years like last time."

"Donnie's not an independent thinker. Who's his boss?"

"Everything points to Duncan. Donnie hasn't done anything since Duncan was killed."

Spike crossed his arms.

I'll hear about this.

"Thank you, Gary. I've got a lot to think about."

We all stood, and I hugged Lillian. I wasn't ready to embrace Gary, and he smiled; I assumed he understood. I didn't shake his hand either. *Too weird.*

On our drive home, I looked at Spike, but he wouldn't look at me.

"What do you think, Spike? Should I have told him Duncan is alive?"

Spike shook his head.

"Good. Thanks."

Spike raised his arms.

I rolled my eyes. "Woo-hoo for you."

When we got home, Lucy was ready to go outside, and I wanted a run to clear my head. While she did her wander, sniff, pee routine, I ran the fence perimeter at full speed until I was winded. When I passed her, Lucy trotted behind me for a bit, then stopped for a rest and waited for the next round. Of the two of us, she was the smarter one.

After my run, I sat on the porch with raspberry tea and texted Kate.

"Call when u can."

My phone rang. *Kate, so quick?* No, it was the lawyer's office.

"Ms. Sloan, this is Shantelle from Ms. Rodriquez's office. We've gone through about half of Ms. Edwards's papers. We found receipts for jewelry. Do you have her jewelry? You may want to have a jeweler match up the receipts with the jewelry and give you a good estimate of the value. If you make an appointment, I'll be happy to go with you."

I didn't even have a lawyer last month. Guess I call Mother for another reference.

"Mother, I need to find a good jeweler. Olivia left me some jewelry, and I need someone to estimate the value."

"I know a good jeweler. I'll make an appointment and go with you. You don't know anything about jewelry."

"Good idea. My lawyer's assistant will meet us there. Let me know when the appointment is, and I'll tell Shantelle."

"I'll get it done now. And I'll call and let Shantelle know when to meet us."

This will work. I can turn the jewelry business over to the two of them.

I called Glenn. "Mother is arranging for a jeweler to examine Olivia's jewelry. I'll pick it up before our appointment."

I spent the rest of the afternoon on the computer. "Come look." The guys leaned over my shoulder. "I searched Parker Coyle and found the sale of sixty acres of land and a hunting cabin to Parker Coyle six years ago. The seller was Jennifer Elizabeth Coyle." I leaned back. "And Reggie's Diner was transferred to Parker and Katherine Coyle two years ago when Reggie became ill. A simple internet search is how Duncan found us. He must have known about Parker and me."

Kate called at five thirty. "You got any beer? I've pulled into your driveway."

I hung up on her to grab two beers. Finally—I got to hang up on somebody, but I'm not sure it counted because she burst through the front door before I closed the fridge.

"Sorry for such short notice this morning. Did you shoot? How'd ya do?"

"We should sit down."

We made ourselves comfortable on the porch. I told Kate everything. The range, Lillian, Gary, jewelry, Everett Duncan's toupees, my job-application database, Ella, love letters, the internet search, and my theories about the bank, cartoon shop, warehouse, and counterfeit drugs. She interrupted a few times for clarification.

When I got quiet, Kate narrowed her eyes. "Anything else?"

"All I can think of for now."

"I've got information for you. Olivia was listed as the beneficiary on John Edwards's life insurance policy. It makes sense in hindsight. I'm sure your lawyer will want to know." Kate's stomach rumbled. "Guess I'm hungry. You got anything here? Want to crash Mom and Dad's?"

"I have some chicken."

"Good, marinate it a bit for the grill, and I'll pull something together."

I threw the chicken in a plastic storage bag and poured in olive oil, apple cider, basil, and rosemary. Kate prepared her oven-roasted potatoes.

"We've got forty minutes. If you pull together a salad, I'll make a dressing and dessert."

I'm the grill master, or at least I am when Glenn's not around. I timed the chicken to come off the grill to rest a few minutes before the potatoes were done.

While we ate, Kate told me about an assignment she was offered. "It involves a lot of travel. I can't talk specifics, of course, but it's an excellent opportunity."

She baked a yellow cake for dessert. She put a dollop of fudge sauce and a scoop of ice cream on top of our still-hot squares of cake. The chocolate fudge melted into the cake and the ice cream slid down the sides.

"Let's see what you've got that I can use to tighten the noose for Mr. Duncan."

We sorted and scanned more documents. Kate copied the scans to her flash drive.

"How safe do you feel here? Should you be somewhere else? Do you need someone to stay with you? Wait. Scratch that. You've got Lucy and two imaginary men. But what about going somewhere else?"

"I'm fine here. I would like to go back to Olivia's apartment for another search. I keep feeling like there's something we missed."

"I can't imagine what it would be, but I'll go with you."

"Good. When? Now?"

"It's after nine, but let's do it."

We put the documents back into the boxes and carried the boxes to my room. I threw on my gray sweatshirt to ward off the chill from the clear night's dropping temperatures before we jumped into Kate's car.

The brightly lit water spray from the bubbling fountains looked like sparkling diamonds. The nonstop night sounds of the tree frogs at the lake and the crickets in the grass drowned out the traffic noise from the street.

"This is even more impressive at night," Kate said.

When we got close to Olivia's apartment, Kate and I froze at the same time.

"Do you see a box at the door?" I asked.

A brown, medium-sized box blocked the entrance.

Kate shined her flashlight down the breezeway and hissed, "Stay here." She moved within four feet of the package and backed away. "There's no mailing label on the box, at least from what I can see. Let's go back to the car."

While we trotted to the parking lot, Kate made a call. I heard her say "suspicious package" and the address.

"Okay with you if we stop by my place to pick up a few things? I'll be fast. We're in for a long night."

I was anxious to get back and check on Lucy, but Kate sprinted into her apartment and reappeared with a backpack.

"I keep a change of clothes and pajamas in this backpack. I hope you have a spare toothbrush. I just grabbed my bag and didn't take the time to pack anything extra."

Kate's phone rang twice on our way back. She confirmed she called in the suspicious package, and the second call was Glenn. He'd gotten a call we'd found something. She handed the phone to me.

I gave her an "Oh fine—make me talk to Dad" look.

Most of the conversation on my end consisted of "We understand" and "Yes, sir."

After I hung up, Kate asked, "What did he say?"

"You're grounded."

She laughed. "Dang it, Maggie. I believe you."

"He's on his way to my house. He may beat us there."

"As soon as we get there, we need to grab a beer. We'll be off duty."

"Can we have cake with our beer?"

"Yep, sounds great."

When we got to my house, Glenn was waiting for us at the gate.

"I walked around the house. Lucy did her hello bark," he said.

"Lucy would have let you know if anything was wrong," Kate said.

Glenn took my house key to open the back door, and Lucy bounded around to the front of the house to greet us. Glenn opened the front door.

"Everything's okay here."

I pulled out three beers, and Kate warmed the fudge sauce.

Sergeant Arrington called me, and I handed my phone to Glenn. I learn quick.

"The girls are fine . . . We're at Maggie's . . . Drinking beer and eating cake."

Spike raised his eyebrows.

I owed them an explanation. "Kate and I saw a box by Olivia's apartment door. No label, so we left. Anything here?"

Spike and Palace Guard shook their heads.

"What'd they say?" Kate asked.

"Nothing here."

Glenn put his hand over the phone. "Sergeant Arrington says someone will be here in the next half hour."

Kate and I took our beer to the back porch while Glenn and Sergeant Arrington talked.

We rocked. "I'll talk," Kate said. "Okay?"

"Yep."

"I'm glad we put everything away before we left for the apartment."

I took a swig of my beer. "It's what we do."

"What's that?" Glenn asked when he came out to the porch.

"Put things away and clean up before we sit," Kate said, but Glenn narrowed his eyes. *Can't fool Dad.*

Twenty minutes later, Lucy growled at a car with two men at the gate. Glenn stood by the door as Kate and I peeked out the front window. The older one had dark hair and was in his mid-forties with dark-rimmed glasses. He was medium height and had a heavyset build with a thick neck. The other man was in his early thirties; he had light brown hair with hints of red. The younger man was slender, shorter than the first man, and looked like a runner. Both men wore khaki pants, white short-sleeved shirts, dark ties, and lanyards that held ID cards and badges.

I whispered. "I don't need a law-enforcement database. Right?"

She snickered. "You're funny. You've already cataloged them, haven't you?"

When they reached the door, they shook hands with Glenn. Glenn introduced us. We all shook hands. Spike and Palace Guard shook hands. I coughed to keep from laughing.

"You okay?" Kate asked.

"Might be coming down with something. Tell you later."

Glenn didn't say "My daughter, the FBI agent," but I could tell they knew. They had the *Wow, Kate Coyle!* look every time they glanced her way.

Kate took my elbow. "Shall I fix you some tea?"

"Thank you. Tea would be nice." I almost said *lovely* but managed to refrain.

Glenn narrowed his eyes at us. Kate smiled and brewed my tea. I think Kate tried for a sweet smile, but I needed to let her know her sweet smile looks more like a lioness gazing at a newborn fawn with longing.

After Kate handed me my tea and sat next to me, the police officer with glasses said, "Ms. Coyle, would you tell us the circumstances of how you found the package?"

"Ms. Sloan and I went to the apartment to pick up a few things. When we stepped around the corner, we saw the box at the door. Packages are delivered to the manager's office, not to an apartment. Ms. Sloan stayed back, and I approached close enough to see the box had no label, at least from my view. We left the area, and I called the police department on our way back to my car. We returned here and waited for you."

"Ms. Sloan, do you have anything to add?"

I thought about diamonds, tree frogs, and crickets. "No, I don't."

"Do you have any ideas who might have left a suspicious package at your apartment?"

"No, I don't."

"Ms. Sloan lives here, not at the apartment," Kate said. "The prior tenant is deceased, and Ms. Sloan manages the estate. The apartment lease is paid through the end of the year."

"Ms. Sloan, how often do you stay at the apartment?" the younger man asked.

"I've never stayed there."

"Never?"

Kate laughed. "It's a fancy place, but it's not Ms. Sloan's style."

The two men looked around at my gray furniture and tiny house and nodded. Glenn glared.

The older man cleared his throat. "That's all we have for now. Unless you have anything else?"

We didn't. They left.

Glenn narrowed his eyes. "Now what?" The two imaginary men stood by Glenn with their arms crossed.

Kate told me to let her do the talking, so I looked at her.

"Maggie said you grounded me."

"Way to throw me under the bus, Kate," I said.

Glenn laughed. "You two are a mess. What's going on?"

"Okay, Dad. We didn't want to start a premature investigation. Sit down, and we can go over what we've got."

We spent the next hour going over our documents, findings, and theories. Glenn frowned and crossed his arms. "Why are you sitting on this?"

"I don't want to move until we've got a tight net," Kate said.

"Let's go through this again," Glenn said. "Some of this is hard evidence. Kate, that's yours. Some of what we know is conjecture. Maggie, that's what you and I can follow up on."

"I don't know, Dad. I'm not crazy about you and Maggie getting into the middle of this."

I raised my eyebrows. "Do you have any suggestions on how I get out of the middle?"

"Let's think about this. Is there any way to shift the focus away from Maggie?" Glenn asked.

The imaginary men sat down and rested their chins in their hands. I closed my eyes. My other option was to laugh, but it would have been rude.

"Maybe we take advantage of me being in the middle."

"No," said Kate.

"When you set a trap for a rat, you don't put the entire block of cheese out. You use a sampling. We don't need the entire me, just a sampling."

"I'm not following. What?" Glenn asked.

"I don't know. I have imaginary men. Why not an imaginary Maggie?"

Glenn laughed. "How many beers have you had?"

"Two beers," I said automatically.

Kate opened the fridge, pulled out three beers, and handed one to Glenn and one to me.

"This is a dopey idea. Where would the imaginary trap be? I don't think it's a good idea for imaginary Maggie to stay at Olivia's apartment. No good way to secure it. And imaginary Maggie can't be here," Kate said.

"What about my apartment? We'd have Mr. Morgan's apartment and Taylor's apartment as observation points. We can set up security cameras and have the lights and TV on timers. I'd go in the front door with my gray Maggie clothes and slip out the back."

"After we get the trap set, how do we lure the rat?" Glenn asked.

"Why don't we tell the rat?" I asked.

Kate shook her head and looked at the ceiling.

"So if I go along with this imaginary plan, besides our imaginary Maggie, what's the bait?" Kate asked.

"The rat we want to catch is the king rat who murdered Parker," Glenn said.

"Everett Duncan killed Parker. I'm sure of it. I'm not sure he's the king rat, though," I said.

"This is the Scotland Yard part, Maggie," Kate said. "I want to tie in all his aliases and all their activities—the bank, the murders of Parker and the auditor, the library explosion and deaths of Olivia and John Edwards, all the attempts on your life, and counterfeit drugs."

"I'm sure we've got all the threads, and if we pull the right one, the rest will follow. I may be mixing my metaphors, but how about, pardon the cliché, the low-hanging fruit?" I said.

"We've got something going here," Glenn said. "What is the easiest thing to hang on Everett Duncan?"

"The most vulnerable thread in his whole organization is Donnie," I said.

"Like it. What's the tightest case we have on Donnie?" Glenn asked.

"He planted the explosives in my car," I said. "Mr. Morgan saw him."

Glenn and Kate looked at each other.

"We can't use Mr. Morgan," Glenn said.

"Oh. Donnie beat up Lillian," I said.

Glenn shook his head.

"Can't use Lillian either? Then why don't we frame him?"

"Are you nuts? I can't sanction that," Kate said.

I turned to Glenn. "We don't know who killed the auditor, right? Wouldn't an official investigation into the murder consider the phony investigator as a prime suspect?"

"Just might shake up ole Donnie. Nothing shady about that, right, Kate?" Glenn said.

"Dang. I'm glad you two are on my side. I'll get my team on it," Kate said.

"I'll get a leak to Everett Duncan that I can identify the person who was in the library on the day of the stabbing," I said. "Which, by the way, I can."

"And you're just now telling me? Who?" Kate asked.

"Might have been Donnie," I said.

She narrowed her eyes and looked at me. I practiced her lioness smile.

"Really, Maggie?" she said.

"Not saying."

"Sorry I asked." Kate grabbed the dishcloth at the sink and wiped down the dining table. I understood. I was a little on edge too; cleaning helps.

"This is pulling together. Maggie, you can't stay here," Glenn said. "Your only presence needs to be your imaginary self at your apartment. You and Lucy need to stay at our house. And your imaginary men, of course."

Spike and Palace Guard nodded. Sagely.

"I'll bring you some boxes and a couple of suitcases in the morning. Pack up your things for our house in the boxes, and I'll take them home," Glenn continued. "You can take the suitcases to your apartment when you're ready to go there. I'll call Sergeant Arrington to make sure your mother doesn't have plans to redecorate your apartment or some other surprise. We'll work out when I pick you up and where. You might want to wear gray going in, and your new colors when you leave."

"I'll talk to Mr. Morgan and Taylor to arrange for the use of their apartments and assign three teams—one to investigate Donnie openly, the second to watch you and the apartment, and the third to investigate Everett Duncan and the dead man on Duncan's boat." Kate counted the three items on her fingers. "Give me a day to get everything in place. Then you can get the word out you're the witness. How will you do that, again?"

"Take a friend to lunch."

Chapter Twenty-One

After Glenn and Kate left, a fog of doubt shrouded me. *Shake it off. It's a good plan.*

"Lucy, I'll call the vet and the groomer, but it's all part of the plan."

Lucy put her head on my foot. After I finished my calls, I scratched her ears. Lucy rolled over for a belly rub, and I eased to the floor next to her. "You're all set, girl. Checkup and a nail trim at the vet's in the morning. Then a bath and haircut at the groomer's." Spike sat on the floor next to us. "I want Lucy to be safe. Why do I feel like I'm abandoning her?" Palace Guard joined us on the floor. He rubbed Lucy's belly while I made the next call on my list. Apartment manager. Mine, not Olivia's.

"This is Maggie Sloan. I'm moving back to my apartment. I'll be there tomorrow."

I rose and stretched. When Lucy whined, I opened the back door, and she and Spike trotted out to the yard. I grabbed a bottle of water, and Palace Guard and I sat on the porch while I called Ella.

"Hey. You free for lunch today? Great. I'll pick you up at noon."

I brushed a few wrinkles out of my gray shirt as I walked to the door to let Lucy back in. *Imaginary Maggie looks a little drab.* I didn't realize I'd become attached to the Taylor-matched colors.

Glenn arrived midmorning. I had stacked my clothes for the Coyles' on the dining table.

Glenn carried in a cardboard flat and folded it into a packing box. "I thought you'd only need one box, and I was right, I see. I'll take the document boxes too, right? I can load them now. When's Lucy's appointment?"

"The boxes to go are by the door, and first thing in the morning."

"I'll pick her up in the afternoon. Were you planning to leave the apartment before or after dark? And do you have a go bag?"

I finished putting my folded clothes into a box. "After I take my suitcases to the apartment tomorrow morning, I'll go to the store and buy groceries then I'll hang out a little at the apartment before I go for a run to leave the apartment for a while. I want to give Donnie every opportunity to do whatever. What do you think? What's a go bag?"

"A backpack with what you'd need for two or three days if you have to travel with no notice. Your plan will give the surveillance team a nervous breakdown," Glenn said.

"I'll pack a go bag. Kate's team will see Donnie if he does anything and get word to her. I'll have my phone—a warning text from either of you and *poof*, I'm gone."

"You tell Kate. If she says okay, I'll go along."

"Dang it. What's with you Coyles? Masters of passing the buck."

"It's genetic. We're good at it, aren't we?"

I called Kate. "Got you on speakerphone. Your dad's here, and we want you to listen to my idea because its success depends on your crack surveillance team. I go to my old apartment tomorrow, and then I leave. Donnie will have an opening to make a move, and your team can catch him. If he doesn't do anything, I'll return. Leave again then return. Maybe three times. I can slip out after dark and meet up with your dad if Donnie doesn't try anything during the day."

"Hi, Dad. Hate the plan, Maggie. But let me talk to the team then I'll get back to you. What do the guys say, by the way?"

Spike and Palace Guard frowned, shook their heads, and waggled their fingers at me.

"They're thinking about it."

After she hung up, Spike grabbed Palace Guard by the neck with both hands, pretended to choke him, and pointed at me.

"She didn't say 'goodbye,'" Glenn said.

"Welcome to my world."

"I'll take the boxes and get out of here. Text me when you leave for lunch. You sure you're okay?"

"I'm fine." My hands were sweating, and my heart was racing. I was so scared my goosebumps huddled together for protection.

Glenn left. I knew he didn't believe me, but he didn't say anything. *He's a good dad. I wonder if he knew my father.*

Lucy and I stepped outside as the crows flew overhead and called their urgent, raspy warning of a nearby predator. A slight breeze brushed the back of my neck when Palace Guard wrapped his arm around my shoulders. I inhaled through my nose and exhaled through my pursed lips. *I can do this.*

"I need to go for a hard run. Spike, will you stay with Lucy? Palace Guard, race ya."

And we took off to the north. The horses caught our excitement and raced us to the end of their fence. We turned around like a choreographed group and headed south. For a minute, I thought the horses might jump the fence to continue their gallop with us as they whinnied to cheer us on. When we streaked past the house, Lucy barked, and Spike jumped around with his arms in the air. We continued to the goat farm, and the bleating goats chased us along the fence. After we turned and dashed back to the house, we careened into the driveway and raced to the backyard.

Palace Guard won, of course. I flopped down on the grass, winded and soaked with sweat. I was exhausted, stinky, and energized.

"I just had a thought."

Spike and Palace Guard made a big O with their mouths and put their hands up to their faces.

"Very funny. I'll ask anyway. Do the horses see you?"

Palace Guard grinned.

"Just curious." I stood up stiffly and headed inside.

After my shower, I left to pick up Ella. While Spike jumped into the back seat, Palace Guard stayed with Lucy.

Ella waited on the curb. She wore a gray warehouse uniform with ELLA stitched in white on her left shirt pocket. She hopped into the car and beamed. "I am so glad to see you. Where we going? What's the occasion?"

"Me too. Let's get a good greasy burger and fries. I'm moving back to my apartment; the whole mess is as good as solved. We'll talk at lunch."

"I know the perfect place. Turn left then it's just a few blocks away. They get real busy at lunchtime, but we'll be just ahead of the rush."

When we walked in, I could smell the years of grease on the walls— ready to self-combust any second. It was an authentic diner, down to the lunch counter with spinning, red-vinyl seats repaired with black tape. We grabbed a booth in the middle—not too close to the front door and not too close to the restrooms, but near the kitchen and an exit in case of fire—my choice. Ella scooted into a booth and faced the entrance. Spike slid into my side before I did and sat sideways. He'd watch my back.

We ordered cheeseburgers with everything, fries, and colas—no diet cola here.

"Diane, put back two pieces of pie for us, would ya? Might be to go," Ella said. "Homemade cherry pie will be a perfect afternoon snack. So what's up?"

"I'm moving back to my apartment tomorrow morning. I've had enough of being out in the country," I said in a clear, loud voice.

Ella cocked her head. "Since when?" she whispered. "This a setup?"

"You know it is." I kept the volume up.

Ella nodded and smiled for the people in the diner. "Being in town is better."

I lowered my voice so I'd have a confidential tone but still be loud enough for everyone nearby to hear. "I give my deposition day after tomorrow. The Big Fish is going down."

Ella raised her eyebrows. "Well, that is news."

Our food arrived, and we dug in. Our conspiracy would have to wait. When grease dripped down my fingers and chin, Ella pointed at the roll of paper towels on our table. "These are more useful than flimsy paper napkins."

I ate almost half of my cheeseburger and a quarter of my fries. Ella ate more than I did, but she didn't finish hers either. When Diane whisked away our plates, she said, "We don't allow our food to be reheated. You get hungry, you come back. Wave when you want your pie. Want coffee?"

She didn't wait for an answer. "Yes, please," must have been plastered on our satiated faces. She returned with two heavy diner mugs of steaming hot coffee. The acidic, fresh coffee bean aroma reminded me of a black and white movie—old-fashioned and timeless.

"So tell me," Ella said.

"Turns out I saw a few things when I interviewed for jobs and didn't realize at first they were related. FBI is very interested." I nodded sagely. *I knew it would come in handy sometime. Thanks, Lillian.*

Ella's eyebrows shot up, and her eyes widened. She coughed a little with a paper towel over her mouth. "How am I doing?" she whispered.

"Great," I mouthed.

"Deposition day after tomorrow, right?" she asked. "And you're moving back to your apartment."

"What about you?"

"My daughter graduated from college and accepted a position with the CIA."

"What? How exciting. I know you're proud of her. You know, I always wanted to be a spy."

"She won't be a spy. She's a computer genius. I don't like she'll be moving to DC, but we have family in the area, so she'll have people to look out for her."

"It's good to have a support system in place." I glanced behind me. "There's a line out the door. Maybe we should wave for our pie."

"And I should get back to work."

I paid for our lunch, and Diane handed Ella two white paper sacks.

When we stepped outside, Ella said, "Can we talk in your car?"

"My car has a GPS tracker on it, but nothing else."

"So what am I supposed to do?"

"Tell somebody at work in confidence you heard the Gray Lady moved back to her apartment and will talk to the FBI at the end of this week. If they press for more, you can mention deposition—up to you. We don't want to be obvious. I suspect you'll only need to say it once. And make sure nobody gets the idea you know anything."

"I know just the person. She'll keep the details straight—sounds like that's critical, right?"

"Yes."

"She'll make herself sound important and spread it before the end of the day with no mention of me. It'll get to the right people. She's good."

Spike patted Ella on the back, and she touched her shoulder and smiled.

When we got back to the warehouse, I tapped Ella's arm with my fingertips. "You stay safe, girlfriend," I said.

"You, too, honey. Call me if you need me." She climbed out of the car with her white sack in her hand.

It's good to have friends. And pie.

I tried to read after I got home, but I was too jumpy. I scrubbed the baseboards in the living room and kitchen. I wore out my arm muscles and knees as I crawled around and attacked dirt. The smell of the cleanser and the sound of the scrub brush calmed my nerves. I got a call from Mr. Morgan.

"Lillian and I want to come over for dinner. We'll bring food, and I'll cook."

"Sounds great. I've got a piece of pie from lunch, and it's big enough for four. We can have pie for dessert."

* * *

Lucy yipped. Mr. Morgan and Lillian were here. I almost yipped myself at the thought of the friendly faces of regular people.

Mr. Morgan opened Lillian's car door and helped her out. My heart melted over the sheer normalness of his old-world manners. Mr. Morgan looked sharp in his khaki slacks and blue knit collared shirt. Lillian was summer personified in her mint green capris and cream blouse with tiny yellow roses. Mr. Morgan toted two oversized canvas bags, and Lillian carried a covered salad bowl. I hurried out to the car and picked up the two grocery sacks on the back seat.

"There's only the three of us." I laughed.

"We might have invited some other people to drop by," Lillian said. "We'll need a little nosh."

Spike, Palace Guard, and I rolled our eyes.

I emptied the sacks and put food in the refrigerator. I peeked into Lillian's deep bowl, and it was filled with her homemade cookies. Mr. Morgan pulled out a chair for Lillian to sit at the table.

"I'm the sous-chef for the evening, dear," she said.

"I hope the army you invited is hungry because there's enough food here for two armies. You do know I'm moving to my apartment in the morning, right?"

"Of course we do. That's why we're here," Lillian said.

Mr. Morgan washed his hands and put on his apron. "I needed to get out of the way at my place, so we came here to be in your way instead. I need a mess of chicken grilled. Can you handle it?"

I tied on my black barbeque apron and fired up the grill as I smiled— nothing more gratifying than chicken with charred grill marks. I infused my hair and clothes with applewood smoke, and my tense muscles relaxed. *Wood smoke and grilling therapy.*

Lillian came outside with two glasses of wine. "He doesn't need a sous-chef. He's Mister One-Man Show in the kitchen. Chicken smells heavenly."

I relaxed in the companionable silence, broken only by chirping crickets and the sizzle of the grill.

"You know, dear, Mr. Morgan and I were spooks. Now we're semiretired. We're investigators."

I knew "spooks" was spy talk for spies. I hoped "investigators" was another word for "good guys." *Also, so much for normal, everyday people.*

"We investigate insurance fraud, a little white collar crime. Nothing quite as exciting as what we used to do."

Mr. Morgan brought out a platter of cheese and a variety of olives, grapes, and his homemade crackers in one hand, a bottle of wine under his arm, and a large empty aluminum pan in his other hand.

"I brought you two some refreshments. Got chicken for me? I'll put some in the oven to stay warm and chop up the rest for chicken-wrap sandwiches. So, Lillian and I accepted an assignment to investigate the bank and Everett Duncan for fraudulent loans."

"We had so many rabbit trails to follow." Lillian held our empty wine glasses in front of Mr. Morgan, who pulled a corkscrew out of his back pocket and opened the fresh bottle of wine. "For example, John Edwards worked for Duncan. Olivia was Duncan's girlfriend and John Edwards's ex-wife. Then Donnie appeared, and you learned he was Olivia's brother. Isn't it interesting how pivotal Olivia was?"

I frowned. "Do you think Olivia was involved?"

"I was never sure if she was involved or an innocent bystander. Also interesting at least to me was how slick Duncan was. His embezzlement passed regular audits for years. I'm sure Donnie killed the auditor." Lillian sipped her wine.

"Maggie, I'm not so certain Donnie killed the auditor, but Lillian and I do agree Parker may have found a link to the bank in his investigation of illegal drug activities," Mr. Morgan added.

"I need to sit down," I said.

Lucy sat on my feet, either to keep them warm or to keep me calm. Spike and Palace Guard sat on the arms of my rocking chair. No rocking for me.

Lillian looked at me. "Would you like a small snack plate, dear?"

"Yes, please." I glanced at Spike and Palace Guard. They nodded, and I laughed. *Goofy guys.*

"Are you okay, dear?"

I laughed harder. *How do I explain my imaginary men wanted a nosh too?*

I fanned my face with my hands. "How can I explain?"

Spike and Palace Guard looked at each other and shook their heads.

"I'm fine. I just remembered something . . ."

Lillian narrowed her eyes. *She knows something is going on.*

I closed my eyes. I tried to look calm. Mistake. *Need a diversion.*

"Mr. Morgan, remember my blushing problem?"

He laughed. "I'll never forget the rimless wall-hung shower toilet."

"What are you two talking about?" Lillian asked. "Just a second. I need to adjust my new hearing aids."

Mr. Morgan went into a long, colorful explanation. I loved how he turned a silly moment into a hilarious story.

After we all calmed down, I asked, "What about the library explosion?"

"We think John Edwards set the explosives and was leaving when Olivia pulled the fire alarm. Didn't you say she had an appointment that morning?" Lillian asked. "She must have returned sooner than expected, and he tried to get her out of the library. Their bodies were found outside the library at the back door. FBI got a positive ID from dental records."

Need to ask Kate how Lillian knew about the FBI and the dental records.

"It's kind of—I don't know—touching? He tried to save her," I said. "Do we know where she went?"

"I'm sure she was seeing her doctor, but we don't have her medical information," Lillian said.

"Would I have access?" I asked.

"Only if she listed you on her forms. Law enforcement has already begun the legal process for her records," Mr. Morgan said.

"There's just so much, isn't there? Do we know the link between the warehouse and the bank?" I asked.

"I think you do," Lillian said. "It must be why you're their target. What do you see as the link?"

Lucy whined and barked. Three vehicles drove past the horse farm and headed to my house. Lucy ran to the fence in the front, near the driveway. I glanced at Spike, and he swept a hand toward the front. I ran to join Lucy.

Glenn's truck pulled into the driveway, and Jennifer and Kate were with him. Sergeant Arrington's car pulled in behind them with Mother in the passenger's seat. I didn't recognize the third car. When the passenger waved, I realized Taylor and her Harry were here too. We were having a party. I was glad I'd changed to one of my new Taylor-colored shirts. Lucy, Spike, and Palace Guard danced.

Oh, what the heck. I joined in.

A fourth car appeared. I didn't recognize it either. I prepared for a dash to the back, but Palace Guard gave me a hand wave to stop. When the car pulled in, Kate showed them where to park. A man and a woman with the look of law enforcement—all business—stepped out of the car.

"Food couriers," Mr. Morgan whispered behind me, "for the surveillance team."

"We are feeding an army," I said.

Kate wore her dark jeans and a black T-shirt. She came up to the house with a tight hold on Jennifer's arm. Jennifer wore jeans and a pink and white striped shirt. She glared at Kate and growled. "I am not a doddering old woman."

Taylor wore dark blue, ankle length slacks and a bright yellow peasant blouse. She grabbed onto her tall Harry with two hands. He wore jeans and a white T-shirt with a black and orange tiger with glowing eyes and BE FIERCE READ! in an arc around the tiger. He stared at Taylor with his eyebrows twisted into almost-actual question marks. I locked arms with Lillian. Glenn looked at Kate, Taylor, and me and broke into a grin as Mr. Morgan turned his back and coughed.

"Girls," Jennifer said in her mom voice, "can we call a truce for just one evening? Kate? Maggie? Taylor?"

I stepped behind Lillian and narrowed my eyes at Kate. "Sure. If they will."

Taylor's eyes widened. She was good at the "Who, me?" look. She had learned from the experts—five-year-olds.

"Taylor?" Jennifer said.

Taylor looked down. "Yes, ma'am."

"Okay, Mom," Kate said. "You beat all three of us."

Jennifer threw her arms up in the air. "I win!"

Spike and Palace Guard did a victory dance for her.

"Harry, welcome to my home. I'm so happy to meet you." I put out my hand.

He grinned and hugged me. Taylor laughed. "Forgot to tell you. Harry's a hugger." Harry emitted man soap.

Spike and Palace Guard did a victory dance for Harry. I rolled my eyes.

"What?" Kate asked.

"Victory dances. For your mom, the winner, and Harry, the hugger." Kate snickered.

Everyone grabbed a beverage and gravitated to the backyard, except for Courier One and Courier Two, who stayed in the kitchen with Mr. Morgan.

Taylor introduced Harry to everyone. I made my way to Mother and Sergeant Arrington. Mother wore a forest-green blouse with palm fronds and pink flamingos, a red pencil skirt, and green strappy heels. Sarge was in his off duty uniform of khaki pants and a white collared shirt. His pale green tie with the pink flamingos, however, was new.

"It's nice to see you. Mother, you look radiant."

When Mother blushed, Spike and Palace Guard punched each other.

"Thank you, Margaret."

Mother and Sergeant Arrington grinned.

"What? What's up with you two?" *I'm acting like a parent.*

Spike and Palace Guard stood next to me with their hands on their hips. I went for an interested demeanor to keep from busting out laughing. I'm sure I just looked dopey.

"We kind of need to talk to you in private," Sergeant Arrington said.

If Mother's pregnant, she's grounded.

"Want to go for a walk?" I asked.

"Well, no. Not with these shoes," Mother said. "Can we go inside?"

We went inside. When Sergeant Arrington gave Mr. Morgan a look, Mr. Morgan stepped to the back door like a sentry. Palace Guard shrugged and stood at attention with Mr. Morgan.

I sat on the sofa. Sarge and Mother stood in front of me like a couple of errant teenagers. Mother hung onto Sarge's arm, and he took in a breath. "I've asked Izzy to marry me, and she said yes. We want your blessing."

Who is Izzy?

Mother giggled. "Big D calls me Izzy."

I forgot Mother's name was Isolde.

"That's sweet. Of course, you have my blessing. When is the wedding?"

"We planned to elope next weekend. Is that okay?"

What? Whoa. I need to shift back to immature.

"It's exciting. Shall we announce your engagement?"

Sergeant Arrington looked at Mother, and she blushed.

"Sounds great," he said.

The three of us walked outside together, and I signaled for Taylor to whistle. Taylor put two fingers to her mouth and whistled while Harry looked at her with admiration. Everyone hushed.

"Excuse me, everyone," I said. "Sergeant Arrington has an announcement."

Sergeant Arrington stepped to the middle of the porch and cleared his throat. "I am proud to announce Mrs. Sloan and I are engaged to be married."

He reached for her hand, and Mother stepped next to him. He wrapped his arm around her, and she all but disappeared in his embrace.

Everyone applauded, and Taylor whistled. The gathering turned into an engagement party.

"I am so pleased for Sarge and your mother." Jennifer appeared next to me.

"So am I. It's turned into quite a festive evening. I should have put up colorful paper lanterns."

"I can't see your backyard with colorful paper lanterns. Maybe gray." She chuckled and hugged me. *Jennifer just teased me.*

My heart was bursting with joy for Mother and Sarge. I joined Mother on the porch while we sipped our wine and rocked.

"Mother, is my father dead?" I asked.

"No, Margaret. Where did you get that idea?"

"When I was young, you said my father was *gone*. I thought gone was a polite way to say he was dead."

"As far as I know, he's alive. I divorced him when you were four. He asked me to. He said the divorce was for 'our protection.' I understood, but I didn't understand. He's an undercover agent. A spy. You've always been just like him."

"Do you have any pictures of him?"

Mother glanced around and spoke in a hushed voice. "I'm not supposed to, but I have one. I'll give it to you. It's our wedding picture."

"You know I like Sergeant Arrington. He's a wonderful man."

"I'm glad you like him, Margaret. He thinks you're amazing, and so do I."

"Oh, Mother. That's nice. Thank you."

"Do you need help packing? I'd love to help."

"I've already moved just about everything. Nothing left to pack but my toothbrush and hairbrush in the morning."

Mother talked about Sergeant Arrington, and I listened. Giving her my full attention was the least I could do after all the years I ignored what she said. I must have slipped into my old ways of zoning out because I thought she said "Tony."

"I'm sorry, Mother. I was distracted. You said, Tony?"

"The explosion might have damaged your hearing, Margaret. You need to have it checked." She spoke slower. "Tony, my friend from church, said I should thank you and let you know his daughter PJ is fine. She's with her aunt and uncle in Nevada and going to college. Tony is very proud of her. She was in a bad situation and wouldn't let anyone step in. He said you gave her confidence to break away. I don't know how—" Lillian signaled me.

"Excuse me, Mother. Lillian needs some help."

Mother patted my knee and smiled.

I can't wait to tell Taylor.

"You're a good daughter," Lillian said when I reached the porch. "Kate sent me because she needs to talk to you inside."

When I reached the door, I glanced back before I went in. Mother smiled as Lillian headed toward her and Sergeant Arrington.

Mr. Morgan was at the sink, where he scrubbed pans, rinsed dishes, and loaded the dishwasher.

"Mr. Morgan, you don't need to do the dishes," I said. "I'll take care of them."

He glanced over his shoulder and waved a soapy hand. "Almost done."

Kate sat at the dining table. "He wouldn't let me help either."

She motioned at a chair for me to join her at the table. "We need to go over our plan. The team is ready to support whatever you want to do. We need two signals. One I can send you to tell you to run away, kind of like Lucy's bang bark. And you need a signal to send me to come get you. I can track your phone, and I have a tracker for you to wear. It looks like a small bandage."

I frowned. "A bandage tracker? Is it new?"

"Not really." Kate rose from the table and strolled to the front window. "About a signal, I have an idea. *Okay* could be our emergency signal word. What if you include okay in your text, like *I'm okay*. Or *I'll see you later okay* means come get you right away."

"Oh. I like that. Would it be the same if you send me a text with *okay* in it?"

"I hadn't thought of it, but good. Simple."

"I can think of a third signal we need. A way for you to come get me if you don't hear from me."

"It's built into your bandage. I'll show you tomorrow."

"I'll be in the backyard unless there's something else I can do," Mr. Morgan said.

I smiled at the hopeful look and the spotless kitchen. "You've taken care of everything. Thank you."

"Call me if you need anything," he said as he stepped out the back door.

"I can't sit anymore." I rose from the table. "How about a walk?"

We ambled out to the front gate and toward the horses.

"What's up?" Kate asked.

"What about before tomorrow morning? What if something comes up tonight? Here?"

"Lillian could stay with you tonight. What do you think?"

A hawk circled overhead and dove into the field across the road. With a shift of its mighty wings, it soared skyward. A snake dangled from its beak as it flew away.

I frowned. "Are you sure about Lillian? She told me the FBI identified John Edwards from dental records. Is that public information? And I don't know how she knew I was at the range."

"Hmm. Need to investigate it. It's your call about Lillian. I do know she's always been unsurpassed in her skills for collecting information," Kate said.

"Whose idea was it for her to stay?"

"Mr. Morgan suggested it. He said he'd rather she stayed here."

We stopped at the fence, but the horses were bedded down for the night in the barn. A breeze blew the familiar smell of horses and hay our way. The pasture looked lonesome.

"Hmm. Let me think." I glanced at the guys. Spike shrugged. Palace Guard frowned.

"If Mr. Morgan wants Lillian to stay with me, there must be a reason. Tell Mr. Morgan thank you."

On our way back to the house, I stopped to listen to the crickets. "Parker should have been here."

"I know," Kate said. "I miss him too."

I didn't miss Parker. I wanted him there. I trudged toward the house. My feet felt as heavy as my heart. *Nobody understands. Not even Kate.*

When we reached the gate, Kate caught up with me then stopped with her hand on the latch. "Does Lillian know about the imaginary men?"

"No. The guys said 'no.'"

"Interesting. Just needed to know. They are a real asset."

"Shh. They'll be insufferable."

"You about ready to call it a night?"

"I am. Thank you," I said.

Kate was a good bouncer. Everyone headed toward their cars. Lillian and I were alone with my men and Lucy in thirty minutes. The spare bedroom faced the front. Lillian set up her "nest," as she called her lookout post at the window.

Lucy and I went out back, and I rocked on the porch while Lucy wandered the yard. My eyes adjusted to the reduced light, and I listened to the night noises and looked at the stars.

It's nice here. The crickets are louder than the far off traffic.

We went inside, and Lucy settled down in my bedroom.

Tomorrow's the day. Don't go into the basement. I fell asleep.

* * *

I woke up to the gurgling sound and beckoning whiff of perking coffee. It took me a second to remember I was at my house, not at the cabin. Lillian was in the kitchen, not Kate.

And Parker is not here. I closed my eyes. A tear escaped then another. Lucy licked my elbow.

"Good morning, Lucy. Thanks for the kiss."

The tantalizing aroma of bacon assaulted my nose, and I threw on my gray clothes for the day.

Bubbly Lillian handed me a cup of hot coffee. I had planned to power up my computer to check the security cameras, but I took Lucy and my coffee out back.

Lillian came to the back door. "Our breakfast is almost ready. When you go to your apartment, I'd like to ride along, if you don't mind, so I can go to Ray's apartment. We have a few things to do this morning too."

Lucy and I came inside, and I sat at the table. "Lillian, I have something I need to tell somebody, so I can get over it, but I might have to swear you to secrecy. Can I tell you?"

"Of course, dear. Just a second while I adjust my hearing aids."

"Mother's name is Isolde. Sergeant Arrington's name is Duane. She calls him Big D, and he calls her Izzy."

"So together they are Big D-Izzy." Lillian laughed.

"Right. I couldn't even let myself think about it last night." I laughed along with her.

While Lillian straightened the kitchen, I loaded my suitcases into the trunk of my car. I walked through the house to be sure I hadn't missed anything.

I need a picture of Parker.

Lillian and Lucy went outside while I locked up, but I left the security camera and computer on.

When we got to the vet, Lillian and the imaginary men waited in the car for me.

When the vet tech took Lucy's leash, I said, "Lucy, after the groomer, you'll go to a new dog kennel and a new home. You'll make new friends."

I hugged Lucy. The vet tech frowned in judgment. *Only a shallow person abandons a dog on a whim.*

When I got in the car, I hung my head. "The vet tech doesn't like people who dump their dogs."

"People don't always realize things aren't as simple as they seem. You'll be safer in your apartment with Mr. Morgan nearby," Lillian said.

So that's the official Mr. Morgan version. Good to know.

When we got to the apartment complex, Spike and Palace Guard got out first. I sat a minute, waiting for their signal.

"You all right, dear?"

"Yeah. This is not fun."

I carried my suitcases to my apartment, and Lillian went to Mr. Morgan's.

When I opened the door, I wasn't surprised to see two men in my living room. Both of them were tall and within the average weight range for their height. The younger man was the taller of the two and had short, brown, curly hair. The other man had thick, straight, black hair. The younger man looked familiar. *Aha. Larry and Moe.*

Kate had warned me they'd be there. "Don't talk to the men when you get home. You are alone in your apartment as far as anyone is concerned. If you have something you need to say, write it down. Turn on your TV or radio. Get on your computer. Put away your things. Make a shopping list. Do normal stuff. Or if you can't, do Maggie stuff." Kate chuckled, and I stuck my tongue out at her. She deserved it.

I put my gray clothes in the closet, swept the kitchen, and checked the cupboards and refrigerator. Red wine, cheese, rolls, and ingredients for soup went on my grocery list.

I scrubbed the bathroom toilet, sink, and shower, mopped the bathroom floor, and changed my bedsheets. All normal for me. More for the list—toothpaste, bathroom cleanser, and air freshener. I sent Kate a text—"Groceries"—and grabbed my keys.

The birds greeted me with chirpy songs when I stepped outside. The yip-yap of a small dog in one of the apartments and traffic noise from the street added to the chorus of normalcy.

I parked my car in the middle of the apartment lot, where no one else parked. Everyone else parked either in the shade or as close as possible to a sidewalk. I walked to my car, and nobody jumped out at me or grabbed my leg by lying on the ground under another vehicle like they did in Taylor's movies.

I climbed into my car and locked the doors. I put the key in the ignition, held my breath, and turned the key. The engine started right up.

Someone's behind me.

I glanced back and stifled a scream. Spike and Palace Guard were in the back seat.

I'll give myself a nervous breakdown if I don't settle down.

The blue sky was clear except for a few puffy clouds. I pretended I was an average person out for a drive with her imaginary men. When we got to the store, I didn't deviate from my grocery list, but Spike and Palace Guard insisted on ice cream. I got two kinds of ice cream because they didn't agree. Spike wanted vanilla, and Palace Guard wanted toffee mocha.

I parked in a different spot when I returned to the apartment. I held my key in my hand when I left my car, but before I approached my door, Palace Guard blocked my way and waved me toward Mr. Morgan's apartment. I knocked on the door, and Kate opened it.

"Nice to see you. Did you get my text?" Kate asked as she grabbed my arm and pulled me inside.

Kate held out her hand for my phone, and I gave it to her.

"Back in a second." She scooted past me and left Mr. Morgan's apartment.

I set my sack of groceries on the counter. After I stashed the ice cream in the freezer, Kate returned. She waved a small electronic device around me, gave me a quick thumbs-up, and stuck the device in her pocket.

"Hi, Maggie," Kate said. "You must have gotten my text."

"Yep." I didn't know how much I should or shouldn't say.

"What kind did you get? Vanilla?"

"And toffee mocha. I wasn't sure." We laughed, but I didn't know why. *Boss laughs. I laugh.*

"I owe Mr. Morgan vanilla. Thanks for picking it up. You don't need to leave the toffee mocha."

"I'll grab it out of the freezer then. I need to get the rest of my groceries into the fridge. Mr. Morgan here?"

"No. I dropped by to see him. The ice cream will be a surprise. Lillian's here."

I walked into the living room. "Hey, Lillian."

She was on the sofa. Her head jerked at the sound of my voice. "Sorry, dear. I must have dozed off. I didn't hear the doorbell. Kate let you in?"

"She did. Didn't mean to startle you, I just wanted to say hi. I've got groceries to put away. I just stopped by to deliver the ice cream Kate asked for."

"I'm sorry, dear. I took my hearing aids out to charge. They're in my room. You delivered ice cream?"

"It's a surprise for Mr. Morgan," Kate said in a loud voice. "Don't tell him when he gets back. We had a bet. We'll see you later."

After Kate closed the door, she glanced at her phone and mumbled. "Phone's acting funny. Must be time for a new one."

Kate walked with me to my apartment. When I walked into the kitchen, my phone was in the sink in a bath of steaming water. I raised my eyebrows.

"I'll help you put away your groceries," she said. Four men hovered while we put the few items away.

Kate turned and bumped into Moe. "So?" she said.

He handed her a piece of paper. I stood in front of her and read the note while she read. The two large imaginary men hovered over her shoulder to read.

"U & MS can talk. Must be code. Everything else write."

Kate grabbed a notepad and pen.

"You staying for supper?" I asked.

I read the note she handed me. "You're clear. I sent text & you didn't respond, so I waited for you. Phone was bugged. The guys swept here. Nothing new. Why did you go to Mr. M's?"

I glanced to my left, and Kate grunted.

"I don't think I can," Kate said. "I need to get back to work."

"How was my phone compromised?" I wrote.

"You wrapping a case up or do you have a new one?" I asked. The concurrent writing and spoken conversations left me off kilter like I'd walked into the middle of an old existential play.

"A little of both. What are your plans for this evening?" Kate said while she wrote.

I read. "Phone not yours. No contacts. Bug on the battery. Anybody bump into you at store?"

I shook my head. Spike smacked his forehead and pointed at the refrigerator.

"Just a quiet supper and some ice cream. I've got a book I want to read," I said.

I wrote. "Ice cream freezer. Reached for IC & man reached past me. Phone in my back pants pocket on his side."

Spike pointed to his eyes and made a walking motion with his fingers.

I walked to my bookcase with the notepad.

"I've got several books I want to read. You have any suggestions?" I said. And wrote. "Saw him a few times. Different aisles. Stalked? Waited for opportunity?"

Spike frowned and hung his head.

"Let me look," Kate said. And wrote. "Don't blame yourself. Pickpockets slick & fast."

I knew Kate's last note wasn't for me. Palace Guard patted Spike on the back.

"Here," Kate said. "You may like this one."

"Thanks, Kate." I inclined my head and slid my eyes to the right, indicating Spike.

I looked down. She had handed me my *Merriam-Webster Dictionary*.

"Only said it because it's true," she said almost under her breath. She looked at the spot where Spike stood.

"Well, gotta run," Kate said in a normal tone.

After she left, Larry and Moe nodded. I interpreted it as a *Welcome home*. My two imaginary men nodded too. I coughed and tried a fake sneeze, but it sounded more like a cartoon clown horn squeak. Spike and Palace Guard laughed. *Need to work on my fake sneezes and coughs.*

Next in my plan was to go for a run. I must have been nuts.

I wrote a note on an old envelope. "I don't have a cell phone." I set it down on the table near the men. They read it and frowned. I picked up the envelope and sat at my computer. I opened a spreadsheet and typed "going for a run." Moe sent and received a text and handed me his phone.

I read the text. "Tell Crazy Lady fine. Give her your phone."

I changed my clothes and stuck the phone in my bra. Palace Guard was ready when I was.

"You're on, bud," I said. Moe and Larry looked at each other.

I grabbed my springy bracelet with the attached apartment key and headed out. Palace Guard ran behind me. He could have passed me, but he had my back. I loved the snick-snick sound of my running shoes on the sidewalk and breathed in the familiar smells of the dumpster, traffic, and noxious weeds. *Ahh, the city.*

I came to the cutoff for my favorite jogging path. Palace Guard pointed, and I broke into a hard run. Palace Guard stayed a few steps ahead of me. We came to a split, and instead of my usual path to the right, he led me to the left. The sound of hard-driving footsteps was behind me, but I put them out of my mind. We ran harder and faster. The path looped back to the sidewalk near the apartment. When we popped out, we raced at a hard sprint to the stairs and ran up to my door. When we were inside, I collapsed on the sofa. Palace Guard slammed down next to me. He would have hurt my feelings if he'd done a little cool-down dance. We grinned.

I pulled the cell phone out of my bra and held it in the air with two fingers. Moe took it, pulled out his shirttail, dried the phone off, punched in some numbers, pointed at the bathroom, and handed the phone back to me. Larry turned on the radio.

I went into the bathroom and closed the door. My two imaginary men crowded me.

Kate picked up. "Hey. Good run?"

"Yep, a great run."

"You left your bodyguard in the dirt, you know, but he claimed he hung back."

I giggled.

"You had your guard, didn't you? We arrested a guy who attacked your double on your usual path."

"Someone attacked a woman on my usual path? Was the attacker anybody we know?"

I gave Palace Guard a thumbs-up.

"Smooth way to tell your guard. We don't have an ID for the man yet. Close to six feet tall, overweight, brownish hair."

Sounds like Donnie.

"So what's next?"

"See what he says. Stay safe."

She hung up. I flushed the toilet, opened the door, and gave Moe his phone.

I wrote a note. "Shower." Spike, Palace Guard, Larry, and Moe looked at the paper. Spike and Palace Guard rubbed their heads and under their arms like they were taking showers.

"Goofballs." Oops, I said it out loud.

Moe frowned. Spike and Palace Guard laughed, doubling over.

No worries, Moe. I'm the crazy lady.

I stood in front of the closet. *Gray or Taylor colors?* Gray won. I gathered fresh clothes and shower stuff.

The hot water was glorious. It had been a while since I'd taken a shower without being in a hurry or afraid. Four men guarded me. I didn't know much about Moe and Larry, but I trusted my imaginary men implicitly.

After my shower, I plopped down on the sofa with a book I'd read a hundred times—or maybe only once. Didn't matter. I was restless and couldn't focus. I wrote another note. "Need a new phone" and handed it to Moe.

He looked at it, and his face turned red. He gave the note to Larry and pointed at his phone.

Larry sent a text and showed it to me. "Crazy Lady wants a new phone."

I smiled. He snickered. Moe frowned.

Those frown lines will freeze on your face, mister.

Larry got a reply. He read it and wrote something on the paper.

I read his phone text: "only if Lillian goes 2"; and the note: "checkmate".

He was right. Kate won the match, although I wasn't sure why she wanted Lillian to go. Mouse watching the cat? And I was the mouse?

I strolled to Mr. Morgan's apartment and knocked. "Hi, Lillian. Want to go shopping with me?"

"What a nice surprise. I'd love it. Let me grab my purse. I'll meet you at your car."

I started the car, and Spike and Palace Guard hopped into the back. Lillian opened the passenger side door.

"Thanks for waiting, dear. I have everything I need." She patted her purse. "Are we shopping for anything special?"

"I need a new phone," I said. "My old one lost all my contacts. I took it as a sign."

Lillian chuckled with me.

After I dropped off Lillian at the door and parked, I entered the store. The store employee helped a young couple with phone selections while a middle-aged woman waited in front of the tablets. Lillian had claimed a chair near the door and sat with her purse on her lap.

I noticed a gray wall in the back of the store. I wandered back and leaned against the wall. *Ah, I had forgotten how much I loved gray.*

The couple completed their transaction and left with a store bag filled with two phones and accessories. The middle-aged woman was next.

A large older man entered the store. He wore jeans, a T-shirt, and a heavy flannel shirt. His cowboy hat was pulled down over his face, and his cowboy boots were squared off at the toe. His left arm hung stiffly from his shoulder, but he was taller than Everett Duncan.

Everett Duncan with cowboy boots. Of course, taller.

Lillian looked at me with her eyebrows raised. I nodded.

As he walked past her, Lillian placed her right hand inside her purse. "Hello, young man. Don't I know you from somewhere?"

His head jerked, and he half turned to look at her.

"No, ma'am," he said in a thick drawl. "I'd never forget makin' the acquaintance of a lovely young lady like yerself."

Lillian giggled and blushed.

She's good.

He walked over to a headphones display and shook his head then left.

Lillian sent a one-handed text on her phone and kept her right hand inside her purse. After she set her phone down, she signaled thumbs up.

The middle-aged woman and the store clerk narrowed her search down to two tablets.

A young man with tattoos on his arms and neck held the hand of a four-year-old girl with a pink tutu over her jeans as they came into the store. The little girl stared at Palace Guard, snapped to attention, and saluted. He returned her salute. Palace Guard stooped down, and the little girl twirled for him. He applauded, and she curtsied. Lillian stared at the little girl and glanced at me. I shifted my gaze to the store employee with great interest.

Palace Guard looked at me and shrugged. The little girl copied him. Spike and I cracked up. Spike did a pirouette. The little girl applauded. Spike curtsied. I laughed like the crazy lady I was supposed to be. If Moe and Larry had walked in, I would have piddled right where I was.

The middle-aged woman looked at me and walked out. The little girl laughed with Spike, Palace Guard, and me.

Her father smiled. "She makes friends everywhere she goes."

"She's delightful," I said as Palace Guard and Spike grinned, and the little girl beamed.

The store clerk and I selected my new phone. He shut down the service to my stolen phone and transferred my contacts to my new one.

The little girl and the imaginary men had a dance-off. She won, of course. When it was time for us to leave, the three of them had identical downturned mouths.

"You have nice friends," the little girl said.

"Thank you. I think so too."

When we left the store, Lillian narrowed her eyes. "What a talented child."

"She was, wasn't she? And speaking of talented, your giggle and blush were magnificent. Who did you text?"

"Kate. I think he followed you and didn't notice me until I spoke to him. I loved his reaction." She smiled.

"Why did Duncan come in?"

"He came inside to show off his disguise for the security camera. But he intended to strike—quick and deadly. It was a precarious move, though, to the point of desperate, don't you think?"

Lillian recognized him too, and he knew her.

"He was shocked to see you, that's for sure," I said. "Why didn't he notice you when he came in?"

"Did you know old people are invisible? We are. The most invisible of all is an old person in a wheelchair, which is why I sat at the door. He missed seeing me. You don't know how much I wanted to say 'Boo' when he came in."

We giggled.

On our way to the car, a young man pushing a train of shopping carts saluted Lillian, and she waved back.

"We're clear," she said. "Your car's fine. Let's go back to the apartments; I need a nap."

Moe waited for me with his usual sour look. No Larry.

Moe handed me a note. "You need a boyfriend. Kevin will be back later. Your new boyfriend."

I turned the note over and wrote. "I don't need a new boyfriend. Who's Kevin? What's he supposed to do, guard me? I already . . ." I stopped and shoved the paper into my pocket.

Is Larry Kevin? I'll still call him Larry.

I sent a text to Kate. "It's me. No one else has this number."

Return text from Kate: "Still cking Lillian. Be cautious."

Time to mix it up.

I signed on to my computer and checked email and social media. No emails except ads, sales, and spam. My social circle consisted of the marketing departments of businesses who sent me pictures of kittens and puppies to remind me to buy their incredible products.

I heard a *tap-tap* at the door. I looked out the peephole. *Larry.*

He gave me a hug when I opened the door. "Mags, I've missed you."

"Haven't seen you in ages, cuz. How's Aunt Katherine?"

Larry snickered. "She's great. Sends her love. Want to go out for pizza?"

"Give me a minute to freshen up, Larry."

"Sure," he said. He grabbed the pencil and paper on the table and scribbled "Larry?"

I glanced at the paper. "Yep, pizza."

"You got it," Larry said.

Moe shook his head. Spike and Palace Guard laughed. Spike raised his arms in victory.

I like ole cousin Larry. He's pretty sharp.

I ran a brush through my hair and grabbed a sweatshirt and my purse. Spike made a slinging motion over his shoulder.

"My go bag too?"

Spike nodded. Moe scanned the room and narrowed his eyes.

"My treat this time. My car or your car? Where we going?" I asked.

"If you're treating, then I'll drive. I've got just the place. You'll like it."

I sent a text to Kate: "U trust Larry?"

"Who Larry?"

"Kevin."

"Yes. No question."

I held my phone up. Spike and Palace Guard read the texts.

Larry glanced in his rearview mirror, at the back seat, and at my phone. "Who knows about Olivia's apartment?"

"Kate, Glenn, my lawyer and her assistant, the apartment manager, and the apartment security guy. Everett Duncan. Donnie. Everybody who works for Everett Duncan. Oh, all the nine-one-one dispatchers and the police and fire departments. And everybody with a scanner. That's all I can think of off the top of my head. Why?"

"Well, good. Glad it's such a narrow list." He rolled his eyes. "We might go hang out there for a bit. What kind of pizza do you like?"

"My favorite is Margherita pizza, and my second favorite is any pizza."

"What's a margarita pizza? With tequila?"

"No." I laughed. "It's a cheese, garlic, basil, and tomato pizza. It's called Margherita because it's the three colors of the Italian flag. You know, white, green, and red. The name references Queen Margherita of Italy."

"Impressive. You know your pizza. We'll get a Queen Margherita pizza for Maggie then. A Maggie pizza. And some beer." He grinned. "Aunt Katherine said I can have a beer. She said to tell you that friends don't let cousins drink alone."

"I'm tired of hiding from Everett Duncan." I frowned while I gazed at the passing scenery.

"Aunt Katherine believes Everett Duncan's boss is putting pressure on him. She wants to test her theory."

"Is she doing something dangerous?"

"Of course not." He waggled his eyebrows and grinned.

"Do you like dark beer?" I tapped my lips and my ear with a finger and raised my eyebrows.

"Sure do."

I pointed to him and then me. He pointed to himself with his thumb on the steering wheel.

Good to know. Larry is wired, and he trusts me.

"Why Olivia's apartment?"

Larry smiled. "It's a luxury safe house. Gotta be the best kind."

"So what do we do?"

Larry moved his hand like he was writing. "Oh, you know. Watch TV. Read. Play cards. Nope, wouldn't work. I bet you still cheat."

I snort-laughed. "You've always been my favorite cousin, Larry. You know me like a book."

We picked up the pizza and beer. Before we got out of his car, Larry motioned two fingers at his eyes. I waved in the direction of the apartment, and he nodded.

He's wired, and the apartment has security cameras.

* * *

Larry opened two beers, and I grabbed plates. We sat at the bar to eat.

"Good pizza. Why did I not know about Maggie pizza?" Larry grinned.

I reached for my second piece. "You know Aunt Katherine has always been a worrier."

"She sure has. Here's to Mom," he said, and we clinked bottles.

"I want to check the apartment sheets, towels, and soap," I said.

Larry sat on the white sofa after he brushed the seat of his pants. Made sense to me. He clicked on the TV, found a war movie, and turned up the volume.

I grabbed a hotel pad and pen out of a drawer in the master bedroom and stepped into the master bathroom. I counted three security cameras—one in the kitchen and two in the living room. I found no cameras in the bedrooms, the bathrooms, the hall between the bedrooms, or the balcony. I wrote a note, flushed the toilet, and stuck the pad and pen in my bra. I switched the TVs in the bedrooms to infomercial channels and turned up the volume.

I returned to the living room and stepped out on the balcony. "Hey, Larry, come on out here. The view is to die for."

Larry rolled his eyes as he walked out with two beers in his hand. Palace Guard elbowed Spike.

He handed me a beer. I waved at the view. "Isn't this great?"

I fished the pad out of my bra and handed him the note I'd written in the bathroom. "No camera out here or in the bedrooms or bathrooms. Two in the living room. One in the kitchen."

"View's nice. It's still a little humid. Want to sit?"

"Sounds good."

Palace Guard leaned over my shoulder while I wrote. "Last time I was here, we saw a box."

I handed Larry the pad and pen. Spike read over Larry's shoulder.

"Apt surveillance cameras had good pic of who left it. K said you'd know him," Larry wrote and then passed the pad and pen.

"Donnie? Explosives?" I wrote.

Larry took the pad and pen. "Yes. No detonator, though. Not the level of expertise of the others. What's the plan?" he wrote.

We wrote and read in silence.

"If I tell you, will you be fired?" I wrote.

"Depends. Will we get caught?"

"By Kate? Probably. By bad guys, no."

"I'm in."

Spike and Palace Guard high-fived. I held up my hand. Spike, Palace Guard, and Larry smacked my hand.

I frowned at Larry and wrote. "Officer Kevin Ewing?"

He stared at the note, shrugged, and handed me his note. "Larry IRL."

I gazed at him, snort-laughed, and spoke loud enough for any listeners. "You are the best cousin in the world."

I raised my bottle to him in a toast.

He clinked my bottle. "Thanks, Crazy Lady. You too."

I smiled and held up my empty beer bottle. "I love how quiet it is here. Want another beer?"

"Sure. I'll fetch," Larry said.

I jumped up. "I'll put the pizza in the refrigerator. Unless you want more."

"Nope. I'm good."

We took our beers out to the balcony, set them down, and resumed our note passing.

"Can you ditch the wire?" I wrote.

"Yes. Take a shower."

"In the morning. Early. Go for run. Take a shower. I can disable kitchen camera. We leave."

"Ok. Then what?"

"Find bad guy."

"Kate's got that."

"Different bad guy."

Larry gazed at me with his brow furrowed. He picked up the pen and wrote. "This a new plan?"

I met his gaze and nodded.

"Still in," he wrote.

"I'm tired, and it's buggy," I said aloud. "Time for me to turn in. See you in the morning."

"I'll take care of our bottles." He stuck the pad inside his shirt. We left the pen outside.

Larry carried the unopened bottles with the tops covered by his hand and put them into the kitchen trash can.

I turned off the blaring TVs, kicked off my shoes, and climbed into the bed. I counted backward from four. I was tired. I was out before I got to one.

I woke up before dawn to the sound of a gurgling coffee maker. The aromatic tendrils of earthy coffee tickled my nose. *I have the best cousin in the world.*

I rushed to the kitchen. Kate sat with Larry at the bar as she sipped her coffee and grinned. When Larry handed me a cup of coffee, I almost refused it, but I was angry, not stupid. "What the heck, Larry?" I ignored Kate.

"Kate said it would be nice for you to get a good night's sleep before we go catch the bad guys, and nothing relaxes you like a good, evil plan. Did I say it right, Aunt Katherine?"

The two of them laughed, and Spike and Palace Guard joined in. I gave all four of them my best glower, but it was a little weak; I need to practice my sullen.

"Don't any of you have impulse control?" I asked.

When they laughed harder, I crossed my arms and glowered.

"So what's your plan, Kate?" I asked.

"We'll follow yours. You're the one with the good plans."

"Still mad," I said. "I need to go back to the apartment and run the usual path."

I looked at Spike and Palace Guard, and they nodded.

Kate said, "What do the guys say? And no lying."

"They agree."

"What guys?" Larry asked.

He looked at the scowls on our faces. "Never mind. Forget I asked."

"What kind of coverage do you need?" Kate asked.

"Just my guard."

"No," Kate said.

Spike stepped over to Kate and patted her shoulder. She looked at her shoulder.

"Maggie, Spike?"

"Yes."

"What do I do, then, while you're the center of the bull's eye?"

"We need to give you a false lead to chase. Maybe you take a team to the warehouse. Maybe Donnie gave you some information. Or maybe the cartoon place. Might be the epicenter."

"I like the idea of the cartoon place. It's been under the radar long enough. If I take a team, can I leave Larry with you?"

I glanced at Spike and Palace Guard. Kate looked in the same direction, and a small smile appeared on her face.

"You agree, Spike?" she said.

When Spike nodded, Palace Guard and I gaped at him.

"Spike said yes," Kate said.

Larry stared at Kate and me. "Thanks, Spike. I think. Somebody tell me later who Spike is, okay?"

Palace Guard, Spike, and Kate laughed.

"I will," I said.

"We need to find a good breakfast place," Kate said. "Too bad Donnie blew up the diner."

"I know a good place down by the warehouse for lunch," I said.

"I know a better place. I'll call Mom," Kate said.

"You know, if we play our cards right, we just might snag Everett and his boss," I said.

"I want to hear your plan," Kate said.

Chapter Twenty-Two

Palace Guard and I rode with Larry to Glenn and Jennifer's house. I suspected Spike caught a ride with Kate.

The welcoming aroma of bacon, coffee, and cinnamon rolls swirled around us when we walked in the front door. Glenn wrapped me in a dad hug, and Jennifer pulled me into a mom hug. Waves of sadness rose in my chest and became tears. I choked them back as Lucy scrambled to the door. I bent down, scratched her ears, and rubbed her face. She gave me a thank you lick and rolled onto her back. Spike rubbed her belly.

Jennifer said, "Sit, eat."

We did. While Glenn poured coffee, we passed platters of food, boardinghouse style.

"I need Spike and Palace Guard," I said.

The two of them crowded me. "Not right now." I laughed. "This is the plan. Nobody at the apartment. Moe leaves."

"Moe?" Kate asked.

Larry narrowed his eyes, and his face settled into a scowl. "She means Detective Ross. And if we had a bald guy on the team, he'd be Curly. Right, Maggie?"

His neck was crimson, and a red flush crept up his face.

He's mad at me.

"No, not at all," I said.

"Not convinced." Larry crossed his arms.

Kate reached for the platter of bacon and took the last slice. "Continue your family fight another time. It needs to look like all protection is gone, right?"

"Yes. I'll go for my usual run and wear oversized gray clothes so I can have my pistol and knife on me. I expect an attack, and I think it will be Everett. Spike and Palace Guard will be with me. I'll be fine. Is Lillian still at Mr. Morgan's? I'll go for another run near dusk. I expect a full-blown attack by the big guy. Spike and Palace Guard with me again. I don't want anybody else because I don't want them to have any leverage against me."

"So far, I don't like it," Kate said.

"I think the big guy has become impatient with all these failed attempts and knows I'm close to exposing him."

"Are you?" Larry asked.

Whew. He's speaking to me.

"Of course, especially if he attacks me." I smiled my best smile. I hoped for a friendly Spike panda smile, not Kate's lioness smile.

"What if there's not a second attack?"

"Then I was wrong, and Everett is the big guy, but we'll have him. I have another idea. Do we still have the use of Taylor's apartment?"

"Yes, and to answer your question, Lillian is still at Mr. Morgan's apartment. I haven't seen Mr. Morgan. He may have gone to visit his sister," said Kate.

"Good. Larry needs to be at Taylor's apartment."

"I'll go along with your wacky plan with one addition. You wear a wire and Larry's listening, and I have one more question. When?" Kate said.

"Yes to the wire if it doesn't show and if it isn't itchy. This morning. You raid the cartoon store at nine thirty, and I'll run at ten," I said.

"Right. Larry, call Detective Ross and tell him to get a search warrant for drug trafficking and meet me at the office. We've got a raid to do. And get a wire for Maggie."

"What do I do?" Glenn asked.

"Nothing," Kate and I said in unison.

"Wait. Bring Lucy to my house, not the apartment, this evening at seven. I'll meet you there," I said.

"Whoa," said Kate. "Is this part of your plan?"

"If Duncan has a boss, we need the final trap. The pit with the sharpened sticks. Lucy and I will be at the house alone. Well, except for Spike and Palace Guard."

"I'm not budging until you tell me who Spike and Palace Guard are." Larry rose and slammed his palms on the table. I didn't have the nerve to point out he just budged. Spike put his hand over his mouth to hide his grin.

"That's insubordination, mister," Kate snarled.

"My cousin is a crazy lady, and I need to know why," Larry growled back.

Spike and Palace Guard stared at Larry while Glenn chuckled.

"Make the call for Aunt Katherine, and I'll tell you," I said.

After Larry ordered the wire and called Moe, Kate gave Moe the background for the search warrant.

Glenn handed Larry a fresh cup of coffee. "You might want to sit, son."

I explained about the explosion, my physical therapy, and how much Spike and Palace Guard helped me then I sketched out the training. I wanted him to understand why they were critical to the plan.

After I finished, Larry looked at Glenn. "You knew about this?"

"Yep, and never believed a word of it at first, but now I have respect for Palace Guard and Spike. They do good work, and I trust them to keep Maggie safe."

Palace Guard and Spike hung their heads; I think they were embarrassed.

Larry looked at Kate. "What about you?"

"I believe everything Maggie said . . ." Spike waved his hand in a circular motion. ". . . and I see Spike too."

Spike did his victory dance. Kate, Palace Guard, and I laughed.

"What's so funny?" Larry asked.

Glenn put his hand on Larry's shoulder. "I've learned it's best to ignore them."

Kate said, "Let's get Crazy Lady's plan cranking."

Kate and I walked out to Larry's car with our heads close and our arms intertwined. Two old friends. Palace Guard and Spike walked along with us.

"One more thing, Kate," I said in a soft voice. "If we do shoot a bad guy, make sure the ambulance rushes away from the scene full-blown lights-and-sirens. It needs to look like the bad guy was wounded, but not dead. Need to keep Everett's boss nervous."

Larry dropped me off at my apartment. "Mags, I'll return with a wire. I called for a dog to sniff your car for explosives."

* * *

I went to see Lillian at Mr. Morgan's. She smiled when she answered the door.

"Hello, dear. Come on in. Mr. Morgan said he had some out of town business to take care of. I'm the temporary apartment-sitter. How about a cuppa? I just perked a fresh pot. So tell me about your young man."

Lillian wore dark-blue slacks and a pale-lavender shirt and looked ready to go to a fancy luncheon. After I followed her to the kitchen, she poured two cups of coffee. I picked up mine and waited while she added cream and sugar to hers.

"He's my cousin, Larry. Mother told him to look after me, and he's hovering. You look like you're dressed to go out. Did I slow you down?" I said.

"My schedule is always flexible, dear," she said. "I plan to check out the new downtown bookstore later."

I sat at the dining table with my cup and inhaled the swirling aroma. "Hazelnut?" I asked.

"Mr. Morgan grumbles when I make flavored coffee. He says he can't stand the smell of prissy coffee. We wind up in a big argument, so I only make flavored coffee when he's not around."

I laughed. "I love prissy coffee. Thank you. I came to check on you. How are you doing?"

I glanced at my phone. And frowned. *Need to talk to Kate.*

Lillian joined me at the table and set a plate of homemade cookies in front of me. "I'm fine. The doctor says my recovery is surprising for my age. I get tired of being reminded I'm old. What about you?"

I laughed. "Lucy and I will move back to the house this evening. Glenn and Lucy will be at the house around six or seven."

"Well, that's good news. I bet you have a ton of things to do at your apartment if you're moving back to your house. Is there anything I can do to help you? Maybe make cookies for your freezer? Pick up some fresh veggies from the farmers' market? Help you pack?"

"No cookies. My stretchy pants would complain," I said. "I came to see if you needed anything because I have a little free time this afternoon. There's a big break in the case. In fact, Kate expects to wrap it up in the next day or so, maybe today, so Larry will return home, and I can go back to my usual twice-a-day runs, as long as there's no rain."

"I'm fine. Don't need a thing. Mr. Morgan told me he could set his watch by your ten o'clock and five o'clock runs," Lillian said.

I grabbed a cookie and waved on my way to the door.

"Thanks again, dear, for checking on me," she said as I left.

She was right. I needed to pack some things to go home.

A few minutes later, Larry came to the apartment with a high school girl whose dark-brown hair was pulled into a ponytail. She wore short jeans and a tiny orange crop top.

"Hey, cuz," Larry said after he closed the door. "Officer Heather will put your wire on you."

My eyebrows shot up almost to my hairline.

"I get that all the time," she said. "Kate didn't want me to show up in a police uniform. The only other clothes I had in my locker today were my working-girl outfits."

"Will you talk to Aunt Katherine anytime soon, Larry?"

He pointed at the wire. "Yep, but you may talk to her before I do. Anything special?"

"No, just a little technical glitch with my phone. A bit worrisome."

While Heather put the wire on me, Larry said, "I'll drop Heather off, park down the street, and walk to Taylor's apartment."

After I confirmed the wire was comfortable, Larry and I checked the sound. The two of them left.

It was nine thirty. I took Lillian's advice and pulled out my oversized gray suitcase then tossed it onto my bed. After I dumped the contents of my dresser drawers into my suitcase, I rearranged and patted down the clothes and pushed smaller items into the corners. I carried pants and shirts, hangers included, to the living room and laid them across the back of the sofa.

I shoved my hairbrush, toothbrush, toothpaste, and shower stuff into a plastic grocery sack and grabbed a couple of towels. I realized I duplicated what was already at the house, but packing helped ease my nervous energy.

"Ten o'clock," I said. "Showtime."

Palace Guard, Spike, and I raced down the stairs, and Palace Guard and I jogged toward my usual path. Spike veered off to the right.

Palace Guard and I ran next to each other. The weather was warm and dry. Puffy clouds dotted the sky, and the birds called to each other. The morning's rush hour was over and only the occasional car passed by. Except for the socializing birds, silence settled on the neighborhood like a comforting blanket.

The bus stop was in front of us. My legs warmed up, and I picked up the pace. We dashed toward the bus stop, where I noticed a gray-haired man in a wheelchair. His head was drooped. I'm not sure I would have seen him if I hadn't known about the invisible people.

I looked at Palace Guard. He narrowed his eyes and quickened his pace until he was a few steps ahead of me. When we were almost to the bus stop, he veered to the right, and I stayed on his heels. We sped toward the woods away from the bus stop.

A loud shout came from behind us. Palace Guard spun around, dropped prone, and held his hand in a shooting position. Just like we had trained, I dove next to him with my pistol drawn. I heard *crack* and then *wzzzt* over my head. The wheelchair was empty, and the man stood next to the bus stop shelter with a rifle at his shoulder. After a second crack of gunfire, the old man dropped to the ground. Palace Guard and I maintained our prone positions. The man didn't move.

Pssst came from behind us. Palace Guard looked back and combat-crawled into the woods. I crawled alongside him. I loved the smell of fresh soil, but crawling through dirt, rocks, leaves, and tree roots was not high on my list of fun. When we were ten yards away from the bus stop, Spike waited for us.

"Was that you?" I whispered.

He shook his head and pointed ahead of us. Larry crouched in the bushes.

"Yes, follow me," Larry whispered.

The four of us made our way through the brush away from the bus stop and came out where the path curved to the parking lot.

"Who shot him?" I asked.

"One of our guys," he said.

"Are you sure?" I brushed dirt and leaves off my legs and shirt.

He cocked his head and narrowed his eyes. "Yes. The acknowledgment was on the radio. Why?"

"Just wondering how deep the schism is between Duncan and his boss."

A siren screamed behind us and roared away.

Larry put his finger up to his earbud. "Ambulance picked up the bad guy," he said. "I'm surprised. Our guys never miss."

"Larry, you can't go with me to my apartment with your department radio hanging on your belt and the earbud wire dangling down your neck."

"I'm not here anyway. Are you okay to get back alone? Never mind. You won't be alone, right?"

"Right. Let's go, imaginary men." Palace Guard saluted Larry, and Spike waved goodbye.

After I closed and locked my apartment door, I told Larry or whoever cared to listen, "Good run. Time for my shower."

Two minutes later, Heather showed up at my door, but this time she looked like a young mom with her Namaste shirt and yoga pants.

"I'm here to help you take off the wire. Smart to announce it, by the way," she said as she untangled the wire and removed it. "You are totally awesome. We got the bad guy. Glad we're all through." She grabbed a pencil and paper.

Is that all these people know? Write a note?

She scrawled, and I read. "K says u keep wire. Can u put it back on?"

I raised my eyebrows and nodded.

"Well, I'm outta here. I'll take the wire with me." Heather waved.

"Thanks for everything," I said as she closed the door.

After Heather left, I took my shower. I didn't realize how exhausting being shot at was. I threw on a gray sweatshirt and sweatpants and flopped face down on my bed. When I woke, it was three o'clock. I rubbed the creases on my cheek and saw drool on my pillow.

Signs of a successful nap.

I searched the cupboards and refrigerator for a snack. I found frozen bread, peanut butter, and raspberry jam. While the bread slices thawed in the toaster, I brewed a cup of peach tea. I smeared peanut butter to the edges of the bread, covered the peanut butter with a scant teaspoon of jam, and cut my sandwich into two equal triangles.

"You are a beautiful sandwich." I devoured a corner and squinted. "Still pretty." I finished it off.

Kate texted me. "Still on for 5. usual route. Car scan ok."

I put on my wire like Heather did, except the excess dangled to my knees. I pulled all the wire out for a do-over. The second time I left more at the top and stuffed the extra wire into my sports bra to take up some of the slack. It looked sloppy when I looked down at my bosom, but I wouldn't trip over the cord when I ran. The afternoon was too warm for a sweatshirt, so I wore a long-sleeved gray T-shirt from my pre-explosion days. I flushed the toilet and whispered, "I hope this is on right."

Text from Kate: "Loud and clear."

I strapped the sheath with my knife onto my left ankle, secured my belt, holstered my pistol, and dropped my phone into my pants pocket. No room in my bra.

I leaned back on the sofa, propped up my feet, and closed my eyes in meditation. A tap on my shoulder woke me, and Palace Guard grinned. Time to go.

"Let's mix up our run with a reverse of what we ran this morning."

Palace Guard raised an eyebrow and nodded.

With Palace Guard alongside, I jogged from the parking lot to the path. We picked up our pace when we reached the dirt. Spike replaced Palace Guard as my running shadow. Palace Guard darted into the woods on the right and then on the left and crisscrossed ahead of us. He vanished into the woods and reappeared on the path in front of me. He stopped and put his hands on his knees. I halted and put my hands on my knees. He pointed to my chest.

"Whew, I'm winded."

Palace Guard led Spike and me into the woods on the right. We hunkered down close enough to see the path without being seen.

"Palace Guard stopped me. We're in the woods. Just past marker five," I whispered.

I got a text: "Why?"

"Don't know," I said. "But we'll stay here and watch the path."

We crouched until I got a muscle cramp in my calf. Spike helped me stand to stretch it out. And we waited.

A man of average height appeared from the opposite direction on the path through the trees.

"Mr. Morgan. Carrying a rifle," I whispered.

Text: "Stay put."

"Will do." I frowned and shifted my weight to ward off another cramp.

Crack. Crack.

"Two rifle shots in the direction Mr. Morgan walked. Was that you? We're okay," I whispered.

Text: "Stay put."

"Not very informative," I grumbled.

Text: "Stay put."

"Repeating yourself," I mumbled. No answer from Kate; it was like she hung up before I did. I gazed at the sky. The clouds changed shapes as they moved past us.

Time to change?

Palace Guard backed away. Spike and I followed him.

"We're walking away from the path. Palace Guard's lead."

Crashing sounds came from the direction Mr. Morgan had gone. The noise grew louder as someone hurled through the woods toward our earlier position. We shifted to a ninety-degree angle and walked parallel to the commotion. Palace Guard motioned *crouch*. Donnie barreled through the woods ten yards from us. The front of his shirt was soaked with blood.

After he was out of sight, I reported in. "Donnie. Shoulder wound. Somebody chasing him through the woods?"

Text: "Stay put."

Palace Guard rose. We shifted to a position a little farther away from where Donnie blazed his trail. Two men in black with bulletproof vests hurried with a quiet crunch on the path behind Donnie.

"Two guys in black behind Donnie. Yours?"

Kate text: "Yes. They c u?"

"Of course not. We're imaginary."

Kate text: "Not u."

"Oh yeah. I'm just gray." I put my hand over my mouth to stifle my snicker. Palace Guard, Spike, and I high-fived each other.

Palace Guard lowered both hands, palms down, to the ground. I sat near an ant hill. *Glad I'm not any closer.* After he left, a hawk called overhead and circled in a thermal. As crows gathered in the trees to warn others, their clamor drew more crows. I don't know if the crows chased off the hawk or if the predator left to go where its presence would be undetected.

"Undetected," I said.

Text: "What?"

"Someone is undetected."

Text: "Who?"

"I'm tired of this. We'll finish our run."

Text: "No."

I ran with Palace Guard in front of me and Spike behind me. Palace Guard scanned our path on all sides, and Spike ran much of the way backward, then spun off to the left and disappeared.

When I was within twenty yards of the sidewalk, Donnie stepped out with a rifle and aimed it at me. Palace Guard and I dropped to our prone shooting position, and I fired twice just as the crack of a bullet zinged over my head. My first shot was a headshot, and the second hit his upper-right abdomen, just below the ribcage. A car screeched to a stop on the street, and Spike and Kate ran to us. I placed my pistol on the ground away from my fingertips and stayed spread-eagled on the ground.

"Oh, get up," Kate said.

"As soon as I stop shaking."

She reached down and snatched me up; So much for empathy.

"Lord, girl, you need to eat something."

"We need to talk." I pointed to my chest.

"Somebody send Heather to Crazy Lady's apartment. Let's go."

I brushed leaves and sticks off the front of my shirt and pants. *Wonder what Heather will wear this time?*

Heather tapped on the door. She wore a gray pinstripe business suit with a dark-gray blouse and black heels. She had pulled her hair into a severe bun, and she wore black-rimmed plastic-framed glasses.

"I love all your looks, Heather." She untangled the wire.

"This is a good quality wire," she said. "It's amazing it worked at all. Well done, Crazy Lady. We should have you test all our equipment. None of us would have tried the stuff-it-in-the-bra technique. I'd love to see what else you'd come up with."

"No," said Kate.

After Heather left, I nodded toward the door. "Should we walk down to the children's playground?"

"Good idea."

Kate and I sat on swings at the old playground. Spike and Palace Guard took turns pushing each other on the creaking merry-go-round.

"What's going on? Who's undetected?"

"What was the rifle shot before I shot Donnie?"

"I don't know. Not us."

I looked at the sky. The buzzards circled overhead. "Something's in the woods. Need to search the area the buzzards are targeting. And unrelated, something extra showed up on my phone when I was with Lillian at Mr. Morgan's."

"You mean like an extra Wi-Fi?"

"Yes. You know what I'm talking about, don't you?"

Kate barked orders into her radio and rose from her swing. "My crack team identified the dead man on the boat. He was homeless. His sister's been looking for him for years. Kind of sad."

She patted the rubber seat. "Sure am sorry to leave you, swing. Maggie, let's get your stuff loaded into my car. I want your car scanned again."

"Thanks. I agree," I said.

Kate and I loaded her car. I locked my apartment, and on our way to her car, Larry joined us. He walked in step with Kate and talked to her in tones so quiet I couldn't hear him.

"Somebody ambushed Mr. Morgan," Kate said after we were on the road. "I'm sure it was Donnie. Larry will notify Lillian because they've been partners for years. He's in surgery, but the docs say his age is against him. It was a good call to search the woods."

"Thanks. He's a fighter."

We rode in silence, and I worried about Mr. Morgan.

Kate stared at the boxes and suitcase we unloaded at the house. "Are you sure about all this? Are you waiting for someone?"

"Yes, I'm sure. I'm waiting for someone undetected."

"What does that even mean?" Kate's cheeks were blotchy, and her eyes narrowed. "Spike, do you know what she's talking about?"

Spike shook his head.

Kate stopped at the door. "You sure about this, Crazy Lady?" She closed the door without waiting for an answer. Kate's version of hanging up in person.

Chapter Twenty-Three

After Kate left, I wrinkled my nose—my little house was musty. I guess it didn't like being left closed up. I threw open the doors and windows to air it out. After I dusted the living room and scrubbed the kitchen sink, I closed and locked most of the windows, so Glenn wouldn't tell on me. I checked the security camera and paced.

Palace Guard tied his running shoes.

"Good idea. Let's go."

We ran south. Seven new kids surprised us as they bounded around their field. We wheeled around and ran north past the four horses, who neighed and galloped ahead of us. The show-off horses turned at their fence and waited for us. We all ran south toward my house. When I was inside, I poured myself a big glass of water and gulped it down. I didn't realize how dry I was. My stomach growled.

Did I eat lunch?

Glenn parked in my driveway. When he opened the back door of his four-door truck, Lucy leaped out. She tore to the house and jumped around the imaginary men. I sat on the front steps, and she waggled to me. I put my arms around her neck, and we cooed together. After I stood up, she rolled over for Spike to rub her belly and cooed to him.

"She's getting a belly rub." Glenn shook his head. "I want to stay here. Jennifer and Kate can come to pick up my truck. Would that be all right with you?"

It would be wonderful.

"No, I'll be fine. Kate agreed everyone would stay away."

"Had to try." He headed to the door. "She said it's your plan and you'd stick to it. And she swept your house. No bugs, no explosives."

Glenn left. I cruised the refrigerator and kitchen cupboards in search of something to fix for dinner. I found ice cream in the freezer; white wine, a steak, and fresh salad fixings in the refrigerator; and homemade thumbprint cookies in the cupboard.

I texted Kate: "Thanks G, J, & K 4 dinner."

While the grill heated, I brewed tea, placed the steak on a plate to come to room temperature, set my table for one, and tossed a small salad. I threw my steak on the grill, and my tummy growled at the sound of the sizzle and the smell of singed meat on the hot metal grid. I didn't realize how much I missed my grill. I carried my perfect, medium-rare steak inside and poured a large glass of iced tea. When I sat at the table, I cut into my steak and popped a piece into my mouth then closed my eyes. *Tender and succulent. Ahh.*

After I finished off my steak and salad and loaded the dishwasher, I scooped a serving of vanilla-bean ice cream into a bowl and added a thumbprint cookie. I stepped back to admire my dessert. *Doesn't look right.* I added a second cookie.

Lucy and I strolled out the front door to the southernmost corner of my front fence, and I sat in the grass cross-legged. I spooned up ice cream, took a bite of cookie, and followed it with more ice cream. I was transformed to when I was eight and sat on the grass and enjoyed ice cream after dinner with Mother. "Margaret," Mother said more than once, "one thing about your black clothes is I don't have to worry about grass stains."

I popped my bowl and spoon into the dishwasher, and Lucy yipped. I peered out the front window. A car headed toward my house from the north. It pulled into my drive and parked near the road. A tall, thin man with sandy hair, graying at the temples, stepped out of the car, scanned the yard, and walked toward the house. He stopped midway and waved his hand.

"Hello, the house," he called.

Lucy and I stepped out. Lucy trotted to him, and he stooped down and held out his hand. She sniffed and declared him acceptable to scratch her ears.

He looked up at me, and his blue eyes twinkled. "Hello, Maggie."

"Hello, Gary," I said. "Come in."

"You aren't very surprised. How did you know I'd be here?"

"Just made sense," I said after he came inside.

He glanced around. My house had three bugs: one in the living room, one in the dining room, and one in the kitchen. He spotted them and signed "OK?" I shook my head and gestured toward the back porch.

"How about some iced tea?" I poured two glasses. We moved to the back porch and strolled toward the gate.

"Tell me what's going on," I said when we reached the back fence.

"You know you interviewed at every one of Duncan's businesses involved in his illegal counterfeit drug operation, right?"

I shrugged. "I was suspicious when I realized how many times I saw Everett Duncan after his supposed death."

"I traced the operation from the original manufacturer of the counterfeit drugs in Indonesia to the warehouse where the drugs were repackaged with counterfeit labels printed at the cartoon business and shipped to hospitals and pharmacies. The bank managed the laundering of the profits, but it's bigger than just one drug counterfeiting operation. The bank became a global center to manage illicit funds. They integrated the criminal funds into legitimate transactions through cooperating banks and European banks who also laundered money. None of this is new. It's been done before because liquid capital is hard to trace, and when it comes to easy money, even major banks can't resist the temptation to participate."

"Why was Parker killed?" I needed to know. I turned, narrowed my eyes, and examined his face. "Was Parker killed because of me?"

"Short answer, no. Bob Zephfer first found evidence of Duncan's embezzlement at the bank, but then he found the tie between the warehouse and the bank during his audit. He dug deeper and found evidence of financial books for multiple businesses and multiple banks—and realized it was more than just one man who dipped into a bank's till. He found solid evidence of money laundering. He contacted Parker—they were old friends—and told Parker what he suspected. When Zephfer was killed, Parker rushed to Bob's apartment and collected his notes. Duncan killed Parker because he had the auditor's notes."

I didn't know Parker knew Zephfer. He would have told me. Later—

I cleared my throat and raised my eyebrows. "How do you know this?"

"Someone close to Parker had a copy of the notes and sent them to me."

I paced. I needed to process. I stood at the edge of the porch, gazed at the field, and listened to the birds. A chickadee chased an owl, and Lucy leaned on me. Spike stood next to Lucy. Palace Guard had my back.

"Mr. Morgan gave you the notes," I said. "But he didn't get them from Parker, did he? He got them from someone else."

I turned; he stared at me. *Thought so.*

"How did Duncan know Parker had the auditor's notes?"

Gary shook his head.

I leaned back in my chair and rocked. I smiled, not Kate's lioness smile, but my feral Maggie smile. "You can tell me, or I'll find out myself."

Gary narrowed his eyes. "I've been suspecting a mastermind, but I'm not ready to say who. I have no proof yet, but I'm close."

"Back to the auditor, how much of this can you prove?"

"All of it. I've been working on this for almost twenty years. Duncan was cautious until you showed up. You spooked him, Maggie, because of your job searches."

I raised my eyebrows. "You mean everything was a coincidence?"

"Only because your recruiter sent you to interview at every job opening in town, but nobody else would have seen what you saw. Your observational skills and memory retention are phenomenal. You were Duncan's undoing," he said. "Duncan's admin arranged the teller interviews and put them on a calendar without any assignments for interviewers. Edwards was scheduled to meet with a courier and was unaware of the teller interviews until you showed up." Gary stepped off the porch, reached down, picked up a small rock, and tossed it high in the air and over the fence. He rubbed his neck and rolled his shoulders.

"We needed an impromptu distraction so the auditor would have the opportunity to give Lillian some critical information, and a teller interview seemed perfect. The timing of the courier introduced a complication. The auditor was under tight surveillance by Duncan's organization. At first, Edwards thought you were the courier and had arrived early. He recovered when he realized his mistake. The real wild card was Duncan's arrogance. We didn't expect him to hang around when an outsider came into the bank."

"Is Duncan dead?"

"No. We don't know where he is. That's another reason I'm here."

"What? Who was in the wheelchair? Did he survive?"

"A paid killer. One of the best, but he didn't survive."

"So the first trap caught a hired assassin. The second trap caught Donnie. I shot Donnie. He's dead, right?"

"Yes, Donnie's dead."

"Who shot Mr. Morgan?"

"We don't know yet, but I'd bet on Everett Duncan. I think Mr. Morgan was after Donnie, and Duncan ambushed him."

"I need to know. Lillian and Mr. Morgan. Good guys or bad guys?"

"It's complicated."

I narrowed my eyes at him. "What are you holding back?"

He fidgeted and rubbed his right hand with his left, like rubbing away an ache. He arched his back, stretched, and sauntered toward the porch.

"When Lillian and Ray retired"—he paced the fence—"they went into business as independent contractors. They sometimes ignored what might be legal when it seemed important to their investigations. In theory, independent contractors have been very helpful in my data-collection process."

It made sense for Lillian and Mr. Morgan to be on the inside helping the good guys, but he still didn't answer my question.

"Lillian told you I'd be here," I said.

"Yes. I think Duncan's obsessed with you."

Palace Guard and Spike stepped closer to me. "Could Lillian be a double agent? Providing information to you and Duncan?"

Gary frowned. "Seeing shadows again." He rubbed his eyes. "Seems to be an indication of somebody working both sides, doesn't it?"

"Do you trust her? Would you stake my life on it?" I asked.

"No. I don't trust anybody when it comes to you," he said. "Let's just move forward on the assumption Duncan knows where you are."

"I trust Kate," I said.

"I'll give you Kate," he said. "Your house is bugged."

"Not by bad guys. Kate checked."

"Understood."

"I need for you to leave, you know. No one can be here with me. Duncan will wait until I'm alone."

"You think he's watching, don't you? Where is he?" Gary asked.

"Of course he is."

Gary narrowed his eyes at me. I think he tried to give me the father look, but only Glenn can pull it off, as far as I'm concerned. He scanned the backyard.

"There's nowhere near your house to hide, is there?"

"That's how it looks." I bit my lip. *Asking for a friend?*

He shook his head. "You win, Maggie. I'll leave."

* * *

After he headed down the road to the south, we went inside. "Well, Lucy. Will Gary spend the night in the field with everyone else? I'll bet it's crowded out there."

My two imaginary men laughed. Lucy grinned and sat, so I gave her a treat. She did ask with her best manners.

I checked the weather forecast. "Hope everybody's dressed in layers. It's supposed to drop to the low forties or high thirties tonight."

I walked over to the front window and peered out. "I might need my car here, just in case. I'll call Kate and see if she can drop it off."

I got a text from Kate: "Ok. On its way."

I put my phone to my ear. "Hey, Kate. Do you suppose you could run my car over to me? They can? I don't want to put them out. Thanks."

Wasn't long until my car drove past the horse farm, followed by a patrol car. I met my car at the gate and took over the wheel from the young uniformed officer. After I parked my car in the driveway, he closed the gate and waited until I stepped onto the porch before he turned away. He climbed into the passenger's seat, and the vehicle remained at the road until I went inside. I peeked out the window as they drove away. The darkening sky in the east pursued the few lingering wispy streaks of dark red and orange from the approaching sundown in the west.

"Here's the plan," I announced to a cast of listeners. "The front and back porch lights will go on at dusk, in about twenty minutes, and off at ten o'clock. I won't turn on any interior lights so it will be dark inside. I'll move the dining table and sofa to provide at least minimum coverage for the front and back."

I scooted the dining table and flipped it on its side. It scraped, bumped, and crashed. I pushed the sofa toward the middle of the room, with lots of grunting. It squeaked and rubbed on the wood floor.

Perfect sound effects for our faithful radio listeners.

I walked to the bedroom and pointed to the south window and motioned out and down. Spike and Palace Guard nodded. I grabbed a hand towel and a book and walked to the back door. I pointed at the lawn tractor in its shed and then at the book. Spike and Palace Guard shook their heads.

Not cover.

When I draped the hand towel over my arm, they nodded.

Concealment. Good to know.

I rolled my dark-blue sleeping bag and old gray comforter together, pulled out my dark-brown yoga mat, and grabbed my backpack. I stepped to the back porch and let Lucy out while I scooted my backpack, yoga mat, sleeping bag, and comforter out with my foot. The sun disappeared with only a sliver of a moon on the horizon, and the crickets sang a slow song. While Lucy sniffed, I rearranged the porch. I scooted the rocking chairs away from the windows, picked up the logs on the back porch, and moved them and my things to the ground. I walked around the backyard as a perimeter check and, in the process, checked the shed and lawn tractor. When Lucy and I went inside, I gave her a treat for helping.

I dressed in layers of dark gray, warm clothes and grabbed my watch cap and gloves. I turned on the radio, not too loud, before I went into the bathroom. Might be my last chance until morning.

I had left my south window open after I aired the house. I rolled out straight to the ground, lay there, and listened. A car drove by as I commando-crawled around to the back, and my heart rate jumped. I crawled to the shed, dragging my gear. I put my yoga mat down for ground cover, set my phone on vibrate, and put it face down in the dirt. I didn't want to get a text from Kate and not respond. The two imaginary men sandwiched me. I braced my back against the wall of the shed with my knees up. The porch lights came on, but my shelter remained in the dark. I put my arms across my knees, my head down, and fell asleep.

A tap on my cheek woke me, and I lifted my head. Still dark. When Spike pointed at my phone, I pulled the comforter over my head and checked my phone for the time. Ten minutes after midnight.

Text from Kate: "U ok?"

Me: "Yes."

Kate: "Somebody near ur car."

Me: "I'm at equip shed." I figured if she came in with guns blazing, I wanted her to know where I was. I held my breath and waited for a long, scolding text.

Kate: "Smart."

I realized the two imaginary men were under the comforter with me. Palace Guard held up one finger and disappeared. When he returned, he mimed a stiff left arm. I sent a text.

Me: "PG cked. Duncan."

Lucy growled and barked from inside the house.

Spike was gone. The back door opened, and Lucy ran outside with a low growl. She headed toward the front, wheeled to the back away from the shed, and was quiet. She was low in the grass with Spike.

Kate: "Where's Lucy?"

Me: "Hiding with S."

The headlights of a passing truck illuminated the front of the house. The back stayed dark. The truck disappeared into the driveway of the goat farm. The air temperature dropped, and the coldness of the ground seeped through my yoga mat.

Me: "Any ur ppl in yard?"

Kate: "No."

Me: "Will shoot any come to back. Ok?"

Kate: "Y."

Someone pounded on the front door, and then a man skulked toward the back on the north side. A flare went off in the front yard, and the man froze in the shadows. I assumed a kneeling position and took my shot. He went down.

Kate: "Your shot?"

Me: "Y."

Kate: "Stay. Don't shoot. Going in."

"I need Spike and Lucy here," I told Palace Guard.

Palace Guard and Spike led Lucy in a low crawl to the shed. I maintained my kneeling position and kept my rifle trained on the man I'd shot. *I'm sure it's Duncan.* Spike coaxed Lucy onto the yoga mat behind me then Palace Guard and Spike guarded my back and sides. I lowered my rifle when the fields came alive with dark figures, who jumped the fence from all directions and headed toward the north side of the house.

Kate appeared at the shed. "Mags, we need you to identify the body. Nobody knows Duncan like you do."

I was stiff from kneeling so long and rose with the grace of a wooden stick figure. I stretched and lumbered to the north side of the house.

I examined the man sprawled on the ground. "Yes, this is Everett Duncan."

"Clean shot," Kate said. "Well done."

When I wobbled on my feet, Officer Heather was at my elbow.

"Want to go inside? Or somewhere else?"

"I'd like to go in where it's warm. My feet are frozen."

Officer Heather, Lucy, Spike, Palace Guard, and I went into the house. Officer Heather brewed tea, and I closed and locked the two open windows. I changed to fresh wool socks, a sweatshirt, and sweatpants. Officer Heather flipped my furniture upright.

When I returned to the living room, I grabbed my cup of hot tea and plopped down on the sofa before I swung my frozen feet up on the cushions. Lucy jumped up and sat on my feet. Officer Heather brought me a plate of cookies and Lucy a treat.

Kate stood in the doorway while technicians disconnected and removed the audio bugs.

"Was this your plan?" she asked.

"Yes. The plan was to catch Duncan and Duncan's boss. We got Duncan."

Kate grabbed my last cookie and sat next to me while she munched. "Do you still believe Duncan has a boss?"

Heather handed me a cookie she had held back and winked at me.

I bit into my cookie and smiled. *Heather knows her regulars.*

"If Duncan didn't have a boss, then your team would wrap up here and leave, right?" I asked as I finished off my cookie before Kate tried to pinch off a piece.

Kate narrowed her eyes. "Yes. You've moved to part two of your plan, haven't you?"

I tried for her lioness grin, but it might have been closer to a hyena's. "You don't want to know, do you?"

She cocked her head, and her stare seemed to pierce my brain like she was reading my mind. "You're setting a Maggie trap. Fine. You whittle, I dig, right?"

I looked away and pondered the wall paint. "Should my walls be a brighter color? They seem a little drab."

She followed my gaze. "Might consider it. You could always ask Taylor or your mother. Make me the imaginary Kate."

I raised my eyebrows. *Hadn't thought about that.*

I brushed a stray strand of hair behind my ear. "Do you think Heather could be Kate?"

Chapter Twenty-Four

Kate went outside and rattled off orders. She brought Heather inside and wrote a long note. After Heather read it, she grinned.

Heather whispered to Larry, and the two of them left. A half hour later, they returned with two large boxes of doughnuts. Palace Guard and Spike laughed.

I stepped in front of Kate, pointed to my elbow like I had a bruise or a scratch, and spoke in a quiet voice. "Good one, Kate."

Heather went into the bathroom with a sack and closed the door. An hour later, the team finished their business and loaded up equipment. I took Lucy out for a nice, long Lucy walk in the backyard. As cars left, Larry came into the house. Kate went into the bathroom, and Heather-Kate came out. Larry and Heather-Kate were the last to leave. I checked the locks on all the doors and windows and turned off the lights. I went into the bedroom, turned on the light, and closed the door. I tapped with my fingertips on the bathroom door.

"All set."

Kate crawled out and sat on the floor in the hallway. I stepped to my bedroom, flicked on the bedside lamp, and arranged the pillows on my bed until I was satisfied with the silhouette on the blinds and dimmed the light. I crawled back to the hallway and joined Kate. Lucy clicked to the living room and flopped down. It had been a busy night. I listened to her soft snore and snuffles while she dreamed.

My phone buzzed. A text. I looked at Kate. "Nobody has this number but you. Did you give it to anybody?"

She shook her head, and we looked at my phone together.

"Give me a call?" The text was from Mr. Morgan.

I shrugged and called. Kate put her head next to mine to listen.

"Maggie, I'll be released from the hospital in a couple of hours. Can you pick me up?"

I raised my eyebrows, and Kate nodded.

"Sure. You want to text me when you're ready to leave? Are you sure you're well enough?"

"Seriously, I'm okay." He hung up.

Kate whispered. "He said seriously. Parker used to always say that. And okay. He was in the kitchen when we discussed okay for *come get me or get out,* wasn't he?"

The four of us sat on the floor and looked at each other.

"We move," I said.

"Spike, can you take care of Lucy?" Kate asked.

He hurried to the living room and woke Lucy while Kate and I dressed for the chilly weather.

I opened the back door, and Lucy and I stepped outside. I sat on the porch and gazed at the stars while Spike and Lucy crawled away. I rose and held the back door open as Kate crawled out. After I stepped inside, I dropped down and crawled out then pulled the door shut.

We had left the back gate open to allow Duncan's boss access. We hadn't planned on an escape route for ourselves, but it worked out. We all crawled away to the field.

"You know this is tick territory, right?" I whispered to Kate.

"Shh."

Over to our left: "Psst."

Kate and I froze, and Palace Guard left.

I'll bet it's Gary. He's the only one who didn't get the all-clear memo.

Palace Guard returned. I mouthed "Gary?" He nodded.

Kate frowned and gave me a *Now what?* look, and I remembered all the times my mother said, "You're just like your father." I crawled toward Gary while Kate crawled to flank him.

"Ray called me," he said. "We needed you out of the house, so I gave him your number. I kind of got it when I came to visit. Sorry."

I snorted. "Right." My voice was just as sincere as his.

We remained still in tick territory. A pop-pop and the sound of breaking glass came from the south side of the house, but we didn't move. Palace Guard left.

When he returned, Palace Guard put his hands over his face. *Invisible.* I said, "Lillian?" Palace Guard nodded.

"Bedroom window?" I guessed. Another nod from Palace Guard.

Gary rose to a crouch. "We'll give her time to pick the lock."

He strode toward the back door of the house.

Kate and I stared at each other and then followed him. Gary waved us to positions on the sides of the house. Kate stepped to the south corner, and I turned north. Gary unlocked the back door. Kate shifted to a position closer to the back door. I motioned toward the front of the house and got the okay from Gary and Kate. As I eased along the side of the house, the silence was broken only by the call of a barred owl off in the distance.

When I rounded the corner to the front, Lillian had opened the door. Her gray eyes were black, and when she looked at me, they narrowed to slits. She squared off and lifted her pistol. Palace Guard appeared next to me. The two of us dove for the ground together. As she fired, Palace Guard and I hit the dirt, and I fired. Lillian crumpled in the doorway.

Kate barreled around the north corner, and Gary flew through the front door.

Gary checked Lillian, and Kate made a call.

I leaned against the house. Gary grabbed my elbow and led me to the back of the house to a chair. "I'm going inside to check."

When he returned, he sat next to me. "She shot the pillows. Would have been a head double-tap to anyone in the bed. The south bedroom's yours, right?"

"I hoped all along it wouldn't be Lillian. She's dead, isn't she?"

"Yes, she's dead."

Kate joined us on the porch. "You'll need time to process. I'll set up a debriefing session."

"Kate, you know I can't be here, right?" Gary rose from his chair.

"I do. Thanks for everything."

"What? What is going on?" I said.

"Kate will explain." Gary hugged me and left through the back gate. I gazed after him, and he sauntered through the field until I couldn't see him anymore.

"Well, finally. A Coyle got out-Coyled. So explain."

Kate moved to the rocker next to me. "I knew Gary had been working a complex international case, drug trafficking and money laundering, for years. I didn't believe Duncan had a boss, but you insisted he did. When I saw Gary tonight, I realized he had something and was close to moving in."

"When your team gets here, I don't talk again, right?"

Kate grinned. "You got it, Crazy Lady."

"Good. Can I have a beer now?"

"It's almost breakfast. I can't have one, so you can't have one. Send a text to my dad. He needs your number since it seems like everybody else already has it. Let's go inside."

The wailing sirens came closer.

"I'll take a fast shower and throw on Taylor clothes. I need to check for ticks."

"No ticks," I announced after my shower.

The first squad car screeched to a stop in front of the house. Larry jumped out of the driver's seat and raced inside. Seeing me, he slowed to a casual walk and put his hand on my shoulder. He gazed at my face. "You okay, cuz?"

"Of course."

He growled. "Right."

The second vehicle to arrive was Glenn's truck, and then my yard was swarmed with marked and unmarked cars. Kate called the group together and barked orders. Larry stared at me, shook his head, and took notes while Kate talked. Moe stood by the door and glowered.

While Glenn and I sat on the sofa, he whispered, "Almost like a television show. As soon as this episode is over, we'll go to my house for breakfast."

When Glenn and I took Lucy outside after a walk, Kate joined us. "They don't need FBI to supervise them. We can go."

Palace Guard, Spike, Lucy, and I rode with Kate.

"You don't think anybody else is looking for me now?" I asked.

Kate checked the traffic and made her turn. "No. It's clear you were Lillian's problem. You knew Duncan wasn't dead and identified him at all the related businesses. The packet Olivia gave you had a wealth of evidence against Everett Duncan and John Edwards. Olivia's evidence pointed to an overall boss, but nothing identified Lillian."

"Actually, she did," I said. "Olivia recorded an excellent profile and left me the code."

"Which you will share with Scotland Yard, right?"

"Yep."

Lucy whined in delight when we pulled into the Coyles' driveway. As Jennifer stood in the doorway, I gazed at her with a twinge of sadness. *How many times has she waited for her family to return safely?*

The Jennifer hug reminded me I was safe.

While we ate, Glenn asked, "What's next for you, Maggie? You're a rich woman, so you don't need to work unless you want to. Olivia left you funds your lawyer confirmed are not related to Duncan's illegal businesses."

Because I had a mouthful of cinnamon roll, I had time to think while I chewed. "I always wanted to be a spy, but I liked being a cook."

"What about being a detective?" he asked.

"Dad, I'm not sure Maggie can pass a psychological test for a police department." Kate raised her eyebrows.

"I'm not police department material," I said. "Unless there's an opening as Officer Heather's understudy."

After a taxi stopped at the front of the driveway, Glenn rose to answer the door.

When Mr. Morgan walked into the kitchen, his face was drawn, and his arm was in a sling. He sat across from me, and I glared.

He peered into his cup while Jennifer poured his coffee. "Maggie, I want to apologize. I didn't know about Lillian's other activities. Sometimes I wondered if she was into something, but I guess I was a little blinded by the years we worked together. When I heard Donnie was near our apartment, I stormed out to find him because of what he did to Lillian. She must have warned Duncan. I know she didn't shoot me, though, because I'd be dead if she'd had me in her sights."

I narrowed my eyes. "Lillian was a master at being unseen. Undetected. She even explained it to me."

"I'm sure she was torn about you," Mr. Morgan said. "She admired you. Did you know that?"

I snorted. "No. I think I frustrated her."

"Here's your breakfast, Ray." Jennifer handed him a plate with two fried eggs, sausage, and a cinnamon roll.

"Thank you, Jennifer."

"Eat first, then talk." Jennifer refilled his coffee.

Mr. Morgan cleaned his plate and scooted his chair back. "Maggie, Lillian told me you were the only one who thought Duncan had a boss. I didn't understand why she was angry and said you'd never quit. I said that was good, but she shook her head. I talked to her about . . . maybe we'd retire and ask you to take over our business. She said you'd be a natural."

"Who told Duncan that Parker had the auditor notes?" I asked.

Glenn refilled everyone's coffee cups. Mr. Morgan looked at the Coyles. He dropped his head. "I'm afraid I might have in a roundabout way."

When Kate slammed her palms on the table and rose, the fire in her eyes was terrifying.

"Wait, Kate." Glenn patted Kate's hand, and she sat. Glenn's eyes narrowed. "Continue, Ray."

"When Lillian and I discussed the auditor's murder, I mentioned Bob Zephfer and Parker were old friends. She made a call soon afterward, but I didn't think anything of it. I'm sure someone stole the notes from Parker after he died."

"How did you get the notes?" I asked.

"When I was supposed to be out of town, I searched our office, found them, and gave them to Gary. I made it look like a break-in. I'm sure Lillian assumed Duncan was responsible. She never mentioned a robbery or what was missing."

Mr. Morgan hung his head and rose. "I should go. My cab's waiting."

Kate narrowed her eyes. "I have a question. Why did Lillian send the 'John Updike' message?"

Mr. Morgan leaned against his chair. "My guess is that after Donnie attacked her, she saw Maggie as her best weapon against Duncan."

"Why did you warn me to get out of my house?" I asked.

"Lillian and I were close. Partners for over forty years. We had a code word. It was similar to your 'okay.'" He rubbed his forehead and stared at me. "Lillian has never failed to respond to my call for help. Forty years. When she didn't—" A long blast of a car horn interrupted him. "I've got to go. My cab."

Glenn stood. "I'll walk you to the door."

"Mom?" Kate asked after Mr. Morgan left.

Jennifer stopped clearing the table and sat next to Kate. "I'm okay. Ray feels guilty, but it wasn't his fault Parker was murdered."

"I guess I agree." Kate hugged her mother and left for work.

"Take us home, Glenn?" I asked. We rode home in silence.

* * *

The afternoon was too hot for a run, but I needed some outside time. I grabbed a glass of iced tea and fresh water for Lucy, and the four of us sat on the back porch.

"When I shot Donnie and Duncan, I felt empowered. Like I avenged Parker."

Spike took Lucy for a slow walk, and Palace Guard sat on the porch next to my rocker.

"When I saw Lillian, my heart stopped. Duncan pulled the trigger that killed Parker, but she gave the order. My only regret is I killed her with a single shot. That murderous bitch deserved a slower death." I slammed my fist on the rocker arm.

After I slid down to the porch to sit with Palace Guard, the tears rolled down my face. Palace Guard wrapped his arms around me while I sobbed for Parker. Lucy leaned on me and kissed away the tears on my arm, and Spike brushed away my hair from my face. I swiped at my dripping nose with my sleeve. "I need a run."

I tied my running shoes and crammed a ballcap on my head in deference to the heat. I took off with a pace that was much too fast for the weather conditions. Palace Guard ran in front of me and stopped with his arms crossed.

"I'll slow my pace to one less likely to give me heatstroke. Happy?"

When Palace Guard smiled, we ran to the horse farm. The horses stayed in the shade of their barn and whinnied but didn't run with us. Palace Guard raised his eyebrows.

"You and the horses win. It's too hot to run. I'll walk back."

The air temperature dropped with a sudden wind shift out of the northwest. The sky darkened, and I caught the distinctive smell of imminent rain. I jumped at the flash and crack of nearby lightning and a sudden boom of thunder. Palace Guard and I sprinted for the house while big raindrops smacked us. We reached the porch just ahead of the fast-moving wall of rain. It was a dark, noisy storm. I brewed a cup of hot tea, and Lucy sat with me on the sofa while I read.

When I woke, the rain had stopped, the sky was clear, and my stomach rumbled. My back was stiff, but it was a small price to pay for a much-needed nap. I opened the back door, and Lucy followed me to the porch.

"I know you're not fond of wet grass, but come on, girl." I stepped to the middle of the yard, and she stared at me. Spike and Palace Guard coaxed her off the porch for her bio break. She relieved herself and dashed to the porch. I sloshed back, and we all went inside.

I opened a jar of Jennifer's home-canned chicken and vegetable soup. While it heated and filled my small house with the consoling aroma of chicken mixed with carrots and herbs, I pulled together a salad. I read my book and ate my comfort food dinner.

After I loaded the dishes into the dishwasher, I dropped my clothes on the bedroom floor and collapsed into bed.

* * *

I woke refreshed. I started a pot of coffee and jumped into the shower. After I dried off, my phone rang. *Glenn.*

"You up? Come for breakfast."

I laughed. "I planned to call you after breakfast. I need to replace my bedroom window. Can you teach me how to do that? We could go to the hardware store this morning if you're available."

I grabbed a cup of coffee for the road, and the four of us went to the Coyles. Glenn opened the door before I reached the steps, and we went inside together.

"Dad answered the door because Mom said I was forbidden to ambush you when you came to the door," said Kate.

I smiled at her lioness grin.

Jennifer hugged me and pointed at the table. "Grab your seat, Maggie. I'm about to put plates on the table. Glenn, would you pour coffee?"

Jennifer set a plate in front of me with two blueberry pancakes and two slices of thick bacon.

"I don't make sausage," she said. "That's Kate's specialty. She needs to make some for my freezer." She waved her spatula at Kate. "Before you leave, right?"

I slathered butter on my pancakes and munched on my bacon while the butter oozed and melted. "You going somewhere, Kate?" I asked.

"I start my new job on Monday. Guess I'll make sausage tomorrow. Want to help?"

When the doorbell rang, I raised my eyebrows, and Kate shrugged.

"I kind of invited somebody for breakfast." Glenn rose to answer the door.

Chapter Twenty-Five

When Glenn and Mr. Morgan stepped into the kitchen, five sets of eyes glared at them. Lucy was asleep.

Jennifer broke the silence. "Welcome to our home, Mr. Morgan. Do you want plain or blueberry pancakes this morning?"

"Just coffee, please. I have a doctor's appointment this morning and can't stay long, and I've already eaten."

"Then I'll just make you a couple of small blueberry pancakes." Jennifer turned to her griddle.

"Might as well sit, Ray." Glenn nodded.

Mr. Morgan sat next to me, and I stiffened. When I glared, he dropped his gaze.

"Maggie, I'd like to talk to you about our . . . my business."

I shifted in my seat to examine his face.

"Lillian and I have—had—a business. We did investigations, on a retainer basis, like contractors. You'd be a perfect detective with your research abilities, self-defense skills, and instincts."

After Mr. Morgan put a manila envelope on the table, Jennifer set a plate with two blueberry pancakes in front of him.

Don't look small to me.

I passed the butter and syrup to Mr. Morgan, and Kate handed him a knife, fork, and napkin while Glenn refilled his coffee.

Mr. Morgan buttered his pancakes then tucked his napkin to cover his tie and shirt. "I brought a contract my lawyer drew up. It's signed and notarized. If you give me a dollar and sign, Maggie, the business is yours."

After he drowned his pancakes in syrup, he cut them into bite-sized pieces and swirled each piece in syrup before he ate it.

I bit my lip to hide my smile. *That's why he tucked in his napkin.*

After he blotted his mouth he said, "The packet has all the information on how to access our files. There's a proposal from a client in the packet."

Glenn reached for the envelope and pulled out papers while Mr. Morgan ate, and the rest of us stared at Glenn.

After Glenn read all the pages, he put the contract down. "Looks good."

The doorbell rang. "That's my taxi. My contact information is in the packet if you have any questions or want a consult."

Glenn left the room with Mr. Morgan. They talked on the way out, but I couldn't understand what they said. When Glenn returned, he grinned. "You owe me fifty cents. Mr. Morgan suggested I might want to partner with you."

"No," Kate growled.

Glenn frowned and crossed his arms. "I was a good police officer and a great detective. Retirement's boring. I wouldn't mind a little work to keep my brain active. What about you, Maggie? Ready for a little work? What do the imaginary men say?"

Spike shrugged, and Palace Guard shook his head. I stared into my coffee cup. *I'm not a detective. I always wanted to be a spy.*

Jennifer flipped two quarters onto the dining table. "You've got a deal, bud. I'll be your partner. I always wanted to be a detective."

I jumped up to hug Jennifer, and her eyes widened. "Watch out!" she yelled, but she was too late.

Kate, the lioness, saw her opportunity and slammed me to the floor.

ACKNOWLEDGEMENTS

Huge thanks to my husband for his patience while I wander off into the world of my imaginary friends.

Thanks to my family and friends for their support, and to my beta readers who don't let me get by with anything.

Thank you for reading. Did you enjoy Maggie's story? Tell a friend, tell your bookseller, write a review, read, and subscribe!

What to read next?

RED IS THE NEW GRAY, BOOK 2
MAGGIE SLOAN THRILLER

The Gray Lady travels to Galveston, Texas, to find a missing spy. After Maggie is shot and friends are murdered, she is determined to uncover the vicious leader. Larry and the men are frantic: Maggie is in the crosshairs.

Subscribe: to the newsletter!

Look for the Subscribe button on www.judithabarrett.com

ABOUT THE AUTHOR

Judith A. Barrett is an award-winning author of mystery, crime, and survival science fiction novels with action, adventure, and a touch of supernatural to spark the reader's imagination. Her unusual main characters are brilliant, talented, and down-to-earth folks who solve difficult problems and stop killers. Her novels are based in small towns and rural areas in south Georgia and north Florida with sojourns to other southern US states.

Judith lives in rural Georgia on a small farm with her husband and two dogs. When she's not busy writing, Judith is still busy working on the farm, hiking with her husband and dogs, or watching the beautiful sunsets from her porch.

Website   www.judithabarrett.com

Subscribe to the eNewsletter via her website

Let's keep in touch!

Made in the USA
Columbia, SC
28 May 2023

17144108R00245